The Kitten Burglar

By
John A. Burnham

Eloquent Books

Eloquent Books
An imprint of Strategic Book Group
P.O. Box 333
Durham, CT 06422
www.StrategicBookGroup.com

ISBN: 978-1-60693-380-0   1-60693-380-9

Printed in the United States of America

Book Design: D. Johnson, Dedicated Business Solutions, Inc.

*All characters appearing in this work are fictitious.
Any resemblance to real persons, living or dead, is
purely coincidental.*

CONTENTS

1

KITTEN

A flash of headlights in the street caused Kitten to flatten herself against the wall. She had little concern about being seen three stories up and in the shadow, but why take a chance?

"The only people who win by taking chances are in the movies," her daddy used to say.

The headlights illuminated a row of manicured bushes parallel to the street, but not much beyond. The car swept by too fast for the occupants to be looking for anything. However, the play of headlights had revealed that a security vehicle prowling down that street couldn't see much beyond the line of bushes; that left at least a hundred feet to the building. Bless the people who put these huge lawns around condos. They had provided her with plenty of working room.

After scaling three stories of wall, Kitten felt a genuine appreciation for the condo architects. The bricks protruding from the face were intended to enhance the aesthetic effect, but they also made her job easier. A climb like this—with all of her hundred pounds supported on fingertips and big toes—would usually have those members yelping. These eye-pleasing protrusions were spaced perfectly for her five-foot-four frame, and they stuck out enough to provide purchase for all five toes or the entire first joint of her fingers.

Once above the doors of the third floor balconies, Kitten paused. She studied the object of her ascent on the next floor up and about twenty feet to her right. It was a good thing that the pattern of the protruding bricks would make a diagonal path faster. The shadow ended five or six feet from her goal.

She negotiated the first few feet of new path with her muscles registering gratitude for the change in load. Reaching for a brick above the balcony, she felt for loose material. Finding none, she transferred her weight to the hand and pulled herself up. With deliberate care, she raised the opposite leg and used her toes to feel along the length of the next brick. Finding nothing loose, she put weight on that foot. The process continued; reach, check, transfer weight, move the other hand or foot and check. It slowed her progress, but she gained the opposite side of the balcony without a single dislodged grain sounding on anything beneath.

Once clear of structures below, she paused to look around. She'd be out of the shadow in the next couple of steps and there would be a temptation to gawk about when the light hit. Neither looking around while moving on a wall nor stopping in the light were advisable, so she took the time to satisfy herself that the surroundings were still friendly.

Kitten's stomach tightened as her hand reached out of the shadow. Look at the wall . . . just the wall . . . concentrate . . . grasp . . . shift weight . . . concentrate. The light, being attenuated by a journey from far away street lamps, wouldn't have revealed her to anyone without binoculars, but the absence of shadow made her feel visible.

Kitten's hand closed around a steel upright. The balcony railing felt good! She fought off an impulse to transfer her weight to the wrought iron structure immediately. Instead, she examined the top of it. There were no flowerpots or bird feeders sitting up there—good. She shook the railing and smiled at the solid feel. A wave of relief rippled through the muscles of her calves and forearms as she vaulted over the railing and landed in a crouch behind a large pot containing a Norfolk Island pine and something with droopy leaves. Ignoring the pleas of her legs for a stretch, she remained in her landing position for a full minute, looking and listening.

Detecting no hostile signs, she slid her backpack off and extracted a climbing rope. On hands and knees, she located an upright in the center of the front railing, tested its solidity, clipped the end of the rope to it, and placed the coiled bundle on the top rail. With a rapid escape route secured, she felt better and allowed herself a noiseless stretch while remaining below the level of the planters, chairs, and other paraphernalia on the balcony.

Settling into a sitting position against the glass doors, she withdrew a stethoscope from the pack, pushed the suction cup end onto the glass, adjusted the earpieces for comfort, and listened intently. Hearing nothing but the sound of her own breathing, she forced her respiration into a slower and deeper mode—still no sound—good. She shifted position to lean against the doorframe and pulled a sleeve back to reveal the luminous dial of her watch. Noting the time, she released the sleeve and leaned her head back. Above, gem-like stars shone from the velvety night sky. The sight of a shooting star gave her a warm glow. Her daddy used to say they were a sure omen of a good score that night.

"It's like what we do," he had said. "Those falling stars don't fall. They wink out of where they are and show up somewhere else in the sky. We aren't taking anything because the stuff we pinch shows up someplace else for a different person to enjoy."

Being a semi-literate thirteen-year-old at the time, she had not questioned either his astrophysics or his ethics. Now, at twenty-two, she knew his understanding of stellar behavior to have been questionable, but the way he had loved her was never in question. She allowed bittersweet memories to fill the minutes while she listened, memories of her daddy trying—for her sake—to go on. At nine, she was not able to comprehend that his ability to face life had died with her mother. Daddy and everyone else in the circus went into a depression after mom fell. That she had understood. Not only was the loss of their premier aerialist a blow, but they had lost a deity. Mom had been considered to be more talented, more beautiful, and more anything than anyone. The death of a queen should cause greater consternation than the demise of an ordinary person, so it was fitting and proper that everybody mourned for several days. They returned to the business of living by small degrees. It had taken a long time for her to understand why daddy didn't return with the others.

Daddy had tried to return to the trapeze, but his heart just wasn't in it. Mom had loved to fly and daddy had loved to help her do it. Now, all he could offer was skill. He no longer had a heart to put into it. Nobody lets go of a bar without knowing that the catch man is applying heart as well as talent. Since nobody would fly to him without a net underneath, daddy had to start working the sideshows. He did a mediocre job as an escape artist for a couple of tours, but people don't return to that type of thing year after year. Working booths in the midway seemed only to deepen his depression.

Kitten closed her eyes to savor the next memory. She could still feel the joy as she walked through the door of their trailer to find her daddy smiling. It wasn't the usual smile, with sadness beneath. This smile went all the way through. Books surrounded him. She could remember the ensuing conversation as though it had happened yesterday.

"Sweetheart, I've got it all figured out."

"What?"

"How I'm gonna look after you."

At thirteen, she had a vague concept of not being prepared to face the world. Although she was an exceptional gymnast, she didn't have the love of flying it took to be an aerialist. She could throw knives and things like that, but it was becoming apparent that she wasn't going to have the necessary figure to fill out one of those sequined costumes. In short, there wasn't any future for her in the circus. However, the idea wasn't a bother to her young mind. She knew it was different for daddy. He was always trying to find her a spot inside the circus and sometimes muttered about how he hadn't prepared her to do anything outside. Tonight, she sensed that he had arrived at a resolution, so she had waited for him to continue.

"This is a course in locksmithing," he had said, gesturing to the books. "You are going to learn all about locks."

Surprised beyond words, she asked, "Why?"

"You've got to be able to make a living and I don't want you to have to do it working the midway or taking tickets for the rides."

"Being a locksmith sounds sorta dull."

"I'm not talking about your becoming a locksmith, honey. I'm talking about you learning about locks. Have you noticed how many of those big motor homes are around these days?"

"Not really."

"Well, I have. There's getting to be scads of 'em. Some time back, I began to wonder if people who could afford something like that wouldn't also be the type of people who would carry valuable things with them. Over the past few months, I've had a look in several. In all but one, I found things that would make a good score. I didn't take anything, because I was just looking, but I could see how you could make a decent living."

"A line of B and Es that followed the circus would have the fuzz on us before the middle of the season."

"That's my smart girl! You are exactly right. If we cleaned out a motor home everywhere we went, the pattern would point right to the circus. Suppose you scored only one thing—a piece of jewelry or a wad of bills—and left other valuables undisturbed. Do you think it would be reported as stolen?"

"Probably not; particularly if it wasn't the most valuable thing in the place."

"You're getting the idea! Even if it was reported, the mark would have a hard time convincing the cops they hadn't just lost or misplaced the missing item."

It had worked out well. She became adept at letting herself into the grand motor homes and daddy had arranged a good fence.

She had hoped that release from the burden of taking care of her would give him a new lease on life, but it didn't. Instead, he became less and less interested in going on. He became useless in the midway booths and spent his last year picking pockets among the crowds. At first, the circus thought about getting rid of him, but decided against it because he could point out the other pickpockets to security.

Although she was sixteen when they buried him, she knew by then she'd actually lost him seven years before.

Kitten pulled the sleeve back again. She had been listening for five full minutes without hearing a sound. Slowly, she brought her feet under her to bear her weight. Crouching in readiness, she scraped her fingernails along the glass to arouse any animal that might be inside. There was no sound, so she packed the stethoscope. Looking around, she stood. Everything still looked dead, so she took a penlight from her pack and examined the lock. It was a simple deadbolt as the lead had said it would be! Smiling about how good these leads were, she went back to her pack and selected a few tools. A single thickness of polished metal affixed to a shaft no thicker than a ballpoint refill with a jeweler's hinge slipped easily through the weather stripping. A pull on the wire hanging from the end of the handle deflected the mirror.

Working with the penlight in her mouth, Kitten used the image in the mirror to follow the mirror shaft with a loop of wire that she looped around the knob of the bolt. She pulled the wire; it didn't give. She put her weight against the door and pulled the wire again. Nothing. She reached into her bag for a suction cup, which she strapped to her knee. Knee against the door to plant the suction cup . . . locate the image of the bolt again . . . tension on the wire . . . pull with the knee. Click!

Fighting off the tendency to turn around at the sound, which had seemed so loud, she examined the image in the mirror. The bolt had rotated. The knob was now in line with the slot. She moved her knee enough to put tension on the bolt again and rotated the mirror until she felt it against the bolt knob. Again moving her knee, she felt the mirror rotate. Repositioning the mirror and penlight, she could see that the bolt had slid toward the unengaged position. After withdrawing the mirror, she moved the bolt along with an ultra-thin knife blade until she could feel that it was clear.

One last time, she checked around the door for signs of security devices. The lead had indicated nothing electronic, but people sometimes rigged tripwires and such; there wasn't any reason to take extra chances. Satisfied, she moved her knee sideways and the door followed it. She was in!

Kitten found the strong box located in the wall where the lead said it would be. The lock was simple; she was through it without breaking stride. Inside was the biggest pile of ice she had ever seen! The bracelet had too many diamonds to count—big ones and little ones in all different cuts. She pulled a jeweler's loupe from her backpack and examined a diamond that was easily two carats. It had flaws. It was real!

She looked at the other contents of the strong box. There was some cash, a few envelopes, and good jewelry, but nothing as extravagant as the bracelet. The bracelet didn't fit with the other stuff—perfect! She put the bracelet in her backpack, made certain that the other contents were exactly as she had found them and locked the box.

Kitten pulled a pleated, short skirt from the backpack and put it on. Funky slippers from the backpack went on her feet. As she pulled the thin toque off her head, ponytails fell past her shoulders. She returned to the balcony, retrieved the escape rope, came back inside, closed, and locked the door. In the bathroom, she used her flashlight to get a look at herself. In the mirror, she saw ponytails, make-up inexpertly applied, tights, and a short skirt—the perfect image of a teeny-bopper. She let herself out the front door of the condo and exited the building as if she owned the place.

2

GARTH

Charles Hollingsworth had led the narcotics division since its formation. All knew him as the Old Man.

Detective Garth Moore began to take an interest in what the Old Man was saying. It sounded as if this first-thing-Monday-morning conversation wasn't going to be another "excessive force" lecture.

Garth never used excessive force. If a problem existed, it was genetic. At six five and two hundred fifty pounds, Garth could be considered excessive. He couldn't help it if what felt like an appropriate level of force to him was mistaken by others for excess. In addition, his take-downs were in question. Too many of them had resulted in the perpetrator meeting his maker instead of the judge. No, his record wasn't the classic image of a sophisticated investigator, but he did seem to get results. That is why the Old Man had, for fourteen years, limited his disapproval to a semi-monthly lecture.

Garth put his fingernail clippers away and tuned in to what the Old Man was saying.

"The head shed has allocated funds for the project you suggested. I'm pleased, but surprised as hell. I'd expect the task force on missing children to protect its turf instead of sharing it with us. Therefore, I want you to be damn careful about honoring their request to be kept in the loop. I want weekly updates with a cc to them, understood?"

"Absolutely," Garth replied.

"And, no cowboy stuff. If things get beyond the data gathering stage, we have to let them call the shots on any action."

"You got it. Since my plate is clean at this point, may I give it full time right away?"

"Not quite right away. I want you to get down to Teula. A thirty-two year old female Caucasian was murdered there last night. They have a suspect. The link is drugs. It might not be of any interest to us, but I want you to have a look around before the local law clabbers things up."

"Isn't that Lew's hometown?" Garth interrupted.

"Yes. In fact, he was there over the weekend. Visiting his mother, I think."

"Ah, we want to ascertain whether or not the local constabulary is looking in any directions that might connect to us."

"More or less. Stop by Lew's office on your way out. He can give you some background on the townspeople."

"Was the victim anybody he knew?"

"I don't know. It is more than likely. Teula is one of those places, how does the song go? 'One stoplight blinkin' on and off. Everybody knows when the neighbors cough.' I'll let him know you're coming by."

Garth stood. "I'm on my way."

The Old Man looked up at him. "Garth, sit back down for a minute. In relation to this missing children investigation, I'm more than serious about the Dirty Harry stuff."

Garth feigned a hurt expression. "Dirty Harry? I've never even fired a .44 magnum."

"You might find this amusing, but I'm having trouble knowing what to think. I can't imagine the task force guys not having a squint at your record. I'd have taken big odds that the number of perps who have perished resisting your arrest, or attempting to escape would queer any chance of their accepting you on the team."

"But . . ." Garth protested.

The Old Man waived his hand. "I know, I know, the cases looked airtight . . . the conclusion that the perps panicked is easy to arrive at. Trying to shoot one's way out is almost an admission of guilt. I've told you before how I admire the tidiness of your cases, but you must promise me that you'll include the task force if you even want to issue a parking ticket."

Garth smiled, "You got it, pop."

The Old Man watched Garth disappear through the door. They both knew that if Garth caught somebody abusing children, that individual would meet a summary end without benefit of the justice system. He hoped that extracting the promise had emphasized the need for making certain that all the ducks were in a row before doing anything. Garth was neither dumb nor impulsive. Probably, it would be as sanitary as a Mr. Clean commercial, but he hoped the extra warning would induce Garth to consider a methodology that didn't involve his personal participation.

✳✳✳

Garth headed for the office of Randall Lewis with more than slight apprehension. Murder is incidental to a narc's work. It had never been his lot to discuss a murder with someone of Lewis' ilk. His reaction was in question because Garth didn't consider him a real cop. Real cops worked in the field, got shot at, pounded the pavement, asked questions, endured boring stakeouts, things like that. Lewis had degrees in both medicine and criminology. He answered questions for other cops, did things with the computer, and wrote books. Garth had plenty of experience in helping other cops through grief, but this guy was more like a civilian or some civilian's mother.

Garth saw that Lewis was still on the phone when he walked in. He seated himself and tried to look casual. The appearance required effort. He was accustomed to people saying he was the biggest, meanest-looking black man they had ever seen. He didn't try to look mean; his face just hung that way. In private, he exercised different facial expressions before a mirror. He tried to remember how his face had felt when the reflection looked bland. He also tried to slow his eyes down. The habit of examining everything in the room while making continual sweeps was good for surviving in bars, but was inappropriate in an office.

The slight, prematurely balding man behind the desk was nodding as he listened to the phone cradled on his shoulder. He answered in monosyllables. His fingers poked at the keyboard. Garth tried to find something in which the screen was mirrored—a window, a picture, anything reflective. He didn't have any particular reason for wanting to know what was on the screen. It was habit.

Lewis hung the phone up and turned to Garth. "So, I guess you want me to tell you all about the good folks in Teula," he said. The eyes and voice were slack like the jowls on a coon dog. The man was numb.

Garth tried to remember what the book said about dealing with people in this state. It was something about being compassionate and trying to think oneself into the position of the bereaved. "Were you close to the victim?" he ventured.

Lewis picked up a pencil and slowly shook his head as he examined the eraser. "No, I hardly knew her."

"Then wh . . ." Garth began but couldn't find the words to finish.

Lewis took a deep breath as he leaned back in his chair. His eyes were getting moist. Garth squirmed. Randall Lewis was one strange duck, but even strange ducks deserve help when they're hurting.

"Give me a second," Lewis said as he looked at the ceiling. "It was a rotten weekend."

Garth tried again. "The visit with your mom didn't go too good?"

"She hardly knew me . . . finally realized that she had to be in a rest home . . . made the arrangements . . . have to go back Friday and move her . . . she doesn't want to go . . . house is the only thing she recognizes . . . tough . . . tough . . ."

"Look, if you don't want to talk, I can wing it."

"No, I think talking about the old home place may do me some good."

"Wanna coffee?"

"Thanks, cream only."

As Garth fetched the coffees, he began to feel he was getting the hang of this compassionate cop thing. He walked back wondering if he might ever get good at it. By the time he was seated, he had reached the conclusion that leaning on slime was more fulfilling.

Lewis sipped the coffee. "Thanks . . . just right. I'll start by telling you about the scene I saw at the airport last night. It's perfect for giving you a feel for the place. As I was waiting for my flight back, I saw lights all over the ramp. The Sheriff had his red and blue lights flashing. The Fire Chief had his rotating red light going. The Mayor had put one of those detachable rotating yellow lights on top of his car. All three vehicles had their headlights pointed straight at the chartered airplane as it taxied off the runway. It was something right out of the movies. Each man was standing in his headlights, motioning at the airplane to park in front of his vehicle. The Sheriff was the best. He had a ten-gallon hat on his two-pint head, trousers tucked into his boots, sidearm on, and those goofy orange tint sunglasses–at night, yet! All these people were there because the airplane was returning the body of the Lieutenant Governor's dad and each one wanted to appear to be in charge. Small town people with small minds."

"What did the pilot do?" asked Garth.

"He located the hearse and parked in front of it."

"Smooth. What can you tell me about the victim? This . . . er . . . Roberta Valdez," asked Garth, as he fumbled with his notebook.

"Not much. She was a couple of years behind me in school. I don't think she was the sharpest arrow in the quiver, but she was quite decorative."

"Ever date her?" It was out before Garth thought. Such questions were ok for the street, but the wrong move here. He covered with another question before Lewis could answer. "Valdez, Spanish American?"

"No, I never asked her out. Her great-great-grandfather was Mexican. The name was the only thing about her father that even hinted at anything other than pure WASP. The town never forgave her mother for marrying him. They're real salt-of-the-earth types. They hate racial prejudice and anybody who's different. She booted out of there as soon as she finished high school. I believe she was in Houston until her dad died. Her mom was sick and couldn't sell the house, so she returned to look after her. She'd been doing something with cosmetics. She set herself up in some type of wholesale cosmetics business there. Gossip abounded about how she actually made her money. Probably, it was jealousy because she was still enough of a looker to make men stand on their heads and stack B-Bs. I never heard of her dating any of the locals."

"Have the Mayor and the Sheriff been in office long?"

"As long as I can remember, Charlie 'Bub' Hollis has been Sheriff and Clarence Lamont has been Mayor."

"Ever regret not sticking around after high school?"

"With all that small mindedness to squeeze me in? Not for a second," Lewis replied with a sardonic chuckle.

"What about the suspect?"

"Norm Bodine is in his early twenties. His parents died in a house fire when he was about twelve. He couldn't explain how he escaped from the burning house or much of anything else about the event. I think he was a normal kid up to that point, but it took him three extra years to finish grammar school. He lives with his aunt now. She works a small farm on the outskirts of town. When he's not working on the farm, he wanders around town. He gets an ice cream here, a pop there–never talks to anyone–just wanders."

"Thanks Lew. I've an errand to run before I catch that plane, so I'd better make a mile. If you think of anything else, can you give me a holler?"

"Sure thing."

"Did you say you'll be there on Friday?"

"Yes, and I think I'll catch the Saturday flight back."

Now, Garth knew what he could do. "If I'm wrapped up by that time, maybe we'll ride back to civilization together, knock back a few en route, and more when we get here."

Lewis brightened. "Sounds good."

"You got a steady girl or somebody you want to bring along?"

"No."

Garth stood. "See you in Tuela, my man." He walked out of the office pleased. Being treated like one of the boys had done good things for Lew.

✳✳✳

Garth waited in front of the receptionist's desk while the ample woman put her nail file back in the drawer.

"May I please see Miss Winters?" he asked, when she looked up.

"At the moment, she's with a client."

"I . . . uh," Garth stammered.

"I know. I know. You gotta ketch a plane or sump thin," said Ample, as she reached for the intercom. "Miss Winters?"

"Yes."

"Kin y' come out fer a minute? Tall, dark 'n ugly's here bearin' gifts."

Garth was disappointed. He had been trying for the suave face.

As Rose walked into the reception area, she noted the small box of chocolates and the flowers Garth was holding. "Let me guess. Those mean you can't tell me where you're going, Thursday night is off, and you don't know when you'll be back," she said, mocking a pout.

"Wrong, right, wrong," said Garth as he handed her the peace offerings. "I'm going to Tuela. I don't think I'll be back for Thursday, but we should be able to do the town Saturday. Howzat sound?"

"As good as can be expected," she teased.

"Another guy may be coming in with me. Do you suppose you could find a friend for him—perhaps one that isn't over five four?"

"Is this another of your therapy projects?"

"Huh?"

"Sure. Now scat before you own that cab."

Rose watched Garth get into the waiting taxi. She would have liked a goodbye kiss, but Garth didn't operate that way. Not in front of the receptionist anyway. She smelled the flowers. This one didn't sound too bad. At least he could tell her where he was going and he wasn't wearing his gun . . ."

"Miss Winters, your clients . . ."

"Yes . . . Yes! Thanks Carol."

✱✱✱

Garth walked into the men's room of the Teula airport terminal. His eyes swept the room. Sink, mirror, urinal, stall—one of each. He straightened his tie and studied the mirror until he had worked up the pleasant face.

The ticket counter and rent-a-car desk were the same piece of furniture. He hoped the pleasant face was holding. He didn't want to frighten the plump little hamster of a man behind the desk.

"I'd like a car, please."

"Yes, sir. Cash or card?"

Garth produced the company credit card.

"You must be here about Miss Valdez."

"That is correct. How do I get to the morgue?"

"If you can wait a few minutes, I'll take you. The body is in my facility. I'm also the town undertaker."

"That would be fine," replied Garth. He looked at the rental car keys. "Blue Taurus. I'll get it and be waiting out front. Is that black Lincoln yours?"

"Yes, sir. Good guess. Perhaps you'd like to phone the sheriff while you're waiting?"

"I'll touch base with him after I've seen the body."

"But the sheriff . . . I'm certain that he would . . ."

Garth looked straight at the little man and relaxed his face.

"But on the other hand . . . state officer and all . . . there shouldn't be any need . . ." the little man continued.

Garth parked the Taurus where it gave him a view through the window of the terminal. He wanted to observe the hamster. Presently, the latter locked the terminal door. He had not used the phone.

When they pulled into the driveway of one of the better-looking structures in the town, the sheriff was not waiting for them. The hamster hadn't called him while Garth was getting the Taurus. That was good.

Obviously, the little man was in a rush to get inside, but Garth was beside him before he got the door open. "May I please use your phone?" he asked as he stepped through the door—practically over the hamster—and headed for the office.

"Yes, yes by all means."

Garth had swung his laptop onto the desk, unplugged the phone, and was plugging the computer into the jack as the little man came through the door. With a pleasant voice and the appropriate face–he hoped–he asked, "Is this your only line?"

"Yes, but that's perfectly all right. Help yourself," replied the hamster, as he mopped his brow with a snow-white handkerchief. His manner revealed that Garth's actions were anything but all right.

"I thought these things were gonna be the cat's meow when we first got 'em . . . instant information 'n all that . . . actually provin' to be more of a pain . . ." Garth said with studied absentness as he tapped the keys. "There, just like I said. Doesn't that beat all! It'll be twenty minutes before they can handle my request. Why don't we go back and have a look at the body while this junk is waiting to do its thing?"

"Couldn't you hang up and call back later?" pleaded the hamster.

"If I do, I'll lose my place in the queue and who knows how long we'd have to wait then. I don't want to keep you from your dinner, so we should have a look at the body while I'm waiting for my turn. Then, I can do my thing here and you can be home on schedule."

"Whatever," replied the hamster in a beaten voice. "The morgue is this way."

It took Garth a good deal more than twenty minutes to examine the body and question the hamster about the handling.

"Much obliged," said Garth as he unplugged his computer from the hamster's phone line.

"Er, are you going to get in touch with the sheriff now?"

"Think I'll get a bite to eat before I drop in on him."

Garth smiled at the haste with which the hamster closed the door behind him. He could go ahead and call the sheriff now. That would keep the little man too busy to see which way he went.

✳✳✳

On the way into town, Garth had noted the location of the sheriff's office and a narrow alley across the street from it. He eased the Taurus into the alley just in time to see the sheriff drive away–probably looking for him. He waited. Slowly, the sheriff drove past going the opposite direction. Yes, he must be checking out the eating-places. Garth waited and munched a candy bar. The sheriff drove past going in the other direction. When the sheriff was safely past, Garth parked in front of the sheriff's office, let himself in, and sat at the sheriff's desk. Garth estimated that the man should be well past the boiling point by now.

Sheriff Charlie "Bub" Hollis burst through the door. Garth wasn't disappointed. His face was florid behind the orange sunglasses. Rivulets of sweat ran out from under the white Stetson. Jowls and paunch bounced in unison as the shiny black boots stomped.

"Boy! Where you been? I don't like to be kept wait . . ." he growled and stopped short as he realized he was talking to a law-enforcement superior.

The ploy had been effective. Hollis was betraying his apprehension about the case. Garth pursued the advantage. "Sheriff Hollis, why haven't you sent specimens from the deceased in for evaluation as required by Mississippi law when the case involves narcotics?"

Hollis blanched. "No need . . . got the culprit . . . open and shut case," he stammered.

Garth looked at him evenly. "Mississippi law and federal statutes require that blood and tissue analysis be performed in cases which involve narcotics regardless of the status of the investigation. You have your undertaker get them off before the day is out. Understand?"

"Yeah, ok."

"Have you had blood and urine analysis done on the accused?"

"Nayet."

"You have until tomorrow night. I'll check with Jackson when I get back to the motel tomorrow evening. If they don't have the specimens, you can take that oversize gold badge to the pawnshop. Unnerstand?"

"Don' push me b . . . that's not reasonable . . . how do I get them there in twenty-four hours?"

"That's your problem. I'd like to see the accused now."

Garth worked on the pleasant face while following Hollis back to the cell.

Norm Bodine was a skinny man of average height. He had a large nose and unkempt straw colored hair. Garth observed that he looked more like late teens than mid twenties. The vacant expression lent the man an air of innocence. It belied his age.

"Gotcha visitor here, Norm," said Hollis. "This here's state narcotics officer Garth Moore."

Norm offered his hand. "Pleased t' meet ya Mr. Moore."

Garth took the hand and began to respond, but Norm turned to Hollis. "All city cops this big?" Hollis locked the door and walked away without answering.

"Tell me about it," Garth asked in a gentle tone.

"Wuz up 't Lyndon Bonner's place in Jackson. Had a few drinks. Next thing I knowed, I wuz in here."

"Nothing else?" prodded Garth.

"Uh uh."

Garth didn't need to work at a pleasant face. He felt compassion tugging his skin around. "Do you know what they are accusing you of doing?"

"Killin' that lady."

"That lady? Don't you know her name?"

"Mizz Valise, or Vallas or sumpin' like that."

"Didn't you know her . . . I mean . . . can you picture who she was?"

"Can't rightly say I can."

Hollis came down the hall with the doctor. "Doc's here to get the specimens. You done yet?"

"No, I'd like to talk with Norm some more, but I'll wait until the doctor is finished."

After the doctor left, Garth again seated himself opposite Norm. "Have you known this Lyndon Bonner long?"

"He wuz grade head 'o me in school."

"You chum around together?"

"Nah."

"But you said you were at his place drinking. Weren't you two friends?"

"Nah. Din see nothin' of 'im fer years. Couple months ago, he invites me 't his place in Jackson for drinks. First time I seen him since he quit school."

"Did you two do that often since?"

"Nah, din see no more of 'im 'till 'tother night. His girl picks me up 'n, we go up to his place."

"Where did she pick you up?"

"Outsida town."

"She picked you up and drove you all the way to Jackson?"

"Yep."

"Didn't it seem odd to you that a casual acquaintance would drive two hours to get here and two hours back merely to have a couple of drinks with you?"

"Din think 'bout it much."

"This Lyndon Bonner denies that you were with him last night. What do you think about that?"

"Things been pretty mixed up fer a fair while now. If he says I wern't, maybe I got it wrong."

"Do you know what will happen to you if you are found guilty of this charge?"

"Lectric chair, I suppose."

"Are you worried about that?"

"If I killed that lady like they said I did, I wouldn't want 't take no chance of doin' it again."

Garth chatted with Norm awhile longer. Norm's rendition of his personal history tallied with what the sheriff had said. They talked about Norm's likes, dislikes, and relationships. Garth couldn't detect any duplicity in the man's answers. He appeared to be exactly what Lew had said—a not-too-bright person whose marbles had been scattered by trauma. He did not seem to be a person who would, or could, plan and commit a murder.

Garth thanked Norm and retired to the motel room. He needed to consider what he'd seen at the morgue and heard here today.

✱✱✱

A short burst came from the siren—not long enough for a full wail to develop, more like a growl. The tent flap was unzipped from the inside and a sleepy head peered out to see a white Stetson and orange sunglasses.

"Good morning, folks. Welcome to Teula. I'm Sheriff Hollis. I'm trying to confirm that you're passing through. Folks around here pay me to know everyone that's in town, but if you'll be moving on soon there's no reason for me asking any questions."

"I believe I understand, Sheriff."

"Good. If y'all need anything, I'll be over in that diner yonder having breakfast."

Hollis walked into the diner and seated himself where he had a good view of the park.

"Shameful, shameful. Bet them two ain't even married," said the waitress, as she brought coffee.

Hollis watched the couple loading their tent on the motorcycle. "As long as they keep moving on, 'tain't no concern of ours, Maude."

✳✳✳

Garth was waiting in Hollis' office when he returned from his morning rounds.

"Good morning Sheriff."

Hollis eyed the fur hat in Garth's hands. "Ain't that the hat Miss Valdez was wearing?"

"Yes it is. Did she favor hats like this?"

"I don't think I ever saw her with a hat on."

"I suspected as much."

"What is that supposed to mean?"

Garth turned the hat inside out. A seam was open. He pulled the rayon lining back. A shiny white cloth was between the leather and the lining. "What do you suppose that is?" he asked.

"How should I know? I ain't no haber-de-whatever-you-call-em."

"My guess would be that it is an exotic fabric used for insulation in space suits. I'd like to send this hat to Houston for confirmation if I may."

"You'll damn well do as you please. Go ahead. But, why is the lining of a hat important?"

"The doctor has estimated the time of death to be around eight o'clock. At that time, you were out at the airport waiting for that casket. Correct?"

Hollis nodded.

"How did the doctor determine the time of death?" Garth asked with a smile.

"That's his business . . . I donno."

"By measuring the temperature of the brain. The rate at which the brain loses heat following death is well known."

Hollis' belligerent expression began to become one of interest. "You mean, if that hat held the heat in, our time of death might be several hours off?"

Hollis' display of nimble cognition surprised Garth. "Precisely. I wondered about this hat when I saw it last night. It is inappropriate for this part of the country, but she did have those Cossack boots on, and you know about the goofy things women wear . . ."

Hollis chuckled. "Did you notice those boots? She hadn't walked anywhere in 'em."

Garth was becoming aware that he had misjudged Hollis. "Yeah, I wondered about that too. I couldn't get it out of my head last night. That's why another look at this hat was first on the agenda today."

"So, if you're right, how far off do you think we are?"

"That, I can't say. I'll need the help of the boys in Houston to tell me how much this thing would have retarded the heat loss."

"When will you know?"

"Day after tomorrow—Thursday."

"Look, Moore, can I depend on you not to breathe a word about this hat business to anyone?"

"No problem . . . until I hear from the lab. But, if I'm right about this stuff, you realize that it will mean that Norm cannot be the guilty party, don't you?"

"Look, we found her blood on his sneaker, a print made by that sneaker beside her body, two envelopes of golden horse on him and six more in her car. If that don't add up to him killing her for the dope, I don't know what does."

Garth decided to back off and retrench. "I won't be around until Thursday anyhow," he said.

"Mind telling me where you're going?"

"Jackson. I intend to have a chat with this Lyndon Bonner. What can you tell me about him?"

"He's a real punk. I'd like put him so far away that they'd have to pipe sunlight to him. I've wanted to nail him since he was in grade school. I hear he pimps in Jackson. He ain't got the guts to do anything heavy."

"If that is your opinion, why do you believe him against Norm?"

"According to Norm's story, Bonner's girl made two round trips from Jackson to here and back that night. That's eight hours of driving in a twelve-hour period. Why? It's too far-fetched. Besides, Norm does have a history of getting time all wrong. Did he mention the fire when you talked with him yesterday?"

"Yes, he mentioned it."

"How did he seem to have it placed in time?"

"About right."

"Sometimes he talks about it as though it had happened yesterday and expresses worry about whether or not his parents are going to pull through."

"Perhaps you don't realize that your scenario is equally hard to believe."

"Whaddya mean?" snapped Hollis.

"The way you have it, he killed Miss Valdez, stole what drugs he found, shot up—doing an overdose—and wandered down onto main street where he passed out. For starters, you haven't found the murder weapon."

"I'll find it. I know I'm lookin' for a small caliber handgun."

"I'm aware that you did your ballistics work," Garth said. Hollis puffed up as Garth had anticipated. "Remember how many shots were used?"

"Sure, one."

"One shot from a small caliber weapon and not in the head. Whoever did that job knew what they were doing. A head shot would have botched the attempt to distort the time of death. We both know Norm isn't capable of anything like that. Besides, people don't go for long walks when they're high."

Hollis squirmed. "A house of cards, Moore. We got our murderer. He's gonna fry. I don't care how much of the taxpayer's money you fancy city types squander trying to make this more than it is."

That caught Garth off balance. Hollis' vacillations between hick town sheriff and intelligent lawman had him on the ropes. He excused himself and headed for Jackson. He was angry with himself for letting Hollis trip him up and angry with Hollis for insisting that Norm was the culprit. Anger called for a long drive, not action. He was pleased with himself for having learned that much over the years.

✸✸✸

Shiny boots propped on the desk, coffee cup at his elbow, Charlie "Bub" Hollis was enjoying the Wednesday edition of the paper. That smart-assed, white-trash-loving nigger cop was out of his hair for the day. He expected to have the whole thing wrapped up before Moore could do anything about it.

The door slammed. Hollis looked over his paper. "Well, if it ain't the local edition of Shoe," he said with good-natured sarcasm as the editor-publisher-reporter of the local newspaper walked in.

"Charlie, I talked with Norm's aunt this morning."

"And?"

"She says she saw a car pick Norm up. She says she told you about that too."

The good-natured demeanor fell from Hollis' face as his boots dropped to the floor. He leaned across the desk wadding the paper and stared into the newspaperman's eyes through the orange sunglasses. "Listen to me Throckmorton, you 'n me both know that Norm's aunt is almost as goofy as he is. You forget all about what she said. Printing something like that would mess things up. Got it?"

"Sure Charlie," replied Throckmorton as he ripped pages out of his notebook and deposited them in the wastebasket. A pleasant demeanor returned to Hollis face as the wads of paper hit bottom. "What can you tell me about that black narcotics guy?" the newspaperman continued.

"Good man. He's very thorough. I believe he's confirming what we already knew."

"Anything else?"

"We should have an indictment along about Friday."

Hollis accompanied the newspaperman out and sauntered over to the bakery.

***

Hollis put the finished newspaper aside and stretched. He regarded the empty coffee cup and doughnut sack with satisfaction. The ringing of the phone interrupted his reverie.

"Hollis here."

"Charlie, it's Doc. I just got a call from Jackson. Norm's blood showed traces of a sedative. They are sending me a fax of the report now."

"Doc, listen up. You burn that fax when it comes in. Then, get your fax machine out of sight. If that big Nigger asks you any questions, play dumb. Got it?"

"Charlie, are you sure? That guy is a state narcotics officer."

"Virgil, when was the last time I questioned the way you were delivering a baby?"

Laughter. "You know better than to do that."

"You ought to know better than to mess with my baby."

"Ok, Charlie, but if I get in trouble . . ."

"Ain't gonna be no trouble."

***

Driving back to Tuela on Wednesday night, Garth was no less mad than he had been on the way to Jackson. Somebody was playing games, the kind of games he played. He didn't mind games as long as he was moving the pieces. Being the moved rather than the mover made him mad.

***

Instead of starting with his rounds, Hollis called Garth's motel on Thursday morning. Garth had already left. That was bad. There was nothing to do but wait. He got some doughnuts and made coffee. The Taurus slid to a stop out front. Garth's steps were rapid and heavy. Hollis took a deep breath and made certain he was taking a sip of coffee as Garth burst through the door. Son-of-a-gun, the man had to be the biggest, meanest-looking, black man he had ever seen.

"Hollis, you were holding out on me!"

"Whatever gave you that idea, Moore?"

"I found Bonner's car before I found him. I had an idea that if he planned to make those two fast trips here and back, he might have had his car serviced before doing them. Sure enough, the sticker showed a service job on Saturday. The odometer now shows too many miles for city driving but plenty to get here and back."

"Very good. Did you catch up with Bonner?"

"No," Garth replied.

Hollis visibly relaxed.

"I didn't need to. I got to his girl," Garth continued.

Hollis stiffened. "What?"

"I leaned on his girl. I explained about the mileage. She changed her mind about Bodine being with her for the whole twenty-four hours. Do you know what else? I checked with the lab while I was there. I know about Norm's blood. I also know that the doctor here is playing dumb. He's so scared that I didn't have the heart to lean on him, but I'm about mad enough to have no such compunction regarding you."

Hollis didn't react to the threat. His eyes searched the room. He twiddled his thumbs. Garth didn't know what to do. If Hollis had denied or tried to cover up, the proper course of action would have been clear. Instead, he was sitting there as if he was calculating something.

Hollis looked at Garth and took off his sunglasses. "You're a lot better cop than I expected," he offered. "I guess I'll have to take you into my confidence."

Garth had been prepared to deal with obtuseness, chicanery, or stubbornness. He had no plan for dealing with this. "If you think you can get me to help you fry that innocent retard back there, you got another think coming," he growled.

"You can drop the crusade for the rights of the unjustly accused. Norm was never in any danger. I needed everybody to think I was swallowing the frame-up so I could smoke out Mr. Big."

"Mr. Big?" Garth asked, beginning to feel he had walked in during the final ten minutes of the movie.

"Yeah, when Roberta Valdez moved back here, the story about this wholesale cosmetics operation looked fishy from the start. She hadn't done well in Houston. She spent eleven years going from one thing to another. She tried hard, but never landed anything worthwhile. A few years ago, her dad died. He left no insurance, but he did leave a modest mortgage on the house. She moved back here driving that Cadillac convertible and started paying all the bills on time, in cash."

"That car has the name of a cosmetics company on it. Don't they give those out as sales incentives?" Garth asked—probing for flaws.

"That outfit gives out Buicks, nothing else. Besides, I checked her sales record. She wouldn't qualify for a roller skate. The routine she established took her out of town for a couple of days each week. When she returned, she shipped about a dozen parcels out. They were to the same addresses every time–lower class whores and poor women in the Jackson area–people that wouldn't buy the pricey line Roberta was supposedly representing. I checked a few out. They didn't pay. She'd told them that she was dumping excess and obsolete inventory. I kept track of the mailings for a spell. In every group, one address got two packages. The address receiving the second package would vary and there would be a different name on it. When I asked the recipients about it, they said that the agreement was for them to hold the package with the wrong name until somebody picked it up. I took some pictures along. The packages were picked up either by Lyndon Bonner or one of his girls."

Garth was impressed. "Be nice to know what was in those packages."

"Coke. Four uncut kilos per package."

"How did you get that data about the addresses and get into a package without a search warrant?"

"It's called trust. The lady who runs the parcel depot knew what I was doing even though I made certain that she never saw me tampering with packages. People around here trust me enough to let me do things like that."

"Do you know where she got the stuff?"

"Yeah, some friends down south tailed her. She pulled a waterproof bag out of the swamp."

"Your tentacles seem to reach a long way."

"People around here pay me to know what's going on. Pity though, I never have been able to get any closer than what I've told you. Whoever set this up did a good job. I don't think she ever knew who put those bags in the swamp. She would send a letter out each week containing the address for the extra parcel, but it was always addressed to a P.O. box. I don't think she ever knew who was on either end. It was clever, to set the mule up so that she couldn't tell anybody anything if she got caught. The quantities that moved showed a lot of planning too. The profit margin was substantial but not enough to make the syndicates want to horn in."

"Do you have any idea where Bonner took it?"

"There's a guy in Jackson named Moser who supplies a lot of retailers. He gets his stock from independents. He employs firm means to keep his suppliers and customers in line. I'm counting on him being the buyer."

"Counting on . . .?"

"Yes, and you can have a part of that action if you want it."

Garth didn't want to seem too anxious. "Maybe you should tell me why they killed Miss Valdez first."

"That was my mistake. After tracking this operation for a couple of years and not getting any closer to who was running it than I am now, I tried the tack of showing Roberta some of those drug education videos. I didn't make any accusations; I just wanted her to know what that stuff did to people. I was hoping she would agree to lead me to the king-pin. The videos rattled her, but she didn't offer any information. Apparently, she talked to the wrong people, and they rubbed her out. Tragic as it is, I think her murder will close this case for us."

"Oh?"

"Sure. Whoever set this thing up is smart. Maybe he out-smarted himself. This murder doesn't look like the work of a hit man. The cover-up is too elaborate. My guess is that Mr. Big did the job himself. Since a professional criminal would have hired the hit, my guess is that we are not dealing with an underworld figure. Such a person probably wouldn't think he needed to secure Bonner."

Suddenly, the lights came on for Garth. "So that's the action you are offering me?" he said through a broad grin.

"Right on, my man."

✹✹✹

Everything was right with Garth as he drove to Jackson early Friday morning. He had that good feeling which comes from knowing you're eminently qualified for the current task.

It was about ten-thirty when Garth knocked on Lyndon Bonner's door. A disheveled weasel of a man peeked through the opening allowed by the door chain. Garth's foot exploded against the door. Weasel and chunks of doorjamb went flying into the room. Garth's gun was out, but there wasn't anybody else in the dingy room. Bonner dabbed at a bloody nose and whimpered as he took the chair indicated by Garth.

"Who 'r you? Whadda ya want? I gave Moser his shipment last night," Bonner whined.

"I'm not with Moser, but you might like to know that the package you gave to Moser last night contained four kilos of flour."

Bonner paled and looked like he was going to retch. "Who . . . why?" he gasped.

"Sheriff Hollis did the switch. That leaves you with a choice. Come over here, but don't show yourself in the window."

Bonner sidled over to the window and looked out.

"See those two guys watching the entrance to this place?" asked Garth.

Bonner started shaking.

"I can walk out of here, and you can take your chances, whether or not they work for Moser," Garth continued.

"Or?" said Bonner, as he stared at Garth with terrified eyes.

"Or, you sing to me about who killed Roberta Valdez and a patrol car will come and pick us up. When you are tried and sentenced, that should convince Moser you didn't scam the shipment."

Bonner became bold. "What's to keep me from telling Moser what you just told me?"

Garth shrugged. "Common sense. Cold fear. Moser doesn't have a reputation for listening when he's pissed. It'll take time and dramatic proof to get him off your case."

Bonner shrank.

✳✳✳

Randall Lewis felt drained by noon on Saturday. Moving his mother into the nursing home was a trying experience. The message for him to stop by the sheriff's office was the only bright spot. He was looking forward to the therapy Garth had suggested.

As Lewis walked into the sheriff's office, he looked around. He was surprised not to see Garth. Hollis looked up from his paper.

"Get your mom settled ok, Randy?"

"Yeah, I guess so."

"You'll let me know if there's anything I can do for her?"

"Yeah, sure. Is Moore here?"

"Before I answer that, you'd better read this," said Hollis, handing Lewis a folded document.

Lewis stared in shocked disbelief. It was a warrant for his arrest. The charge was the murder of Roberta Valdez. "How? . . . Who?" he stammered and began to lose his balance.

Hollis sprang to his feet and guided Lewis to a chair as the latter crumpled. Lewis sat with his face in his hands sobbing for several minutes. Hollis was waiting patiently when Lewis lifted his head.

"How did you find out?" Lewis entreated.

"It makes no difference, but I'll tell you how if you tell me why."

"That's fair enough, I guess."

"I've known for a long time that Roberta was making her money by being a mule. Your operation was good. I never could find anything that pointed to the brains. I had no reason to suppose that Bonner even knew who ran things. The murder put it all together. Bonner's involvement meant he had to know. We made Moser think Bonner had tried to scam him. Bonner fingered you in exchange for protection from Moser. Now, suppose you tell me why you did all of this in the first place."

"I first thought about doing it for the money, but I was scared, and I couldn't figure out how to move the stuff from the bay to Jackson. Roberta . . . I'd tried to date her since high school, but she'd never give me a tumble. When her dad died, I even proposed but that high and mighty little spic broad turned me down. Me! A white man! Offering her a good name and a secure future–and she turned me down! Something snapped and I decided that I was going to make the deal with her pay off. I set it up through another party. She never knew who she was working for."

Hollis nodded. "Did she come to you after I showed her those videos?"

"Yeah, she was scared, real scared. She didn't know what you were doing. Since she knew I was a policeman, she came to me for advice. At last she came to me for something, but it was too late."

"Trying to enlist her help was a mistake. At least I could tell her mom that she wasn't a pusher. I could say that she was working undercover for me. It wasn't exactly the truth, but not too far off."

Lewis looked around the office. "Uh, is Moore still around?"

"No, after he brought Bonner in yesterday, he mumbled something about the 'compassionate cop business' and not wanting to see you now. Do you know what that was all about?"

"Not a clue."

✳✳✳

Rose looked across the table at Garth. "I'll have to admit that I was relieved when you called to say that the other guy wouldn't be coming into town with you. I was having difficulty finding anyone that short. What did you say changed your plans?"

"I didn't say."

Rose saw that Garth was troubled and didn't feel he could share the why with her. He had promised to "do the town" with her tonight, but the town wasn't going to have much done to it if she couldn't brighten his mood. "I don't believe that you said anything about your new project beyond it being something you had suggested. Can you tell me any more?" she prompted, trying to get his focus beyond whatever was troubling him.

Garth brightened. "Sure, I meant to tell you about it anyway. Some new computer technology recently became available to us. I was taking a course in using it and one of the assignments was to design a search through data that was outside the area in which we usually work. I chose to look at missing children. The exercise was to use a specific set of data while changing search parameters. If we saw a pattern, the idea was to refine the search parameters to see if the pattern got stronger or disappeared. The instructor called it an exercise in separating real patterns from statistical some-thing-or-others."

"I believe that 'statistical anomalies' is the term you are looking for," Rose offered.

"Yeah . . . yeah . . . that's it. Anyway, the first few runs didn't seem to show any pattern that I could see, but when I used male, Caucasian, age five to twelve, the incidences seemed to be greater in cities surrounding us than right here. So I played with the parameters some more and when I added unsolved and no witnesses, the data pattern looked like a doughnut around this city."

Rose began to look alarmed. "Do you mean that, at a certain radius from this city, the incidences go up significantly, stay high for awhile as the radius increases and then drop off sharply?"

"You got it, babe."

"Does the size of the radius suggest anything?"

"Unfortunately, yes. It represents the approximate travel time for which a person could be sedated without risking any ill effects."

"Could it mean that someone is abducting children, drug-ging them, and bringing them here?"

"That hypothesis does fit the data."

"Whatever for?"

"These are all cases where the victim has disappeared. That makes any guess about the 'what for' ugly."

"So, you've been assigned to this case?"

"No, it isn't 'my case.' I wrote up a proposal to do some fieldwork. I suggested that, with my street contacts, I might be able to find out if there was anything to the pattern. My boss didn't think there was any chance of the head shed buying the idea. It surprised the hell out of him when funds were allocated. I'll have to admit that—with bureau politics being what they are—I was surprised myself. I had made a call to a friend. He's on the task force for missing children and was the one who gave me the idea of looking at data on missing children. Well, he was able to explain it. The task force has received a couple of tips about a child porn ring operating out of here. They didn't get anywhere with the tips and lost interest in them until they saw my data. My friend suggested that, since their contacts hadn't been able to give them anything on the tips, they might do well to let me try mine. My role is limited to snooping around. I have to keep them informed and let them decide what to do if I get onto anything."

Rose raised an eyebrow. "At first, it sounded like you were going to be doing what I've heard you refer to as 'computer weenie stuff.' I couldn't see you in that role. Now, you tell me you're going to be somebody else's legman. I have a harder time seeing that."

"Hey, if there's some scumbag out there abusing kids, I'm willing to play any part to bring him down."

"I don't doubt that you are sincere in that, Galahad, but let me propose a scenario. Suppose you caught somebody dead-to-rights. Would he be turned over to the justice system or would we find him dead because he'd pulled a gun on you?"

Garth looked hurt. "How can I say what might happen? I don't have control over those things."

"Perhaps you don't, but let me tell you this: If the family of that last dealer who pulled a gun on you came to me, your record would make me think I could make a pretty good case that you somehow provoked him into resisting instead of submitting to arrest."

"Fine thing, take a lady out on a date, and get lawyered."

"Look, bozo, it's hard enough being in love with a man who might get killed on his next job, let alone one who might get convicted of being a vigilante." Her expression took on an edge. "I'm going to level with you."

Garth winced. Rose's "Level with you" lectures happened with about the same frequency as the Old Man's lectures on excessive force. For an instant, Garth wondered why the important people in his life felt it necessary to lecture him regularly, but he caught himself and began forming a strategy to deflect the looming lecture. Commitment–

women always groused about lack of commitment–maybe reminding her that he wasn't lacking in that department would do the trick.

"Why's that necessary? I've leveled with you more than once that I want to spend the rest of my life with you," Garth said innocently.

"That is precisely the problem," she burst. "I can't see myself living without you, but I can't see myself spending the rest of my life wondering if you are going to come home from work or not."

"C'mon, now, the stats ain't that bad. There are a lot of professions that have higher life insurance rates."

"I'm not talking about Mr. Average cop. I'm talking about your high incidence of shoot-outs."

"I can't help it if some scumbag pulls a gun on me. I've got a right to defend myself."

"Granted, but it always seems to be the suspects you've got cold who resort to gunplay while those whose guilt is in question wind up getting arrested and standing trial. Do you have any explanation for that?"

Garth's eyes became narrow. "How do you know that? It sounds like you've arranged to have a snoop at my record. That isn't legal . . . you got no right . . ."

Rose's eyes flashed. "You encourage me to fall in love with you, and then you tell me I've no right to find out if my fears for you are justified?" she snarled, and fell silent.

"Damn, she's good," thought Garth. She'd made a stinger of a statement and not diluted the effect with more verbiage. Garth knew better than to make an attempt at matching wits with either ladies or lawyers. That made him two strikes down going into this conversation. "Wull, I'm not saying whether you are right or wrong, but you have to admit that, the way things have worked out a couple of times, a social menace was permanently removed from the streets and the taxpayers were saved a lot of coin."

Rose relaxed. "I thought so and I appreciate your candor." She took a deep breath. "I have no idea how you provoke these people, but you have to quit doing it if we are to go any further."

"Hey, I didn't say . . ." Garth began.

"Put a sock in it," she interrupted. "I can understand why you do it. I can even agree with your reasons up to a point. However, now that it's out in the open, I expect you to think about it, to put yourself in my place. How can you expect me to make a life around a person who deliberately provokes combat with dangerous, dysfunctional people who may be under the influence of anything from weed to meth?"

Garth didn't reply right away. She waited. Finally, he looked at her and smiled.

"Madame Prosecutor, the defense has nothing to say. It's a brand new concept that will take awhile to assimilate. But, he promises to give it top priority."

Rose smiled back. "Good boy. Now, let's get on with doing the town."

3

FRANK AND ROSLYN

His finger hesitated over the mouse button. Pressing it could change his life unalterably–perhaps in several directions. A worst-case scenario was that he might lose life as he now knew it. And, life as Frank Grant now knew it was not shabby in the least. He didn't share ownership of anything with a financial institution. In fact, he owned little pieces of several. The house in which he sat was valued within the top ten percent in the city. His wife was one of the best-looking women around. He was on better than amicable terms with his grown children who were all doing well. He made a better than decent living, working few hours in pleasant surroundings with no stress. It had happened without striving. His circumstances had progressed from one level of comfort to another in a manner that was almost predictable. That was why he was here, with his finger poised over the mouse button. It was all so predictable . . . and . . . so insufferably boring. His finger smashed the button down.

Two weeks later, as he walked toward the restaurant, Frank experienced the same sense of foreboding that had preceded his hitting the mouse button. Stepping through the door would be crossing a personal Rubicon–no turning back. At this point, he could still turn around and return to the status quo. He'd erased the incriminating emails and exchanges of information that had brought him to this point. Nobody knew that he'd used Discreet Encounters to set up a meeting with a woman. The process had been titillating. DE had asked all sorts of questions about his interests, aspirations, and inner thoughts. It had even questioned why he was interested in meeting someone outside his marriage. The process had been professional with constant reminders that the service was not there to facilitate affairs, but to connect people who "were in need of intellectual companionship not available in their marriages." In fact, the service claimed to have salvaged many marriages by broadening a member's circle of friends.

Without addressing the matter of why he had requested an introduction to a woman—rather than to another man with similar interests—Frank had rationalized that it was all innocent. At least, he could claim that he was playing along with what he thought to be a joke. Now, if he walked through the restaurant door, there would be no turning back; he'd be guilty of a tryst with another man's wife. DE had suggested from the onset that if he and the woman "clicked" that the ideal situation would be for the couples to become friends. It had sounded innocent enough and perfectly plausible to a man bored out of his skull. Although there had been moments—like this one—of trepidation, the excitement had made him feel alive!

The restaurant building had been a grand old house at one time. The treed front yard, now manicured in a professional manner, wasn't the work of a loving, resident, gardener. He'd had to look twice to find the sign. "The Victoria House— fine cuisine served in a private atmosphere." It was small and tasteful to the point of invisibility unless you were looking for it. He looked around to see if anyone was watching and pushed through the door.

The foyer was, indeed, that of a grand old house. The wood paneling bespoke of artisans no longer available. The closed doors on either side featured ornate casings and inlaid panels. Nevertheless, the atmosphere was cold. Items like umbrella stands, coat racks, vases, and bric-a-brac were absent. Without those signs of habitation, the beautiful wood tried in vain to comfort. It was like the yard–beautiful but sterile. The single piece of furniture was a small desk adjacent to the winding staircase at the far end. From a distance, it looked antique. In other circumstances, Frank would have taken the time to inspect it. Had he been in a less excited state, he'd have also wanted to examine and savor the artistry of the curved railing and pilasters on the stairs.

The maitre d' rose from behind the desk and, to Frank's astonishment, offered his hand.

"Good evening sir. Would you be Mister Grant?"

"Uh, yes," replied Frank, taking the beefy hand. Since Frank shook several hands during a normal business day, he had become adept at reading a lot about a person from the handshake. This hand felt like it was more accustomed to handling barbells than menus.

"And, may I have your membership number please?"

"Uh . . . 5X21Z."

"Thank you, Mr. Grant. My name is Carlos and I have the pleasure of serving you. Mrs. Cornelius is already at your table, if you will follow me."

Frank followed Carlos up the stairs. At the top, they started down a hallway. On either side were doors. The first two were marked "Sierra" and "Teton." The woodwork was nowhere close to the quality of that in the foyer. This level had undergone recent renovation.

"Carlos, are these conference rooms?" asked Frank—more because he was employing the salesperson's technique of using a name as soon as possible after introduction than because he wanted to know.

"No, Mr. Grant, they are all private dining rooms."

Frank made his living by sizing up people, so he noted the use of "Mr. Grant" instead of the customary "Sir." This guy was fixing the connection between his face and name. Did he take the maitre d' business so seriously that he wanted to be able to greet patrons by name the next time they came in? Or, was he the maitre d' at all? He'd said that it would be his pleasure to serve—an odd turn of phrase if his sole function was to show patrons to their table.

Carlos opened the door of the "Mojave" room. Frank found the view captivating–she had to be the most interesting thing he had ever seen. Standing by the window, she appeared to be slightly over five feet tall with long dark hair and light olive skin. The conservative green dress was neither too low in the upper nor too high in the lower . . .

just . . . just . . . nice. The amount of shoulder, arm, and leg showing were well-proportioned firm muscle. Had the dress been more revealing, it would have been quite a show, but this lady didn't seem to have a need to show off, a quality Frank found most attractive.

Warmly, Carlos addressed her. "Mrs. Roslyn Cornelius, may I present Mr. Frank Grant."

Frank's fascination escalated as she turned and walked toward them. She was graceful and knew how to walk in the tall heels. She didn't stride or glide. Frank searched for a word—"athletic" presented itself. A walk that appeared athletic but graceful in spike heels seemed a contradiction, but there it was, approaching him.

"Pleased to meet you Frank," she said in a matter-of-fact voice as she offered her hand. Frank fought back embarrassment as he realized that his hand was still hanging at his side.

"My pleasure," Frank replied as he took her hand. It was small and smooth but firm. The grip betrayed no hesitation; she wasn't as off balance as he.

Carlos seated her as Frank took the other chair. Menus materialized in Carlos' hand. He placed them on the table, beyond the line of sight between the two of them. "May I offer you something to drink?" he asked.

"Chianti," she said simply.

"Uh . . . er . . . Grande Marnier," Frank blurted, trying to match her decisiveness.

As Carlos disappeared, Roslyn looked at Frank with a twinkle in her dark eyes. "Grande Marnier as an aperitif? I thought liqueurs were for desert."

"I thought Chianti went with red meat. You haven't even looked at the menu."

"Bravo," she said softly, intertwining her fingers. She put her elbows on the table, rested her chin on the intertwined fingers, and looked at him. Her voice was soft but firm. "This is your first sample. I know what I like and couldn't care less about what convention dictates. Right now, Chianti sounds good, so that's what I'm having. Other people's opinion regarding what it should go with doesn't enter the equation for me."

"What a voice," thought Frank. It was lower than average, but still feminine . . . how did that work?

Carlos appeared and placed a wine glass before Roslyn. As he uncorked the bottle, she looked at him and said, "Top it up, pal. I don't do the sip and slosh thing. I probably wouldn't know a good bottle from a bad one."

Frank's eyes went to Carlos, expecting the prince-serving-a-peasant response. Instead, Carlos smiled broadly and replied, "Darn, if that's the case, I could have brought a bottle of the cheap stuff." The quip brought a laugh from Roslyn, so Frank joined.

After placing Frank's glass on the table, Carlos took a step back from the table and said, "You two enjoy. When you are ready to order, or if you'd like anything else, Mr. Grant can push the button on the arm of his chair, and I'll be right with you. Would you please try it now, sir?"

Frank looked at the right arm of his chair. Sure enough, there was a button on the end. He pressed it and a soft chime came from somewhere on Carlos.

"Ah, my leash is in good order," Carlos said, as he nodded and disappeared through the door.

"Not exactly what one would expect," observed Frank, as he cocked his head toward the door through which Carlos had exited.

"Most refreshing," she answered. "When I walked in, I expected to encounter someone who, as the song says, 'Talked kind of snooty and walked sort of fruity . . .'"

"And they won't bring you what you want," Frank finished.

Gently, she clapped her hands. "Wonderful, you know Ray Stevens!"

"Just because he happens to be my all-time favorite comedian."

She arched an eyebrow. "How do you feel about the rest of country music?"

"It's my preference. I may have everything the Hag and Possum ever did."

"And your wife?"

"She hates it."

"What music does she like?"

"Classical—for background—I couldn't say that she is 'into' any type of music."

"Well, since the subject is open, I guess that now would be as good a time as any to follow DE's recommendation that we level with each other regarding our marriages."

Frank leaned back, took a sip of the Grand Marnier, sighed, and said, "Yeah, I guess you're right. But, before we do, I want to ask you something, lest I forget it."

"Umm, I do think that we need to get the spouse thing out of the way, but shoot."

"Bang!"

They exchanged grins.

Frank gestured toward the window. "When I came in, you were standing over by that window, but you didn't seem to be looking out. Mind telling me what you were doing?"

"I can't imagine why you would be interested, but I was examining the woodwork," she replied, with a shrug.

"And . . . go on."

An expression of incredulity covered her face. "For real? You want to know why I was inspecting the carpentry?"

"Yup."

She sat up straight and took a deep breath as she turned her head to look somewhere to the side of him. "I love wood and I'm fascinated by what people can—or used to—do with it. That's all."

"No, that isn't all. Go on."

She looked at the ceiling. "I can't believe this. I'd love to talk about wood, but nobody has ever asked me."

"I'm asking."

"Ok. Did you notice the exquisite wood work in the foyer?"

"Yes."

"Well, the craftsmen that did that not only had to know how to measure, cut, and fit; they had to understand the nature of the wood itself. Wood twists and shrinks over time, so they had to place the types of wood and the grain orientations in a manner that would cause the changes in one piece of wood to counter the changes in the other. The window in this room survived the renovations—it was done by the same artisans who did the foyer. When you came in, I was appreciating how the joints in it are as tight as they were 100 years ago."

Frank could see in her eyes that she—in spite of herself—expected him to be bored and want to change the subject. He looked over at the window. "Uh, yes, the renovators did spare that casing. Why didn't I notice?" He felt a flush creeping up his neck. "I . . . I . . . guess I was . . . otherwise distracted."

She smiled. "Yes, I noticed. I thank you for that. A girl gets to experience having that effect on men less and less as she gets older. Honestly, I don't remember the last time it happened. But, tell me, would you have noticed the beautiful work on that window casing in other circumstances?"

"Oh, yeah. I was so preoccupied with looking at the work in the foyer that I didn't see Carlos until he stood. And, that faux antique desk he was behind! Putting a laminate construction next to that beautiful staircase is . . . is . . ."

"Insulting?" she offered.

"Yeah, I was fishing for something like chutzpah, but insulting works."

She took a firm pull on her Chianti and studied the glass as she put it down. "Whew, this is a little much. DE promised to put me in touch with someone who shared interests, but country music and wood in one package is hard to believe."

"I have to echo that sentiment, but if this is a harbinger, it's gonna be fun."

"I find the prospect exciting, but we should get this spouse thing out of the way."

"Yup, you're right. Following DE's lead has turned out great thus far. I guess we should play by the rules. Ladies first."

She toyed with the wine glass as her expression became pensive. "A.P. is five years older than I. He's an attorney—has his own firm."

Frank blanched.

"What's wrong?" she asked.

"Nothing. Please continue."

"We don't have any children. I was ambivalent about whether or nor I wanted the parent trip when I was younger. I feel the same about not having any progeny at this point. I might have found parenthood cool, but I'm certain A.P. would never have found time to be a dad."

"Does A.P. have a name?" Frank interrupted.

"Alphonse Percival, but everybody calls him A.P. He's pretty sensitive about it. It seems that his parents were on some misguided trip about honoring certain relatives. They didn't pay much attention to what effect the name would have on him. In fact, it seems typical of them. I don't think that they ever paid much attention to the effect any of their decisions might have on the child."

"A.P. was an only child?"

"Yeah, not inflicting themselves on any other children is about the only thing they ever did right as parents."

"So, your in-laws are not exactly your favorite folks?"

"Past tense—both deceased. Does my lack of reverence for the departed bother you?"

"No, I find it refreshing. This deal of sugar coating statements about a deceased person—particularly when you've never said anything good about them when they were alive—is odious."

"Giving him that name did turn out to be a backhanded favor. The teasing he took as a child made him tough and ruthless in a battle of the wits. His courtroom performances are pure virtuoso. I guess he got good with the put-down while he was in grammar school, but he really found his identity on high-school debating teams."

"Along the lines of Cash's 'Boy Named Sue'?" Frank asked.

"Exactly, but it didn't do anything for his social skills. It seems as though he was a person who nobody wanted around unless they needed a mouthpiece who could devastate an adversary. I think that his few forays into romance were situations where girls wanted somebody who could serve a vicious put-down to a former boyfriend."

"I notice the use of terms like 'it seems, I guess, and I think.' Am I correct in deducing that you two haven't talked much about his younger years?"

"That would be a big ten-four pal. In fact, we don't 'talk' about much of anything. We discuss and analyze matters of mutual interest, which car to buy, whether to get new carpet or go to hardwood, who to vote for, and so on."

Frank's ears perked up when he heard "car" and "buy." "Do you mean that he helped you pick out your car?"

"Yes, but I also helped him select his."

"Amazing. How did that work?"

"He knows from nothing about technical matters. He knows that he doesn't know and doesn't want to be bothered. He relies entirely on me to make sense out of technobabble. When we were looking for his last car, it turned into a neat game. We got a pair of walkie-talkies. I rigged them up so that his looked like a hearing aid and mine looked like a hands-free rig for a cell phone. As the salesman started explaining the features of the car, I faked receiving a call. He was obviously pleased to have the little woman occupied so that he could lay all this macho stuff on A.P. When he said 'turbo intercooler,' I said 'unnecessary maintenance headache'. When he said 'GPS,' I said, 'This is not a submarine that you want to drive under the polar ice cap'. It was fun. It didn't take us long to get the timing down. When he'd nod to let me know that he understood, the salesman would think he was nodding assent. It got rich when A.P. started asking him questions. I remember the bit about the GPS because it was a particular riot. The exchange went something like this:

"A.P: About that GPS, you say that I push a few buttons, and it will tell me where I am and where I need to turn to get where I want to go?

"Salesman: Absolutely.

"A.P: I don't see why I'd need such a thing. My wife always knows right where we are and where we need to turn.

"Salesman: But, when you are on the road by yourself . . .

"A.P: Son, if you'd taken the time to find out anything about me and what I need in a car, you'd know that I don't drive out of town without my wife. Thank you for your time."

Frank's eyes rolled as he pictured the scenario. "From what you'd said, I wasn't picturing A.P. having much of a sense of humor, but he must have one to go along with something like that."

"I appreciate your patience. A.P. is a difficult person to explain, but you need to see all sides of him, or you'll get the wrong idea."

"Perhaps you could tell me what attracted you to him in the first place."

"That's easy. Integrity. Pure and simple, he has more integrity than anyone I've ever known. A good example is the reason for the one failing grade on his university transcript. One of the jocks asked him for help in preparing for a test. When they got together, the jock handed him what he called a 'study guide' saying that these were his weak areas. The 'study guide' had one hundred paragraphs, but A.P. didn't notice. He took the guy through them one by one.

"When the test was handed out, A.P. realized that the one hundred paragraphs on that guy's 'study guide' were the questions on this test, paraphrased. So, A.P. didn't take the test and explained to the teacher that he'd unwittingly seen all the questions beforehand. The teacher demanded that he finger someone, but he refused. The teacher then refused to give him another test and failed him."

"Sounds like a case of misguided loyalty."

"How can you say that? The overwhelming probability is that the 'study guide' no longer existed. Something like that was almost certainly the product of someone on campus who ran an exam scam. Jocks depend on the services of such people to pass courses. Thus, if one of them allowed the products of a scammer to fall into the hands of the authorities, said jock would suffer serious consequences at the hands of his peers. The guy that A.P. helped would have destroyed the 'study guide' that same night. Without it, fingering the jock would have been pointless."

"Hummm . . . a lawyer with integrity. Will wonders never cease? Do you mind if I ask how practicing law has affected this 'integrity'?"

"Not at all. He doesn't take cases unless he believes in them. Consequently, he has passed up some good bucks. He's a good man who takes bad cases because he thinks that the litigant needs his ability to make an argument."

"He sounds like a good guy, so I guess I need to ask why you are here. I'm damn glad you are, but you've got me wondering."

"A.P. and I are compatible, and we have fun, but there's no real intimacy, no sharing of minds and hearts. At first, I thought he'd come around, but now I know that I fell into the trap of seeing him as raw material."

"That's not unusual," Frank observed.

"Yeah, but I've always loathed the way other women would talk about the changes they planned for their men rather than appreciating what they are. Sometime ago, I woke up and realized that I'd been doing the same thing–perhaps on a more subtle level, but essentially the same game." She took her glass in hand and regarded it pensively. "At first, we were so busy launching our careers that I didn't give it much thought. We'd get home from work, chatter about how the day had gone, watch some tube and zonk. At the time, it was comfortable."

"What happened on weekends and other leisure time?"

"I was busy training."

"Training?"

"Yes, I discovered triathlon in university. During my senior year in high school, I found that intense physical activity made me sharper. Therefore, I experimented with various sports as I began university—triathlon turned out to be the best fit. By my junior year, I was enjoying it for its own sake. By the time I started post-grad, I was doing Iron Man."

Frank's eyes widened as he sat back in his chair. "You're one of those that do a long swim . . ."

"Just two and a half miles."

"Jump out of the water, onto a bike and pedal . . ."

"One hundred and twelve miles."

"Pile off the bike and run . . ."

"A marathon—twenty six miles."

"M'god," Frank observed. "And you do this in one day?"

She sighed and sat back. "It's part of the whole picture. To do any good at Iron Man, a person has to train constantly. Your whole life becomes focused around planning for the next run, swim, or bike ride. When we were first married, I was concerned about the effect that being a permanent part of another person's life would have on my training. At the time, I thought I'd lucked out because A.P. didn't seem to mind at all. Instead, he encouraged me. Now, I can see that it was a crutch–one of the things that enabled us to learn how to live at the same address without ever being really 'together'," she said, biting her lower lip as her eyes became moist. She leaned her head back to contain the tears and continued. "As is typical for professionals, our career paths dominated our time and effort in the early years. Again, the way that A.P. was happy to have me around without asking for much seemed like a good deal. He didn't seem to mind when I brought work home, worked late, or had to make business trips. At the time, I rationalized that we were giving each other space to become established in our professions. In addition, it was great—we never had issues about the time we gave to the job, the time I spent training, or that the closest thing to vacations we ever took was attending Iron Man events. Now, here we are–both comfortably established in our chosen fields of endeavor. Now, we could spend more time with each other, but we don't. Although we could start staking out time for 'just us', it has become quite clear that A.P. isn't interested."

The ensuing pause lasted for more than a couple of sips, so Frank asked, "What is your profession?"

"Applied mathematics. I work in the research department of a firm that manufactures compact disks. My role is to help the physicists reduce their findings to formulae that the chemists can use to produce the next generation of CDs."

"Wooo," Frank said, in mock surprise. "A genuine egg-head!"

"I'll have to admit I was geeky in school, but 'egghead' doesn't fit. I don't have much to do with the academia any more. I've always loved the sciences, but pure research or teaching never appealed to me."

"You must have a serious IQ–people like that usually have research aspirations."

"Serious research requires a lot of interaction between others in the field. The popular notion of the lone wolf scientist isn't accurate anymore. Pioneers like Newton and Einstein worked alone, all right, but the expansion of knowledge has changed the environment. Newton could know everything about physics at the time; nobody could do that today. Now, a single lifetime is hardly enough to master everything about any specialty. Therefore, researchers have to rely on other scientists because any investigation will eventually touch areas outside their expertise. Ergo, you have to get on well with the rest of the community to have access to what you need for your own project . . ."

"And . . .?" Frank prompted.

"And? The 'and' is that I realized from the get-go that 'getting on with the rest of the community' isn't my strong suit!" she blurted, and fell silent.

Since she was obviously uncomfortable, Frank waited awhile before gently saying, "Please shut me down if I'm out of line, but is that because of your disdain for convention?"

She looked at him with widening eyes. "You understand!"

"Yeah, I do. I've always wanted to be like that, but never had the guts."

"It's nice of you to say that," she said with a hint of disbelief, "but you didn't have to."

"There is no 'have to' about it. I don't like most wines or gourmet cheeses, but I sip and nibble at wine and cheese parties. Even though I think the stuff stinks, I smile and nod and agree with everybody else about how good it is. I do it to ensure acceptance while wondering how many others are also lying."

"Are the wine and cheese parties related to your business?"

"Mostly."

"So, what is it you do for a living?" she asked, trying to deflect his discomfiture.

"I sell cars. We refer to them as 'Motor Cars' because they are stupid expensive."

Her eyes brightened. "Like Jags and Beemers?"

"More like Lamborghinis and Ferraris."

"Well, color me impressed. I always knew that somebody sold the top of the high end, but I never thought I'd meet one of them. I appreciate the technology in the exotic stuff, but I'd never even consider owning one–too impractical."

"Do you mind telling me why you think them impractical? I agree, but I'm surprised that you understand. So, I'd like to hear your take."

"Uh . . . in order to maintain the . . . the . . ." She became pensive and began to examine the corners of the ceiling. "The . . . I guess . . . panache, is the closest I can come; the vehicles have to use state-of-the-art technology and manufacturing techniques. Since the reliability of any mechanical device is a direct function of the number of units produced and the experience gained thereby, state-of-the-art vehicles are way down on the reliability scale. Ergo, these exotic machines can pass anything but the maintenance shop. I'd like to drive something that looked that cool, but the maintenance bills–even if they were no financial burden–would grate on me to the point of destroying any pleasure of ownership. That's just me. I've got to feel that I'm getting value."

"Hey, that's well put. I'd never thought of using 'panache' instead of 'snob appeal' but the idea of flashy and flamboyant works. I agree with you completely, but I'm glad that everybody doesn't agree with us—if they did, I'd starve to death."

"You're refreshing," she said, with genuine admiration. "Most guys would go to great lengths legitimizing what they do. So, tell me, how does a guy with your attitude wind up selling exotic cars?"

Frank grinned mischievously. "It was mostly my wife's doing."

"Pardon me?"

"I thought that'd catch you off guard, but it's true. I have an MBA, but I didn't set the business world on fire after graduation. On the other hand, Catherine's career took off like an ICBM. When we found out that the first child was on the way, we had to make some decisions. I never thought for a second that Catherine would make a good mom. That's not a slam, it's just the way things are–I'll explain more later. I, in contrast, have always liked kids. The idea that a nanny might raise mine was revolting. So, I volunteered for Mr. Mom duty. Catherine was some relieved but I think that she didn't believe I'd carry through with it. I'll have to admit that I had my doubts too, but I surprised both of us by taking to it like a duck to water. Caring for Jerry and watching him change day by day was a grand adventure. I was so caught up in the whole thing that I didn't miss working at all.

"Catherine couldn't believe that I wasn't chafing about not being the breadwinner. She kept looking for things that I could do from home. Lord knows, we didn't need the money and most of the schemes would have required a lot of time to get going. Jerry wasn't a year old when we discovered that she was pregnant again. I was delighted, but she became even more concerned about my developing an identity crisis. Well, with knowing I'd have another baby to look after, I became even less interested in devoting time to a business start-up.

"Somewhere along the line, she found out that people were making nice coin by brokering exotic car sales. I agreed to look into it—more to give her relief than anything else. It worked out well because we didn't hear anything more about my looming identity crisis throughout the pregnancy and delivery. I've always liked cars, so educating myself about the current crop of exotics was fun. She gathered the legal details together and even dug up some contacts. I didn't think it would go anywhere, but going through the motions seemed to meet a need for her.

"I was so delighted when Katie was born that I pretty much forgot about the exotic car brokering business for the following couple of months. To my utter shock and amazement, one of the contacts Catherine had made called to set up an appointment. I'd traded a few letters with this guy never thinking that he'd decide to use me. I'll have to admit that the idea of brokering a deal on a car that sold for more than most houses scared me to death. I went to the meeting determined to do what I could for the guy but to steer him toward someone who had a track record in the business. As it turned out, this guy came equally determined to make a deal. He felt that Catherine's legal expertise would ensure him of a clean transaction. He said he'd been 'very impressed' with my efforts to make certain he understood what the car was, and, more importantly, what it was not. Actually, I'd simply approached the correspondence as if I was chatting with another enthusiast. I wound up making that deal for him, and we've done five more since.

"It went from there. I'd say that over eighty percent of the people I now deal with have bought from me before. But, you see, it was Catherine's idea to begin with, and it was her legal expertise that gave the whole enterprise credibility."

Roslyn had grown pensive as Frank talked. "Ummm . . . Catherine . . . Catherine Grant. Would that be Judge Catherine Grant?"

"One and the same," Frank grinned.

Roslyn sat back in her chair and regarded the chandelier.

"Whowee . . . How dumb can a couple of people be? Both married to lawyers and having a tryst."

"C'mon now, we're not doing anything wrong. If this evening ever came into question, I could say you were a client," Frank offered weakly.

"Hey, pal," she retorted, "imagine yourself on the stand being questioned by either A.P. or Catherine. How long do you think your story would hold up?"

"Not more 'n a few milliseconds," he answered, grinning again.

"You got it, pal. Even if we're not here for unauthorized nookie, either one of 'em could nail our hides to the barn door."

"You're right—this is a crazy thing to do, but it's more fun than I've had in years."

"Crazy . . . people used to call me that all the time . . . haven't heard it much in the last few years . . . but this is crazy . . . and it feels good," she answered softly.

"A little bit crazy's alright," Frank said, and hummed a few bars of the tune.

She regarded him with intensity. "Is that your honest opinion?"

Frank's brow wrinkled. "Look Doc, this isn't the first time you've asked me if I meant what I said. Even though you probably have a right to, I find it slightly annoying. Therefore, I'm gonna make you a promise. I will never say anything to you that is not my honest opinion."

"Doc?" she asked. "I don't remember mentioning any advanced degrees."

"You do have a Ph.D. don't you?"

"Yes. You're scary."

"Hey, I didn't need to be a mental giant to figure that out. Anyway, Doc, do we have a deal? I promise to shoot straight and you take what I say at face value."

"Deal," she said with a broad smile, as she reached across the table to shake his hand. "But, there's a rider on that deal."

"And, what might that be?"

"Don't call me 'doc' or 'prof' or any other title. It's a thing of mine; I hate stuffy. In fact, I regard 'Roslyn' as too stuffy. I prefer 'Roz'; it seems much more me.

"Hey, I'm down with that," Frank said through a grin. "The more I learn about you, the worse 'Roslyn' sounded."

As Frank refilled her wine glass, Roz noticed his watch. "Good grief," she exclaimed, "we've been here over an hour and haven't ordered yet."

"Yeah, and Carlos hasn't bugged us. This place is certainly different."

"That it is," she said, picking up the menu.

After they decided what to order, a press of the button on the arm of Frank's chair brought Carlos within the minute. He disappeared with the order and reappeared with the food sooner than either of them expected.

"I've had to wait longer than that at McRaunchy's," Roz observed, as Carlos set the plate before her.

"Have a nibble and tell me if it tastes anything like fast food," Carlos replied.

Roz's eyes widened as she sampled various items on the plate. "This is out of this world," she said, looking at Carlos.

"How could your chef put something like this together in such a short time?"

"Zat, madam, is our little sec'ret," he said with perfect Gallic accent and inflection.

"That's the closest I've heard him come to sounding like a fancy waiter," Frank observed, after Carlos' departure. He took a few bites. "This does taste like the chef labored over it for hours."

"So, what about you and Catherine?" Roz prodded.

"Well . . . we knew each other in university . . . nah, that's not the way to put it," he began, groping for words. Everybody on campus knew who she was. The girl who'd rate ten for looks on anybody's scale, but never dated. There were at least six pools that would be won by the guy who could get a date with her."

"Don't tell me you won a pool?"

"No, I can't say that I was successful enough in the dating game to think about going into one of them. I got to know her because we wound up on the same debating team. I'll admit to surprise when we began spending time together that didn't relate to debating. At first, I didn't think of it as dating because I couldn't imagine her being interested in me, but other people saw it as such. And, it worked out to be kind of neat for both of us. I gained a lot of prestige among the guys for being the one who was melting the ice queen. She had political aspirations, such as class president, but she kept running into the question of why she didn't like boys. Being seen with me gave her the stamp of normalcy. She got the nomination and, eventually, elected."

"Was she gay?"

"No, but I do think that she was emotionally crippled or perhaps deficient. She just wasn't interested in men. She loved the law and craved power, but men didn't turn her crank. She recognized that they should, so she sought some counseling and therapy. It didn't seem to do much good; I think it was because she didn't put much into it. I can't fault her lack of effort because I suppose her family or friends nagged her into going. Other people were always more concerned about her lack of interest in men than she was.

"I guess the pressure to address why she wasn't 'normal' got intense at times and—as I've already mentioned—was hurting her political aspirations. When we began hanging out together, that pressure disappeared. At first, I didn't have the foggiest idea why I was hanging with her. I was in awe of her, so getting cozy didn't seem a remote possibility. I wasn't hoping for sex.

"The more time we spent together without my making a pass, the more relaxed she became and the more fun we had. On a relaxed evening, after a few beers, she asked me if I was ever going to 'try anything.' We were both surprised when my spontaneous answer was, 'Not without an invitation.' She got real serious and said, 'The odds of that happening are quite remote.' She couldn't believe it when I told her that I understood, that I had become empathetic with her situation and was cool with things as they were.

"After that, she opened up about how much easier her life had become since she began to be seen with me. It was as though the whole world had relaxed because she now 'fit.' At first, it was difficult for me to grasp. Not being a high profile person, I had no concept of the pressures she was experiencing. As the days went on from there, I paid more attention and was amazed to realize how much scrutiny goes with the limelight. Her every move and motive were analyzed. Having a man in her life made the evaluations much kinder.

"As time went on, it became apparent that the only thing her critics could ever sell was the possibility that she was a sexual deviant. With that out of the way, she became unstoppable. After winning the election for class president, she confided that–as far as she was concerned–I had made the difference. She even joked about owing me a tumble in the sheets, but we both knew it couldn't happen. We had become close enough to talk at length about why she couldn't handle the idea of physical contact with men. We even went through some psych texts, but never came close to finding a reason."

"But . . . you two finally married. Were your children adopted?" Roz puzzled.

"Nah, that was the ultimate gas," Frank laughed. "After graduation, I thought we'd go our separate ways. I figured that she wouldn't need me anymore, and I wanted to get on with the home and family thing. It came as the biggest shock of my life when she asked me to marry her. She'd obviously been thinking about it for a long time and had concluded that she couldn't get to where she wanted to go as a single woman. She didn't even grouse about how unfair it was. She had analyzed the situation and decided what she needed to do. When she laid all this on me, I was flabbergasted. I didn't know what to say, think, or do. Mercifully, she had anticipated this reaction. I can still hear her words today."

"'I know you are thinking my proposal is absurd because of the sex thing. Ok–just as you have understood and appreciated my problem with it–I now understand and appreciate your problem in the light of a marriage proposal. After a long talk with myself, I believe that I can learn to handle the conjugal aspects of marriage. It will be a process, but I know you have the patience to make it work. Wanna try?'"

Roz's eyes were wide. "That has to be the damnedest story I've ever heard. I'll admit to a certain amount of difficulty in keeping our deal at this moment."

"I don't blame you. I was dreading this explanation. I know it all seems far fetched."

"That it does, pal. So, go on. Obviously, you accepted, but was it right there, or did it take you awhile to come to a positive conclusion?"

"You give me too much credit. The idea of dipping my wick in that luscious thing dominated everything else. Somewhere in the back of my big head, I knew the process would take time and patience, but that didn't enter the decision. The little head was in complete control. I accepted on the spot."

Roz closed her eyes and shook her head. When she opened them, she had a mischievous look. "So, you 'wanna' tell me how it worked out?"

Frank sat back and chuckled. "Like everything else she's ever done, she researched the subject, and applied the information with true diligence."

"Diligence—now there's a word I never expected to hear applied to a discussion of sex."

"It's the only word for it. I don't think she has ever enjoyed sex, but she became a most satisfactory partner. In fact, I think it worked out to make me luckier than most guys. I hear my friends complaining about wanting it when their wives are not in the mood, but being 'in the mood' has never been an issue with us. I guess she regards it as something that needs to be done–kind of like laundry–whenever I express the need, she does it."

Roz's eyes went wide again. "Laundry—how did you come up with that simile?"

"Well, I don't do the laundry because I like to do it, but I don't dislike doing it either. I find a comfort in meeting the needs of those I care about. While the laundry isn't something I look forward to doing, I don't resent having to do it. I think that's Caroline's attitude about sex. While she doesn't enjoy the act per se, she finds meeting my need agreeable."

Roz wrinkled her nose. "Doesn't sound intimate."

"You're right about that. While I've always had all the sex I want, I don't think I know what sexual intimacy is."

Roz grew serious. "Do you love her?"

"I don't think I know. I respect her and I know that I want to do whatever I can to make her life pleasant."

"Probably, there would be fewer divorces if more marriages were based on respect," Roz observed. "So, you raised the kids and sold cars while she pursued her career?"

"Yeah, it was great. I was the pivotal point of the kids' lives as they grew up. I was involved with everything: preschool, PTA, little league, music, dance, you name it."

"It sounds like Katie and Jerry had a great childhood. Few kids get to grow up with a dad who has both the time and inclination to devote himself to them."

"If I'd written the script for our lives, I don't think I could have come up with anything better for them."

"What are they doing now?"

"Both in university."

"And now, dad finds himself at loose ends—wondering what to do now. Is that what this is all about?"

"Well . . . er . . .," Frank stammered.

"Hey, not to worry. It's the same with me. I'm here to-night, with you, because I'm at loose ends. I've finally ad-mitted that the intellectual intimacy that I thought would de-velop between A.P. and me is a fantasy, but I want someone with whom I can share my thoughts and feelings."

Frank brightened. "This has been a good session of that."

"Indeed it has."

Frank stood at the window watching Roz get in her car. Following the suggestion made by DE, he wouldn't leave for a while. They had worked to make this whole deal discreet, he realized. His instructions had been to park on the street and enter by the front door. He hadn't even been aware of the parking lot in the back, but, apparently, she had been instructed to park there.

As he descended the staircase, Frank pulled out his wallet. Carlos was on his feet before Frank got to the desk. "Ah, Mr. Grant, I trust you had a pleasant evening. No need for the plastic, your card has been charged."

"And your tip?"

"Thank you for asking, Mr. Grant, but we don't do that here. Our goal is to make your meeting as pleasant and free from anxiety as possible. Were we successful?"

"I'd give you top marks for that."

4

GRAM

Kitten reached out and swept the alarm clock off the nightstand. Instead of going silent amid satisfying sounds of breakage, it continued its electronic chirping from across the room. Coarse expletives tumbled through her mind as she stumbled out of bed to bring her foot down on the lid of the travel alarm. That shut it up, but the hard plastic case prevented damage. She made a mental note to pick up a couple of real alarm clocks—the kind that disintegrated when thrown against the wall. The first morning home after a job was always a particular bitch; it helped to break something for openers.

She sat on the edge of the bed and massaged her temples. After several days of adrenalin high, her body screamed for rest, but Grandma required her presence at breakfast. She insisted on a complete report the first day home. Talking was the last thing Kitten wanted to do; the thought of doing it cheerfully was nauseating. Why in hell couldn't the gab wait until afternoon? Why was Gram unable to understand that mornings were an ordeal at the best of times and cut her some slack?

As Kitten's morning bitchiness edged toward a full-fledged mad, mom came to the rescue. One sensible lady— that had been her mom. "Don't do anything without thinking it through, regardless of how you are feeling. If your feelings are strong, inaction is the best plan," she had said on countless occasions. Yes, this was the time to get things in perspective instead of giving vent to one's feelings.

She took a deep breath, pulled her hair back, and reminded herself that the first day after a job was critical. After spending several days worrying, Gram had a right to hear how things had gone. The important thing was to control the conversation. "How long are we going to do this?" or "Have you thought about starting your education?" or "Wouldn't it be nice to live a normal life?" were topics to avoid.

Under the shower, Kitten answered those three questions aloud to herself. "Forever." "For what?" and "No damned way!" It felt good to verbalize her feelings. For perspective, she reminded herself that Gram viewed the current arrangement as temporary. She saw her late son as a tragic character who taught his daughter the trade because it was the only way he knew to give her a start in life. In Gram's mind, the name of the game was to facilitate enough jobs to finance Kitten's education.

Kitten brushed her teeth while preparing to walk the tightrope. She regarded her daddy's gift as the best thing a man ever did for his daughter. She loved what she did, and couldn't imagine herself doing anything else, but it had to remain hidden from Gram. She had to maintain the charade of trying to gather an education grubstake until she could operate without Gram. That thought always gave her chills. Gram's dislike of what they were doing imparted a meticulous care just short of paranoia to her planning. It was a prime ingredient in their recipe for success. The fear of functioning without Gram did its job. Although morning conversation ranked somewhere below last on her list of desirable activities, she headed for the kitchen, ready to give Gram the obligatory rundown on how the job went. Experience had taught her that an amusing anecdote was useful to truncate the episode; she reviewed the details of the tire incident.

"Mornin'" she chirped, breezing into the kitchen.

"Good morning dear, how did it go?"

Kitten noticed that Gram's brow had furrows. She heaped on the cheer. "Perfect. Everything was exactly as you said it would be."

"Well, that's a relief. You know, I worry so about you when you're out; won't it be nice when . . .?"

"Gram, I don't mean to interrupt, but I've been dying to tell you about the trip back."

"Oh! My goodness, was there trouble?"

"No, no, it was hilarious—I had a flat."

"What was funny about a flat tire? Did it happen close to the job?"

"No, no, I was somewhere in Iowa. I'd just passed through some little Podunk Junction."

"I don't remember that town being on the route. Did you deviate?"

Kitten fought back anger. "No, Gram, that's what you call a berg when it's too small to pay any attention to the name. Anyhow, I'd just passed through it, rain was coming down in buckets, and I realized that the car wasn't handling right. I pulled over, checked the tires, and sure enough, one of the rear tires was low. I turned around and went back to that wide spot . . ."

"That was dangerous, dear. Why didn't you change the tire yourself?"

Patience, Kitten reminded herself. "Gram, it was pouring rain and we both know that I can jump up and down on the end of a tire iron and my one hundred and three pounds often doesn't budge the lug nuts."

"Well, we do have that electric impact wrench in the car, and we did go to the expense of modifying the alternator to drive it," Gram stated reasonably.

"Gram, that would have meant being on the side of the road with both the hood and the trunk open in the pouring goddamn . . . I mean, with the rain pouring down. Now, wouldn't that look curious?"

"Perhaps we wouldn't run into such situations if you drove something that didn't need those great big tires."

"The 'Vette doesn't have anything to do with my not wanting to get myself and everything in the trunk soaked. Anyhow, one of the three buildings on Main Street was a garage. The place was an unbelievable mess. Piles of parts and stuff were everywhere. One dog lay sprawled by the door, another curled up by the stove, and a cat lay on the books and papers covering the counter. The place smelled of wet dog, wet cat, and wet shoprat."

"The place was infested with rats? Didn't the other animals do anything about them?"

"No gram; I'm being funny. Shoprats are those young guys who work in automotive shops."

"I see," said Gram with the beginnings of the smile, which appeared when Kitten mentioned young men.

Inwardly, Kitten sighed. Gram was loosening up. "This grizzled old coot was behind the counter. I told him what I needed, he petted the cat and drawled, 'Well, lady, we don't have time to do it, but I'm afraid one of the boys in back has seen either you or that car you're drivin' by now. If I don't give them the opportunity for a better look, I'll never hear the last of it.'

"I pulled the car into the shop, and before I was all the way out, this young shoprat had a floor jack under the front of the car and was pumping away like fury. He was watching me get out instead of paying attention to what he was doing. You won't believe this, Gram, but one of the wheels of the jack was on his foot! How anyone could get into that position is beyond me, but there he was, about to transfer the weight of the front end of my 'Vette onto the toe of his boot. I considered waiting until it happened, but decided he might injure himself."

"Very good," observed Gram. "Injuries result in records being made."

"Careful," thought Kitten and continued, "Well, I just said 'The low tire is on the back.' His stupid grin changed to an expression of acute embarrassment; he let the jack down and got the right tire fixed without ever looking back at me. The old guy in the front must have seen the whole thing because he was still chuckling when I paid him."

5

Roz and Frank Get Nailed

As Frank dialed the number, he felt the same delicious mixture of anticipation and trepidation he'd felt as a teen when calling girls. He settled back, waiting for the connection to be completed. This was dumb, but it sure was fun. Last night, dining with her at the Victoria House was more fun than he remembered having in a long time . . . rring . . . Did she feel the same? . . . rring . . . In the cold light of day, would she brush him off? . . . rring.

"Hello, Roz here." The voice was cool and professional.

For the first time in many, many years, Frank felt tongue-tied. Finally, "Uh, hi Roz, this is Frank," came out.

"How ya doin' pal?" This time, the voice was softer.

"I'm doing great . . . uh . . . uh . . . that sure was a nice place we ate at last night," Frank replied, feeling the fool.

"Indeed it was. Did you know it was there before last night?"

"The first I heard about it was through DE."

"Same here. I wondered why I'd missed it, because it would be a great place to take a colleague for a working lunch. I asked around when I got in this morning, but nobody here knew of it either. I checked the phone book, but there is no listing for Victoria House."

"Man, I don't see how a layout with that overhead survives without advertising. In fact, I'm not certain how they survive at all. I checked my Visa account this morning to see how much they nicked me, and it wasn't bad at all."

"Well, pal, I think I can shed some light on that area. I'm in the habit of checking my credit card activity first thing in the morning to charge back business expenses. They also pinged my card for an amount that was reasonable for two people but on the rich side for one."

"Ahh, so we needn't worry about the Victoria House's finances," replied Frank, feeling more relaxed.

"No, we shall be able to enjoy their hospitality numerous times in the future."

Frank's stomach tightened again. "Would you go for that?"

"Yes, last night was most enjoyable, the best evening I've had for a long while."

Frank pulled out his PDA and tapped some keys. "Ummm . . . how about next Thursday?"

"Hang on."

Frank heard her fingernails clicking on the keys.

"Won't work," she said.

Frank felt a sinking feeling. Had he misjudged? He groped for words, but none came. Her voice broke the silence.

"I said that it won't work, not that I didn't want to. The following Sunday works."

Relief washed over Frank. It was almost palpable. He tapped some keys. "Yeah, that works for me too."

Their conversation fell into the same easy exchange of ideas and opinions they'd enjoyed the night before. It wasn't until the low battery warning on his cell phone began squawking that Frank realized they'd been talking for almost an hour. "Oops, I think I'm about to drop off the air," he said.

"M'gosh—I just looked at the clock—have we been talking that long?" she replied. "I'd best get to work before I find myself unemployed!"

✳✳✳

The following morning, Frank struggled with twinges of guilt as he sipped his coffee and tried to read the paper. The titillation he felt at the prospect of again dining with Roz kept intruding on what he was trying to read, but he fought it off. He needed to get his mind off her. Catherine would be along in a few minutes and the idea of trying to make breakfast talk while thoughts of another woman flitted about in his head didn't seem a desirable exercise.

"Do you have any plans for Sunday?" Catherine asked, as she breezed through the door.

Frank almost choked on the current mouthful of coffee. "Ah, er, no," he lied.

"I was wishing you did," Catherine began, as she seated herself across from him. "I'm going to a meeting of the party's steering committee on Sunday, and I might be returning late."

"Big decisions to be made?" asked Frank with studied nonchalance as he pushed a plate of fruit and yogurt toward her.

"I'm going to announce that I want to run for that House seat coming open in the next election. The ensuing discussion might extend into Monday."

The news didn't surprise Frank. He'd known that becoming a judge wouldn't satisfy her appetite for power. He'd been waiting for her to announce the next step. The fact of the matter was that he was ambivalent about her going into politics. He was accustomed to his opinion having little bearing on her doing what she wanted to do. This was her way of telling him what she was going to do next. Somewhere along the line, she'd initiate a "discussion" to help him feel comfortable with what she was going to do in any case. This time, though, instead of feeling the usual mild annoyance, he felt elated. She wouldn't know or care where he was on Sunday. His mind raced. The campaign would have her insanely busy for the next months. His role was to stay out of the way. He could do that while getting better acquainted with Roz! He shook his head. He shouldn't be entertaining those thoughts. "Um, no worries," he replied. "I'll dredge up something to do."

Tenderly, Catherine looked at him. "Babe, this 'empty nester' thing isn't easy for you is it?"

"It has been a big change, but I'll get it sorted out."

"I've been concerned—you seem bored and at loose ends."

"Thanks a bunch for noticing," Frank thought. The kids' departure hadn't affected her in the slightest. She was going ahead with her life plan. She was 'concerned'. So what? It wouldn't influence anything. Maybe it was the best she could do.

✴✴✴

One of the private dining rooms at the Victoria House featured a fireplace. Roz and Frank were relaxing in front of it after a fine gourmet meal. Since meeting, they had dined here almost every week. Their friendship had matured. They didn't need to fill the air with small talk. Pauses in the conversation were not pregnant. They were times to enjoy being together quietly.

"This is more like it," Frank said contentedly.

"More like what?" she asked.

"Oh, I was thinking about Catherine. Her shirttail hasn't hit her butt for about six weeks now. Every night it's go, go, go. Maybe she's compelled to do it. Maybe she likes it. But, I think that this is so much better."

"How long is this going to continue?"

"Until after the election. Why do you ask?"

"Well, I was thinking that we should try to ease our friendship on Catherine and A.P."

"I don't think there's any chance of getting together as a foursome until after the election. Speaking of A.P., how is he taking your having a night out almost every week?"

"I don't think he's noticed."

"How does that work?"

"I don't spend more than three nights a week at home. He's not there any oftener. Actually, we sort of make appointments to spend time together. He often accompanies me to Iron Man competitions, and we plan vacations together. Outside of sleeping and breakfast, we go weeks without being home at the same time. This morning, he begged off going with me to an Iron Man practice next weekend."

"Practice?"

"Yeah, there are about a dozen IM competitions world-wide per year. The next venue is particularly hot, so competitors go there to get acclimated."

"When is the competition?"

"Next month. I'm going to try for three weekends there between now and then."

By this time, Frank had pulled out his PDA and was tapping on it. "Uh, I ain't A.P., but would I do as a companion for this weekend?"

"Hummm . . .," began Roz thoughtfully. "What did you have in mind regarding the accommodations?"

Frank turned toward her. "I'm pleased that you got right to it. I'm not suggesting anything beyond what we enjoy right now. You stay wherever you stay, and I'll get a motel. No hanky-panky, just friends."

"Color me like the firefly that backed into the fan."

"Whaaat?"

"De-lighted. I'd be delighted to have you with me during the weekend. I'll have to warn you that I'll be running, biking, or swimming during the day, and I'll be hot and tired and maybe not good company in the evening, but having you there sounds exquisite."

✳✳✳

During the rest of the week, the word "exquisite" kept popping up in Frank's thoughts. In his wildest dreams, he'd never thought that anyone would use that word to label something connected with him. However, she had.

✳✳✳

On Friday evening, Frank drove into Palmdale and pulled up in front of the house where Roz and some of the other competitors were staying. She was leaning on her car looking radiant and like a million bucks, tax-free. Frank had to remind himself that the current task was to park the car. This was the first time he'd seen her in shorts, and it was some treat.

"Hi pal, the gang is all going to Salty's Fish and Chips. Could we join them?"

Frank was surprised. This was something new in his experience. She had stated her preference in a way that left him feeling free to express his. "Uh, do you think that's a good idea?"

"I know what you're thinking. Don't worry. This bunch is cool. They won't care or even think twice about who you are."

The evening meal was fun. The talk began about carbohydrates, training regimens, equipment, and diets. After Roz deftly let them know that this was Frank's first exposure to their sport, the banter switched to general topics. Frank was impressed with their level of education as the conversation flitted over an eclectic mix of subjects. He was not able to detect who was "with" whom; the talk avoided relationships.

After the meal, Frank and Roz excused themselves to go for a walk along the lakeshore. A cooling breeze off the lake moderated the oppressive heat as they walked.

"I hope you brought some shorts," she said.

"Yeah ah did," he said in a Ray Stevens mockery. Then, without thinking, he added, "I'm sure glad you brought yours."

She stopped, looked up at him, and smiled.

Frank was seriously embarrassed. He fidgeted. "I . . . I . . . didn't mean . . ."

"I'd be disappointed if you didn't . . . thanks."

✳✳✳

The next morning, Frank sat in Roz's car and watched her pedal away into the shimmering heat. "Exquisite," he thought. The sight of her in the Lycra biking outfit was breathtaking. Watching her unload the bike from the roof rack and sort out her gear had been an experience he had no difficulty calling exquisite. Up to the present moment, he would have objected to the idea that the rear view of any bicyclist could be called exquisite. Now, there it was, in front of him, disappearing into the heat.

He started the car and fumbled with the unfamiliar air conditioning controls. Once cool air started moving, he dug into the door pocket for the map she'd given him. Her route was marked with points of interest along the way. He hadn't thought much about it when she said it would take her a little over four hours to get to the half way point where they planned to meet. Now that he was looking at the map, he began to wonder. He checked the scale. Black River Junction was over 50 miles away!

When Frank passed Roz, she gave him an enthusiastic wave and a smile. Farther along the road, he passed a pair of cyclists and then a threesome. At a roadside fruit stand, he pulled over. The heat hammered him as he opened the door of the car, but he wanted an unobstructed view of her as she went by. He went to the stand and selected a few items. The threesome went by as he was walking back to the car. Good, the pair would warn him when to watch for her. He was wiping off an apple when a whistle alerted him. He raised his head in time to see her approaching. With another smile and wave, she passed and was gone. Returning to the car, he regarded the map. Somehow, none of the points of interest looked as interesting as watching her go by.

Frank found the ice cream stand at Black River Junction. All the tables were full of people in cycling togs. He bought an ice cream cone and sauntered around until he could score a table. It was sharp of Roz to recommend this tack, he thought as he settled down.

Roz parked the bike and took off her helmet. "Man, whatta built," thought Frank as she shook her hair out. She had no makeup on, she was glistening with sweat, and her hair hung in soggy strings. To Frank, she looked like something right out of Playboy. "Why'd ya come in here lookin' like that?" he quipped.

"It's not hard to look a mess," she said, plopping into the chair opposite him.

"On the contrary, I think you are proof 'that you could stop traffic in a gunny sack'," Frank continued with the song line.

Her face took on an expression that Frank hadn't seen before. It was . . . was . . . sort of . . . he searched for the word. Gooey, he decided. The thought of her having a gooey expression on her face, was difficult to accept, but it was right there, looking at him.

"Thanks," she said. "That's nice to hear."

"C'mon, you must get compliments all the time."

"Not ones that I enjoy hearing."

Frank felt a stirring that frightened him. This was going somewhere they'd both agreed to avoid. He was glad to have an alternate subject at hand. "When you said that you were going to practice the bike route, I was thinking in terms of a couple dozen miles. Exactly how long is the biking portion of this event?" he asked.

"One hundred twelve miles."

"And the run portion?"

"Twenty-six miles."

"And the swim?"

"Two and a half miles."

"And you do this in one day?"

"Yessir," she said with a grin.

Frank shook his head. "I can't believe it. How long does the whole thing take?"

"The pros do it in about nine hours. I hope to break twelve this year."

Frank shook his head and worked on his ice cream while watching her eat and drink unrecognizable concoctions— probably the "performance food" he'd heard them talking about last night. "Want an ice cream?" he asked.

"Yes, medium vanilla would be nice."

Frank brought back a cone for each of them, but the over-dessert talk that he'd anticipated didn't materialize. She wolfed the ice cream and began putting on her gloves and helmet as she offered, "Gotta get truckin' before I cool down."

"Exquisite, positively exquisite," thought Frank as he watched her pedal away. He didn't make any of the points of interest along the rest of the route either. Instead, he leap-frogged ahead of her and waited for her to pass. Watching her go by was more fun than anything he could imagine.

As Frank waited at the end of the bike route, he began to wonder. For most of the day, she had been passing the other cyclists, but the order of people at the last couple of stops had indicated that she was losing ground. At this point, several of the cyclists that she led at the last stop had passed by without a sign of her. Frank began to worry as a guy in an electric blue outfit, riding a bright yellow bike, stopped alongside. "You waitin' on Roz?" he asked.

"Yes."

"She fell about five miles back. She doesn't appear to be hurt, but a couple of the girls are staying with her . . . she sent me to find you."

Frank was in the car and on the way before he realized that he hadn't thanked the man or asked for specific directions. He growled at himself and punched the trip meter. She wasn't hard to find. A dozen or more bikes marked the site. A woman was out on the road to waive him down. Roz was propped up against a tree, cushioned by the gear from other cyclists. One gal was applying a wet cloth to her forehead. A guy was tying stuff back on her bike. Two others were fussing about trying to make her more comfortable. Others stood close—ready to do whatever. As he approached her, the group backed away. One leg had a bloody scrape, but she looked ok otherwise.

The gal who had the wet cloth on her forehead looked up as he approached. "Dehydration—zoned out for a second and ran off the road. There do not seem to be any injuries other than the abrasion on her leg."

A man's voice behind Frank said, "Here it is, Lilly." He turned to see a man holding out a first-aid kit. The guy looked at Roz, grinned and said, "You got enough stuff in that trunk to get Santa Anna's whole ragged-assed army bikin'."

Roz smiled weakly at him and grimaced as Lilly began to clean the wound.

Feeling like the fourth wheel on a tricycle, Frank knelt down beside Roz. She reached out and grabbed his hand.

"Wha . . . wha," Frank stammered. He couldn't remember ever being this frightened.

"Like Lilly said," Roz began in a weak voice. "I pushed too hard, didn't pay enough attention to the signs of dehydration, and blanked out for a second . . . that's all it took."

Frank didn't know what to say. He covered the hand that Roz had in his and held it.

After completing the bandage operation, Lilly stood and got Frank's attention. "The fall doesn't seem that bad. Other than a little cosmetic damage here, she seems ok. Take her home, put her to bed, and you sleep on the couch. Make sure she gets rest and fluids."

Frank started to protest, but Roz squeezed his hand and shook her head slightly. "Thanks, Lil," she said. "He'll take good care of me. If I feel a twinge of anything, I'll call you."

The expression on the face of the tall, angular woman softened as she looked from Frank to Roz. "I'll take that as a promise."

One of the men came and knelt on the side of Roz opposite Frank. "Here, we'll help you up."

"I can walk ok," she protested.

The man looked toward where Lilly was mounting her bicycle. "With Dr. Bitch in attendance?" he said with a sly grin.

"Roger that," replied Roz, as she lifted her arms. "Ok boys, haul the invalid to the passenger side of the car."

As they approached the car, Frank noticed that Roz's bike had been loaded and that her helmet and gloves were in the back seat.

With Roz comfortable in the passenger seat, and the vehicle headed back for town, Frank turned to Roz. "That wasn't nice, him calling the person who gave you first aid a bitch."

Roz laughed. "We all call her that. She's a first rate physician—a trauma specialist—but she doesn't have much use for men; she thinks they are all sex mongers. She's brusque about telling people what they need to do to get better."

"A lesbian?"

"Donno for sure, but I think so. Nevertheless, if you are ever in an accident, hope that she is in the ER. Uh, could we go to your place for a while? Right now, I don't feel up to explaining what happened to the gang at the house."

Frank redirected the car toward the outskirts of Palmdale.

✱✱✱

Roz let out a low whistle as they entered Frank's room at the motel. "This is some layout. Have you been here before?"

"No, I've never been to Palmdale before. DE's website steered me to this motel."

"They're a travel agency too? I didn't notice that."

"It's not too obvious, but there is a link. I thought it might be worth a try—like the Victoria House, a place nobody's heard of."

"Well, it is more than nice," she said, settling into a chair.

"What now?" he asked.

"If you don't mind, I'd like to curl up in that comfy bed over there. I might be able to snooze, but I should have more water."

"I'll go out and get you some of the bottled stuff. While I'm gone, you can get into my pajamas. I'll run your bike stuff through the washer downstairs while you rest. Do you feel like anything to eat?"

"A grease burger sounds good."

"Ok, a six pack of Disani and one Whopper coming up."

"Hey, I could get used to this," she called as Frank went out the door.

"I could get used to having you get used to it," thought Frank as he went down the hallway. He shook his head in an attempt to clear the thought.

When Frank got back to the room, she was snoring softly. Her clothes lay in a pile by the door. He put the Whopper and a bottle of water on the nightstand. After gathering her clothes, a few of his own, and the novel he'd purchased, he headed for the laundry room. With the washer sloshing away, he opened the novel. It was a piece of luck to find a new "Prey" novel by John Sandford. One could rely on ole JS to deliver an absorbing novel. He needed something that would pull him in and get his mind off the beautiful thing in his bed.

When Frank returned to the room, almost two hours later, Roz had not stirred. The burger and water were untouched. She was still snoring softly. He ate the cold burger, put on the headset, and selected a movie from the PPV. After the movie, he made himself a cup of coffee and prepared to settle down with John Sandford when she mumbled, "Coffee? Mmmmm, smells good." Frank looked at the bed, she was stretching. He opened a bottle of water and took it to her. She downed half of it in one shot.

"The burger got cold, so I ate it. Do you still want one?" he asked.

"Kinda."

When Frank returned with the fresh burger, she was sitting up in bed with a drink in her hand. He looked at the water bottle; it was still half-full.

"Do you think that's a good idea?" he asked.

"Hadda piddle . . . couldn't get back t' shleep . . . havin' luscious dreams . . . only way t' avoid reality."

"Smashed," Frank thought. A couple of swallows of liquor on an empty stomach, in a dehydrated state, had sent the alcohol straight to her head.

"Gimme th' burger," she commanded.

As Frank set the sack on the nightstand, he noticed the pajama bottoms draped over the chair. What was going on here? As he reached into the sack for the burger, she grabbed him around the neck, pulled him down and kissed him fiercely. With his last vestige of resistance, he mumbled weakly, "But Dr. Bitch . . ."

✸✸✸

Frank lay in bed staring at the ceiling. Roz was again snoring softly beside him. It wasn't supposed to be like this. He hadn't been looking for an affair; he just wanted to meet someone he could to talk to. Shit! Who had he been kidding? He'd asked to meet a woman. Where did he expect it to go if they hit it off?

After midnight, Roz stretched and threw the covers back. Frank was still awake.

"Gotta get back to th' house," she offered. "The gang does the swim together for safety reasons. We're hitting the beach at zero eight hundred." She turned on the light and began dressing from the neat pile of clean clothes. "Thanks awfully for doing these up for me."

Frank didn't acknowledge. He lay with his hands under his head, staring at the ceiling.

"Trying to figure out whether or not you still respect me?" she asked playfully.

"How can you be so flip when we've just screwed up our own lives beyond repair and taken two other innocent people with us?" he growled.

She walked over to the end of the bed and regarded him earnestly. After a couple of minutes, he met her eyes. "I do understand your feelings of guilt, and I respect you for them," she began in a level tone. "But, I don't share your premonitions of doom and gloom. I think that this whole business will work out to the benefit of all concerned."

Frank was astounded. His lashing out hadn't touched her. He closed his eyes and shook his head. "How can you possibly say such a thing?" he moaned.

"You're in no shape for an explanation right now. I'll be out of the water around ten. I'll forego the run this afternoon if you want to talk."

Frank started to protest, but she was on her way out the door. He lay back and stared at the ceiling again. She'd warned him that many people thought her crazy. Well, he had to admit her reactions were anything but typical. But crazy? Hardly. Sure, some people would label her impenetrable confidence crazy. Nevertheless, didn't her accomplishments justify it? Everything—her talk, her walk and now her reaction to the specter of total disaster—radiated total confidence. He loved it . . . loved what other people called crazy . . . loved her . . . loved the whole package . . . the time had come to admit it.

✳✳✳

Frank searched the beach. It was past eight. He hadn't taken time to catch a coffee in his rush from the motel to the lake. His fears of being late subsided at the sight of a group of people down the beach. Was it the right bunch? Roz's car wasn't there but she was. She came running over as he pulled up. Even in a wetsuit, she looked smashing.

"Hi pal, I didn't think you'd make it, but I was hoping you would."

Frank put his hand over the one she'd placed on the sill. Her grin softened into a smile. She turned her hand over and squeezed his.

"Wanted to see you off," he said simply.

"This will take a couple of hours. Will you be here when I get back?"

"No question."

"Great!" she exclaimed, disengaged her hand, and ran to one of the parked cars. She returned with a small bundle that she threw over Frank into the passenger seat. Putting her hand on his cheek, she said, "See you in a couple. And, I meant what I said about foregoing the run if you want to talk."

Frank was out of the car, leaning against the fender, watching the group of swimmers. As they got farther out into the lake, they seemed so tiny. His heart jumped into his throat the first couple of times they disappeared over the crest of a wave, but it got easier after they reappeared each time. He couldn't imagine swimming in water that rough, or for that far, or any of it, for that matter. After they faded from sight, he got back into the car and drove around until he found a purveyor of bagels and coffee.

✳✳✳

Frank couldn't explain his anxiety as he scanned the water. He'd been gone from the beach for a little over an hour, so he couldn't expect to see them yet, but the absence of swim caps bobbing in and out of the water filled him with dread. The sense of relief he felt when he spotted the first cap was enormous. He had to wait another fifteen minutes before he could count the caps, but they were all there. The last time he'd felt a comparable sense of relief was when his daughter had returned from her first solo drive with all the fenders intact.

Roz was among the first out of the water. Breathing heavily, she trotted up to him. "Say, you are some good luck charm," she began, between breaths. "I'm usually a midpack swimmer, but I almost kept up with the front runners today—I can't ever remember feeling this strong in the water." Frank didn't know what to say, so he smiled. She reached into the car, retrieved the bundle, and started around the car. "C'mon, help me out of this thing," she said.

Several of the other swimmers were now in the grassy area across the road, getting out of their wet suits. Roz unzipped her wet suit as she went around a clump of bushes. She was wiggling her arms free when she turned around. There wasn't anything underneath! "Don't just stand there and stare," she said with a laugh as she sat on the ground. "Grab the legs and pull!"

Frank loosened the leg zippers. Grabbing the ends of the legs, he tugged as she wiggled to get free. In addition to getting her out of the wet suit, the process had considerable entertainment value. Fascinated, he watched her towel off and dress.

✳✳✳

On Monday afternoon, Frank sat in his home office staring out the window. Throughout the morning, he had tried to work, but it was hopeless. His mind kept going back over breakfast. Had Catherine suspected? No, he couldn't think of a thing that betrayed her detecting anything out of the ordinary. True, he had made it home only minutes before her. His head had barely hit the pillow when she came in, exhausted, from whatever political shenanigans had claimed her evening. She hadn't initiated conversation or anything else after collapsing into bed. Breakfast had been the usual chitchat about the campaign and a brief question about how his weekend had been. As usual, she wasn't concerned about the details of what he'd done, just that he had found something to keep himself from being bored. He found no reason to think that she suspected anything.

Frank picked up the ringing phone "This is Frank Grant, how may I help you?"

"Mr. Grant, this is Jamie Herron, I need to speak with you today, if possible."

"Uh, Mr. Herron? The name doesn't ring a bell."

"We've never met."

"What is it that you would like to see me about? Are you interested in a motor car?"

"Mr. Grant, I'd prefer not to discuss my business over the phone. I understand that you operate your business out of a home office. Would it be acceptable if I came over in a few minutes?"

In this business, Frank met more than his share of eccentrics. He agreed to be ready for a meeting at one thirty.

Frank watched from the window. At one twenty-nine, a beautiful Avanti pulled to the curb in front of his house. That would be a fun—and profitable—deal to negotiate. An athletic, youngish man stepped out. The doorbell rang at one thirty on the dot. When Frank opened the door, the man was tucking sunglasses into the pocket of an Armani suit that didn't need shoulder pads. The guy looked to be thirtyish, well groomed, and big enough to burn diesel. The handshake was powerful. The smile had difficulty covering his mouth and gave up before reaching his eyes.

Frank led the way to his office, gestured his guest to a chair, and offered coffee.

The man seated himself, took the coffee, set it on the table, and opened an attaché case that had cost both the alligator and the purchaser dearly. He withdrew a folio and handed it to Frank. "Please look at this," he said without expression.

Frank opened the folio, expecting pictures of the Avanti, and turned pale. The photographs were of him and Roz on Saturday night. The whole tumble had been photographed! Enlargements of the face shots made identification positive. He sat back and took a few minutes to compose himself. He felt anger rising and reminded himself that care was the operative word here. "Is this a shakedown?" he asked.

"Let's say that I represent interests that propose to establish a mutually beneficial relationship."

"I pay you and you keep quiet doesn't sound like a 'relationship'," Frank replied, barely able to control his anger.

"The interests whom I represent are not interested in your money, Mr. Grant. They ask that you run an occasional errand for them in exchange for discretion."

"What sort of 'errand' are we talking about?"

"Each month or so, you will receive a small package in the mail. Inside, will be a wrapped DVD and a set of instructions. You will meet a person at a place specified in the instructions. If that person uses the password in the instructions, you are to give him the DVD."

"And then?"

"That's it. My interests will guarantee that nobody sees these photographs."

"What if something goes wrong, and I can't deliver the DVD?"

"You are to call a number that will be in the instructions. You will be told what to do from there."

"What's on these DVDs?"

"That is of no concern to you. Under no circumstances are you to open the DVD wrapper. The interests whom I represent will know if you tamper with it. Should you attempt to play the DVD, it will self-destruct and ruin the machine. In either case, the interests I represent will reveal these photographs at their discretion. May I have the folio back please?"

Frank shoved the photographs into the folio and handed it back. After placing the folio back in his attaché case, the man began to sip his coffee. His eyes never left Frank. It was all clear now. DE was a front. It trapped people into delivering stuff for these guys. As he studied the man sipping the coffee, Carlos came to mind. Carlos was darker, but both men were large, powerful, guys who subscribed to the same dress code. "Do you know a person named Carlos?" Frank asked.

The man's expression didn't change. "Carlos who?"

"I don't know his last name. He's a waiter at the Victoria House Restaurant."

"Neither name rings any bells," the other replied, his expression never changing.

"That makes sense," thought Frank. "I'll bet your name is not 'Jamie Herron' either," he said with irritation.

"Perhaps."

"And, I'd venture that if I ran that vanity plate on the Avanti you're driving, I'd come up with zip."

"Perhaps."

"And, I'd further bet that Carlos' profession isn't that of waiter," Frank blurted, realizing he'd said too much.

"Since I'm not acquainted with anybody named Carlos, I can't reply to that. Do we have a deal?"

Frank felt hemmed in. "Yeah, I guess so," he muttered.

As the man departed through the front door, he paused and turned to Frank. "Do you recall the Nicholson scandal?"

Frank did remember. Last year, a story accused Alderman Nicholson of liaison with unauthorized poontang. His wife walked out of the divorce with everything but the bills. City council asked for his resignation and the loss of political contacts almost ruined his business. "Did you guys have something to do with that?" Frank asked.

"Let's say that it was an unfortunate case of pulling the trigger too soon. It was thought that he was reneging on his part of the bargain when, in fact, he was not."

"B . . . b . . . but," Frank started with alarm. The man ignored him, turned, and walked to the Avanti.

Frank stood in the doorway, feeling like his gut was full of cold lead. As he walked back to his office, he realized that he was shaking.

6
KITTEN VISITS SCHOOLS

Kitten and Desiree sat at a table in the student lounge.

"Wow, nobody'd know that you're like old," Desiree said.

"Thanks," thought Kitten. Thanks for nothing. She'd tried for the late teen look. In the opinion of this seventeen-year-old airhead, she was successful.

"You're like getting some serious looks. Wonder what they'd say if they knew you were almost as old as some of the teachers around here?" Airhead continued.

Desiree was someone Gram had dredged up–a grandniece or something of some friend. She wasn't quite sure of the connection and really didn't give a damn; she was putting up with this to please Gram.

Airhead nattered on, "That serious hunk over there in the khakis, the one that's like to die for . . ."

Kitten turned her head to see who Desiree meant.

"He's been lookin', but don't look back."

"Why?"

"He 'n Lisa are an item. You don't want to get on her bad side."

"What?"

"She's real 'in'; she thinks you're like messin' with her guy, and you'll like never get friends who are worth anything."

Kitten didn't understand, but she didn't need to. She'd agreed to let Desiree show her around the campus to please Gram. Desiree had a class within the hour. A few more minutes of this nonsense and she'd be gone. While Airhead nattered, Kitten looked around. The majority of the people in the lounge appeared to be trying for a bored, sophisticated look. In contrast, a group at a corner table was having a lively, animated, discussion. She motioned in their direction

"That bunch appears to be the only group in here having a good time."

Desiree looked horrified. "They're like nerds. Don't even get close to them. You don't want people even like thinking you know they exist," she said, closing her eyes with a shudder.

"Why is that?"

"Nobody'd want to hang with you."

Kitten began to feel irritated. "Do you mean that, if I went over and joined that group for a few minutes, nobody in this school would want to be seen with me?"

"Oh, the nerds'd be glad to have you around, but you'd never make any good friends."

"Why would talking with them influence the quality of relationships I might develop in the future?"

Desiree began to look exasperated. "I mean 'good,' like people who can be your in with people who are like more 'in'."

Kitten pondered for a few minutes before the lights came on. "You're using 'good' to mean advantageous rather than intimate, aren't you?"

"Huh? I don't get you."

"You're talking about the pecking order. A good friend would be one who would help you climb the pecking order."

"Man, what planet are you from? 'Pecking order'; whazzat mean?"

"I see," Kitten said slowly. An evil gleam grew in her eyes. "Why don't we invite that guy over there, the one sitting alone in his wheelchair, to join us?"

"Him? Ugh? Are you outta your mind?"

Kitten smelled blood; she pressed in. "Ugh? What is it about him that disgusts you?"

"Well, er, ah . . . lookit him!"

"You don't know anything about him do you?"

"Of course not!"

"You don't have the slightest idea what kind of person he is, do you?"

Desiree squirmed. "Look!" she said in a voice that was too loud. Heads turned their direction. She lowered her voice and continued. "I donno what your thing is, but you're outta line—big time."

Kitten's countenance turned feral. She considered choking the living shit out of Airhead. Then, she thought about getting up and spending a little time with both the crippled boy and the nerds. Desiree's frightened look reminded her that she wasn't here to piss in Airhead's cornflakes. It was best to leave her as she'd found her. Without a word, she got up and walked out.

✳✳✳

Gram was sitting in the living room as Kitten slammed her way into the house.

"How did it go dear?" Gram called out. The banging door didn't surprise her; it explained the lack of answer. She hadn't expected this to be easy for Kitten. She waited. After a few minutes, Kitten walked in with a bottle of beer in her right hand. Two more bottles dangled between the fingers of her left hand. Gram surmised that "hadn't been easy" was an understatement. Kitten plopped down in a chair. Gram didn't say anything while Kitten downed the first beer in agitated pulls.

"That little twit was unbelievable!" Kitten growled as she started on the second beer.

"Desiree?" Gram asked.

"Yeah, she talks about people as though they were stepping stones or rungs on a ladder."

"Do you mean that she regards friendships as means to advance her social standing?"

"Good way to put it. That's all she talks about."

"I was afraid of that. I hardly know the girl, but I was concerned that she'd be that way."

"What made you think she might be?"

"These days, most young women seem to be preoccupied with status."

"It was gross . . . made me wanna puke . . . she dismissed people who were different or handicapped as though they were dirt to be avoided."

"Dear, dear," Gram said, almost to herself. "I expected you to be put off because I thought Desiree's conversation would be dominated by boys or clothes. I didn't think she'd find your mad button."

"She didn't 'find' anything; that's the way she is," Kitten pouted. She turned the bottle in her hand—studying it. Gram waited. After several minutes of contemplation, Kitten asked in a subdued tone, "Gram, you said 'most young women' a few minutes ago. Do you mean that most of the girls in that school would be like that little bitch?"

"I'm afraid so, dear."

"So, acting that way is normal to them? It's the way everybody is?"

"Unfortunately, yes."

"But, it's wrong, wrong, wrong. Whether people are good or not has nothing to do with their appearance. Am I wrong to think that way? Why am I so different from them?"

"Yes, it is wrong. You are right. You are different because you had the privilege of growing up in an environment where 'different' did not equate with bad. The majority of people in the circus family are there because they are different. You grew up evaluating people based on what they were without reference to their appearance."

"Yeah, you've told me that before, but I can't seem to get over taking it wrong. How can you expect me to function where people are like that? I'd be up for Murder One within a month."

"Well, dear, I don't expect you to."

Kitten brightened, looking at Gram.

Gram continued, "So, I've arranged an interview for you at a private school."

Kitten darkened, "Oh, no, Gram!"

"Yes, they are expecting you at two-thirty tomorrow. It's a completely different environment. Please be a good girl and give it an honest appraisal."

Kitten stood, her jaw clenched.

"Please don't be angry with me dear," Gram entreated, but her voice was resolute.

"I'm gonna get me some videos and something stronger than beer. See you when I get back," Kitten said, as she walked out.

A screech of tires told Gram that the 'Vette was leaving the driveway. She sighed. She didn't like to see Kitten turning to drink when frustrated, but it was the lesser of evils at this point. From a moral perspective, Kitten's position and reaction were unassailable; she was proud of that. From a practical standpoint, however, she grieved over her granddaughter's lack of the social skills she'd assumed to be instinctive.

✱✱✱

Kitten awoke with her head feeling larger than the great pumpkin. She wondered if her arm was long enough to scratch her ear. It hurt to move her head as she tried to focus on the clock. It was half past noon. She had two hours to get to that dammed appointment. She carefully swung her legs out of the bed. Pulling on her robe, she made her way to the kitchen.

Gram was at the table, reading the paper with a cup of tea in front of her. "Good morning, dear," she said brightly.

"I know it ain't mornin' no more, but thanks for the space," Kitten muttered. She ran water into a glass, sloshed some around in her mouth, and spat it out. "Uggh, mouth feels like Poncho Villa's whole ragged-assed army marched through it with dirty socks."

Gram hid a grin behind her paper. "That coffee will be ready in a minute."

Kitten regarded the perking pot. She'd have loved to smash the damned cheerful thing. Finding some tomato juice, she downed it as the pot finished perking. After pouring a cup of coffee, she turned to Gram. "Your tea ok or do you need a top-up?"

"I'm dry, dear," Gram said, pushing her cup toward Kitten.

Kitten removed the cozy from the teapot and refilled Gram's cup. She seated herself across from Gram. "Thanks for puttin' the coffee on," she said into the cup as she drank.

"It was the least I could do," Gram said quietly, and turned to the paper while Kitten finished her coffee.

As Kitten returned to the table with her second cup of coffee, she said, "Ok, tell me about this place that you got me an appointment at today."

Gram put her paper down and her glasses aside as she looked at Kitten. "It's a private institution that offers instruction from the ninth grade up through junior college. They don't use classrooms per se, the instruction is individual, and the students progress at their own pace."

Kitten began to look interested. "That sounds cool. How does it work?"

"I understand that the curriculum is packaged into modules that each student works through. There are tests within and at the end of each module."

"Kinda like that correspondence course in locksmithing that daddy got for me?"

"Yes . . . yes, I supposed so," Gram replied. The similarity to Kitten's pittance of formal education hadn't occurred to her until now.

"Does that mean I could do it at home—without havin' to go to school?"

"That, I don't know about dear. I understand the students attend on a schedule similar to public school. They each have a cubicle where they do their work. I did explain some about your unique situation, and they offered to work out an arrangement that would be comfortable for you. In fact, the person that I talked to said that she would discuss your needs with the principal and come up with a proposal before you got there. I believe they are surmising that you are regularly employed; I didn't tell them any different."

"Sounds ok," Kitten said thoughtfully. "They say anything about getting me up to speed?"

Gram was encouraged. This was the first time Kitten had been willing to talk about her need for the basic skills. "We talked briefly about that. Their approach is to assign modules based on a battery of tests. You might be working on a module that is, say, ninth grade English while you were doing grade twelve math."

"Mmmm, sounds great for a person like me," Kitten reasoned, as she toyed with her cup.

Gram fought to control her elation. This was the first time Kitten had seemed anything other than overwhelmed at the prospect of starting her education. Gram knew that her obstinate attitude was more fear than anything else, but she hadn't known how to help.

"What's the name of this outfit?" Kitten asked.

Gram winced. "Calvary Christian College."

"What? No way! I ain't goin' to listen to someone tryin' to convert me all the time!" Kitten fumed, and rose to refill her coffee cup.

When Kitten returned to the table, Gram turned a stern look on her. "Please give me some credit, dear. I'm no more interested in your having to endure religious claptrap than you are. I've done a lot of inquiring about this institution. Although they are associated with a church, any religious instruction is optional. As near as I can tell, their only goal is to provide quality education."

"They don't think the schools are good enough?" Kitten grumped.

"No, they are of the opinion that the public system is deficient."

"Well, from what I saw yesterday, I'd have to say that they are right on. I—me, with no education—was getting over Desiree's head. I figured it was just her."

"I don't know, but from what these people say, it is possible to graduate from the public system without being able to spell or read above a third grade level. They claim that to be their motivation for providing the school."

"Sounds kinda pie in the sky to me, but we'll see this afternoon."

"Thank you, dear," Gram said, with considerable relief.

✳✳✳

"Whatta plant," thought Kitten as she turned into the parking lot of Calvary Baptist Church. The sanctuary was a huge glass and brick affair that couldn't have been more than a few years old. Attached via a covered walkway, a less imposing structure bore the label "Calvary Christian School." Kitten pulled into one of the visitor parking places. She sat for a moment, took a deep breath, got out of the 'Vette, and walked through the school building doors. Kid-done projects and various displays lined the foyer walls. Portraits of graduating classes on one wall faced a trophy-filled cabinet on the opposite wall. She walked through a door labeled "Office."

"Good afternoon. How may I help you?" came from a pleasant looking lady in a blue skirt and white blouse.

Unsteadily, Kitten answered, "Uh, Jefferies is the name, I . . . uh . . . had 'n 'pointment at half past two."

The lady extended a hand over the counter. "Pleased to meet you Ms. Jefferies. I'm Arlene. I shuffle paper around here. Mr. Collins will be with you in a minute or two. Would you like a cup of coffee, tea?"

"Coffee'd be great." Kitten smiled back. It hurt to smile, but Arlene's warmth was infectious.

"Please make yourself comfortable while I tell Mr. Collins you are here and get us some coffee," Arlene said as she gestured toward one of the overstuffed leather chairs placed around a low table. Arlene pressed a button somewhere under her side of the counter and said, "Stewball, Ms. Jefferies is here."

"I'll be right there," came from an unseen speaker.

Arlene came around the end of the counter with two cups of coffee and condiments on a polished wooden tray. She set a cup in front of Kitten, the condiments in the middle of the table, and took a seat across from Kitten.

Kitten took a grateful sip of the coffee. It was good coffee, brewed strong and black–just what the doctor ordered. "Stewball?" she questioned as she lowered her cup.

Arlene looked up from doctoring her coffee. She flushed slightly. "Uh, yes. Mr. Collins' given name is Stuart. We all call him 'Stewball' . . . I don't know where it started . . . I think it's because he's so funny. I try to watch myself because it doesn't sound very professional, but I slipped . . . sorry."

"Hey, nothin' to be sorry about."

"Thank you, but expressions of familiarity can make a person here for the first time feel like an outsider. I should have been more careful."

Kitten, preoccupied with the pounding in her head, hadn't thought about it one way or the other. Now that Arlene had explained, she thought, yeah, it could have had that effect on her.

"That's a lovely suit," Arlene said.

"Thanks," Kitten replied, and stole another glance at the crisscross tie around Arlene's neck. It was the same blue as her skirt, bordered in red with a logo on the corner, and pinned smartly to one side. Kitten puzzled for a moment at the look it gave Arlene's outfit. Uniform, that was it. It made the outfit look like a uniform. It was smart and pretty, but a uniform, nonetheless.

A girl whom Kitten judged to be about the same age as Airhead, looked up from the pile of paper she was carrying as she came through the office door. "Mrs. Montgomery . . .," she started to say and stopped when she saw Arlene seated at the table. "Oh, I'm sorry. I didn't know you had company. Please pardon my interrupting you."

Arlene smiled pleasantly. "No harm done, dear. Ms. Jefferies, I'd like you to meet Trina Nordstrom. Trina will be graduating with our associate degree in accounting this year. Ms. Jefferies is considering joining us," she said, looking from one young woman to the other.

Trina smiled warmly at Kitten. "I do hope your decision is positive. Calvary Christian has been wonderful for me, and I'm certain it will be for you."

"Uh, thanks," was all Kitten could think of to say. The oddity of a student acting as an impromptu commercial for the school turned in her head.

Arlene, sensing Kitten's awkwardness, turned to Trina. "What may I help you with, dear?"

"Oh, I have the supplies list from the teachers."

"Is there anything you need my help getting?"

"I don't think so."

"Good, get the key out of my desk and load up."

As Trina turned, Kitten finished her assessment. The girl was wearing the same outfit as Arlene! She wore the same crisscross tie at the neck of a white blouse. The skirt was tighter, shorter, but of the same blue material.

Arlene settled back and sipped her coffee. "Lovely girl, Trina."

"Yes, she seemed nice," Kitten replied.

"Hi, ladies," Stew said jovially, as he entered the office. "I see you have coffee, so I'll get myself one before I join you."

Kitten was stunned. The figure rounding the counter toward the coffee bar had the tightest little tush she'd seen in years. He wasn't a tall man, but his well-tailored white shirt and blue trousers revealed a fine bod. She was still watching as he turned back toward them with his coffee. He was dark with rather mid-eastern features. White teeth glistened through a grin. As he approached, Kitten noticed that the tie falling between a magnificent set of pecs was the same pattern as Arlene's.

"Ms. Jefferies, may I present Mr. Stuart Collins," Arlene said, with obvious pleasure.

"Ms. Jefferies, it is a pleasure to meet you," Stew said, as he put his coffee on the table and offered his hand.

"Likewise," Kitten replied, taking the hand. It was a good hand; it felt strong, like her daddy's.

"I'd like to apologize for taking a few minutes to get down here," Stew began as he seated himself on the edge of the chair. "One of my students had shown himself to be . . . quite . . . um . . . creative in his research. I needed to point out to him that he'd expended more energy disguising plagiarism than he'd have used doing the report from scratch. You can't hurry those conversations." Then, he sat back and sipped his coffee.

Curiosity got the better of Kitten. "What's with the uniforms?" she asked.

"Helps level the playing field," Stew replied. "We are here to provide an education, not a forum for status games. We want our students to relate to one another as people, not extensions of how much their parents can spend."

"Hummm . . . that's kinda cool," Kitten responded.

"So, what are your educational goals?" Stew asked.

"Keep my Gram off my back."

Arlene's eyes grew wide.

Stew looked puzzled. "Pardon me, I don't think I understand."

"Gram's got this bee up her butt about me needin' an education. I'm just here to keep her off my trail."

Stew looked thoughtful. When he didn't reply, Arlene got up saying, "If you will excuse me, I'll leave you two to discuss in private."

"Thanks Arlene," Stew said pleasantly. Kitten didn't say anything.

"Guess I kinda shocked her," Kitten said, when Arlene was out of earshot.

"Was that your goal?"

Suddenly, Kitten felt self-conscious. "Donno, 'zactly," she mumbled.

"So, you are here to please your grandmother, not because you are desirous of an education, is that correct?" Stew asked.

"Yeah, that's about it."

"Well, in that case," Stew said pleasantly, "there's no need to take any more of your time. You can truthfully say you have been here. Should your grandmother call, we can truthfully say that we had a pleasant chat with you. The length of our conversation and the contents need not be mentioned."

Kitten felt the unfamiliar urge to backpedal. "Long as I'm here, I might as well look at whatcha got."

"You'd find it boring if you're not interested in furthering your education."

"Well . . . I guess it's sumpthin' a person ought to think about," Kitten said, without understanding why she was prolonging the conversation.

"Fair enough. Could you tell me about your education thus far?"

"Not much to tell . . . raised in the circus . . . mom taught me to read 'n write . . . lost her when I was young . . . daddy didn't push for no more education. Came to live with my Gram when we lost him."

The genuineness of the concern on Stew's face warmed Kitten. "How old were you when your mother taught you to read?"

"Can't say . . . always had books around . . . we all liked to read . . . mom and dad were always discussin' somethin' that they'd read . . . remember feelin' real big when I could join in those conversations," Kitten mumbled, trying to recall, as her eyes grew moist.

Stew's dark hand appeared before her offering a brilliant white hankie. "Please," was all he said.

"Thanks," she said, taking the hankie and dabbing at her eyes with it.

Stew waited for a few moments before asking, "May I ask you a few academic questions to ascertain your level?"

"Sure."

"Please don't be offended if you don't know an answer. Just say so."

"Fire away."

"What are the eight parts of speech?"

"Uh, there's nouns and verbs, but I don't know what else."

After making a notation on the pad he'd brought with him, Stew ripped a blank page out and wrote 2 X 3 = 6. While showing it to Kitten, he asked, "What is that?"

"I'd guess you'd call it an . . . uh . . . expression."

Stew nodded, "Very good." He then crossed out what he'd written and put down 2 X Z = 6. Turning the paper back to Kitten, he asked, "What is that?"

"A formula."

"Mmm, good." Pointing to the X he asked, "What do we call that?"

"An operator."

Pointing to the Z, he said, "And this?"

"A . . . um . . . er . . . ah . . . a," Kitten said, wrinkling her brow, "a factor."

"Excellent! Do you enjoy math?"

"It's kinda fun."

"And you've picked it up on your own—you've never taken any courses?"

Kitten thought about telling him that she'd had to learn some math fundamentals to get through the locksmithing course but decided against it. "Yeah."

Stew scribbled more notes onto his pad and then asked, "What is a dinosaur?"

"A seriously large, ugly creature with a mega bad attitude, now extinct, currently thought to be the predecessor of the chicken."

Stew roared with laughter.

Kitten grinned as she said, "Don't like that definition eh? How about Zeppelins or the Soviet Union?"

Stew erupted with fresh laughter. His eyes began to water. Kitten handed the handkerchief back to him. "Thanks, that's rich," he said, dabbing at his eyes.

Kitten enjoyed watching Stew's genuine, unaffected laugh. She began to search her memory. "Lemme ask you sumpthin'," she said as his laughter died away.

"Ask away."

"What's your take on Descartes?"

Stew looked surprised. "Well . . . ah . . . his thesis that the mind exists separately from the body makes me wonder if he ever looked down."

"Beautiful," Kitten laughed.

Stew watched her with a smile. "Do you pursue philosophy?"

"Sometimes it's fun to read, but I don't get most of it."

"If the truth be known, the rest of us don't either. The tendency of philosophers to restrict their communication to other philosophers has resulted in an internal dialect few care to try penetrating. Mind if I ask you why you asked about Descartes?"

"Wanted to see how seriously you take yourself."

"That's good," Stew responded, "really good. You must read a lot."

Kitten thought about the time she spent in various libraries around the country. They were a good place to await nightfall, so she could go to work. "Yeah, I like to go to libraries," was all she said.

"Do you like science?" Stew asked.

"Yeah, it's cool too."

"Let me guess, I'll bet you go for books by people like Carl Sagan or Timothy Ferris."

"Yeah, there's not too many authors in the science section that I can understand."

"Ever try anything by Einstein?"

"Ha! No way."

"How about Peebles?"

"Mmmm . . . yeah . . . big thick thing . . . didn't get past the first coupla pages."

"How would you like to be able to pick up any book on one of those shelves and understand it? Don't answer me right away—I'm going to put our coffee cups away—think about it until I get back."

As Stew gathered up the empty cups and condiments, Kitten imagined being able to understand any of those delicious looking tomes. The warm feeling that filled her was marvelous. She'd never considered the possibility. Thinking of it now, she found the idea enthralling.

"Do you think I could?" she asked Stew as he sat back down.

"In all honesty, I do," Stew replied. "You're smart. With guidance, you can probably understand anything you want."

Elation rumbled around inside Kitten—elation at the idea that the contents of those books were not beyond her reach—elation because Stew had said it. She didn't know why she'd enjoyed hearing it from him; she just did. The warmth lasted but a second before the old suspicion took over. "You sure you're not blowin' smoke up my butt because you want me to sign on?" she asked, without thinking. She was sorry she'd put it that way as soon as it was out.

Stew didn't flinch. "I believe you have sufficient I.Q. to excel at any academic endeavor regardless of where you pursue it."

"You can tell that from those few questions?"

"Your answers were good. In fact, they were astounding. Your use of the English language reveals a high I.Q. You start with street slang and a lot of contractions, but when you are putting an effort into expressing something, you use the proper multi-syllable words."

Kitten knew she was flushing but didn't know what to do about it. Mercifully, Stew looked at his watch and said, "My troops are about to be dismissed for the day. I should bid them adieu. It will only take a few minutes. Do you have time to continue this discussion after I take care of that?"

Kitten was elated. "Sure," she answered.

"Great," Stew began as he rose. "I'll get one of the students to show you around while I close up shop."

The student turned out to be a striking young woman; she was tall and stacked. Long auburn hair set off rich blue eyes.

Although her skirt was the same shade of blue as the other women wore, the fabric looked more expensive.

"Ms. Jefferies, I'd like you to meet Ms. Kensington," Stew said.

"Pleased to meet you," the tall girl said, extending an immaculately manicured hand.

"Uh, likewise," replied Kitten, accepting the hand.

"Ms. Jefferies is considering becoming a student," Stew explained.

"How nice," the tall girl said with genuine pleasure.

"Could you show Ms. Jefferies around while I dismiss my troops?" asked Stew.

"I'd be happy to," the tall girl replied. Turning to Kitten, she said, "Please call me Kristin."

"Uh, ok . . . Kristin, I'm Kitten."

"The library is around this corner," began Kristin, "so we can start there."

Kristin moved with a cultivated grace as she led Kitten into the library. She introduced Kitten to the Librarian, demonstrated the electronic resource center, and pointed out other resources in hushed tones. Kitten drooled inwardly. Although the library wasn't large, the ambiance was perfect for enjoying a good book. She could envision herself spending many a pleasant hour in this place.

"Now, we'll have a look at the tutoring center," Kristin said, as she and Kitten walked out of the library. Not wanting to appear stupid, Kitten bit back the urge to ask what a tutoring center was. As they walked down the hall, three boys approached. They all wore blue pants, white shirts, and the uniform tie, but the breast pockets of their shirts were loaded down with calculators, pens, and other unidentifiable paraphernalia. Their shirts–two of which looked like something from last week–were unbuttoned at the neck and the ties were loose. Two of the boys wore thick glasses and the other one suffered from acne. Not one of the heads had felt a comb in recent memory. They were quite a contrast to Kristin. Kitten watched, expecting her to look away. Instead, she smiled and raised a hand to meet the high five offered by one of the boys. "Knock 'em dead," she said, slapping the hand.

Kristin turned to Kitten. "That's the geek squad. They're taking a project to the science fair this weekend. I hope they do well."

"Project? Science Fair?" asked Kitten.

"Yes, it's an intramural competition. Students from all over the city enter projects."

"What are those guys entering?"

"Something to do with lasers. Beyond that, I wouldn't have a clue."

"Do you . . . ah . . . talk with them much?"

"I try, but they are still frightened of girls. I was glad to see Clarence high five me–that's progress–but, if you noticed, the other two didn't even look at us."

Kitten had noticed.

"It must be tough for them," Kristin continued. "That type of guy seems to get into the girl thing later than his peers. They must wonder what's wrong with them."

"Do you think that anything is wrong with them?"

"Hardly. People mature at different rates in different areas. It's unrealistic and unkind to expect the conformity pushed by our society."

Kristin led Kitten into an area that had enclosed offices around the periphery and a large table surrounded by chairs in the center. "This area," explained Kristin, "is used to tutor students who need one-to-one help. Time in the offices is scheduled by tutor and student."

"Don't the teachers have offices to do that?"

"Yes, each teacher has an office, but the majority of the tutoring is done by other students."

The door to one of the offices opened. A girl whose spiky hair seemed out of place with her uniform emerged. She smiled shyly at Kristen, ignored Kitten, and left the room.

Another girl, wearing her hair pulled back into a tight bun, and no makeup, followed her out. The latter brightened at seeing Kristin. "Hey, I was just about to look you up. I can take Amy tomorrow after all."

Kristin looked mildly disappointed as she said, "No prob. Mae Klassen, I'd like you to meet Kitten Jefferies. Kitten may join us."

Mae offered her hand. "Hey, pleased to meetcha! You'll love it here. This place is a gas."

"Uh, same here," Kitten replied.

"I gotta run, but before I go, do either of you know why Mennonites don't approve of band music?" Mae asked.

Kristin looked amused as she shook her head. Kitten didn't know what to do, so she shook her head.

In a conspiratorial stage whisper, Mae said, "Too much sax and violince."

Kristin laughed but Kitten was stunned. She watched the girl in the ankle length skirt disappear through the door.

"Isn't she . . . a . . . a . . . I mean the dress . . . the bun?" Kitten stammered.

"Yes, she is a Mennonite. In fact, her father is a minister. They're great people. They know how to laugh at themselves. She said this place is a gas, but anyplace with her around would be fun."

"You looked disappointed when she said she'd take 'Amy'; mind my askin' why?"

"Not at all. Amy has fetal alcohol syndrome. Her learning difficulties are severe. She loves to have us read to her. I was going to take Mae's shift tomorrow."

"You're disappointed that you don't have to do that?"

"Amy's a real sweetheart, loving and appreciative. It's a joy to be able to make her happy. There's never a shortage of volunteers to work with her."

"Uh, how 'bout that girl Mae was workin' with?"

Kristin thought for a time, weighing the options.

"If you don't wanna or can't tell me, it's all right–none of my business," Kitten offered.

Kristin looked apologetic. "You do have a right to know, but I don't think I'm the one to tell you. Would you mind terribly if I referred that question to Mr. Collins?"

Kitten was surprised at Kristin's reluctance to share what must be a juicy bit of gossip, but she replied, "Nah, I understand; I'll nail Stewball with that one."

"Stewball? How did you know that people call him that?" Kristin said through laughter.

"Arlene let it slip."

"We're not supposed to use familiar forms of address around here, but Stewball fits much better than Mr. Collins. I really have to watch it. Anyway, let's go have a look at the cafeteria."

As they walked along hallways, and down a set of stairs, Kristin had a smile and friendly nod for everyone they passed; Kitten was impressed. "Man, do you know everybody in this place?" she asked.

"Not really. They all would know who I am, but I'm not personally acquainted with the majority of them."

Kitten noticed a tinge of embarrassment in Kristin's voice; she couldn't resist pressing in. "High profile, eh? Class prez., Homecoming queen, Valedictorian?"

A flush crept up Kristin's cheek. "Guilty on all counts."

Something about Kristin's name had been niggling at the back of Kitten's mind, now the lights came on. She turned to Kristin. "Kensington . . . Kensington GM. You're not . . .?"

The flush on Kristin's cheek deepened. "Yes, my dad owns Kensington GM."

"Boy, that's a nice layout," Kitten said brightly. "I was over there lookin' at 'Vettes."

"Are you a customer of daddy's?"

"Nah, the guys at WestPark made me a better deal on the same 'Vette," Kitten said with a laugh. "Sorry. Are we still tight?"

"Tight?" Kristin asked and then started to laugh as the flush drained from her cheeks. "Sure, sure, I don't care whether you bought from daddy or not."

The cafeteria turned out to be large, airy, and pleasantly appointed.

"Perhaps we could get some refreshment and sit for a while," Kristin offered.

For the first time today, food sounded good to Kitten. She looked at the serving line. "Uh, yeah, I think I'll get a munchie too."

"Ok, I'll score us a table."

The farther along the attractive serving line Kitten pushed her tray, the better the food looked. She settled for a bowl of tapioca and a muffin, which appeared to contain every grain known to man. With her coffee on the tray, she turned from the till and scanned the room. Kristin was at a table in the corner.

As Kitten sat across from Kristin, the latter looked at her mischievously and said, "Introducing your stomach to the idea of food gradually?"

"Huh?"

"Good party last night?"

"Uh . . . yeah . . . did get a little carried away. Howdidja know?"

"The nose. That's a nice perfume you've got on, but it doesn't hide the alcohol coming out."

Kitten felt embarrassed. "Rats," she said between bites of muffin. She sensed something unexpected in Kristin.

"So, what year is your Corvette?" asked Kristin.

"Last year's model," Kitten answered knowing that the girl wasn't making idle conversation.

"And, that's a beautiful suit. Your tailor's good."

"Oops," thought Kitten. Kristin had realized that the suit didn't come off the rack. Her way of letting Kitten know was clever. She was going somewhere.

"Thanks," Kitten replied cautiously.

"Who does your nails? They are great, but is there any reason why they are so short?"

Kitten bristled, but Kristin cut her off with a kind smile. "See, quid pro quo."

"Fair enough," thought Kitten. She hadn't been gentle with her probing into who Kristin was. She smiled and said, "Yeah, I guess I was a little heavy. Sorry. You just look so much like . . . like . . . Miss Everything that I was curious."

Kristin's countenance became businesslike. "You mean, beautiful, popular, and rich?"

Kitten was stunned. "Uh, yeah, I guess."

"Yes, that's what I am; I hope that I can live up to the obligation it puts upon me."

"Obligation?"

"Aren't we gifted so that we can use those gifts to make the world a better place?"

"Well . . . I guess . . . in a way."

"So, those of us who are blessed with everything, bear the heaviest burden."

"Jeeez . . . that's a good way to look at it. Izzat what your parents are all about?"

The last trace of sweet innocence disappeared from Kristin's face. "My parents are good people, but I came to that realization on my own. Perhaps I'll share it with you if we ever get to the point where you can tell me why a girl who drives last year's Corvette and wears tailored clothes needs basic education."

Kitten looked directly at Kristin and grinned. "Yeah, sis, there is a good possibility we might come to Jesus with each other if I wind up around here."

Stew walked up to the table. "Thought I might find you girls here." Turning to Kitten, he asked, "Did you get a good tour?"

"Better than you can imagine."

Puzzlement flitted across Stew's face, but he replied, "Great. If you are ok for time, I'll grab a cup. I need downtime at the end of the school day."

"No prob," Kitten replied.

The sweet innocent glow returned to Kristin's face. "I really should scat. It was a pleasure meeting you, Ms. Jefferies. See you tomorrow, Mr. Collins."

Stew headed for the serving line. Kristin smiled with genuine warmth at Kitten before she got up and headed for the door. As she watched Kristin walk away, Kitten thought, "Wow, that's graceful."

"Beautiful, isn't she?" asked Stew, as he set his coffee cup on the table.

"Yeah, if there was a speck of lint on her, it would be exactly where it should be."

Stew barely avoided spilling his coffee as he erupted in laughter. "I meant that she is an unusually beautiful person. Yes, she is attractive, but her character far outshines her physical attributes."

"I'll bring my sunglasses next time."

The thinly disguised pout wasn't lost on Stew. "Well, what is your opinion of our facilities?" he asked, turning the conversation.

"Pretty cool. Not what I expected at all."

"Care to elaborate?"

"I donno, everything is . . . sort of . . . comfortable. Schools always struck me as polite jails. This place doesn't register that way. Those classroom layouts are foxy–divided into those little cubicles. Does every student have one?"

"We call them offices. Yes, each student has their own office."

"If I came here, would I have to sit in one of those all day?"

"Well, for starters, our students do not spend more than four hours per day in their offices; and they are rarely in them for more than an hour at a time. There are periods of classroom instruction, physical education, and labs. In your case, the answer is that you wouldn't have to spend any time in an office if you didn't want to. You could work through the modules at home and come in to the school for a couple of hours each week to take tests. We are currently working with about a dozen students on that basis."

"Mmmm . . . that sounds interesting."

"I'd hope you would eventually take the opportunity to interact with the other students, but we wouldn't push it. You'd need time to get to know us, to become comfortable, and to feel your own way, as it were."

"Yeaaah . . . that sounds cool. Do you pump iron?"

The abrupt turn of conversation took Stew aback, but he found himself fascinated by it.

"No. Why?"

"Just wonderin' what a guy with a built like yours is doin' teachin' school. You don't look school teacherish."

Stew chuckled. "Yeah, you're right. I get that a lot."

"You teach P.E.?"

"No," said Stew softly and busied himself with his coffee.

Kitten waited for a few moments before saying, "C'mon, give. I know there's somethin' interestin' here."

Stew looked at the ceiling, sighed, and said, almost to himself, "I don't know why it always comes to this."

As he looked back down, Kitten met his eyes. "Hey look, I didn't mean to . . . to . . . whatever, but if it makes you uncomfortable . . ."

Stew's face twisted with consternation, "No, it's ok. It's my problem. I need to learn to deal with it better. In a previous lifetime, I was a Navy SEAL."

"You believe in reincarnation?"

"No," Stew continued, as his face relaxed. "It seems like a different lifetime even though it's only been a few years. The story is that I loved the Navy, the training, the camaraderie, the constant physical and mental exertion, but, after a few missions, I grew a conscience. I began to wonder if anyone had the right to do what we were doing."

"But, weren't you ordered to do it?"

"Yes, but I was also wondering if anyone had the right, the information, or the wisdom to order those things done."

Kitten's eyes began to shine. "Ever kill anyone?"

"Can't say."

"Ever blow anythin' up?"

"Can't say."

"But I'll bet you liked the danger, didn't you?"

Surprise flashed across Stew's face. "Yes, it was an incredible rush. How did you know?"

Kitten smirked. "Can't say."

"I guess that's fair."

"But I know it was hard to give up. Mind tellin' me why you did?"

"Questioning what I was doing led me into questioning what had led me into doing it. I concluded that the society I'd grown up in had taught me the wrong set of values. Once I realized that, it wasn't hard to make whatever changes were necessary to do my bit to change things."

"So, this Calvary Baptist outfit has the straight scoop, and you can straighten the world out by teaching kids their party line?" Kitten blurted, without thinking. Again, she regretted the antagonistic tone.

Stew laughed. "No way. The best I can do is to encourage them to think, to evaluate everything presented to them. I'm not omniscient. I don't know what the ultimate answers are. Each one has to find what is right for his or her self. I think that has to start with appreciating the worth of the individual. If there is a 'party line' around here, it is that each individual is important and precious in a unique way that deserves our respect. That's what I stand for without apology."

"I'm sorry I put the 'party line' thing that way."

"You needn't be. You were simply being honest—expressing your religious convictions."

"I don't have a religion."

"Yes, I think you do," Stew grinned. "I'd label you an antagonostic—mention religion, and you are ready to fight."

"Yeah, I guess so."

"Do you have anything more you'd like to talk about, or do you want time to mull over what you've seen and heard?"

"I think I'd like to give it some thought."

"Fine. With your permission, I'll walk you to your car. I'm on my way out myself."

As they approached the 'Vette, Stew whistled, "Nice wheels."

Kitten smiled.

Stew offered a hand. "I sincerely hope you decide to further your education with us."

Kitten took the hand. "Thanks, this looks better'n anythin' I've seen yet."

As Stew released her hand, his went into a pocket. A look of puzzlement crossed his face. He began reaching into other pockets. "Darn, I don't seem to have my keys." He started walking toward his car. Kitten reached into the 'Vette and extracted a small leather case.

Stew was grumbling and pulling on the door handle as Kitten approached his car. "Problems?" she asked.

"Yes. Old stupid here has locked his keys in his car. They are in the ignition with the doors locked. Guess I'll have to call AAA."

"Here, use my cell phone," Kitten said, handing the instrument to him in a way that caused him to turn his back on the locked car.

While Stew was busy fumbling in his wallet for the card, Kitten used a tool from the case to open the lock. Stew turned abruptly as he heard the door open.

"Guess you don't need to complete that call," said Kitten.

Stew looked from her to the door and back again, dumbfounded. "Phone," she said. As she took it from his hand, she winked, turned on her heel, and walked to the 'Vette.

7

ROZ AND FRANK SCOOP A DISK

Frank took a seat at a sidewalk table, ordered a cappuccino, and settled in to wait. The day offered a pleasant breeze. The plantings along the boulevard were in their glory. It should be a great day to be alive. However, he did not feel that way at all. That's why he'd suggested meeting at the coffee spot down the street from Roz' place of employment. He knew the sight of her walking toward him would lift his spirits. He didn't feel fit to talk and hoped the sight of her walk would put him in a civilized frame of mind. The coffee was good. He sat back, took a deep breath, and tried to relax. It didn't work. He drummed on the table, hoping she wouldn't be too long.

He could tell who it was before she was close enough to recognize. The dark hair swinging back and forth, the cotton print dress swishing deliciously, and that walk–the picture didn't disappoint. His spirits lifted and his frame of mind brightened. While his thoughts might not be considered civilized by puritans, he felt himself becoming fitter for conversation.

"That's a nice dress–haven't seen it before," he said pleasantly, holding a chair for her.

"Thank you, kind sir," she said, taking the chair.

The waiter appeared; she ordered a latte and turned to see Frank looking at her. "What?" she asked.

"Have I told you recently that I ain't never seen the likes o' you?"

"Not today anyway, but go ahead, I enjoy hearing it."

"Lord, I ain't never seen the likes o' you," he repeated. They both laughed. As their laughter died down, they sat looking fondly at one another. The arrival of her beverage broke the moment.

"This is nice, but I guess we'd better talk about what's on your mind," she said quietly.

"Yeah, I guess so," he muttered. He took a deep breath, but couldn't find the words to start. "Uh, have you been contacted by, uh, anybody asking you to do something odd?"

"You mean like kinky?"

"No, no, I mean like anybody from DE?"

She began to look concerned. "You're not making sense."

"I know, I know, well, damn it all, I just don't know where to start," he said in exasperation, and then told her about the visit from "Jamie Herron." As he finished, he was surprised that she wasn't registering any alarm. Instead, she looked thoughtful. While he waited for her to comment, he wondered how anybody could look so sexy by thinking.

After some seconds, she said, "No, I haven't received a similar contact, but it does make sense."

"Make sense?"

"Yeah, the whole DE setup. We've wondered how they keep going. No advertising, limited promotion, and those expensive facilities we don't see anybody else visiting. The whole biz must be a net for mules."

"Mules?"

"Yeah, people to courier those disks."

"What could be on a disk that is worth all this trouble?"

"That's what we are going to find out."

Frank sat bolt upright. "What in the hell do you mean by that?" he growled.

"I mean we need to find out what is on those disks."

Frank's eyes went wide. "Weren't you listening when I told you what they did to Alderman Nicholson?" His voice rose. "Why would we want to make them mad?"

Roz looked around. She caught people looking away. "Shhh, you're attracting attention," she said quietly. "We are going to find out what is on those disks because it is the right thing to do."

Frank felt deflated. His outburst hadn't fazed her. In the few moments after hearing about the DE scheme, she had decided upon a course of action; it's direction scared him to death. It might be cowardly, but he couldn't remember ever having been this scared. His only hope was to reason with her. "Look, we don't know what these guys are up to. Maybe it's nothing at all," he offered. It sounded lame coming out— he cursed himself.

"Forcing you to become part of their delivery scheme amounts to extortion."

"So?"

"Submitting to intimidation isn't the right thing to do. It will encourage them to intimidate somebody else. The right thing to do with bullies is to put them out of business."

Frank's fright escalated to full-scale alarm. "You're not talking about trying to take these guys down, are you?" he asked in desperation.

"Whatever is on those disks must be illegal—that means they are taking advantage of somebody—we can't let that happen. Besides, I don't like being pushed around."

Frank felt the world closing in around him. First, the indiscretion that would ruin them both. Now, this nutcase was going to incur the ire of some very bad people! The bile of panic rose in his gut. She reached over and gently put her hand on his.

"Relax, pal."

"Relax? I told you what those people would do if I mess with the disk! You are suggesting we do exactly that!" he said, without realizing that his voice had risen again.

She squeezed his hand. "Calm down, I'm not suggesting anything stupid. Remember, compact disks are my business. I also have some experience with tamper detection. I don't have a scheme in mind yet, but I'll figure out how we can get a peek without the bad guys knowing."

At that moment, Frank knew he didn't want to hear any more. What he didn't know was whether he ever wanted to see her again. He rose. His fight-or-flight reflex was in control and had decided on the latter. "When you do, let me know, ok?" he said sullenly. Without waiting for an answer, he turned and walked away.

✷✷✷

The next couple of months were not good ones for Frank. He got a package as promised and made the delivery. It made him sick. He didn't see Roz and that made him feel worse. Catherine, busy with the campaign, didn't seem to notice his discomfiture. For that, he felt worse yet.

When Roz finally called and suggested a meeting, Frank jumped at the chance. He came away from the tryst with a deepening sense of doom.

✷✷✷

Frank sat in the seat of a beautiful restored Corvette. The chrome gleamed, the paint shone, and the new leather smelled exquisite, but it was all lost on him. His hands were clammy with sweat and shook as he gripped the wheel. Would this work? What if it didn't? Was the chance worth it? He took a deep breath and exhaled in steps. After a careful look around the back parking area of the dealership, he took the package out of his pocket and leaned out the door to put it against the tread of the rear tire. The tires chirped as he let the clutch out sharply. The package slapped against the wall of the building. He backed the car into its previous position, stepped out, and keyed the electronic lock.

The package–mangled as expected–was against the wall. He pulled a paper bag out of his pocket and carefully gathered the remains of the package into it. Then, he pulled out his cell phone and dialed the contingency number that had come with this package. A flat voice told him to be on a certain park bench in three quarters of an hour.

As Frank approached the park bench, he wasn't surprised to see it occupied by a powerfully built youngish man in an expensive suit. Although it wasn't "Carlos" or "Jamie Herron," the similarity was, apparently, deliberate. "Nice day," he offered, in compliance with his instructions.

"Not in Afghanistan," the young man replied. It was the right reply. Frank sat next to him and handed him the bag containing the mangled package.

The man opened the bag and looked inside. He moved the bag around to get a better look at the contents without reaching inside. When he looked at Frank, his eyes were cold. "What the hell happened?"

"It must have fallen out of my pocket as I got into the car. I ran over it."

"How long between the time you lost it and the time you picked it up?" The eyes were cold, searching Frank's face.

Frank swallowed. "Seconds. I was pulling out of a parking place at the dealership and reached in my pocket to make sure it was there before I got to the gate."

"You're saying that nobody could have picked this up between the time you lost it and the time you retrieved it?"

"That's right. It wasn't out of my possession for more than a minute."

"I'd a thought running over it would just squash it. This thing is trashed."

"It was a client's car–a 'Vette. I hadn't driven it before. I left a little rubber."

Frank thought he saw a trace of a smile playing around the man's mouth. His next words didn't have the edge. "Just clumsy or scared?"

Frank felt himself relax slightly. The words "Vette" and "left rubber" had done the job on this young man. "Some of each I suppose. I'm not comfortable with doing this."

The young man rose. "As long as it stays that way, we'll be alright. We'll be in touch," he said, and walked away.

Frank rose and began walking around the park. He didn't have any direction; he was just walking, thinking. Had he pulled it off? More to the point, had Roz pulled it off? She had done her part, getting the package back to him in the early morning hours of the day after he'd received it. She must have worked all night. Had she been successful? Had she been able to read it? Was all the tamper detection stuff back in place? Had the destruction of the disk been complete enough? The idea of grinding it under the wheel of the 'Vette was a brilliant piece of insurance. He had to hand it to her for that; but he knew she was brilliant–that's one of the reasons he loved her. His cell phone buzzed.

"This is Frank."

"Hi pal, you up for coffee?"

"Nothing I'd like better. You at work?"

"Yep."

"How 'bout that place down the street from your sweatshop?"

"Thirty minutes?"

"You got it."

✳✳✳

As before, Frank sat at a sidewalk table enjoying the sight of her walking toward him. It stirred both his heart and groin. Today, she was wearing a suit. Had the light cotton dress she wore to their previous meeting been for his benefit? There was a good chance; that meeting was before she went to work and this one was impromptu. The suit was more in keeping with her professional status, but he wished for the dress. The idea that she had dressed to please him produced marvelous feelings, incredulous feelings. What did a dish like her see in him?

He was up and holding a chair for her as she approached. "Nice suit," he quipped. "You goin' to a marryin' or a buryin'?"

The smile he expected in appreciation of the humor didn't happen. She looked troubled. This was a new side of her. He sat and waited for her to speak. As he studied her, he realized that troubled wasn't the right word, serious was more like it.

"We need an evening. Do you know of a place?" she asked.

Frank pulled out his PDA and began tapping on the minuscule keys. "There's a muscle car show down at the Continental Convention Center this weekend. I'll be expected to make an appearance."

"What evening would be best?"

"Doesn't matter. Catherine's so busy that she won't notice whether I'm home or not. Ah, Saturday I guess. That'll be the busiest, so a cover story will be easier."

"A cover story?"

"Yeah, be seen by someone who knows both Catherine and I–tell 'em that I'm there to hook up with a client."

"Ummm smooth. I don't know whether or not I like the acumen you are developing in this area." She pulled out her cell phone and used it for a couple of minutes. Putting it back in her purse, she said, "We've got room 1137 for Saturday night."

"I think we're both getting too good at this sort of thing," Frank observed. They chuckled at each other.

After a sip of her latte, Roz got serious again. "I've had a peek at some of the stuff on that disk–don't have much of it decoded yet, but I should have the whole thing by Saturday."

"So, what is it?"

"Porno–that much I know, but it's broken into sections and the encryption scheme changes for each section. I'm not beyond the first section."

"Sounds sophisticated."

"Not really. Changing encryption schemes on the fly is appropriate for things like radio communications, but there's no good reason for doing it on something that's not happening in real time."

"You lost me," Frank complained.

"Ok, sorry. We use computers to break encrypted information, but it takes time. If the encryption scheme of a secure telephone connection changes every few seconds, there is less chance that a computer can figure it out in time to allow eavesdropping. The transmission could be recorded and decoded later, but the nature of oral communication is that it would be useless later. On the other hand, by its very nature, the information on something like a CD is valuable anytime. It doesn't matter if it takes some time to accomplish the decoding. And, it can be decoded, given enough time and computing power."

"So, why would they go to the trouble?" Frank asked.

"I've been pondering that one and I think that the answer is clumsy."

"Clumsy?"

"Yes, the encryption scheme itself isn't too sophisticated, and the tamper proofing wasn't top drawer."

Frank registered alarm. "You don't suppose they could have made it look like that to throw you off, to make you miss something really sneaky."

"Well, I did think just that when we were working on the tamper proofing."

"We?" Frank interjected.

"Sure, although I know something about this stuff, you didn't think I'd go poking around without the help of somebody who was into it everyday, did you?"

"Uh, I guess not, but how do you know we can trust him?"

"Her," Roz corrected. "For starters, she's a geek's geek. I don't think that she has any interest beyond figuring out how to outwit the safeguards. It's a game to her. Once she's in, she loses interest, has no desire to see the contents."

"That's hard to believe. I'd think that seeing what is inside would be the motivation—everybody's curious."

"Perhaps, but do you know anything about the I.S.P.E?"

"Who?"

"How about Mensa?"

"Yeah, that's the club for real swifties."

"Yes, one needs an IQ that is above 98 percent of the population to be eligible for membership in Mensa. One needs an IQ above 99.9 percent of the population to be eligible for membership in I.S.P.E. She's one of those and, believe me, a lot of them march to the tune of a drummer we don't hear."

"Ok, I guess I'm a bit paranoid. Go on about this 'clumsy' business."

"Actually, the whole security scheme of the package and the disk look to me like the work of somebody who is in over his head. The scheme for triggering the self-destruct was dead simple to defeat. Anybody who knows the details of CD structure could have done it if they knew it was there. It was so simple that we thought it must be a red herring–put there to throw a meddler off guard–but it was the real first line of defense. However, the encryption scheme is the give-away. It's nowhere near state-of-the art. There is no heavy math–strictly Spook 101 stuff. Here you have a simplistic first line of defense and a completely ineffective and un-needed encryption of the data. It looks to me like the work of someone who read 'Encryption for Dummies' and sold himself to these scumbags as a security expert."

As Roz finished, she noticed that Frank had drifted some-where else. He was studying his cup as he toyed with it. She waited.

"Uh . . ." Frank began, "I . . . ah . . . I guess I owe you an apology for the way I left our last meeting here."

Roz returned a warm smile. "I was hoping we'd get around to that–not because I think you do, but because you don't."

Frank smiled back. "You're confusing me again."

"Get used to it pal. I confuse everybody. I guess one of the reasons I love you is that you don't dismiss me as being crazy when I fry your circuits."

"I can't understand why people would dismiss you. I haven't known you to be wrong yet. It's hard on the male ego to admit it, but your way of thinking produces better results than mine," Frank said matter-of-factly. Roz's reaction sur-prised him. She dissolved into a grateful puddle.

She put her hand over his and squeezed it. "That, sir, is the nicest thing anybody ever said to me–thanks." She fished in her purse with her free hand, extracted a hankie, and dabbed at her eyes. "You can't know how I appreciate your thoughtful evaluation. I'm not used to people taking the time to understand me."

"Aha, she is vulnerable after all," thought Frank. A new emotion washed over him. It felt good to know that she had a need he could fill; here was an area in which he could protect her. He had never felt such a man. For the first time in their relationship, he knew exactly what to do next. "This talk about 'the right thing' was what spooked me. It hit me like religious hocus-pocus. Coming from you, I know it's not. Why don't you tell me what it is?"

"Boy, you're getting good," she smiled. "I've spent every minute since you called trying to come up with an opening to explain that to you."

"Yeah!" thought Frank. "I'm getting it." Notification that he'd won the lottery wouldn't have sounded any better. He became aware that he was happier than he'd ever been. He turned his hand over and squeezed hers.

"I knew this talk about 'the right thing' would shock you," Roz began. "I'd have spared you the shock if I knew how, but I don't. I've tried to soft peddle my reasons for doing things to people, but it's always proven counter-productive. It's always worked better to hit them right between the running lights with it."

Insight flashed in Frank's head. "How's A.P. with it?" he asked.

"I think he was my major failure. I tried to go easy; I explained it to him in stages. Instead of accepting the little bits I was feeding him, he became more disconnected."

"But, this is basic to what you are . . ." Frank puzzled.

"Yeah, I know it sounds weird in the extreme that you can share a house, a bed, a life, with a person who doesn't understand your basic motivations, but that's how it is. He never objects to what I do, but he has no idea why I do it. I used to think I could live without that connection, but I guess I can't. Probably, the lack drove me to DE and . . . to you." She lowered her eyes and dabbed at them again.

Frank wanted to take her in his arms and tell her it was all going to be alright. He was experienced in doing that for his kids, but the idea of doing it for his woman filled him with a tenderness he'd never known. He again knew exactly what to do. "Ok, how is it that you know what 'the right thing' is?" he asked.

She brightened and her composure returned. "Well, I guess it is a sense of knowing that you are playing your part. The goal of most eastern religions is to experience a sense of connectedness with the universe. They have different names for it, but it all boils down to experiencing a connection with the cosmos–perceiving oneself as an integral part of the grand design in contrast to something apart from it. When I get the sense that a particular course of action is the part I should play in fulfilling that grand design, I feel it's the right thing to do."

"The Quakers talked about an 'inner light.' Is that what you mean?" Frank prodded as he tried to grasp what she was saying.

"I don't think so. It's more a sense of comfort, a feeling that you are properly meshed with your circumstances."

"Meshed like parts of a machine? Are you saying that somebody put all this together? Why would anybody create this mess?"

"I do think there is a reason for everything that happens. However, it stops right there; I'm not presumptuous enough to think I can understand the reason. I think that, in any given set of circumstances, there is a response that is consistent with what the universe, god, cosmos, divine intelligence–call it what you want–is doing."

"You're not hearing voices? You're not talking to God?"

"Hardly. Carl Sagan is credited with saying that the universe is not only stranger than we think it is, but it is stranger than we CAN think it is. For instance, one cannot precisely describe the principles of quantum physics with words. The only way to describe them is via the language of mathematics. Our visually-oriented brains are incapable of getting

around the reality. Whoever, whatever, put all this together–
and I'm not saying there is any particular agency–is so far
beyond my ability to grasp that the idea of having a conversation with him, her or it, is preposterous."

Frank released her hand, sat back, and regarded the tops
of the trees lining the boulevard. She waited.

Looking back at her, Frank said, "I think I'm getting my
head around what you mean, but I need to ask you a few
questions."

"Go ahead."

"Did you feel that getting mixed up with me was the 'right
thing' to do?"

"At the first, no. I was desperate. I wasn't paying attention; I was grasping."

"How about jumping in the sack?"

"That was also a mistake. I was enjoying the ride, not paying attention."

"How about now?"

"Passing the point of no return woke me up. I've been
working hard at paying attention since then. I've spent a lot
of time thinking, meditating, and trying to understand what
the 'right thing' is now. I've been surprised to find that continuing the relationship with you seems to be the answer.
Since we've seen what DE is, I think I'm beginning to get a
glimmer of a reason."

"Kinda sounds as though you're justifying what we did.
We let rampant hormones cause us to betray trust and promises, but it puts us in a position to save the day. Hi-ho Silver
and such."

She smiled and toyed with her cup. "Yeah, I knew it
sounded that way as soon as I said it. Nevertheless, that is
not at all what I'm saying. I shouldn't have messed with DE.
Contacting them was not the right thing to do; I'm not mini-
mizing that mistake. I'm not justifying the way I boozed up
and lured you into bed. It was wrong of me to do that. I did
wrong and our present situation is the result. We can't go
back and undo that which put us here. It's normal to scrab-

ble about trying to regain one's status before the act, but it cannot be done–it is futile to try. That which was the 'right thing' to do before the act may not be the 'right thing' to do after."

"Are you talking about some divine wind turning bad into good? I can see why you'd have a hard time explaining this."

"That's because most people are ingrained with this Judeo-Christian concept of punishment for wrong and reward for right. I don't think that the universe works that way. I think that wrong has consequences because it violates natural laws. I also think that the universe, or whatever, is always waiting, ready to nudge us in the right direction whenever we choose to listen."

"Whoo, wee," Frank whistled. "That's heavy. Why would it do that?"

"That, my dear, is the crux of the whole thing. I don't have any idea why things are as they are. I'm a scientist. I understand the laws of physics, but I do not understand why they are as they are. I don't know any reason for the law of gravity, and I don't presume that I could understand the reason if there is one. I know what works and what doesn't. I don't concern myself with the why. That's for theologians. I equate their quest with a vacuum cleaner trying to understand the mind of an engineer—the ultimate form of futility."

Frank looked at her fondly. A truly marvelous creature, this woman. Although she was the most intelligent person he'd ever met, she freely acknowledged that she didn't know. Although she was the most self-confident person he'd ever met, she admitted that she'd made errors. She didn't try to justify herself, make excuses, accept guilt, or assign blame when she made the wrong choices. God, he loved her.

8

Roz Shows Frank the Disk

Frank circled the Continental Convention Center parking lot. He chose a space close to the entrance. He wanted people entering or leaving to see his car there. The marquee proclaimed "Muscle Cars: A Trip Down Memory Lane to The 60's". Vintage cars weren't his thing, but he wasn't there to look at the cars. He often used these affairs to meet with clients. Guys who didn't want their wives to know that they were considering the purchase of an outlandishly expensive car thought them a good meeting place. Tonight, however, he wasn't there to meet a guy about a car. He was looking for someone with a couple of specifics. After greeting a few people, he saw a person who would do. Approaching the husband of the court recorder, he stuck out his hand and said, "Hi Charlie."

"Hello Frank, long time, no see," replied the other, taking the offered hand.

As they shook hands, Frank inched closer and lowered his voice, "Uh, yeah, Charlie, we need to catch up. Right now, I was hoping you could tell me if there is a john upstairs. The stalls down here are packed, and I got a case of Montezuma's revenge."

"Yeah, sure, there is one right up those stairs and to the right."

Frank faked a grimace. "Thanks, Charlie, I was looking for a client, but he'll have to wait."

At the door to the men's room, Frank looked back. He couldn't see the floor of the center. He'd hoped this would be the case; he did not want to be seen going in. After entering, he looked around; he had the place to himself. He pulled off his reversible jacket and turned the more somber shade out. A cap pulled from the pocket went on his head, the bill down over his eyes. Exiting the men's room, he walked down the

121

hall and took the elevator to the eleventh floor. The door to room 1137 was ajar, so he went through it. Inside 1137, Roz was playing a DVD, but she shut it off as he walked in. "I can join you," he said.

She came toward him with that beautiful walk. "Now, would that be a proper way to greet you?"

"No, it wouldn't," he said, gathering her in his arms. Upon arrival, he'd been full of curiosity about what was on the disk, but his priorities were beginning to change. About the time he'd decided that the disk could wait, Roslyn started to disentangle herself.

"Having a look at that disk better come next," she said.

"Awww . . ."

"Trust me on this," she said firmly.

As Frank seated himself in front of the screen, Roz went to the bar and picked up two drinks she'd prepared in advance. Handing him one, she seated herself on the opposite end of the couch and pressed the play button. As the play progressed, Frank's eyes grew wide with horror, and his expression turned to anger. When it was over, he felt drained and sick. Reaching for his glass, he realized there were three empty glasses at his elbow. "I didn't even realize you were keeping me supplied," he said weakly.

"I figured you'd need them," she replied in a matter-of-fact tone.

"I . . . I . . . can't believe it," he stammered. "Those sickos sexually abused that kid for almost an hour and then staged killing him!"

"I don't think it was staged," she said in a hard voice.

"Y . . . You . . . mean, we watched a murder?"

"It's called a snuff vid."

Frank sat back and closed his eyes. He began to perspire. Roz removed the disk from the machine, put it in a jewel case, and put the case in her purse. Picking up her glass and the three at Frank's elbow, she took them to the bar. After returning to her position at the end of the couch, she waited for him to speak.

"We need to call the cops, right now," he said at length.

"I think not—not quite yet, at least."

Frank shot bolt upright and stared at her in disbelief. "Whaddya mean?"

"Priorities pal. Think it through. The important thing is to shut down the scumbag who made this thing—to get him off the street and behind bars."

"Isn't that what cops do?"

"C'mon pal, think. These people have tons of money, they are smart, and their methods are very sophisticated. Their elaborate scheme for delivering the product shows that they have an early warning system in place."

"Early warning? Whazzat?"

"Do you know who sends you those disks?"

"DE, I assume."

"If you were asked, could you supply a name?"

"No."

"Do you know who picks them up?"

"No, it's never been the same guy twice, but they all look like money. One of them was interested in the car I was driving. When I offered him my card, he wouldn't even look at it. 'Not knowing who you are is part of the deal,' he said."

"See, the delivery scheme is a chain. Let's assume that you are delivering the disks to the end users and not to another mule. If the guy came under investigation, he wouldn't know who gave him the disk, but you can be certain that he'd have a way of alerting the supplier. If somebody started asking you questions, you couldn't tell them who sent you the disk or who you gave it to."

"Yeah, and that 'contingency' thing is likely their means of finding out that the cops are sniffing at my chain."

Roz smiled. "By Jove, I think he's getting it. It's going to take an investigator with unusual talent to get close without tipping them off. They would seem capable of monitoring all the usual channels of investigation, so your average flat-foot would probably trip a warning without knowing it. If this scoop got to a clumsy cop who did that, they'd make their present setup disappear without a trace. The investigation would wind up in a blind alley. They would regroup and keep on doing what they are doing and this little guy's death would be for naught. No, this info must go to the right person and no one else."

"I see what you mean," Frank sighed.

"But I do think we should tell Catherine and A.P. immediately."

"Huh?"

"Sorry, babe, I didn't mean to put one shock on top of another; I should have waited before bringing it up."

Frank looked at her with eyes that were pools of misery. "Please don't call me that."

"What?"

"Babe is Catherine's pet name for me."

"Oh, I'm sorry. I didn't know. I was just trying to be tender."

"And I appreciate that. But why tell them right now?"

"Because we involved them with some bad people. They have a right to know, and they need to be a part of any decisions we make."

Frank rose and paced the room. He banged his fist into his palm, the furniture, and the doors. He swept a glass off the bar and hurled it into the hearth. He thrust his hands into his pockets and stared out the window. Spent, he slumped down on the couch and put his head in his hands.

Roz had been watching the performance without expression. "Feel better?" she asked.

"Feel better?" Frank mumbled without raising his head. "Our lives, our futures, our marriages, you and me, all in shambles. How can I feel better?" He raised his head and looked at her. "I knew we'd have to tell them eventually. I didn't expect it to be pleasant, but I didn't think it would be an end-of-the-world scenario."

"End of the world?" Roz asked, a smirk beginning to play on her face.

"Damn right!" Frank shouted. "We're caught between spouses we've betrayed and people who trade in murder. No telling what the bad guys may do to us if they discover we've seen the video. We have no choice but to tell Catherine and A.P. We can admit that it was a mistake, but there's no telling what they will do. It can't be good. I think that's a damn fine definition of the end of the world for us!"

Roz straightened and faced him with a cool gaze. "The only part of that I agree with is that our relationship is a mistake. Furthermore—to quote Tusseman's law—nothing is as inevitable as a mistake whose time has come."

"Roz, I'm in no mood for your quips," Frank growled.

"I'm not 'quipping,' I'm trying to maintain perspective."

"Whaddya mean 'perspective'? We're done for, finished, gonzo, kaput. What perspective can road kill have?"

"Ever hear of Rudin's law?"

"Who the hell is Rudin?"

"Someone who said, 'In crises that force people to choose among alternative courses of action, most people will choose the worst one possible.'"

"You're making me angry," Frank pouted.

"Sorry pal, but it's the only way to get you thinking. Can you trust me enough to let me explain?"

Frank began to rub his temples. "Ok, out with it."

"You are talking as if all these terrible things have already happened to us when, in fact, nothing has happened yet. People normally react to a crisis this way, but my experience has led me to think that it is the worst thing to do."

Frank looked up, into her eyes, with interest. "You are talking as though I'm making a choice. Faced with a deal like this, how else can I react?"

Roz smoothed her hair and looked somewhere beyond Frank. "First, I need to give you a little background. I don't talk to many people about this, because they'd think me kooky. I've been waiting for the time to share it with you, and I think the fear has made me wait too long. What you think of me has become so terribly important in these past few months, that I've missed many opportunities. Now, I'm forced to explain under the worst of circumstances."

She looked into his eyes and saw them soften, so she continued. "There is a theory that our feelings have a lot to do with what happens to us. It states that when we think about negative things, we attract negative events into our lives. Conversely, it says that if we think about positive things, we attract positive events into our lives. As a little girl, I began to practice something akin to this. I noticed that happy things happened to me during the periods I concentrated on things that made me feel happy and that bad things happened to me during the times sad thoughts dominated my thinking. I don't mean to say that I studied and rationalized all this out, but the awareness grew upon me. By the time I was in my teens, I was practicing techniques to keep myself feeling good. That is how I run my life. People say that I have a dream resumé, a dream job, and live in a dream home. I can't argue with that, but I truly think it's more the result of this philosophy than luck, ability, or hard work. Right now, the idea of putting this scumbag in the slammer makes me feel good. Imagining how good it is going to feel when our relationships are worked out makes me feel good. That's what I mean by 'perspective'—keeping the thoughts that make me feel good dominant and resisting the slide into the slough of what-ifs."

When Frank raised his head and looked at Roz, his face was a mask of incredulity. "Relationships worked out? Are you trying to tell me that feel-good hocus-pocus is going to result in Catherine running off with A.P. so that we can be free to carry on?"

A sly smile played around the corner of Roz's mouth as she said, "Finish the line, 'If you want to hear God laugh . . .'"

"Tell him your plans." Frank replied.

"I can't argue that the situation looks hopeless. I don't claim to have any idea how it's going to work out. I just imagine what it's going to feel like to have all this amicably resolved. Turning over possible scenarios and scheming to make them happen puts one into negative feelings."

"So, you honestly believe that this is all going to work out?"

"Yes I do."

"And we don't have to do anything?"

"Au contraire. We have a key part to play, but our understanding is too limited to know what it is. The 'right thing to do' will be shown to us at the right time. We will know it when it comes along if our heads are clear. When we feel good, we are receptive; if we get clouded up with negative feelings, we won't know what to do next. Therefore, it's important that we shepherd our feelings."

"So, God's gonna tell Pollyanna what to do—how to straighten out something that she has royally screwed up—if she just keeps smiling?" Frank mocked. He studied Roz's face, unable to detect any of the impatience or exasperation he expected.

"I know that it flies in the face of the reward-for-good and punishment-for-bad ethic that our culture teaches, but I've always found it to work that way. There are a number of books written about the phenomena that we seem to attract good things when we feel good and bad things when we feel bad. Each of them advances a theory of why it works. Unfortunately, all the theories are bad science, so I can't buy any of them. I think of it as turning the situation over to the universe. I don't bother with the explanation. I think the important thing is to keep myself in a position to recognize the next step."

"Sounds like a mishmash of Zen, New Age, and maybe some Sung Ming Moon."

"I know it does, but it is a win-win situation."

"Win-win?"

"Sure. Finish the line 'The best laid plans of mice and men . . .'"

"Usually amount to about the same thing."

"Right on. Have any of your carefully laid plans or schemes ever worked out as you thought they should?"

"Not that I remember."

"Ergo, all the anxiety associated therewith was for naught."

"Hadn't thought about it in those terms, but I guess you're right."

"Therefore, you've nothing to lose. Regardless of how things work out, all you've lost is a period of feeling down, and who needs that?"

Frank grew pensive. Roz waited. After a few minutes, he offered, "Y' know, I often close the deals that I feel good about and rarely close one that I don't. If I'd thought about it, I'd have said it had something to do with subconscious vibes that I was receiving from the client, but I guess that's no more outlandish than thinking that how I feel affects the outcome."

"Let me put one more thing in the hopper for you to chew on."

"I feel a severe case of overload already."

"I understand, but this goes along. The best explanation I can offer is that all this is a matter of cooperating or getting in tune with the universe. The goal of most eastern religions is to get in harmony with the cosmos. Recently, science has admitted that it is getting closer to mysticism all the time. It seems the mystics understand the roots of reality while scientists understand the branches. Some thinkers have even postulated that the universe itself is a conscious being. These ideas aren't the products of unrestrained speculation. Trained, disciplined minds see them as the difficult consequences of pushing the limits of our current knowledge. There is good science—albeit rather esoteric—which would confirm that we attract things by the way we feel."

Frank sat looking at the fireplace. It was decision-making time. He could strap in with her for whatever ride she was taking or back out of their relationship altogether. Neither option was appealing. As he turned the situation over in his head, anger over the young life he'd seen snuffed out eclipsed thoughts of personal consequence. She was right, by god!

He couldn't let that happen without trying to do something about it. Once the thought took root, it felt good. It became clear to him that this crazy broad's program was the right thing to do. Supporting it in any way he could was, for him, the right thing to do. He turned to her. "What's next?"

She smiled at him. "Tell A.P. and Catherine, I suppose."

"And leave that big, comfy bed over there undisturbed, I suppose."

"I suppose."

9

Frank Tells Catherine

Frank sat at the breakfast bar with a death grip on his coffee cup. He couldn't believe what his eyes and ears were telling him. He'd told Catherine about DE, Roz and the disk. In preparation, he'd thought long and hard about what he'd say if Catherine's initial reaction had been outrage, hurt, or the numerous other ways a woman might react. Instead, she had simply looked surprised and said, "This may work out well." She was now looking past him, out the window. He waited for her to gather her thoughts.

She looked back at him. "I've been concerned about you for some time," she began.

"Whaa . . .?" Frank almost shouted.

"Hush," she said quietly, "let me finish. After I win the election, I won't be spending much time here. I know you won't want to come to Washington with me. You'd chafe in the 'Mr. Representative-Catherine-Grant' role."

"Damn right," thought Frank. Since she'd announced her intention to run for congress, he hadn't given much thought to how things would play out between them if she won. Probably, he had been too busy with Roz. She was right, the role of a congresswoman's husband wasn't the least bit appealing. He smiled. This was his ice-queen all right; instead of doing the betrayed wife thing, she was calmly calculating the effects.

"I have given it a lot of thought," she continued, "and, honestly, I was at a loss. If I'm in Washington and you are here for long periods, I can't expect celibacy from you. However, if my opponents discovered that you were running around, it could be damaging. Campaigning as the happily married woman is perfect, but the aftermath had me buffaloed. Now, I'm beginning to see some light. After I've been in office for a few months, we can announce that my service to my country is taking a toll on my domestic life. We will announce a trial separation. Campaigning for reelection as a woman sacrificing her home to serve her constituents will be an absolute ace."

"How can you . . .?" Frank stammered, "Our life together . . . don't you care . . .?"

She reached out and took his hand. "Sure I care, babe. I care about you being happy, but it's time to move on. We've had a good run, but you are bored to death. At least, you were until you met Roz." She grinned. "I was worried about you when the kids left for university; you were so at loose ends. I was pleased when you started trying all these new things, and I was even more pleased to see the way it was brightening you up. I should have suspected there was more to it. The reality is that the next step for each of us does not include the other." She released his hand and sat back.

"Do you want me to move out?" was all Frank could think of to say. Wasn't that what husbands usually said after confessing?

"Absolutely not!" Catherine replied. "And, that's not the politician protecting images. I appreciate what we've had together, and I don't think there is another man alive who could have pulled it off. What I want is that we share the same house and the same bed—like we have for years—until I move to Washington."

Frank couldn't say anything for several minutes. He moved the coffee cup about in his hands. When he did speak, his voice was shaking. "I . . . I . . . I'm so sorry . . ."

Catherine took pity and interrupted him. "No need to be. Politics is the next step for me. It's what I'm supposed to do. I could never be a complete person without answering the call. Nevertheless, I understood, when I decided to go into politics, that being a congresswoman's husband would never work for you. In a sense, my embracing politics was being unfaithful to you."

"It's not only the infidelity thing that I'm sorry about," Frank replied in a more even tone. "It's the matter of this disk. I'm afraid that I involved us with some very bad people."

"Have you been to the police?"

"No"

Catherine raised her eyebrows. "And, why not?"

"Roz," began Frank, almost choking to use her name with Catherine, "is afraid of the wrong cops. Whoever made that disk is very sophisticated, and their recruitment methods show that the organization is big and has plenty of money. Since they employ elaborate means to prevent tracing back through their clients, it's logical that they also have an extensive early-warning system in place. Roz is concerned about a clumsy investigator tripping it and letting these guys jump slick."

Catherine grew pensive. "I can't disagree. She sounds like some smart lady. Odd to find an academic with street smarts. We'd probably hit it off well."

Frank paled. "I . . . uh . . . I . . . I . . . don't . . ." he stammered.

Catherine grinned at him. "Just jerking your chain, babe. For the present, there's no need of us meeting. Hang on, I'll be right back."

Frank watched her disappear through the kitchen door. His beautiful ice queen. What other woman would have understood? To be certain, their relationship had been unusual, but it had been great. He suddenly felt an overwhelming sense of gratitude for their life together. His ruminations ended as she came back through the door tapping on her PDA.

She sat across from him, looking at the small screen. Lights blinked on the instrument, indicating that she was using wireless to access a computer somewhere. Frank refilled their cups with coffee. After stirring precisely one quarter teaspoon of sugar into hers, she reached for it without taking her eyes off the PDA and said, "Thanks, babe."

Frank remained silent while she worked.

"I thought so," she said, looking up. "I think I may have an answer to the dilemma."

"Vintage Catherine," thought Frank. She doesn't offer solutions; she has answers. "Which is?" he asked.

"It seems that the federal task force on missing children has enlisted the help of a local narcotics officer. He's somewhat of a John Wayne type. He gets involved in a lot more gunplay than the average cop, but the interesting thing is that his cases are textbook tidy."

"Tidy?"

"His record for convictions is higher than average because he does a thorough job of making certain there are no loose ends for a clever lawyer to pull. The odd thing is that, in instances where the individual under investigation turned out to be particularly ugly, he never got to trial."

"A vigilante?" Frank asked.

"The records read that the persons resisted arrest by threatening this officer with a weapon and died as a result of his defending himself."

"You said 'particularly ugly.' What does that mean?"

"Long rap sheets with few convictions, histories of brutality, that sort of thing."

"Sounds like he may be saving the taxpayers some money and making the streets safer in the process."

"You know I can't comment on that, but the whole package—if it didn't say anything else—says that this guy has finesse. Following the trail from that disk back to the maker is going to take finesse if it is to be done without tipping them off. This guy might fill the bill. I'll get you guys an appointment so you can size him up."

Frank was still sitting at the breakfast bar long after Catherine left. Was he in a Douglas Adam novel? The fabric of reality had unraveled. If there was anything as certain as death and taxes, it should have been the reaction of a betrayed woman. Catherine had just referred to he and his mistress as "you guys," and expressed confidence in their joint judgment. It was a Richter scale 13 jolt to his concept of reality.

10
ROZ GETS ON THE TEAM

The intercom on Garth's desk buzzed. "Ms. Cornelius and Mr. Grant here to see you."

"Be right out," he answered. Stopping at the mirror on the back of his office door, Garth worked up the pleasant face and tried to fix how it felt in his memory.

The appearance of the dark haired woman standing by the receptionist's desk made the pleasant face thing less of an effort. The ordinary-looking dude with her struck him as a salesman.

"Hello, I'm Detective Moore," Garth said, extending a hand in their general direction.

"Roslyn Cornelius," the woman said, taking his hand in a firm, confident, grip.

The man's handshake was more tenuous, "Frank Grant," he said.

"Please," said Garth, motioning down the hall. "My office is the second one on the left." Following Frank and Roz down the hall, he wondered why the woman was the leader of the pair.

After seating them in his sparse office, Garth smiled as he offered coffee or other refreshment.

"No thanks," replied Roz. "I'd rather get right to it."

"Great," said Garth, maintaining the smile as he seated himself behind his desk. "It's always a pleasure when citizens come forward to offer information," he continued, aware that interviewing citizens wasn't his forte.

The woman regarded him with cool confidence while the man fidgeted. "Judge Grant informs me that you are in possession of an alarming video," Garth said, groping for words.

"Yes we are," Roz said, "but before I show it to you, we need to discuss the price."

Garth looked at the dark haired woman in disbelief. She didn't look like the kind of person who would be selling information. He stole a quick glance at Frank. The man was in shock. He hadn't come here with the idea of selling information. Garth relaxed his face as he looked back at Roz. The change in his countenance didn't seem to have the usual effect. Switching his attention back to Frank, he saw terror mingled with the shock. Unless the guy was an accomplished actor, they hadn't discussed how this was going to go. "Ms Cornelius, if you have evidence regarding a criminal act, I don't have to bargain with you," Garth began in an officious tone.

Roz waved him off. "My husband is an attorney. I came in here with a good idea of what you can or cannot do."

"Lawyer?" thought Garth as he looked at Frank.

"Mr. Grant is not my husband, but he is my lover," snapped Roz. She took Frank's hand, saying to him, "I'm sorry, but I had to do that. I'll explain later."

Garth felt the surprise registering on his face. He was losing control of the interview. The imponderables were piling up faster than he could deal with them. Grant . . . it hadn't registered during the introduction . . . could this character be the judge's husband? He couldn't help feeling sorry for Frank. The dude looked positively ill. It fit though. If this guy was the judge's husband, and he'd been found out fooling around with this toughie, he had every right to look sick. The judge had to know since she'd called about the disk. Yet, this Cornelius broad—married to a lawyer, having an affair with a man married to a judge—was sitting there, cool as you please, delivering verbal punches with admirable precision. "Some tough bitch," he thought as he tried to regroup. She had outmaneuvered him. The only tack left was honesty. He sat back in his chair and made eye contact with her. "Gotta admit, you're some tough broad. Let's talk price." The nice smile he received from Roz felt like a reward.

"That's better. The genteel policeman thing didn't fit. I hoped you were a street cop."

"That's what you got . . . about the price . . ."

"The price for the information is part of the action. I want to see the scumbag that made this DVD taken down, and I want a slice. I have some expertise that I think you will need to make an airtight case. I don't want to see it wasted."

Garth didn't like his ability to make a case questioned, but he restrained his annoyance. "Give me a taste of what you mean by expertise."

"I can tell you who made the disk."

Although interest surged inside Garth, he maintained a cool outside. "And how do you suppose that would help?"

"Ok, the original disk would self-destruct—ruining itself and the machine—unless it was played on a particular computer and supplied with a password. Only one manufacturer makes that type of disk. Ordinarily, government spook outfits are the only customers for them," Roz stated calmly and then paused.

Garth was certain that his eyes were betraying his interest by this time. She was good. She had paused at just the right time to let his brain go wild with the possibilities. He had relinquished control of the conversation to her, but he tried one more feint. "If this perp uses self-destruct disks, he's sophisticated. He'd probably go to ground if we subpoenaed the customer list of the disk maker."

Instead of looking deflated as Garth anticipated, Roz looked pleased. "That's the way I hoped you'd think—we can do business. I've already obtained a list of organizations that buy that type of disk."

"How many people know that the list was requested?"

"It wasn't 'requested.' The only persons who know about it are the person who obtained it and me."

"How did that work?"

"Well, let's say that it pays to know who the competition is selling to."

"Competition?"

"Yes, I'm employed by a manufacturer of disks."

"Are we talking industrial espionage here?"

"We prefer to think of it as market research. Everybody does it. I'm certain that they nip our customer list from time to time."

"How many names are on the list?"

"Ninety-seven."

"Not a bad number. I could have them checked out in a couple of weeks."

"There is no reason to check ninety two. They are either government spook outfits or fronts for same."

Garth didn't try to hide his surprise. "How do you know that?"

"Made some calls."

"You'll have to do better than that."

Roz grew pensive. "Let's just say that it is important for people in my industry to know whether or not they are dealing with the government. We have ways of tipping each other."

"Like a secret lodge handshake?"

"In a manner of speaking. Would you like to see the disk now?" Roz asked, pulling a small DVD player out of her handbag.

Garth grew dark as he watched. By the time the disk ended, he was shaking with rage.

"Now you know why I need a piece of this guy," Roz said icily.

"Yeah, welcome to the team," Garth answered. He knew he was reacting out of anger, but he needed Roz's expertise. Yes, the bureau had people with similar talent, but he didn't know any of them. A plan for whoever made the DVD was forming in his mind. The foot soldiers in the bureau would approve of it, but not the admin types. Techno-weenies in general didn't enjoy a good reputation for knowing when to pass information upstairs and when to keep their mouths shut. Roz had not only come to him with breakthrough information, but she provided a way of not having to use people he didn't know. In addition, she had proven that she knew when to talk and when not to. "How did you come into possession of this disk?" he asked, picking up a pencil.

Garth scribbled as Roz told him of meeting Frank through Discreet Encounters. She threw the ball to Frank for his version as she approached the point where they had become sexually involved. Talking relaxed Frank. By the time he reached the same point she had, his wits had returned and he realized that the gentlemanly thing to do was to let her explain the next part. Without hesitation, she admitted their indiscretion and handed the narrative back to Frank for a description of his being approached to mule the disks. Frank was visibly angry by the time he handed the story back to Roz for a description of how they had obtained a look at the disk and then destroyed the original. Garth was impressed with the dance. He held up a hand. "Whoa, could you go back over why you destroyed the original?"

"Certainly," answered Roz. "I was able to read the thing without it self-destructing, but there remains the possibility that the maker could detect the unauthorized read. That would send them running for cover. The only way to be certain of keeping them in the dark was to wreck the original."

"You are aware that you committed an offense by destroying material evidence, aren't you?" Garth asked, grinning in spite of himself.

"Yes, but I'm also aware that taking the chance put us one step closer to nailing this guy before he has a chance to disappear."

Garth couldn't help being impressed. "Lady, I like the way you think. But, there is a hole in what you are telling me."

"And that would be?" replied Roz, calmly flicking a piece of lint from her skirt.

"It appears that those people at . . . at . . ." Garth fumbled with his notes. "Discreet Encounters displayed a thorough knowledge of you two when they approached you to carry their disks."

"They didn't ask me to carry," corrected Roz.

"Yeah, that's just it," said Garth, as he began to nibble on the pencil eraser. "Since their whole operation hinges on the delivery of product via DVD, do you suppose they didn't ask you because you work for a disk manufacturer? In fact, I'm finding it hard to believe that your being in the business didn't scare them off to begin with."

Roz's expression became mischievous. She began to examine her manicure. "Do you suppose it could be because they don't know I work for DiskTech?"

"What?" blurted Garth. "You said that Dis . . . dis . . ." Garth looked back at his notes.

"Discreet Encounters," prodded Roz. "We call 'em 'DE'."

"Yeah, yeah, you said that this DE required extensive background information, employment and the whole enchilada."

"That's right, but I gave them the name of my consulting company. They think I'm an academic."

"Mind telling me why you did that?" Garth said with considerable interest.

"I enjoy controlling what people know about me . . . no good reason . . . just makes me feel more comfortable. Had I told them I work for DiskTech, dispersal of information about me would have been at DiskTech's discretion. Using my company gives me control over what they can find out. They probably think I'm an egghead who prowls the halls of academia discussing esoteric mathematical concepts."

"So, they don't know you have anything to do with disks?"

"Bingo, they think I'm a mathematician. People consider such creatures mostly harmless."

Garth was more than impressed. He began to look forward to working with this lady.

Frank, on the other hand, was again unsure whether he wanted to continue working with the same lady. As they walked into the parking garage, he turned to her angrily. "What the hell was that 'lover' business all about?"

"Keep your voice down," she said quietly. "Let's sit in my car and I'll explain."

Seated in the car, Frank didn't look at her. He was good and mad. He wanted to stay that way.

Roz's tone of voice was neither apologetic nor entreating. "I had to say something that would get him off balance. I saw that he was struggling with the genteel police officer act. I needed to knock him off his perch so we'd see what he really is."

"But, he will put two and two together, realize who I am, and now he knows we've been messing around . . ."

"Relax, pal. He already knows. He made you as soon as I said you were not my husband. I saw it in his eyes after he'd looked at you. I think the realization is what pushed him into playing straight with us."

Frank felt his mad fading. She was right as usual—damn. He looked at her and felt his mad evaporate. "Yeah, I will admit that you handled him. He kept trying to get control of the conversation but never quite made it."

"Basically, he is calm and centered. Such people are hard to get off balance. That's why I had to call in the shock troops. He wasn't comfortable trying to act like something other than the street cop he is, but that's what he thought we'd be most comfortable with. I had to overload his circuits, so he had no choice but to regroup around his real persona."

"You think he's the guy we need?"

"Absolutely; he's tailor-made for this job. Catherine steered us right. Am I right in assuming that her arranging this interview with Garth is the result of your telling her about us?"

"Yes."

"How did she take it?"

"Unbelievably. I thought I was prepared for almost anything, but I wasn't ready for her to be pleased about it."

Roz's head jerked around to look at Frank. Her eyes were wide. "Pleased?"

"Yeah, she figures the election is won. She knows that I'd never be happy in the role of congresswoman Grant's husband. It sounds like she's been wondering what to do with me." Frank paused and shook his head. "No, that's not what I meant it to say. It sounds too heartless. In her own way, she loves me and wants me to be happy. However, she's moving on and she couldn't see where I fit in the next step. So, she actually seemed pleased that I'd developed new interests."

Roz's expression was still incredulous. "Wow, I expected things to work out, but I would never have imagined this scenario."

"Gotta admit, I thought you were crazy as a shithouse rat when you told me things were going to work out, but this has me thinking that I should replace my stewing with working at feeling good."

"You will be the better for it. If nothing else, it releases stress; your body wasn't built to handle constant stress."

"Uh, did you tell A.P. yet?"

Roz looked down. "No, our schedules aren't meshing. We've set up a date for next Tuesday."

"Man, that's weird, making an appointment to talk with your husband."

"Yeah, but that's the way it works with us."

✳✳✳

Garth sat at his desk, thinking. He'd spent the last three days checking out the companies on Roz's list. Three days was a lot of time to spend checking five companies, but he had to be careful. He thumbed the pile of notes. Nothing had jumped out. "Jumped hell," he thought, not even a nose poked out. He sat back, put his hands behind his head, looked at the ceiling, and took a deep breath. This was no time to get frustrated. He needed to focus, to get centered. He inhaled deeply and let the breath out in stages. He felt calmer. Good, a few minutes of this and the thread to pull or the dot to connect would occur to him. Over the years, the technique had never failed. He continued to relax.

Damn! There it was again! Instead of an insight, the thought "Call Roz" had popped into his mind. "Probably a waste of time," he thought, but it appeared that the only way to get the annoying thing out of his head was to call her.

Roz's phone rang. "Roz here," she answered.

"Ms Cornelius, this is Detective Moore. Could I get a few more moments of your time?"

"Sure, I can be at your office in ten or fifteen."

"I don't mean to inconvenience you. I can come to your office or meet you somewhere close."

"No problem. I want an excuse to get out of here and the walk will be refreshing."

"Well, thank you. There is no need to stop by reception on your way in. My door will be open."

"TTFN."

"TTFN?" thought Garth as he hung up the phone. Oh, yeah, Winnie-The-Pooh, Ta Ta For Now. So, she was on her way. What was he going to say? Why had he called her? He didn't have the slightest idea.

Garth's over-large feet were propped on the desk and he was deep in thought when Roz walked through the door. He lifted his feet from the desk, but she held out a hand. "Stay comfy," she said, seating herself.

Garth put his feet under the desk and folded his hands on top of it. He pursed his lips while looking about the room.

"What?" she said.

Garth met her eyes. "I . . . ah . . . don't . . . er know why I called you. I don't quite know how to explain it, but checking out the five businesses that buy those self-destruct disks didn't turn up anything that I can put my finger on. What I need to do now is to focus, to get centered, but every time I try, I get this thought to call you." He searched for something else to say, but he was so uncomfortable that his mind was a blank.

Garth's discomfort was obvious to Roz. She wanted to reach out and give him a hug. Instead, she favored him with her sweetest smile. "Don't struggle with it. Let me finish for you. You know that you don't have the capacity to know what to do next, so you are trying to tap into something bigger than yourself for direction."

Garth grew lighter in his chair. He smiled back at her. "Yeah. How did you know?"

"During our first meeting, I thought I sensed that about you. Can you tell me more?"

"There isn't much more. Before going into any situation, I try to get quiet. If I try to plan it out, it never plays the way I planned; I wind up being unprepared. If I get quiet and focused, the thing I need to do occurs to me at the time I need to do it and things seem to turn out ok."

Roz smirked. "Pardon me if I say that doesn't sound like sophisticated investigative technique."

"That's why I don't tell many people. In fact, I don't know why I'm telling you."

"Perhaps it's because it gives me an opportunity to tell you that I think this world would be a much better place if more people operated that way."

Garth thought for a minute. It was nice to hear. Nevertheless, the fact remained he was still smarting from the way she had wrested control of their previous conversation from him. Perhaps if he tried some shock tactics of his own . . . A mischievous grin formed as he said, "What would be your reaction if I told you that I've closed seven cases by killing the suspects because they were resisting arrest?"

Roz didn't flinch. "I'd say I'd need a few more details. Were they armed?"

"Yes."

"Who drew the weapon first?"

"They did."

"Did you always get the first round off?"

Garth was shocked. Her tone of voice carried no judgment. Nobody had asked that one before. "No."

"Well, I guess that I'd say it was a good thing you were centered going into those situations. If you'd been relying on training or skill, we probably would not be having this conversation."

Garth couldn't believe his ears. Her assessment was bang on. It was exactly what happened, but he'd never had the courage to put it into words.

She smiled. "This is fascinating. May I ask you a couple more questions?"

"Sure. I can't promise to answer, but ask away."

"Thanks. I wouldn't want you to answer if there is a legal reason you can't, or even if you feel uncomfortable. Anyway, were the cases against these people good?"

"Yeah, I was fairly certain of a conviction."

"How would you have felt if one of them had beaten the rap?"

"Disappointed, but, hey, I could be wrong. That's what the legal system is all about. I'm not omniscient. I don't know everything." He paused for a moment, looked down, studied his hands, and then regained eye contact. "I've got an idea where you are going, so I'll cut to the chase. People usually get the idea that I'm a vigilante. The god's honest truth is that I hadn't judged those people. Although I built the case, I had not judged them; I intended to turn the case over to the people who do that. I went to make the collar with the intent of delivering them intact to the next step. When they pulled a weapon, I just did what seemed to me, in that split second, to be the best way of staying alive."

"How do you feel about killing seven human beings?"

"The number's bigger than that because some of them had help. I'm comfortable that I played my part in the situation."

Roz was pensive for a few moments. Garth waited, wondering. Had he said too much? Why had he told her at all? This was weird. Were all conversations with this person bizarre affairs?

"This missing children thing isn't your usual gig?" she asked.

"No, I'm a narc."

"Ahhh, that fits better. I was having trouble equating missing children with all that gunplay."

"People who mess with drugs have a tendency to play rough."

"I don't see a wedding ring. You married?"

Somewhat surprised, Garth answered "No." Without knowing why, he continued. "I'm sorta engaged. Well, I've asked her—more than once—but she hasn't said either way."

"May I ask if her hesitation has anything to do with those seven cases involving gunplay?"

"Yeah, everything."

"Mmm, I thought as much," Roz mused. "Do I understand that she's not satisfied with your explanation?"

"Nah, she thinks I provoke the confrontation—a misguided effort to save the taxpayers money, or something of the sort. She's a lawyer and committed to the ideal of due process, so it rubs her fur the wrong way."

"Do you mind if I ask how you got started approaching situations by getting quiet? That's not the way most people do it."

"You into jazz?"

"No, my tastes run more toward country."

Garth threw up his hands. "And here I was beginning to think you were ok."

Roz bristled. "A person's taste in music shouldn't . . ." she began, but stopped short when Garth winked and grinned.

"Gotcha! I was wondering what it would take to get a rise out of you."

"Touché," she replied and grinned back.

As he began speaking, Garth folded his hands comfortably on the desk. "My great uncle composed wonderful music. The instruments talked when they played his stuff. One time, I asked him if it was hard to put something that beautiful together. I can still hear his answer. 'It's the mos' easiest thing inna worl. I jes' gets real quiet and th' whol' thing happens in my head like it was there all along.'

"I decided on the spot to try it myself. It took some coaching from him to be able to get rid of the thoughts buzzing around in my head, but once I was able to, my grades, my relationships and everything else improved.

"When I saw it working, I was so excited that I wanted to share it with everybody. That proved to be a mistake. I asked the old man why. He said that I shouldn't share unless asked because most people weren't ready to hear it."

"Have you explained this to your lady?"

"Rose is her name. Rose Winters. Yes, I did explain, but she has a hard time getting her head around anything that she can't find in a textbook. She still thinks I provoke those confrontations."

"Does she think that the answers—even to the big questions—are something that we, as humans, can figure out for ourselves?"

"I've never given it much thought, but, yeah, I'd guess she thinks that way."

"What do you think?"

Garth struggled within himself. This broad was getting too personal. He knew what he thought, but couldn't remember telling anybody . . . ever. He took a deep breath, turned inward and found the same answer—tell her.

Roz saw his struggle. "Let me make it easier for you," she began. "Multiple choice, do you think that the answers to the world's problems are: A, political, B, spiritual?"

Garth relaxed and grinned. "Although I'd never have chosen that word in a thousand years, given the choice between those two, I'd have to go with B. If all the books that propose political solutions to the world's problems were laid end to end, there'd probably be no end to laying books end to end. Yet, this country still spends enough on defense every two weeks to eradicate hunger worldwide. Things like that tell me we have been looking in the wrong places for answers."

Roz smiled warmly. "Garth, I can't tell you how much I appreciate your openness. Now, I'm certain our collaboration will put those scumbags out of business."

"Which little matter, Ms. Cornelius, we'd better get to."

"Hey, please call me Roz. And, yes, we'd better get to business."

Garth thumbed the pile of notes. "I checked out those five companies you tagged for me. Four appear to be spanky clean. They operate out of established premises; the principles are people with no police record, whose names are in the phone book. The fifth outfit, this 'Acme Enterprises,' is interesting because it is a blind alley. It doesn't appear to be anything more than a rented office in Scada Towers. The rent for the office is paid by a check from a numbered company."

Fear gripped Roz. "Weren't you afraid that snooping into the finances of Scada might tip them off?"

"Hey, give me some credit! For all we know, the scumbags own Scada. I wouldn't go anywhere near it."

"Then, where . . .?"

Garth's smile became sly. "Remember our discussion about how you got that list of the people who bought those self-destruct disks?"

"Oh yeah," Roz responded. "Forget I asked. I'd agree that Acme is the company to start with. What else about it?"

"That's the problem. That's all I've found out. I'm having trouble figuring out where to go from there."

"Does that numbered company have any holdings?"

"None that I can find. I can't even find records of any business dealings."

"Does that name 'Acme' ring any bells?"

Garth frowned. Had he missed something? He thought for a minute. "Uh, no. Should it?"

"You know—beep, beep, zoooom."

"Whaat?"

"The roadrunner cartoons. Acme this or that is where Wiley Coyote buys the stuff for his wild schemes to trap the roadrunner."

"If you say."

"M' man, your education is sorely lacking," Roz chided. "May I use your computer for a minute? I might be able to provide some direction for the next move."

"Uh, sure," said Garth, as he vacated his chair.

Roz slid into Garth's chair and adjusted the position of the monitor. "You logged in to access the net?"

"Yep."

"What's the number of that company?"

Garth rifled through his notes and put one on top of the stack. "Right there."

After tapping the keys for a few minutes, Roz exclaimed, "Good, it's there!"

Garth looked over her shoulder. "What's where?"

"The program I need. This will take me a few. Would you mind getting us a cup of coffee?"

Garth began to feel irritated again. First, this broad plays him like a banjo and now she wants him to fetch coffee. "Er . . . the cop swill will be battery acid by this time of the day."

Roz was engrossed in what was on the screen. "I noticed a Second Cup in the lobby downstairs. I take mine with a dab of real cream and no sugar."

Garth didn't know what to say. Several things ran through his mind, but he discarded each as counter productive. She'd ordered him to trot down to the lobby and fetch her some coffee like . . . like . . . someone from the steno pool! The indignation he'd felt at first changed to discomfort as his mother's scowling face appeared in his mind. Roz hadn't looked up. The look on her face told him that she was in a space he couldn't understand. He turned on his heel and headed for the lobby. On the way down, he realized the rightness of the situation. Getting them a cup of coffee was the best contribution he could make to the investigation at this point.

Garth felt a nudge from one of the other men in the elevator. "Hey, it'll cost you a beer to keep me from telling Rose about that hot little piece you got in your office." Although the man was merely making guy talk, Garth had the strongest of urges to choke the living shit out of him.

Garth returned to his office, coffees in hand, to find Roz sitting back looking at the screen. "Coffee for the lady," he said, placing the cup before her. The characters dancing on the screen meant nothing to him.

"Thanks," Roz said, reaching for the cup without taking her eyes off the monitor.

Garth sat in the other chair and started to work on his coffee.

Roz held her cup in both hands, sipping without taking her eyes away from the dancing characters.

Garth was about a third of the way down in his cup when Roz asked, "Where is the printer located?"

"Down the hall," he answered.

"You may want to grab this as it prints; nobody else should see it."

Garth walked down the hall, his admiration for Roz growing with each step. She was some swift to realize that their quarry could have a mole on the force. He was disappointed to see that the document coming off the printer was columns of numbers.

"What's this?" he asked, coming back into the office. Roz had vacated the chair behind his desk, so he took it.

"A list of the numbers that the person who owns 'Acme' might use for another numbered company. The highest probability is in the upper left decreasing toward the lower right."

"Whaaat?"

"People are pretty predictable when it comes to assigning passwords. It's tough to get them to use passwords that are not easy to decode if you know something about that person."

Garth looked incredulous.

"Whether it's conscious or subconscious, people are afraid of forgetting passwords, so they tend to repeat or alter familiar patterns."

"You said something about 'knowing the person.' What do we know about the guy who made that video?"

"For starters, he's successful. It is an unpleasant fact that the legality of an enterprise makes no difference. Success depends upon the same set of personality traits. We also know that he's ruthless, he disregards conventional ideas about right and wrong, he's a sexual deviant, and very smart. Finally, if I'm right about the 'Acme' connection, he's a predator who never feels satisfied."

"Wuff," said Garth. "You'd make a good cop."

Roz was pleased to hear him say that.

"Uh, what do you do for Disk Tech?" Garth continued.

"Applied mathematics. I work in the research department. My role is to help the physicists reduce their findings to formulae that the chemists can use to produce the next generation of CDs. That also gets me into security issues. A behavioral scientist did the program I used to produce that list for his Ph.D. thesis. We use it to test the strength of passwords."

"Strength?" Garth puzzled.

"Yes, the definition of a strong password is one that is at least seven characters long, has no real words or abbreviations, contains both upper and lower case letters, as well as numbers and symbols."

"How would you ever remember something like that, particularly with the number of them you have these days—bank machines, debit cards, internet services and who knows what?"

"That's the problem. People resist strong passwords. We use this program to test passwords for clients. We give it a password from the client, add personality traits, and it generates a list of passwords the client is likely to use. The list is organized according to probability. Passwords with the highest probability are at the top of the left-hand column. The same principles apply when people are choosing the number for a numbered company. I started with the number of the company that pays for that office in Scada Towers, and added the personality traits of our quarry. I'll bet you will find the number for another of his companies in the first column."

Garth frowned. "I'm not followin' ya. Since I can't seem to find the names for the principals in 'Acme,' how am I gonna recognize if one of these numbers is a company belonging to the same guy?"

Roz shook her head. "Sorry, I'm not filling in all the blanks. I'm afraid I tend to do that. I'd suggest that you look for odd patterns of electrical usage in buildings owned by those numbered companies. It took professional quality studio lighting to produce the video. That stuff needs a pile of watts. I'm hoping they are using a facility not used in that way on a routine basis. Ergo, there would be an unusual spike in electrical usage."

"Mmmm . . ." replied Garth, "I do have a rough idea of how often they produce the things. It wouldn't take much to have a look at the consumption of premises we found to be owned by companies on this list . . . if we found a match . . ."

"You know how often they make those things?" Roz said in surprise.

"Yeah, I've got a rough idea," replied Garth before he related how he'd become interested in the pattern of missing children.

"Wow, that's good. You're a lot further ahead than I thought," Roz observed.

"I don't know about the good part," Garth replied. "I was pushing the data around as the assignment said to do when this pattern showed up."

✳✳✳

Two days later, Garth sat at the sidewalk café down the street from DiskTech. Watching Roz walk toward him was as entertaining as anything he'd done in a long time. She certainly was one fine looking woman. He was glad Rose didn't have access to his thoughts at that moment. He stood and pulled a chair out as she approached.

As Roz took the offered chair, she noted the cup of coffee at the place. She took a sip. "Mmm . . . Right on . . . you remembered."

"Hey, legs like mine ain't gonna get no tips; I gotta be efficient," he quipped while returning to his chair.

Roz smiled. "You said on the phone that you had something?"

Garth pulled the list of numbers from his pocket and spread it out before her. About a third of the way down in the first column, yellow highlighter marked a number.

Roz looked at it, then, up at him, waiting.

"A company with that number owns a building down on Industrial Street. There's good correlation between those kids going missing and electrical spikes in that building."

"How well do the spikes stick out from the background consumption?"

"That area is run-down. Over half of the buildings are unoccupied and boarded up. That's the case with this one. The electrical consumption for most of them is what it takes to keep the pipes from freezing and sometimes not even that. At this building, there is an occasional jump in electrical usage for that lasts for a few hours."

"A few hours? How can you cut it that fine? I thought those meters were read monthly."

"A lot of commercial buildings are now fitted with automatic reporting devices. It's getting to be common in run-down areas because meter readers don't like to go there and access to the buildings is iffy."

"I wonder if the people who own that building know that their electrical consumption is monitored on that basis."

"My guess is that they haven't given it a second thought. But, their pattern of paying for it is also interesting."

"Paying for it?"

"Yeah, the bills for that property are paid smack on time. Typically, owners of buildings in that area are sloppy about paying the bills. They are hoping urban renewal or something like that will enable dumping of them. There are properties in that area that haven't had the taxes paid for years and the owners still have them because the city doesn't want them. In contrast, the taxes, utility bills, and everything else on that particular building get paid right on the dot."

"Hummm . . ." Roz observed, "It looks as if somebody doesn't want to attract attention but their methods have resulted in the opposite effect."

"Not unusual," replied Garth. "A lot of cop work is waiting for the bad guy to outsmart himself; criminals usually do."

"What's next?" she asked.

"Gonna have to get a look inside that building."

"How do you propose to do that without alerting them?"

"Can't say at the moment. I got a scheme cookin' but I can't say anything more right now."

11

KITTEN MEETS THE DON

At precisely one forty-five, a long burgundy sedan rolled to a stop in front of the shop. Kitten was disappointed. She turned to Uncle Ted who was fidgeting behind the counter. "I thought you said he was sending his personal car."

"I believe that is his car."

"I thought big time hoods rode around in black stretch Cadillacs or Lincolns."

"That is a stretch and I've never seen him in anything else," the old man replied in a weak voice.

"Yeah, but it's an Olds or maybe a Buick. And, I think he sent some retiree to fetch me," Kitten pouted.

"That man is anything but retired," Ted replied as his frightened eyes darted between the figure approaching the door and Kitten. "He's anywhere something big is coming down."

"But, he looks so old and harmless."

"Keep in mind that each one of his socks is worth more than enough to buy either one of us and that everything else on him goes up from there."

"Good afternoon, Mr. Jarwoski," said a voice which was as clear and cheerful as the chime which had sounded when the door opened.

Ted moved to Kitten's side as he addressed the greeter. "Uh, hello, Mr. Vertolio. Uh, allow me to introduce my niece. Ah, Miss Jefferies, Mr. Vertolio."

"Pleased to meet you, Miss Jefferies," said Vertolio. He removed his hat, hooked his cane over a forearm, and offered a hand to shake in one motion.

Kitten began to feel she was missing an awful lot. "It's nice to meet you," she said as she accepted the proffered hand. Although Vertolio's handshake had all the mechanics associated with a warm, hearty greeting and he had the

154

appropriate facial muscles contracted for a smile, the encounter was anything but amicable. As Vertolio released her hand, she watched his eyes move to Ted. "Cold as a penguin's butt," she thought.

"I wasn't aware of your having any siblings, Mr. Jarwoski," Vertolio said in a cooler tone.

"Umm . . . No, that's right; I'm an only child. I've . . . er . . . been acting family for her since she lost her dad. He was one of my best friends."

Kitten thought she saw a flash of approval in Vertolio's eyes as he replied, "A fine and noble project."

Ted's face failed to register any relief.

Vertolio replaced his hat, opened the shop door and, standing aside, addressed Kitten. "Shall we, my dear?"

She was anticipating a well-built young man with Sicilian features to be attending the door of the limo, but Vertolio moved from behind her and opened it himself. She settled in and observed the opulent interior as Vertolio came around to the other side of the car. The driver pulled away from the curb as soon as Vertolio closed the door, though he hadn't turned around to look at either one of them through the glass divider.

Why was she here? Kitten wondered. Without elaborating, Uncle Ted had told her she needed to be at the shop before one-thirty. Thank god, he'd waited until she got to the shop to tell her the Don wanted a meet. If Gram had been listening on the extension, it would have sent her into a genuine tizzy. At Gram's insistence, it was part of the original arrangement that she have no direct contact with the underworld. Uncle Ted was to take care of the fencing. So far, the arrangement had worked, but it was naive to think it could last forever. The steady stream of high quality ice coming from Ted was certain to attract the attention of somebody who wanted part of the action. Did Vertolio intend to ask for his share?

Kitten couldn't have articulated what she expected a Mafia Don's house to look like, but the ranch style structure at the apex of the curving driveway didn't fill the bill. It looked like any other upscale residence with the possible exception that the landscaping was severe. A few well-tended but small bushes and shrubs were scattered over a lush green lawn. As any professional would do, she began processing a potential business related approach. The landscaping goal became clear. The possibilities for approaching the house undetected were on the minus side of nil. One could not sneak up on this layout. When the car stopped, Vertolio hopped out and came around to open her door. As soon as she was out, the driver moved the car toward the rear of the house. Kitten was impressed by how well orchestrated the whole deal seemed.

The unimposing front door opened into an opulent foyer. Light from seriously expensive chandeliers bounced off the marble floor and illuminated various paintings and objects d' art. It was obvious that they had entered a different world when a servant silently materialized and took Vertolio's hat, coat, and cane. Vertolio himself morphed from the nondescript older gentleman who had opened doors for her into an imperious figure that she couldn't imagine opening his own doors. She was so fascinated that she hadn't heard a man come up beside her.

"May I take your wrap, Miss Jefferies?" he asked.

Startled, Kitten turned toward the voice. It had come from a figure like the one she had hoped would be driving the limo—young, athletic, and darkly handsome. "Uh, yeah," she stammered, as he deftly helped her out of her jacket.

"Please come with me," said Vertolio, as he led the way to a library-looking room. She didn't miss the subtle difference in his tone. He was no longer the grandfatherly type who had picked her up, but the undisputed master of this turf. Stepping through the door, she surveyed the inlaid wood floor, expensive rugs, and genuine leather furniture. At the end of a low table sat the biggest, ugliest Black man she had ever seen. She'd never heard of these guys having Negro goons, but a lot of this was blowing her stereotypes. Vertolio reinforced her impression of the man being a heavy by offering her a chair on one side of the table without introducing him.

As soon as Vertolio took a chair across from her, a woman about Kitten's age and about half a head taller glided in carrying a tray of cookies. "Miss Jefferies, may I present my granddaughter, Monica?" Vertolio asked, as she placed the tray on the low table between them.

Monica gave Kitten a superior smile and nod as she straightened. She was beautiful, the epitome of a high-maintenance, pampered, young woman. Kitten instantly hated her but froze when she noticed the bracelet; she'd purloined it a few months ago. "Would you like coffee, tea, juice?" asked Monica. Her tone made it obvious that she was not happy with the hostess role.

"Uh . . . uh . . . coffee, I guess . . ." stammered Kitten.

"And coffee for me, my dear," said Vertolio. Although his tone was civil, Kitten didn't miss the reprimand in it.

Monica turned to the Black man and smiled, "And for you, Mr. Moore?"

"Coffee'd be great."

"So, the man seated at the end of the low table isn't an employee," thought Kitten. "Who could he be?"

"I see that you recognized the bracelet that Monica is wearing," said Vertolio in a noncommittal voice. His eyes remained on Kitten as he reached for a cookie.

Kitten's mind raced. The bracelet was, without question, one-of-a-kind. There wasn't any doubt. She'd lifted it from that condo. Ted had fenced it to or through someone connected to these people. That's how they got it. So what? Why had he used the word "recognized?" She tried to play it cool. "Yes, it's lovely," she answered.

Vertolio looked amused. "Please don't play games with me, my dear. When you saw it on Monica, you recognized it as the one you took from a condo in Jersey City. Monica told me it had been stolen from her aunt's safe while she was visiting there."

Kitten felt a cold anvil take up residence in her gut. She felt the color drain from her face. Up until now, Gram's network of domestics had provided the perfect targets, but their first miss had been big time; she had burgled the residence of someone related to a Mafia Don! A possibility existed that "Mr. Moore" was there to fit her with concrete shoes.

"I must compliment you, my dear," Vertolio continued. "Monica told me that she had put the bracelet in her Aunt Edna's safe on Tuesday and found it missing on Saturday. Edna told me that nothing else was missing. I'll admit that I thought the girl was trying to cover up some carelessness, but I did send a couple of people up to check for signs of forced entry. They couldn't find any sign of entry or exit. I'd still think that she lost it if an associate of mine hadn't spotted it in some of the merchandise that your uncle was negotiating. You are very skilled and professional."

Although she was shivering inside, Kitten looked at him steadily. "Thank you. But, you didn't bring me here for compliments. What do you want from me? Is this about 'wetting your beak' or whatever you guys call it?"

Vertolio laughed heartily. Kitten found his laughing face pleasant. "No, no, my dear," he chuckled. "We've been aware of your activities for some time and have no wish to interfere with an independent entrepreneur."

"What then . . .?" Kitten began, but Vertolio continued.

"On the other hand, my dear, Mr. Moore, over here," he said as he gestured at Garth, "wishes to interfere because he's a cop."

For the first time since she could remember, Kitten felt utterly lost. A cop in a Mafia Don's house? What was this? The amusement on Vertolio's face enraged her. She couldn't see anything funny as she looked from one man to the other.

At length, Vertolio said, "I'm sorry, my dear, it isn't kind to leave you dangling this way, but if you could see your own face . . . Mr. Moore is here regarding a common interest. We brought you here because we believe you can offer us valuable assistance."

The sense of relief that washed over Kitten was indescribable; she felt as though she'd received a pardon while on her way to the gallows. "Me?" was all she could manage to say through the mixture of relief and her inherit distrust of the law.

"You see, my dear," Vertolio continued, "there is a group of unspeakably depraved people abusing children and selling videos of their crimes to others that are equally sick. Even though Mr. Moore and I are in different businesses, we share the common desire to see this activity eliminated and the perpetrators punished."

Garth tried for the pleasant face as he finished Vertolio's explanation. "We are not dealing with some schlock bunch of sickos. They're sick all right, but also smart and sophisticated. The way they do business indicates they have an elaborate early warning system."

"Early warning . . . huh?" blurted Kitten.

"They have insulated themselves from their clients," Garth began. "If we started asking questions, they'd know about it and disappear before we got close."

Kitten continued to look puzzled.

"They use mules to deliver the DVDs to the clients. Neither the client nor the mule knows the other and there is a new combination for each delivery. You can bet that if I questioned either the client or the mule, that lead would dry up like the Great Salt Lake."

"Uh, you said 'DVD?' asked Kitten. "Couldn't you use that DVD as evidence and squeeze the recipient for further information?"

Garth looked pleased. "Under ordinary circumstances, yes, but their DVDs self-destruct if played on an unauthorized machine."

"Why not grab the box too and have your techno geeks do their number?"

"Seizing the client's computer wouldn't do any good. It's a safe bet that a new password is required for each play. The probability that our technical people could access the DVD without triggering the self-destruct is remote. If the DVD fried itself, it would do considerable damage to the computer. Then, we'd be stuck with destroying a citizen's property without discovering any evidence of wrongdoing."

"Yeah, I see. Is this leading to where I come in?"

Garth brightened. "Yes, we may know where they tape their activities. My problem is that I don't want to ask for a search warrant until I'm certain. The premise seems to be unused unless they are making a video. It is a safe bet that it's clean at other times. In addition, the building is large and has been modified to give whoever is doing what inside a fair window between the time the front door is down and the team could find where the action is taking place."

"Time for them to shut down and scram," Kitten interjected.

"Exactly. However, their escape is not my greatest fear. These appear to be snuff videos."

"What?"

"Snuff videos; the person being abused is murdered at the end."

Kitten's eyes widened. "They'd do the kid before they left! Is that what you're saying?"

"That is what I'm saying. I do not know for certain, but it is my best guess," Garth replied quietly.

Kitten closed her eyes for a moment. She felt nausea coming on.

"Please, my dear, relax, have a sip of your coffee," Vertolio said kindly.

Kitten spooned sugar into the untouched coffee. As she lifted the cup, she noticed that her hand was shaking. The coffee was lukewarm, but still soothing. She sat back and looked at the ceiling.

Silent moments passed before Vertolio offered, "My dear, I continue to be impressed."

"About what?" Kitten asked, lowering her eyes to meet his.

"Your demeanor. That was the first display of uncontrolled emotion I've seen from you. You were shocked to see the bracelet, but you recovered beautifully. I wouldn't have seen it if I hadn't been watching."

"Rugrats aren't my thing. I guess they're ok if they belong to somebody else, but the thought of 'em bein' tortured makes me sick."

Disapproval flashed across Vertolio's face when she spoke, but the smile returned as he sat back and made a steeple with his fingers. "Is your revulsion sufficient that you would be willing to assist us in putting an end to this business?"

"Betcher ass. But I think we need to do some negotiatin' with the law over here, don't we?" Kitten replied, gesturing toward Garth.

Vertolio rose and looked down at Kitten. "Please be advised that your response did not convey the respect to which I'm accustomed, but yes, you two do have things to discuss, so I'll excuse myself," he said, and left the room.

"Getting lippy with him wasn't smart," observed Garth.

"Yeah, I know. The thought of what they're doin' to those kids . . . it really rattles me . . . I'm not thinkin' straight. Gimme a second here," Kitten said, reaching for the cup.

Garth waited.

Kitten sipped the now-cold coffee and looked about the room. She knew Garth could take advantage of her discomfiture. He wasn't; she noticed and appreciated the courtesy.

It took several minutes for Kitten to gather her thoughts. "Now, if I agree to help you guys nail these scumbags, are you gonna offer not to bust me or what?" she asked.

Garth withdrew a small notebook from his pocket. "Do the names of these cities mean anything to you?"

Kitten fought rising panic as Garth reeled off the names of a dozen places in which she'd made scores. Satisfied that her face wasn't revealing anything, she waited until he looked up and said simply, "Should they?"

Garth grinned mischievously. "Yeah, thefts were reported there and the MO looks the same as for Monica's aunt. Most of the valuables were left and no sign of forced entry was found."

Kitten felt the foundations of her world shaking. Cops kept records of that stuff? She and daddy had dismissed the idea of a record being kept when it appeared that the plaintiff had misplaced the article in question. She fought for control. "Best to go on the offence," she thought. "Lemme get this straight," she started. "The sites of these reported thefts, there was no sign of B and E, right."

"Yes," agreed Garth.

"And, you said that other items of value—to which this alleged thief would have had access—were left undisturbed when the supposed theft occurred?"

"Correct."

"Doesn't that look more like the plaintiff misplaced the items?"

"Yes, that would be my take if I was investigating one of these complaints."

"Why would a record be kept?"

Garth's expression became indulgent. "CYA, pure and simple. Gotta Cover Yer Arse in case the complaint was a ploy in the process of initiating an insurance claim. Insurance investigators love to find the law derelict."

"But . . . but how did you find time to search through all those records . . .?"

"Piece of cake these days. Law enforcement agencies share each other's databases. I entered the circumstances of Aunt Edna's complaint and the computer gave me matches."

"Sonofabitch," thought Kitten. All the care that she had taken to cast doubt upon whether or not there had actually been a burglary at all had, itself, become an identifiable, traceable, MO. Damn computers anyway. Damn this information age all to hell! It had scuttled her sweet little operation!

Kitten pouted as she said, "I ain't sayin' that those names mean anything to me, but what gave you the idea of making that search?"

"In order to find out if we are right about that building, I need the services of a cat burglar. I asked Vertolio if he knew of a particularly good one."

"You guys tight?"

"Not at all. I approached him because I knew he's old school, very protective of women and children. This case is our first, and will probably be our last area of cooperation. If you agree to help me, we may never see one another again."

"But he fingered me."

"Not exactly. He said that someone was operating out of this city with a MO that sounded like what I was looking for. He required that I promise to not prosecute that person if he found them for me."

A puzzled expression crossed Kitten's face. "So you ain't puttin' some kinda plea-bargain squeeze on me to help you?"

"If you help me . . . us . . . it will have to be because you want to. The people we're after are smart, well financed, and have no regard for human life. Hunting them is dangerous. I would never coerce a person to face that degree of danger."

"From the looks of you, I'd say that coercion would be part of your bag of tricks."

Garth grinned. "I've been known to lean on people from time to time but only when I know they are taking advantage of someone weaker."

The last trace of petulance disappeared from Kitten's expression. "Tell me what you need done."

Garth took a deep breath, put his notebook away, and made eye contact with her. "The building we think contains their 'studio' is large. Recently, it has received extensive modifications and a sophisticated alarm system. The windows on the lower floors are boarded up. We can't find anyone who has ever seen a light in any of the upper floors. In fact, we can't find anyone who has seen anybody except maintenance people come and go."

"Mind my askin' what makes you think this is the place?"

"At irregular times, the electrical usage for that building spikes. Consumption will be what you'd expect for utilities in an unoccupied building for days or weeks and then, for a few hours, it'll look like a bolt of lightning is being used."

Kitten was thoughtful. "That is curious, especially if no one sees lights."

"More than curious when you consider that the frequency of the spikes matches that of young boys disappearing."

"From where?"

"In an area roughly a day's drive around Jackson, Mississippi."

"More computer geekery tell you that?"

"Yes."

"You don't look like the type."

"I'm not. This pattern emerged while I was doing an assignment for a course I had to take."

"Mind if I ask what got you interested in that building in the first place?"

Garth was silent while considering how much to tell her. If he left out a key and she noticed it, that would mean she was good at thinking on her feet. If she didn't see the hole, she probably wasn't the one for the job and he wouldn't have told her too much. He began carefully. "I'm a narc. We receive routine reports on unusual patterns of electrical usage. Sometimes they point to marijuana grow operations. Since the pattern of the spikes seemed to correlate with the disappearances, I called City Hall to see if I could find out who was paying the taxes. It turned out to be a numbered company, but the payment pattern was unusual, so I checked with the phone and utility companies. Same thing, the bills are paid smack dab on time."

"What's unusual about that?" Kitten queried.

"That part of town is pretty run down. Owners of buildings in that area are usually hoping for a sale or urban renewal. I'd say that most owe a stack of back taxes and other bills."

"Mmmm . . ." Kitten mused. "So, it could be that the owner of that building pays everything on time to avoid drawing attention, but it has had just the opposite effect."

Garth felt a glow; she was buying in! "Hey, sharp! That's exactly what happened."

Kitten fell silent for a few minutes. Garth noted that she seemed to be sorting information. He wasn't surprised when she turned to him and said, "I don't buy it."

Garth feigned surprise. "Don't buy what?"

"The part about the electrical usage being what gave you the initial tip. The rest of the story makes sense, but I'm havin' a hard time believin' that the power company sends you guys reports that have that much detail. Maybe I'm a little dense about where this computer stuff can go. I can see them tippin' you guys when the bill for someplace suddenly doubles, but spikes once in a while—that don't go down so good."

"Wow," thought Garth. It would be a serious miscalculation to assume that this chicken was ignorant about any particular subject. Although it was obvious that she was uneducated, the things she knew revealed an IQ way above average. She was looking more like the one all the time. He turned and grinned at her. "Damn good. I left that part out to see if you'd catch it. You are so right—there's no way we would want, or could get, reports of every power usage anomaly. What happened is that we know that the disks self-destruct. There's only one outfit making them, and they have a single customer in Jackson. The disks get delivered to an office rented by a numbered company. I started checking the power usage of buildings showing a high probability of being owned by the owner of that numbered company and this one popped out."

"You said, 'high probability.' More high-powered computer geekery?"

"Not mine, that time. The idea and execution came from someone who is smarter than both of us."

Kitten was silent for more than a few beats. She shook her head and whistled softly a couple of times. Garth didn't interrupt her thoughts. Turning to Garth, she said, "Wouldn't that be a gas? These guys get tripped up by the very thing that makes them so hard to track; they outsmart themselves."

"That's the way it usually works," Garth replied. "A lot of cop work is connecting the dots until you find out where they outsmarted themselves."

"What you've done sounds damn swift to me. Why are you always downplaying your part?"

"I'm not 'downplaying,' I'm just being factual. I was sitting there, thinking about how the dots might connect when I realized that the pattern of bill payment was unusual for that neighborhood. My best deductions come like that. I try to be quiet and wait for them to come, and they usually do."

Kitten continued. "Sooo . . . there's a lot that points to this building being the place, but if you got a search warrant, these guys would probably go to ground. You need to find out more about this building before you can figure out the next move. Is that where I come in? Do you want me to snoop this place out?"

"Aahh . . ." said Garth, the glow brightening. "Exactly so. From what I can find out, that building has a ventilation system with large ducts. The building inspector tells me that it should be possible to gain access through roof vents."

"I guess I could come to Jackson with you to case . . . er . . . check this place out."

"Yes, that would be move I propose."

"There's one problem; my Gram."

"Who?"

"My grandmother. She'd go nuts if I disappear, or if she knew I was doing something like this."

Garth put his hands on his knees and began to rise. "Let's go see her. I believe that I may be able to settle that issue for you."

12

GARTH CONFRONTS GRAM

As Garth drove them down the Don's driveway, Kitten asked, "May we stop by my uncle's shop to pick up my wheels?"

"Sure. Where is it?"

Kitten gave him the address.

"It doesn't mean much to me. You'll have to navigate."

"Uh, I'm not all that familiar with this part of town."

Garth extracted a map from the door pocket and handed it to her. "Here you go. Please write your Gram's address on it in case we get separated after we get your car."

Kitten began unfolding the map. "They must employ sadists to package these damn things," she muttered.

"Or, at the least, someone who has never tried to use one in a car," Garth observed dryly.

"I'd think you big city cops would be rigged out with GPS."

A grin played at the corners of Garth's mouth. "Umm . . . there is one, waiting to be installed in my car."

Kitten remembered Garth's downplaying of his computer expertise. Still, the results he'd achieved had him a techno-whiz in her mind. This was puzzling. Why wouldn't somebody like that jump on a GPS? Maybe knowing would help her understand the guy. Since he knew a great deal more about her than she did about him, she felt at a disadvantage. Perhaps probing would level the field. "Well, if you had it in here, we wouldn't have to deal with this damn thing," she said, rustling the map. "Busy schedule prevent you from getting it installed?"

The grin again played at the corners of Garth's mouth. "Can't blame the schedule. I could get another car to use. To be honest, it's more procrastination. They made the mistake of giving me the manual for it—thick as the first volume of

War and Peace. I thumbed through it, put it on the corner of my desk, and it's been there ever since. The last time the Old Man—er, my superior—bugged me about it, I reminded him that if it had been installed in my last car, we'd have to pay another installation charge for my current vehicle."

"You wore out a car while putting off getting the GPS installed?"

"Not exactly. My last steed was totaled by some people who resented my interference in their business affairs."

Kitten became fascinated. "A high speed chase that ended in a crash?"

"No, more like munitions."

"Are you talking about exploding projectiles?"

"Yup."

"Hey, that sounds choice, tell me all about it."

"Sorry, I can't. The people who did my car didn't survive the encounter. That's all I can say about it."

"Now, that fit," thought Kitten. She'd sized Garth up as a person who would be much more comfortable with action than a keyboard. It looked as though she'd been right. Perhaps her inclination to trust him was also correct; she'd have to see.

"This person you refer to as 'Gram,' is she your natural grandmother?" Garth asked.

"Yes, paternal unit."

"And your parents?"

"Both dead. Mom was an aerialist . . . killed in a fall. Dad wasn't able to go on after losing her . . . just kind of withered away," she replied. It was more than she needed to say, but it seemed right. She stole a glance at his profile. Genuine emotion played on his face.

"Uh, you don't need to tell me if you don't want to, but I'd like to know how old you were when your parents died," Garth asked quietly.

"Mom died when I was nine; we buried Dad when I was sixteen. I've been livin' with my Gram since." Again, it was more than necessary, but she couldn't seem to help herself.

Garth thought for a minute or two before asking, "And . . . your relationship with your Dad, after your mom died . . . how was it?"

Kitten bristled. "If abused is where you're goin', Mr. Cop-shrink, forget it. My Daddy was the kindest, sweetest, most caring man that ever . . . ever . . ." Her voice faltered as tears began. She lowered her head and wiped at her eyes with the back of her hand. "Ever wasn't worth a damn."

"Hey," Garth began softly, "I'm not trying to pry, and I damn sure ain't doin' no psycho-shit. I'm trying to understand who you are and what you're about."

"Why? I already said I'd help."

"But, I haven't decided yet whether or not I can accept your help."

"Huh?"

"You appear to have the skills to do the job, but I don't yet know if you have the emotional fiber. I know how dicey things might get, but you don't. I need to know you can stay cool if things start going to hell. I think you're smart enough to handle almost anything. However, I'm still weighing your method of handling unpleasant surprises. I don't know whether it will help or hinder your ability to use those smarts. I know the final years with your Dad couldn't have been easy. That's why I asked you about them. Please believe that abuse had not occurred to me."

"Sorry," said Kitten—unsure of why she'd apologized. "Daddy never was much. He was an aerialist too—mom's catch man. Mom was the star; the show revolved around her. He was always in the background. I don't remember any fighting or even arguing. As a child, I thought all kids had moms and dads that thought the world of each other. When mom died, the whole circus went into a blue funk. They cancelled shows and even bookings. Over time, things returned to normal, but Daddy didn't. Before her death, he laughed a lot, always ready with a joke or wisecrack. After, he rarely smiled. When he did, it wasn't like before; there was always sadness lurking just underneath. I guess he tried, but he didn't have what it took to get through losing her. He went from one thing to another, doing ok for a while and then messing up because his mind wasn't on it. Lord knows, the circus tried everything to find him a slot. I can't say that we had it tough, because circus people are a family; they look after each other. If I'd had mom's built, I'd have stayed with the circus, but there isn't much market for a buffed up Twiggy in tights and sequins."

Garth laughed. "I wouldn't have described you as 'a buffed up Twiggy' but its darned good."

"What else would you call ninety-four pounds of bone and gristle?"

"I don't normally make characterizations about women's appearance."

"Yeah, I've noticed. You are quite the gentleman, aren't you?"

Garth chuckled. "The credit belongs to the ghost of my mother. She used to whop my black ass something fierce if I referred to a lady in an uncomplimentary manner."

"Anyway, after Daddy died," Kitten began, not knowing why she wanted to continue the narrative, "I went to live with his mother. She was up front about him never being much for ambition or direction. She told me that she'd reconciled herself to the idea of his being a drifter all his life. He surprised her by finding a place in the circus. She's such a sweetie that I never laid my take of that situation on her. I figure it had more to do with mom making a place than him finding one. Nevertheless, you gotta give him credit for being able to catch mom's attention. Men were always trying, but as far as I know, he was the only one that ever did. Anyway, my Gram, bless her heart, has been real good to me. She's particularly good at helpin' me understand that the rest of the world ain't like the circus."

"Does she encourage you to go to school?"

"Always buggin' me about it. Howdja know?"

"Well . . . please understand that I'm not putting you down, but a person can tell that you don't have much in the way of formal education. It's obvious that you're some swift, but little things in the way you talk give you away."

"Yeah, I know," said Kitten, studying her shoes. "But the thought of startin' school at twenty-two don't sound much good."

"I wondered how old you are. When I first saw you, I couldn't believe you were the one Vertolio told me about."

"My uncle told me that the little girl look would go down best with the Don."

"I'll have to say that he was bang on. Those pigtails, no makeup and pleated skirt had him struggling to remember that he was talking to a college rather than a little girl."

"Looking the kid is better than big boobs for getting what you want."

Garth laughed. "Is that an original observation?"

"Betcha—born of necessity. I clean up ok. I get lots of looks, but you gotta be padded in the right places to sustain interest."

"That last statement is an excellent example of what I meant earlier. The mixture of slang and multi-syllable words bespeaks high intelligence and little education."

Kitten was surprised at her own response. She expected a wisecrack or put-down to come out, but nothing did. Talking with someone—other than Gram—who cared was a strange experience. However, she couldn't be lulled; maybe it was just an act to get her to admit to something.

"I think I've got what needs to be said to your Gram figured out," Garth said after some moments of silence. "Will you promise to not interfere until I've finished?"

"Why?"

"We need to build confidence in your Gram so that she won't fret. At first, you'll think I'm doing the exact opposite, but I need you to trust me."

Thoughts rushed through Kitten's mind. Concerned about Gram's feelings too? Able to manipulate her? She'd have to see this. "Deal," she replied.

Garth whistled softly as he watched Kitten climb into her Corvette. He was gratified that she drove away at a leisurely pace. He'd feared that getting her car was a ploy to ditch him, so he'd dropped a little homing device into the pocket of her sweater. It didn't look like it was necessary.

Kitten pulled into the driveway of a tidy bungalow. Garth parked at the curb. As he got out of his car, Kitten put something on the ground in front of her right front wheel, got back in the 'Vette, drove forward a couple of feet, backed up to her original position and got out. As Garth approached, she pointed to the flattened homing device with her toe, winked at him and turned for the front door.

"Gram, I'm home; I got somebody you need to meet," she shouted, breezing through the door.

A plump, graying lady came into the room. Her expression of radiant anticipation faded as she looked Garth up and down.

"Mrs. Alma Jefferies, I'd like to introduce Detective Garth Moore," said Kitten.

Gram's expression, which had been moving toward disapproval, became one of abject fear. "Wha . . . what's . . . this about?" she stammered.

"Gram, why don't you plant it in your easy chair? Garth, please," she said, gesturing toward the sofa. "I'll get some coffee while you chat."

Regaining some composure as she seated herself, Gram looked at Garth. "I assume you have some identification, young man."

"Yes ma'am," said Garth, as he handed her the wallet with his badge and identification. He was pleased to see her scrutinize it carefully.

"What business would a policeman from Mississippi have with law abiding citizens of the state of Florida?" Gram asked, as Garth seated himself.

Garth pulled the small notebook from his pocket as he said, "Mrs. Jefferies, do these mean anything to you?" He noted Gram's increasing anxiety as he read the list of cities.

Kitten put cups and condiments on the coffee table.

"No, young man," Gram began, "I've never been to most of those places."

Kitten returned with a teapot, a coffee pot, and a bottle of beer. She filled Gram's cup. "Tea for the Gram." She filled Garth's cup. "Coffee for the cop." Settling into a chair, she raised the bottle. "Me, I'm gonna have a beer."

Garth noticed Gram's hand shaking as she raised her cup. He busied himself with sugaring the coffee. He had to admire the way the old lady was trying to maintain control, but she didn't have Kitten's grip. He took a sip of the coffee. It was putrid—probably what Kitten had made for breakfast. He looked at Gram. "Please understand, Mrs. Jefferies, that I'm here because I have your granddaughter's interests at heart."

"Then, why are you accusing . . .?"

"Please, I haven't accused anybody of anything. Nevertheless, allow me to make a couple of observations. I'd bet that beautiful car she drives is paid for."

"It certainly is. I don't believe in debt," Gram said proudly.

"I'd also bet that she isn't a student?"

"We've talked about that; I'm confident that she will be continuing her education soon."

Kitten's eyes rolled to the ceiling.

"And, I'd further opine that neither of you are employed."

"I am a pensioner. At my age, I have a right to leisure."

"I could not be more in agreement with that. But, I cannot be in agreement with the way you are sacrificing your granddaughter's future."

"Now you see here, young man . . ." Gram started.

"No, you see here," Garth interrupted, his expression clouding. "Things may be going your way now, making you a cozy living. However, I can guarantee you that, sooner or later, your activities will run afoul of either the law or the criminal element. In either case, she loses, and you have a good chance of jumping slick."

"Young man! I would never jeopardize my granddaughter's welfare!"

"Maybe not to your knowledge, but think it through. She has demonstrated remarkable talent. Many people would love to have her working for them. She would take all the risk while they skim the proceeds. She can't go on forever without attracting their notice. Those people wouldn't care a thing about her when she was no longer useful to them. There is doubt that she would survive the relationship."

"I'd never . . ." Gram began, and then turned to Kitten. "See, I told you . . . I didn't . . ."

"Put a sock in it, Gram!" Kitten blurted. "I haven't told him anything. Hear him out."

"On the other hand," Garth continued reasonably, "if the law became involved, a young woman with a criminal record and no education wouldn't have much future, would she? Certainly, not nearly as good as someone coasting along on a secure pension."

Gram lowered her eyes and began shaking her head slowly.

Garth continued. "It's obvious to me that neither of you understand how things work in the society which operates outside the law, so let me make it plain. Don Vertolio didn't even have to take time to think when I asked him if he knew of a cat burglar. That means he's been watching you for some time. You can bet that he's not the only one. Eventually, someone of his ilk will make you 'an offer that you can't refuse' to become part of his organization. The jobs they'd assign you would get bigger and riskier over time because you—not being a relative—are expendable. If you got pinched or if you avoided being caught until you were too old, the result would be the same. Their interest would change to making certain that you were not able to reveal what you knew about them."

Gram wilted. "What can we do?"

"In exchange for help, I believe that I can offer you a fresh start. I need the assistance of someone with your grand-daughter's unique skill set. I think that I can offer both of you immunity from prosecution."

"Prosecution?" Gram blurted. "We haven't done anything!"

Kitten rolled her eyes again.

"Yes, yes, of course," Garth began gently. "Let's just say that we'd be grateful for her help, and consider it a contribution to society to the extent that . . ." He stole a glance at Kitten. She mimed gagging. "We'd ensure that, should any of her . . . er . . . past activities come to notice that the applicable authorities wouldn't be able to press charges."

"How about me?" Gram asked.

"You'd be protected against being named an accessory."

Garth rose. "You ladies have a lot to talk about. I'll see myself out. Let me know what you decide."

13

GARTH GETS IMMUNITY FOR KITTEN

For a moment, Garth thought the Old Man was going to have an apoplectic seizure. His face was red, the vein in his forehead stood out.

"You want me to what?" the Old Man shouted.

Garth put a finger in his ear and wiggled it as he cocked his head to the side. "Pretty piercing, chief."

"I ought to do a damn site more than yell at you for suggesting that. Immunity from prosecution for a couple of petty thieves! Moreover, in another jurisdiction! Stupid, ridiculous! I don't think it could be done!"

"Not by most people," Garth drawled, "but I'll bet you can do it on the backstroke."

The Old Man fished a bottle of pills from his desk drawer, turned around to the credenza, poured a glass of water, popped two of the pills, washed them down, and turned back to Garth. He put an elbow on his desk and rested his forehead in the upturned palm. "Ok, run it by me again," he said in resignation.

"I've got excellent reasons to believe I know where the scumbags are making the videos, but I need to get inside the building to verify them. I can't use conventional means for fear of tipping them off. I want to employ the services of a cat burglar. There's this little gal in Florida who's been boosting ice for several years. She is a class act. She doesn't leave any signs of entry or egress. Some of the hits have been ten or twelve stories up in buildings with state-of-the-art security systems. I can't find any criminal record for her or her family, so I don't think she appreciates where this could lead her. I'd like to offer her immunity from prosecution in exchange for getting a look at the inside of that building."

The Old Man lifted his head and looked knowingly at Garth. "Stop right there. I thought I'd missed something the first time through. You 'don't think she knows where doing B and E might take her.' Do I detect another of your projects?"

"Both of her parents were circus people. She grew up in the troupe. They both died before she was seventeen. She doesn't appear to have much education. I'm sure she's doing this because she doesn't know any other way of making a living."

"And you want to help her become a law abiding citizen. Is that it?"

"Well, jeez, the way she's going, she will wind up with a criminal record or as a foul play statistic, and she's only twenty two . . ."

The Old Man rubbed his face with both hands. "Why me?" he mumbled.

"Pardon?" asked Garth.

"Dirty Harry and Mother Teresa in the same package," the Old Man mumbled. "Maybe I need counseling." He rubbed his eyes again, looked about the room, sat back in his chair, and turned to look out the window.

Garth waited.

The Old Man's voice came from behind the chair. "What do you suppose the task force will have to say about this idea?"

"I don't intend to tell them."

The Old Man whirled around to face Garth. His face was getting red again. "Not going to tell them? Keeping them in the loop was part of the deal!"

"Right, but I don't have anything tangible yet. I have some good ideas, but I need confirmation before I have anything I can take to the task force."

"Your lady would be proud of you."

"Huh?"

"You sound like a damned lawyer. Technically, you are correct, but the spirit of this agreement is broader than that."

"I'm only being cautious. I don't want the first thing I hand them to turn out to be a dud. That place smells good, but it's mostly instinct. I want more before I go to them with it."

A knowing expression crossed the Old Man's face. "Is that all or are you afraid they'd do something to tip the bad guys off?"

Garth started to grin. "Well, there is that possibility . . ."

"Possibility, my ass. Get out of here. I'll see what I can do."

***

The hostess looked up brightly as Rose and Garth approached. "Table for two?"

"We're meeting a Ms. Jefferies. Is she here yet?"

"No sir. Will that will be a table for three?"

"Yes, in a quiet corner, if you have one. Here's my card."

Rose looked over her wine glass at Garth while he explained about Kitten. "You've been a busy boy."

"That I have. I didn't expect her to get back to me this soon, but she called yesterday to say she'd help. I offered to send her a ticket, but she said she'd drive."

"Where are you putting her up?"

"I offered to provide lodging, but she said she'd find her own accommodations."

Rose studied her wine glass as she ran a finger around the rim. "I don't like the idea of your involving a young girl in this business."

"I didn't think you would. That's why I wanted you to meet her. I need some hostile input."

Rose looked up, puzzled. "Hostile input?"

"Yeah, I'm keen on using her. I think she has what it takes to do the job. My enthusiasm could cloud my judgment—cause me to miss something important. That's why I need you to get to know her. I know you'll try to talk me out of using her. You'll provide a balance to my enthusiasm.

"Well thanks," Rose replied, raising her eyebrows. "I'm glad to know I can be of service."

Garth reached across the table and put his hand on hers. "Hey, you know I'm not trying to use you. I'm asking you to do this because I care about what you think. It'd be easy to disregard the opinion of most people, but not yours."

Rose smiled softly. "And, I suspect, because you care about her too. You probably feel she needs some girl-to-girl."

"Yeah, that too."

Rose turned her hand over and squeezed his.

"Uh, I hate to interrupt . . ."

Neither Rose nor Garth had been aware of anyone approaching. Surprised, they looked up to see Kitten standing by the table. Her blonde hair fell below her shoulders in a graceful flip. Tastefully applied makeup gave her a twenty-something professional look.

Garth jumped to his feet. "We were waiting for you." He whipped a chair out and held it for her. "Please."

As she moved to take the chair, Garth made mental notes: She was unaccustomed to having her chair held. Her suit hadn't come off the rack. She probably looked best in suits because she sure didn't have anything to show off. She was wearing spike heels . . . how had she been able to sneak up on him in those things?

"Ms. Jefferies, may I present my fiancé, Rose Winters," Garth said grandly.

"Why don't you guys call me Kitten? Everybody else does. When you say 'Ms.' I feel like I need to look around to see who you're talking to."

Rose offered her hand. "I'm pleased to meet you . . . Kitten."

"Likewise," Kitten answered. She looked at Rose's other hand. "Hey, no sparkler! Is tall, dark and ugly over there cheapin' out on ya?"

Rose was taken aback by Kitten's brusqueness and instant familiarity, but she hid it behind a laugh.

"Funny . . .?" said Kitten.

Rose touched her napkin to the corner of one eye. "That's what my receptionist calls him. It stuck me funny. I'm flattered that he would introduce me as his fiancé, but the truth is that I haven't answered his proposals yet. Therefore, a ring is inappropriate."

"Proposals . . . he's asked you more than once?" asked Kitten.

"Yes, we've discussed the matter on more than one occasion."

"Woowee . . . that's one for the books."

The waiter's arrival interrupted their exchange. With a French accent, he described the specialties. Rose ordered the light version of one. Garth opted for something that sounded to Kitten like fish. "And for Mademoiselle?" the waiter said to Kitten.

"Bring me a big, rare steak."

"Ah," responded the waiter, "That would be ze Grande, bleu, wis . . ."

"Look slick, I don't know what you're askin'. Just bring me a steak that ain't cremated and a baked potato with lots of butter, sour cream, and such, and whatever for rabbit food."

The waiter started to protest, but Garth held up his hand and winked. Rose was laughing as he left.

Kitten looked at her. "French accent! Gimme a break!"

"You don't think it's genuine?" asked Rose.

"Hey, he was raised on pierogies and cabbage rolls."

"What makes you think that?" asked Rose, intrigued.

"Donno, exactly. Just the looks of him, I guess. I'd say he was about as Gallic as borscht."

Garth and Rose looked at each other.

During the meal, Rose had to fight resentment. While she nibbled at her minuscule entrée, Kitten gobbled the fats, carbs, and calories covering her plate with abandon.

"Donno what to do with more'n one fork," Kitten said between bites. She looked at Garth. "Wouldn't mind learnin' if this rehab program includes table manners."

Garth's chewing slowed. He began to look confused. At length, Rose took mercy on him. "I'll be happy to coach you," she said to Kitten.

Kitten started to answer, but the ringing of Garth's cell phone interrupted. He answered, listened, said a few mono-syllables, and closed it. "Damn," he said. "If you ladies will excuse me for a few minutes, I have a little business to take care of."

After Garth left the table, Kitten looked at Rose with a puzzled expression. "Cop stuff," said Rose. "You get used to it."

Kitten put her cutlery down and looked at Rose. "Girl-friend, are you nuts or sumpthin'?"

By this time, Rose was beginning to realize how much she appreciated social niceties. Kitten was getting on her nerves. She fought for control. "By that you mean?" she asked.

"That guy's a serious hunk and as sweet as he can be. What's the holdup on telling him yes? Most women would have had him down the aisle before he finished askin'."

Rose sat back and tried to compose herself. "How much has he told you about his record as a police officer?" she asked.

"Not much."

"Ok, then, here it is. He has an excellent record for clos-ing cases, but seven of them were closed because the sus-pects died resisting arrest."

"So?"

"So, it's highly unusual. Many police officers go through an entire career without ever drawing their weapon in anger. It's . . . it's almost as if . . . as if . . ." Rose bit her bottom lip. "As if . . . it's planned."

"What's that got to do with him and you?"

"Everything! I'm committed to the principles of the rule of law! How can I condone the actions of a . . . a . . . vigi-lante?"

"You mean, you think these are Have-Gun-Will-Travel deals? He takes the bad guys out so they don't beat the rap?"

"Yes, how would you feel about him shooting people in-stead of arresting them?"

Kitten grinned mischievously. "Makes me feel kinda horny."

Rose sat back, took a deep breath, looked at the ceiling and sighed. Lowering her eyes to Kitten, she said, "Ok, let's approach it from a different angle. How would you feel, sitting at home in the evening, knowing that he's putting himself in situations from which he might not return?"

Kitten pursed her lips thoughtfully. "I'm with ya there, girlfriend. That'd be a bummer. The queeksdraw thing sounds excitin' but it wouldn't do for the long haul."

Rose raised her eyebrows as she reached for her wine glass. She took a thoughtful drink. "Well, I'm glad we are finally communicating." She looked up. "Good thing, too, himself is on the way back."

"Sorry about that," said Garth as he seated himself. "Did you girls have a good chat?"

"Yeah," Kitten offered. "I was getting the scoop on some of your more spectacular take-downs."

Rose looked alarmed. "I had to tell her . . . there's no way I could let her become involved in one of your operations without knowing . . . knowing . . ." she bit her lip.

Garth reached across the table and took her hand. "Relax, I expected you to," he said gently. "You're right, she needs to know. I wanted it to come from you."

Rose smiled weakly while looking puzzled.

Garth turned to Kitten. "Did it frighten you?"

"Frighten?" Kitten asked, wrinkling her nose.

"May I now give you my side?"

"Fire away."

Garth looked into Kitten's eyes. "The god's honest truth is that I never planned for any of those take-downs to end the way they did. I went in with the intent of making a routine arrest and hauling the perps off to the cooler. I can't blame people for thinking that I somehow provoked those guys into resisting arrest, but the truth is that I did not."

14

ROZ TELLS A.P.

Roz struggled with a bad case of nerves as she sat in her library. The blaze in the fireplace had warmed the room, but it hadn't dispelled the chill from her heart. She'd asked A.P. for a get-together the day after she'd shown Frank the disk, but their schedules hadn't meshed for over a week. Even though she'd tried to keep the right frame of mind during the intervening days, she felt a chill whenever she thought about this conversation. As she sat there, going over—for the thousandth time—their relationship and what she was going to say, she realized that the one bright spot in the last few days was that A. P. hadn't been interested in sex. She had been spared that awkwardness. Come to think of it, he hadn't seemed interested in sex for some time. He'd never been much of a cocksman, but in thinking about it, she realized that he'd been tapering off for quite awhile. The sound of the front door closing interrupted her ruminations. She glanced at the clock. He was almost an hour late.

"Sorry I'm late," A. P. said, lowering his almost three hundred pounds into a comfortable chair across from Roz. "I think you will find the delay warranted because it is pertinent to this discussion."

"Pertinent?" she thought. When she'd asked for the time, he'd indicated that he also had a matter to discuss. Being preoccupied with her own subject, she hadn't given his topic much consideration.

"Mind if I go first?" he asked.

She did mind—terribly, but his manner aroused her curiosity. Did he have a girlfriend? Wouldn't that be a gas? How would she react? "No," she lied.

A. P. extracted a bottle of pills from his pocket and handed it to her. "Know what those are?"

Roz examined the label. "Nitro," she said, looking up at him with furrowed brows. "Have you been having trouble with your heart?"

"Trouble isn't the word. Crisis is more appropriate. I need three or four of those a day."

Roz's eyes grew wide. "My god! Anything over two should mean hospital, right now!"

"Yes, yes, I know. Doctor Graham has been monitoring me closely. I see him every week now. That is why I was late. I wanted the results from the latest battery of tests for this discussion."

"Is this what you wanted to talk about?"

"Yes. I felt the first twinge about eighteen months ago. I don't know why I didn't tell you then. When you asked for time together last week, I realized how long I've been putting it off. That was inconsiderate on my part. Please forgive me."

Roz struggled with a potpourri of emotions: tenderness, shame, alarm, and—most of all—embarrassment at being asked to forgive. Fighting for control, she stammered, "I . . . uh . . . had no idea."

"How could you, when I've all but hidden it?" A. P. asked with an uncharacteristic softness in his voice.

Roz looked at him in surprise. This sounded like they were going to have a real sharing. "I . . . uh . . . uh," was all she got out.

"This has caused me to think a lot about us," A. P. began in a shy voice.

Roz waited in shock for him to continue.

"Thinking about how I've not told you about my heart condition has caused me to reflect upon our life together and to realize that I shall never be able to compensate you for my lack as a husband."

"I . . . er . . . don't . . ." she protested.

A.P. held up a hand. "Please hear me out. I know this relationship hasn't been easy for you. I know you will be surprised to hear me say that I have some understanding of what a woman needs, but I do. Even though I've never been able to deliver it, I've been aware that you need a connectedness, a feeling of sharing. I've always hoped that I could somehow develop the ability to fulfill that need. But, now, it appears that I'm too late."

Fear gripped Roz. "What do you mean by that?"

"The delay in my arrival was because Dr. Graham wanted me to fully understand the results of the latest tests. They indicate that I may not have to pay taxes next year. You will have to, on the estate, but I shall rest beyond the reach of the IRS."

"Classic A. P." thought Roz, talking about his own demise in terms of the tax implications. "What about bypass, transplant? There must be options! Why haven't you seen a specialist?" she blurted.

"Dr. Graham is in consultation with cardiac specialists all over the country. My prognosis is a consensus from the best in the field. I have no doubt that you will research this matter with typical ferocity, and I won't be surprised if you turn up something others have overlooked. In the meantime, I'm comfortable that the medical team is doing everything possible. My main concern at this time is for you."

"Why? You're the one with the heart condition."

"I think not. I don't think your heart is in any better shape than mine is. Mine may be in bad shape physically, but yours is suffering emotional damage. We've had a good run. Professionally, we've been able to do what we wanted. We have a comfortable lifestyle. As I look back, my only regret is not being able to satisfy your emotional needs. Now that the end is in sight, I know that I'll never be able to do it. Therefore, I want you to go out and find what you need."

Roz heard the words, but couldn't assimilate the meaning. "What the hell do you mean?" she retorted.

"I mean that I want to see you happy before I go. If I get to see you with someone who fills that hole in your heart, I can go without any regrets."

Roz was stunned as the meaning of what he was saying sank in. "Are you talking about separation?" she asked.

"Not unless staying here with me would hamper your looking for someone."

Roz took a deep breath. "That's not a question because the truth is, it hasn't," she said, without being able to look at him.

He smiled and quietly asked, "What?"

"That's what I wanted to talk to you about; I've been seeing someone."

A.P. began to look uncomfortable and reached for the bottle of nitro pills. "Would you mind whipping me up a drink before you go on?" he asked.

"Booze and nitro aren't a good idea."

"Then make it a weak one."

After handing A.P. the drink, Roz told him about Frank, DE and the disk. She fearfully watched for signs of anxiety as she talked, but his expression grew more peaceful as she continued. Although she was revealing her unfaithfulness to him, she expected his legal mind to seize upon the disk situation. Upon finishing, she waited for questions, but he sat pensively for a while.

Finally, A. P. asked, "Do you love him? Does he make you happy?"

Roz didn't know what to say. It was out of character for him to ignore the legal questions while remaining focused on the emotional issue. She appreciated communicating with him on a deeper level than ever before, but she didn't know how to handle it. She nodded.

"Would you like to move out of here so you two can move in together?" A. P. asked in the kindest tone she'd ever heard from him.

Instantly, things fell into place for Roz. "No, I want to stay with you for whatever time you . . . we have left."

"You have no obligation . . ." A. P. began.

Roz cut him off. "I'll slap your puss if you ever say anything like that again! For me, this last hour has been the best of our married life, and I'd be a damn fool not to see where things go from here."

"But what about Frank?" A.P. protested.

"There's a whole caboodle of issues that need resolution before Frank and I can continue. Once those are out of the way, who knows? We'll both be different people then. Who can say how we'll feel?" She walked over to his chair, sat on the arm and kissed him softly. Neither one mentioned that his life span—or lack thereof—was part of the caboodle. They were content to enjoy a togetherness they'd not known before.

15

GARTH FINDS TERRY

Garth sat at his desk pondering the next move. His phone buzzed. The call display showed it to be from another narcotics officer. "Hi, Mort. How's it hangin'?" he answered.

"No better than usual," came the droll reply. "I think I have something for you. Some months back, one of my sources saw a van from Arbutis Security parked in front of that building you're interested in."

"Yeah, interesting is right. That would make it the only building in that area with a security system. Most people who own buildings there are hoping that some homeless squatter will set up housekeeping and start a fire that would burn the thing down."

"That's why I thought you'd be interested. My source says that all the street people avoid the place because they're scared of what might be going on there."

"How so?"

"The timing is hard to nail down because this source isn't all that well connected to chronology. He's dead reliable as to what, but the when is always vague with him. Anyway, extensive renovations happened inside that building before the Arbutis Security truck showed up. Nothing has happened since. The locals avoid it because they figure it's a cop or CIA thing."

"Hey, that does sound interesting. Thanks, Mort. What did this tip cost you?"

"Does your interest in that building have anything to do with the missing children detail you've taken on?"

"Everything"

"In that case, this one is on the house."

Garth found the Arbutis Security building in an upscale technological center. He smiled and patted the dog on the seat next to him. "This looks good, Bugsy," he said while pulling into a visitor's parking stall. The dog sat quietly while Garth got out, came around to the passenger side of the vehicle, and opened the door. He clipped a leash onto the dog's collar and said, "Out, Bugsy." The dog hopped out of the car and took up station by Garth's left shoe. The leash remained slack as the animal maintained position a few inches from Garth's left foot while they walked to the door.

The receptionist caught her breath. Coming through the door was the biggest, ugliest Black man she'd ever seen, accompanied by a big, shaggy, dog. "I . . . I'm sorry sir, animals aren't allowed . . ." she started.

As though he hadn't heard, Garth approached her desk holding out his police identification. "Detective Moore, here for my one o'clock appointment with Mr. Arbutis."

"But the animal, sir . . . he . . . or . . . she will have to . . ."

Garth reached into the fur at the dog's neck and pulled out a police identification badge that hung from his collar. "He's part of the team. Please tell Mr. Arbutis that we are here."

Garth smiled as the owner of Arbutis security approached. The guy was exactly as he had hoped—smallish and fastidious. Few men still waxed their moustaches, but every hair remained in place as he nervously held his hand out to Garth. "Oliver Arbutis, I'm pleased to meet you, Detective Moore."

"Good to meet you, Mr. Arbutis, and this is Bugsy." Garth was pleased to see that Arbutis' nervousness abated as he looked at the dog. People who were calmed by animals were often trustworthy.

"Mr. Arbutis, I tried to tell him . . ." the receptionist interjected.

"That is alright," Arbutis assured her. Turning back to Garth, he said, "If you and Bugsy will please follow me . . ."

Arbutis' office was spacious and tastefully appointed. Obviously, it was a place for conversation and negotiation rather than work. As Garth took a chair, Bugsy laid down at the left side of it.

"Since you declined to discuss the reason for your requesting this time," Arbutis began, "I couldn't prepare whatever records or documents you want to see. I hope there isn't any problem . . . irregularity . . ."

Garth tried hard for the pleasant face. "No sir, this is not about Arbutis Securities as such. It is about one of your employees."

"Which one?"

"That, I do not know at this point."

"Then, why . . .?"

"Please let me explain. Do you have a customer at 1295 Industrial?"

Arbutis pulled a keyboard from under his desktop and tapped a few keys.

"No, it does not appear that we do."

"Have you been experiencing any inventory shortages?"

Arbutis looked alarmed. "Can you be a little more specific?"

"Are there any gaps in the list of the serial numbers for the systems you have installed?"

"Yes, we are missing a few. How did you know?"

"One of your trucks was seen parked in front of 1295 Industrial."

"But my check of our customer list didn't show anything there. I'll have our sales invoices checked."

"No need. I think you may have a moonlighter nipping a system here and there."

"How can you be so certain? I'm of the opinion that the missing serial numbers will turn out to be a paperwork problem of some sort."

"That is one possibility, but here is why I think theft is a better one. None of the monitoring services has a customer at that address. If a system is in place, a private party does the monitoring. That would lead me to think that the purpose of the alarm is not to inform law enforcement. Which, in turn, would lead me to the conclusion that said person did not want the normal records kept. Therefore, he would obtain it from a moonlighter."

Arbutis looked thoughtful for a moment. "I'll have to admit that I haven't been able to find any problems with our record keeping. Apparently, we did receive those systems from the supplier. Given that, your scenario sounds plausible. Do you suspect that one of our employees is the moonlighter?"

"It would explain both the missing systems and the presence of your truck in front of that building."

"May I ask what prompted your interest in that particular building?"

"All I can say is that it involves an ongoing investigation regarding missing children."

"Well, I certainly want to cooperate with that. What would you like?"

"For starters, I want to let Bugsy here, sniff around your employee's locker room."

"Could I ask you two whys? Why do you call him that and why are you asking that he sniff lockers?"

"Sure. What else would you call a Big, UGly, ShaggY dog? He's a narcotics sniffer. This moonlighting operation suggests the work of someone who is trying to support a habit. Bugsy can tell us if any of your people have been handling narcotics. If one of them has, I'd like to question him."

"What happens if he doesn't smell any narcotics?"

"Donno, why don't you think about that while he sniffs?"

Arbutis showed them to the employee locker room. As they approached, Bugsy perked up and began sniffing as he turned his head from side to side. "He's getting a whiff of something interesting already," observed Garth. Once inside the locker room, Bugsy began to look excited. Garth removed the leash. "Check it out, Bugsy," he commanded. The dog went straight to one of the lockers, sat in front of it, and began whining.

"Can you let me into that locker?" Garth asked.

"It belongs to Terry Roquefort. I believe he's in the building at this moment. I can get him to let us in."

"I'd prefer to have a look first; can you do that for me?"

"Why, er, ah, yes, give me a second," Arbutis replied and left the room.

While he waited, Garth cased the room. Only one door, the one they'd come in through. He left Bugsy in position and stood so that he would be behind the door when it opened. He didn't know whether it was necessary, but bases were there to be covered. In a few moments, he was glad he'd covered that one. The door opened and a skinny figure in coveralls stopped in his tracks when he saw the dog. He whirled and started for the door that Garth was slamming shut.

"Mr. Roquefort, I presume," said Garth with a devilish grin.

"Who the hell are you?" Terry blurted. He reached for his cell phone. "I'm gonna call security and the cops."

Garth continued to grin. "I think you should call security, but as for the cops, you don't need to call. We're already here."

"We?" asked Terry, looking around.

"Me and the dog."

"Narcs, I suppose?"

"You catch on quick."

"And I suppose you want to look in my locker."

"Actually, what I want is to talk with you. Whether or not we need to go into the contents of your locker will depend upon how cooperative you are."

"You ain't bustin' me?"

"At this point, I'm asking a citizen to volunteer some information of his own free will."

"Yeah, ok. May I change outa these coveralls?"

"Certainly," Garth said agreeably. "Bugsy, back off." The dog returned to his position beside Garth's left foot. As Terry opened his locker and began to change, Garth felt he was looking at Gollum from the Lord of the Rings trilogy. Although Terry was short of stature, his head was larger than normal. His large eyes bugged out slightly. Spindly was the kindest word for the rest of him. His long hands didn't seem to have any meat on them and neither did anything else. The clothes that he put on were of reasonable quality, but they hung like a scarecrow's rags.

The locker room door opened suddenly and struck Garth in the back. He stepped aside. A florid man in a Smoky Bear hat and a blue uniform followed his paunch into the room, but froze upon hearing the low growl from Bugsy. "Relax, Bugsy, he's a cop too," said Garth, as he petted the dog's head. The uniformed man came farther into the room followed by Arbutis.

"As I was coming down the hall, I heard the door bang shut, so I thought there might be a problem that would warrant security," Arbutis said as he fidgeted.

"I don't think there is a problem," said Garth. "Is there, Terry?"

"Uh, no, not at all," replied Terry, buttoning his shirt. "This officer wants to talk to me, boss. I'll need a couple of hours off. I'll come back as soon as we're done and finish that stuff for Lancaster."

"Thanks for your time," Garth said to Arbutis as he followed Terry out of the locker room. "I'll be in touch first thing tomorrow."

When they got to the car, Bugsy stood expectantly by the passenger door. "Uh, uh, boy, we have a guest," Garth said. Bugsy hung his head as he moved to the back door that Garth was opening for him.

As they drove downtown, Garth couldn't help feeling sorry for Terry. He was one peculiar looking dude. His hair was thin and scraggly. The skin on his head seemed stretched too tight and veins showed underneath. He must have taken a lot of ribbing as a child. Before he had his shirt on, Garth had noticed the tracks on his arm—he wasn't a heavy or long time user. Garth pulled into the lot of a city park and opened his door.

"Why are we stopping here?" Terry asked.

"Bugsy needs a run, and this is a nicer place to talk than my office," Garth replied.

They sat at a picnic table across from one another. Bugsy ran about acting like a happy dog.

"I suppose you want to know who my supplier is," Terry said.

"Supplier of what?" Garth replied with mock innocence.

Terry looked at Garth, startled, but quickly regained composure. He studied Garth's face. Garth noted that the eyes didn't dart furtively, but moved slowly, studying, analyzing. This guy wasn't an ordinary junkie.

"What do you want?" Terry asked.

"Does the address 1295 Industrial mean anything to you?"

Terry looked away from Garth as though he were pondering. He looked back and studied Garth's face. He repeated the sequence several times. Garth waited. Finally, Terry's face indicated that he'd reached a decision. "You can probably tell that I don't have much experience dealing with police," he said.

"That would be my take," answered Garth. "I'd guess you for someone who doesn't have a record."

"You'd guess right, so I'm going to have to trust that you'll do right by me."

"Do right by you?"

"Yes. I want to make a deal."

"Give me the particulars."

"Get the monkey off my back. Protect me from the people you want to know about."

"Is that all? How about immunity from prosecution?"

"Yeah, that too, I guess."

Garth was impressed. "I don't see any problem, but you'll have to explain more before I can commit."

Terry closed his eyes and took a deep breath. "Those guys you want to know about are real bad mothers. I don't know who they are, or what they're up to, but I don't doubt for a second that they'd kill me for talking to you. I really, really want to kick this habit. I have a little girl, you see, and I want to be part of her life as she grows up. Her mother doesn't think much of me, and I can't blame her. We both know that the shit will take over if I don't kick it. I've tried, but I can't. I need help. Those guys at 1295 Industrial offered me a deal that I thought would be my way out. I install a few things, test them every so often, and they supply me with shit. I thought it was perfect. I thought I'd be able to taper off if I wasn't anxious all the time about affording the next hit. You probably know that wouldn't work. I haven't been able to taper off. In fact, I want more. I don't want to go down as a junkie. I want to be a dad."

As Terry talked, Garth also came to a decision. It was a gamble, but the payoff would be huge. "That operation on Industrial may have something to do with missing children," he said flatly.

Terry's eyes went wide as he said, "Oh, my god!" He buried his face in his hands. "Kids, little kids . . . what have I gotten myself into?"

"Bingo," thought Garth. "You have involved yourself with something damn ugly. Tell me what you know about them."

"Well, as you probably know, I've been nipping a few systems to support the habit. Usually, I make the deal in a bar. People know I do this. Guys I don't know come up to me, we agree on a price, I install the system, get paid, and that's all there is to it. These guys were different. They approached me with 'an ongoing arrangement.' I install a system and test it whenever they ask. For that, they supply me with shit. They bargain hard. I hoped for enough to get a stash going for when this thing fizzles out, but they know how much will keep a guy barely going. At first, it was very good. I didn't have to nip systems anymore. Mr. Arbutis is a good guy to work for, so I don't like stealing from him. But, you know how it goes; the monkey doesn't stay satisfied. I need detox, but I need it in a context where those guys can't get to me."

"I think that can be arranged. About this 'testing.' How often do they ask for a test?"

"Roughly, every month."

Garth fished about in his memory. Monthly was good correspondence with the power spikes. "How does the test come down?"

"Real kooky. These guys are some paranoid. They have me climb the pole, disconnect the phone pair, and listen as they set off each sensor."

"Why don't they listen to it go off at the other end of that phone line?"

"The only clue I have is that they're paranoid about using cell phones. I'm piecing this together from things I've heard them say. They'd have to maintain cell phone contact with whoever was on the other end of that line as they set off the sensors, and they don't want to do that."

"How do you tell them that you've heard the alarm?"

"I use an infrared beacon that a guy monitors with night vision goggles."

"How about the alarm installation? What can you tell me about it?"

"Some friggin' strange place. It's like a fortress. There are alarms on all the outside doors. You should see those doors. They are solid material with deadbolts as big as an elephant's cock. There is the same type of door at the head of each flight of stairs, and they're alarmed too. The alarm tone is different for each floor."

"Each of the six floors is alarmed?"

"I can't say for certain. They didn't have me put alarms in anything above three."

The more Garth heard, the more interested he became. "Let's suppose somebody wanted to force entry. How long do you suppose it would take to break down those doors?"

"I don't have a clue. I'm not into that stuff. I'd think it would take quite a while. The hinges look like something from a drawbridge. I'd think the studs on either side of the door would give before any part of the door did. I can't imagine any manual battering ram that would do that job. Moreover, the doors at the top of the stairs are right at the top; there is no landing. Anybody trying to break one of them down would be swinging against gravity."

"Was there anything out of the ordinary on the third floor?"

"I couldn't say. They kept a tight leash on me while I was installing the system. A guy who looked like a wrestler in an expensive suit was with me the whole time. He wore an earpiece and a throat mike. He'd call to verify that all the doors on a particular floor were closed before I was allowed onto that floor. I had to run extra wire because there were places they wouldn't let me near. Those doors are the only detail I can give you about the place."

Garth noted with interest that Terry's eyes darted as he said the last. The guy was probably holding something back. That was ok. He needed an ace in the hole. "Would you care to tell me about your daughter?" he asked pleasantly.

Terry grinned as he pulled his wallet out. He flipped it open to a picture "That's little Karen," he said with pride. Garth noted the family resemblance. The kid was going to need some help. "Her mother's a prostitute," Terry went on. "I was one of her johns. She didn't know who the father was until after the kid was born. I don't think she was going to tell me, but the madam she works for is sort of a friend. She let me know. I asked the mother to quit the life and take care of the kid. I offered to support them, but she was smart enough to ask how I could take care of them and my habit too. She's right. That's why I've got to get clean."

"Given your motivation, and your realization that you need help, I have no doubt we can get the monkey off. Are you ok with the idea that you won't be able to start rehab until we deal with those scumbags at 1295?"

"Sure, I don't have any future anyway as long as they are around. But, here we are, talking as though they are behind bars. What happens if you can't pin anything on them? If they jump slick, they'll know for sure I ratted them out."

"My agreement to get you treatment and to protect you is not contingent on anything beyond the information you have given me. Whatever it takes to get you beyond their reach will be provided."

Terry was thoughtful for a few minutes. Garth whistled for Bugsy. The dog returned to Garth's side immediately. Garth smiled as he reached down and petted the animal.

"You work with that dog all the time?" asked Terry.

"No, his handler is off duty today. He's good with my taking his partner out on occasion."

"That dog really likes you. You must be an ok guy."

Garth didn't know how to respond. He grinned and continued to pet the dog.

"You must know what being different is like too, don't you?" Terry asked.

During grade school, Garth hated his appearance. Since finding his calling, and discovering his looks to be an asset in fulfilling it, he had come to be grateful for them. Nevertheless, he still recalled how it felt to be mocked and teased. That had been a long time ago. When he returned from summer vacation to begin the seventh—or was it the eighth?—grade, he was the biggest kid in the class. People didn't tease him much after that. They avoided him. The recollection still stung. "Yes I do," he said warmly, wanting to make connection.

"I . . . ah . . . er . . . er just remembered something else." Terry began, "There is a tunnel from the basement of that building to a building in the next block. It's big enough for a car. You'll have to cover that too."

Garth made eye contact with Terry. "Terry, I know you didn't 'just remember.' Give me more credit than that. I know there are some things that you haven't told me yet. That's cool. I intend to earn your confidence. Before I take you back to work, there is one more little item I need to ask about. You mentioned that you climb the pole and disconnect the telephone pair. Could you explain to someone familiar with telephone technology how to identify that pair?"

"I could explain that to you, but if you need it done for the takedown, I'd be willing to do it."

"I'm going to need it done within the next couple of days. I'll have it done by someone in a telephone company uniform. There's no need to expose you to the danger."

Terry grinned at him. "I guess the dog is right."

16
KITTEN CASES 1295

Garth walked into Kitten's room at the Bed and Breakfast with a roll of documents under his arm. Terry followed him. "Nice digs," he said to Kitten.

"Not bad. And, the lady that runs this place is a mean cook."

"Good breakfasts are a start, but what do you do for the other meals?" Garth asked.

"I went out for the first couple of days. After that, she invited me to share meals with her whenever I was gonna be around."

"I didn't know B and Bs did that for their guests."

Kitten's grin turned sly. "Only when they look like skinny little girls."

Garth turned to Terry. "Miss Jefferies, this is Terry Roquefort. He also has specialized talents we'll be using."

Terry offered his hand. "Ms. Jefferies, I'm pleased to meet you."

Kitten took the hand. "Good t' meet ya too. Call me Kitten; everybody else does."

Garth unrolled the documents on the table. He watched Kitten look at them without recognition.

"What'r these?" she asked.

"Blueprints of the building at 1295 Industrial," Garth began. "This is a side view through the middle of the building. Here is the front door. These are the stairs leading to the second floor," he continued, pointing to the graphics. Kitten began to show understanding. "And, this item," he said, pointing to a shaft that extended from the basement to the roof, "is a service plenum. Pipes, wires and anything else that goes between floors runs through it."

"Yeah, large too," Terry offered. "I was in there, running cable. There is a nice ladder along one side and everything is in good order. Often, those things are a rat's nest of pipes and wires, but it doesn't look like much has been done in this one since it was built."

"You were in there?" asked Kitten.

"Yes, I installed the alarm system."

Kitten looked at Garth. "Damn, you're good, to come up with the guy who did the alarm."

Garth shrugged, "Just . . ."

Kitten interrupted. "Connecting the dots. I know, I know, Mr. Modesty."

Garth and Kitten shared a laugh. Terry appreciated the interplay. He was feeling better about Garth all the time.

Garth leafed through the stack, selected another print, and put it on top. "This is a roof detail. Here is the air-conditioning enclosure. The duct goes along here and down into the plenum."

Kitten studied the drawing, lifted it up, and studied the one underneath. Several times, she went from one to the other. Understanding registered in her eyes. "Uh," she began, "this thing shows that a person could get into . . ."

"The air-conditioning enclosure," Garth offered.

"Yeah, and then go along this . . ."

"Duct," Garth prompted.

"Yeah, along this duct. But, could ya get outta the thing?"

"This indicates a door which would allow a person in the plenum access to the duct," Garth explained, pointing to a symbol.

"How 'bout a person in the duct? Does that door open from the inside?"

Garth turned. "Terry?"

"Those aren't 'doors'; they are access panels. The answer to your question is yes. The handle to open the panel is located on the plenum side of the duct, but the mechanism is exposed on the inside; it can be activated from within the duct."

"I imagine you know that 'cause you were in there, but can you tell it from these papers?" Kitten asked.

"There is a duct detail that supplies that information," Terry replied.

"And this . . . this 'air-conditioning enclosure' . . . ain't it locked somehow?"

Terry rifled through the drawings, extracted one, and studied it. "No, this type of intake grate is secured by screws. It can be modified to be lockable, but I've never seen that done."

"Whoo wee!" Kitten exclaimed. She looked at Garth. "Is there a buncha paper like this for every buildin'?"

Garth frowned at her.

"Hey, just askin'," she said, holding up her hand. "Academic curiosity, nothin' more."

"Academic, my ass," said Garth. "Remember our deal; you shouldn't need this information any more."

"Maybe I wanna learn to build buildings or sumpthin' like that," Kitten pouted.

Terry smiled as he watched the exchange.

"It looks to me," Garth began, "like you can get into the duct through the air conditioning enclosure. Before the duct goes vertical, there appears to be an access panel here. You can use it to get into the plenum. From there, you'd have to search each floor by using the access panel for that floor to get into the horizontal ducting."

Kitten nodded approval as Garth talked.

"I'd suggest you search the third floor first," Terry offered.

"Because that was the last door you alarmed?" Garth asked.

"Yes and because there's a wad of new wiring running into the third floor ducting."

"In the ducting?" asked Garth. "That doesn't meet code, does it?"

Terry smirked. "No, any inspector looking at that installation would begin writing a violation. It's a quick and dirty way of getting new wire around—I've been known to run the odd cable in ducting—but it violates code and the wire is vulnerable to damage if the ducts are ever cleaned."

"Ahh, the Tlot Phickens," said Kitten.

Garth looked at her, puzzled for a second, and grinned as he switched the first two letters. Turning to Terry, he said, "You're suggesting she go to three and follow those new wires?"

"Yes, I'd start there. You may find what you want at the end of them."

Both Kitten and Terry noticed that Garth looked relieved as he said, "That's the best news I've had in a long time. I was damned worried about the time it would take her to check out all those rooms."

Garth pulled out the sheet for the basement. After studying it for a few minutes, he turned to Terry. "I don't see that tunnel that you mentioned."

Terry studied the sheet. "It's not on here. It is right about ... uh ... about there. This shows solid wall at that point."

"Would it be easier," Garth began, "if we got Kitten into that other building, so she could go through the tunnel into 1295?"

"Uh, I don't think that's a good idea," replied Terry. "They had me alarm the door in that other building. It's another heavy mother. It doesn't have any outside hardware. I don't think it can be opened from the outside without damaging it."

"Did you see any access to the tunnel from the other building?" Garth asked, looking at Terry.

Terry's eyes shifted. The nervous look again, thought Garth.

"Uh ... no. It's a spooky setup, just a concrete tunnel from the wall of 1295 to that other door. I know it opens to the outside because they had to open it for me to install the alarm. There is no way to get in there from the other building."

Garth studied Terry. The latter's nervousness was increasing.

"Terry," Garth said gently, "there's something you're not telling us . . . c'mon . . . give."

Terry hung his head. "There's a bunch of C4 planted along that tunnel. They had me rig a remote control trigger. The electronics aren't top drawer—I don't trust them."

"So," Garth pondered aloud, "someone busts through the front door, they beat it to the basement, drive out through this other building, and blow the tunnel down behind them. That's probably the real reason for the heavy doors at each floor, to buy them time."

"That's the way I'd figure it," said Terry. "When, if, your team raids that place, don't let them follow into the tunnel."

"I won't; we'll be waiting for them outside the door. But, as things stand now, we'll continue with plan A and send Kitten in through the roof."

***

"A perfect night," thought Kitten as she scaled the wall of 1295 Industrial. The warm temperature meant that she didn't need any extra clothes. Clouds formed a high overcast which blocked starlight without reflecting the city lights—ideal working conditions for a kitten burglar. She started wondering who she would be if she were no longer the kitten burglar. She couldn't remember when she'd started thinking of herself in those terms, but she couldn't imagine another identity. "Whoa," she thought, "focus." Thinking about something else while scaling a wall was a good way to get put out of the kitten burglar business for good. She resumed concentration on the job at hand.

"I'm on the roof. I see the air-conditioning thingus," came over Garth's headset.

"Damn, she's some good," he thought. He keyed his mike. "Don't go in until I get confirmation that the alarm is disconnected."

"Rog."

Garth keyed his mike again. "Did anyone see her?"

The lookouts stationed on the roofs of adjacent buildings responded in rotation:

"#1, negative."

"#2, negative."

"#3, negative."

"#4, negative."

Garth shook his head. He keyed his mike again to contact the operative who had climbed the telephone pole to disconnect the line. "Pole, status?"

"Disconnected and monitored."

"Got that," said Kitten. "I'm takin' the panel off."

Garth keyed his mike. "#3, you should be looking right at her. Don't you see anything?"

"Negative. I'll get the night vision glasses up. There she is, but you'd have to know exactly where to look."

The next voice was Kitten's. "I'm in; can you still hear me?"

"Perfectly," said Garth. "What do you see?"

"Big fan."

"Can you get through the blades?"

"No prob."

"Don't try until you have those clamps in place."

"Don't look like that mother's turned this decade."

"All the same, clamp it."

"Yes, Gram."

After several minutes of silence, Garth heard, "Fan's clamped . . . I'm beyond it . . . that whatever panel is in front of me."

"#3 to Kitten. Did you use any light?"

"A little."

"I didn't see any."

"Ain't polite to not close the door behind ya."

Garth was glad his chuckle was not going out over the air. He keyed his mike. "Can you open that access panel?"

"Done, I'm in that . . . that . . . plun . . . whatever outfit that goes up and down in the center."

"Great, start down, but call me every few steps. If you even think you've lost me, get out of there."

"Kitten to Grandma Garth from the fifth floor."

"Thank you."

"Kitten to Gram from the fourth floor."

"Thank you."

"I'm at three. Just like Terry said, there's a wad of wires and stuff coming up from below and going into the duct."

"Is there an access panel?"

"Yeppir . . . uh, gimme a sec . . . friggin' handle's stuck . . . gonna have to get a tool . . . yeah, that did it."

"Got your dust mask on?" Garth asked.

"Do now. Can you hear me through it?"

"Well enough. Don't take it off while you are in the duct."

"Yes, Mom. Hey, this thing's big enough for me to go on hands and knees. It's clean in here; the guys who put them wires in must have worn the dust out on their coveralls. This bunch of wire is goin' down through the first grate. Yeah, it does—everything's real dirty beyond."

Terry was with Garth on the rooftop, listening. Garth turned to him. "Got any idea where she is?"

"I'd think that she is above the first room toward the rear of the building from the service plenum."

Kitten's voice came over their earpieces. "I'm at the grate. There is a hole in the corner of it for the wires to go through. The hole's big enough that I'll be able to get that spy thingy through without touchin' the sides."

"Don't do anything until you've made certain you won't knock any dust through the grate!" Garth almost shouted.

"Hey, who's the pro at not leaving any signs that they've been there?"

"Carry on," Garth answered quietly.

Kitten started a running commentary. "Big room, white walls, no windows, photography stuff scattered around. And . . . and . . . there it is! It's the place where they had that little guy tied up . . . straps and chains and stuff hangin' from the wall."

"Bingo!" said Garth. "Now, get out of there."

"Uh, wait," began Kitten. "There's sumpthin' else. There's only one door. At the other end, there's a hole in the floor with a pipe comin' up through it."

"Pipe? Like plumbing? What about it? You need to get out of there."

"No, not exactly a pipe. It's shiny, like those poles the girls in the clubs use. And the hole, it's big."

Suddenly, Garth made the connection. "Does it look like those poles firemen slide down?"

"Yeah, yeah, that's it . . . the setup you see in pictures of fire stations."

"Can you see if there's a hole in the ceiling of that room?"

"Uuummm . . . lessee if I can get a better angle . . . uh . . . no . . . that pole is attached to the ceiling of this room."

"Good job, Kitten, now get out of there."

"Yessir, getting as we speak."

Garth keyed his mike again. "There's a beer waiting for anybody who spots her on the way down."

"#1 rog."

"#2 rog."

"#3 rog."

"#4 rog."

"I think I saw that pole when I was in the basement of that building," offered Terry.

"Yeah?" answered Garth.

"The basement is cleaned out, nothing much down there. If there were any walls, they are gone now. I did notice that pole coming down about twenty feet from the plenum. I couldn't tell what was at the bottom of it at the time, but I think I know now. It was a pad, the type found at the bottom of poles in fire stations. The chaperone goon tried to put himself between the pole and me, so I didn't get a good look, but I'm certain now."

"That's interesting," Garth pondered aloud, "an elaborate escape scheme."

From their position atop the building across the street from 1295, Garth and Terry strained for a glimpse of Kitten. Garth propped his elbows on the parapet wall and studied the front of 1295 through binoculars. "I'm sure she won't come down the front, but let's keep a close eye on it. I'd love to catch her."

Terry was also scanning the front of the building. "I don't think there's much chance of our seeing her," he observed.

"Out," came over their headsets.

"Look sharp, everybody," commanded Garth.

"She won't get by us this time," one lookout said without identifying himself.

"#3 here. Don't be too sure. I didn't see her come out of the air-conditioning enclosure, and I had the night vision gear trained on it."

"Tee hee," crackled in everybody's headset.

Terry and Garth squirmed to get comfortable. It had taken her about thirty minutes to gain the roof. They didn't expect her at the pickup point in less than that amount of time. After ten minutes, they were having trouble concentrating. Garth keyed his mike. "Hasn't anybody seen anything?"

"#1, negative."

"#2, negative."

"#3, negative."

"#4, negative."

"Tee hee."

Garth looked at Terry. "You get that?"

"Yes, the transmission was broken; she must be down already."

"Can't believe that," remarked Garth, as he keyed his mike. "Check the ground everybody. That last transmission sounded like she was down."

Garth and Terry searched the streets, then the building face, back to the streets, back to the building . . . nothing.

"Can I have a look too?" came a voice from behind them.

Startled, Garth began to whirl and reach for his gun. Halfway around, the voice registered. "Damn you," he growled.

Terry began to laugh.

"Now, is that any way to greet a lady?" Kitten asked. "I anticipated some congratulations or acknowledgement of how good I was."

"You are a fourteen-carat brat is what you are," Garth replied. "Let's get off this roof." He keyed his mike. "Secure, everybody."

As they were driving out of the area, Terry turned to Kitten. "If he's not gentleman enough to compliment you, I'll say that the way you got down was sweet. How did you do it that quickly?" Garth was glad to see Terry loosening up enough to initiate some repartee.

"Took the rope down," replied Kitten.

"Did you leave the rope?" asked Terry.

"Hey c'mon, that'd be a dead giveaway that we were there."

"But, then, how?" Terry puzzled.

"Rope releases."

"Really?" said Terry with obvious interest. "Could I see it?"

"Sure," Kitten replied, pulling the coil from her backpack.

Terry made sounds of "ooo" and "ahhh" as he examined the device. "Super sweet, where did you get this?

Garth looked sharply at both of them. "Enough, you two. You won't need that stuff anymore—remember our deal."

"Tell him it's academic curiosity," Kitten said to Terry in a stage whisper.

Terry and Kitten began to giggle. Garth gave them a moment before he joined in their laughter.

Terry handed the rope back to Kitten. "May I ask you something?"

"Sure," she replied, puzzled.

"When Garth introduced us, you were not shocked at my appearance. Most people are. They try to hide it, but I can tell. Why it was different with you?"

Kitten pondered the question before answering. "I donno . . . guess it has sumpthin' t' do with my growing up in a circus . . . always a lot of . . . er . . . unique looking people around. I don't suppose I think that a person's appearance has much to do with what type of folks they are."

"You and this policeman are a unique pair of people. I appreciate getting to know you," replied Terry.

17
GARTH TELLS THE TASK FORCE

Garth awoke from a restless sleep. The clock showed 1:30—less than an hour since his last look. It was the dream; the task force had assumed direct control of the investigation. The thought was unpleasant in the extreme, but it was their prerogative. He put his hands behind his head and stared at the darkened ceiling. Perhaps he had played his part. Perhaps, in the grand scheme of things, his role was to bring the investigation to this point. Perhaps it was now time for the legal owners of the jurisdiction to take over. Perhaps bah! Even though he didn't know the name of the guy who made that video, he smelled a collar around the next corner. He didn't even have a vague idea of how it would happen, but it felt close. The Old Man had been right to bug him about updating the task force. He'd forced the issue by setting up this appointment for tomorrow . . . er . . . later today. Garth couldn't argue with the rightness of the move. As he thought about it, he found himself formulating arguments he'd give the task force to leave things as they were. When he realized what he was doing, he swung his legs out of the bed and padded off to the kitchen. He took several deep breaths as he poured himself a glass of milk. What had Rose said to eat with milk if you were having trouble sleeping? Banana that was it! He peeled himself a banana. What he needed was to get himself centered and focused so that he could sleep. However it went, later in the day, he needed to be alert and at the top of his game.

Garth sat uneasily in the conference room. The Old Man sat at his side. The latter had said little while Garth reported to the federal agents from the task force on missing children.

He'd given full details regarding the part played by Frank and Roz. He'd offered less detail regarding Terry. He hadn't mentioned Kitten at all. Across the table, the agents now watched the DVD. Garth knew where they were as he watched shock turn to disgust and ultimately to rage. The agent who had introduced himself as Martin was the head of the task force. The other two, Dan and Cliff, hadn't mentioned their roles. They didn't look like foot soldiers; they smelled like lawyers. Garth pondered whether that was good or bad. He didn't want to lose control of the case, but he had no choice. The time had come to update the task force and let them decide where to go from here. He wanted a continuing role desperately, but his mandate had been vague from the beginning. They could take over, limit his role, whatever; it was their call. He hadn't slept well last night for worrying about it. He'd get centered and calm and go to sleep, but he'd wake up with various scenarios churning in his head. He knew stewing about it wouldn't do any good. Again, he'd work at getting calm and centered, but it was harder this time than it had ever been before.

As the agents looked up from the DVD player, Martin seemed particularly enraged, but Dan spoke first. "You say, Detective Moore, that this disk is not the original?"

"That is correct."

"And, you say that your source destroyed the original because he feared that the originators might be able to tell that it had been viewed."

"Also correct."

Dan shuffled some notes. "That's understandable, but also unfortunate. The material on the DVD is not admissible unless we establish that the disk was owned by the originator."

Cliff spoke next. "But, you say that you have seen the premises where this video was made?"

"Not personally, but my source described it exactly."

"And, this source," Cliff continued, "would you put that person on the stand?"

"No. In my opinion, it would open too many rabbit trails the defense could use to distract the jury."

Dan and Cliff looked at one another. Martin smirked.

"Aha," thought Garth, "these two are from the legal department."

"Detective Moore," Martin began, "you haven't given us much detail regarding how you obtained the details of the site where you think these videos are being made."

"I've told you as much as I think you want to know."

A knowing look crossed Martin's face. "I see," he said and turned to look at the Old Man who returned a shallow nod.

Martin flipped through the notes he had been taking. "This Mr. Grant, from whom you obtained the disk. I believe that you mentioned that his wife is a judge. Is that correct?"

"Yes," said Garth pleasantly. "It makes this investigation problematical. Her hat is in the ring for a congressional seat. Although she's a complete innocent, her opposition could make hay out of any connection with this."

"How do you feel about putting Mr. Grant on the stand?" Cliff began.

Martin cut him off. "Hold that thought for a minute, Cliff. I need to get this nailed down." He addressed Garth. "You said that Mr. Grant was involved with a Ms. Cornelius?"

"Yes."

"And that they got together through this . . . this . . ." Martin said flipping through his notes.

"Discreet Encounters," Garth offered.

"Ah yes, Discreet Encounters, and it appears to be a scheme for trapping people into participation in the delivery of their . . . er . . . product?"

"That is about the size of it," Garth replied.

Martin turned his attention to the Old Man. "Do you concur that Judge Grant had nothing to do with Mr. Grant's becoming involved with this Discreet Encounters?"

"There is no question; she's an innocent bystander."

Martin turned to his two associates. "You guys need a smoke. Give us about ten, would you please?"

Garth had to look away as the two agents rose with obvious displeasure. He had to admit that the sight of an uncomfortable lawyer gave him a tickle of perverse pleasure . . . unless that lawyer happened to be a particular lady, of course.

After the door closed behind the two agents, Martin fixed earnest eyes on the Old Man. "Charlie, off the record, what do you think of Judge Grant's chances?"

Garth was shocked. He'd never heard the Old Man's given name before. He and Martin must go back a long way.

"Sure Marty, we're on the same page. I'd say she's a ninety-seven percent bet," the Old Man replied in a confidential tone.

"Suppose her opposition got wind of her husband's indiscretion. Do you have any guess about how that would affect her chances?"

"I don't think it would do more than inconvenience her. She's never done anything without having her ducks lined up like marines on parade. I'd guess that she already has contingency plans for this thing breaking."

The familiar talk between the Old Man and Martin continued. Garth felt like an ignored child. A soft knock on the door interrupted the exchange. "Come on in," Martin said.

Cliff and Dan took their seats uneasily while looking from one face to another. Martin broke the awkwardness by addressing Cliff. "You were asking Detective Moore about putting Mr. Grant on the stand when I interrupted. Please excuse my rudeness and continue."

Cliff preened. "Yes, Detective Moore, how do you feel about putting Mr. Grant and, for that matter, Ms. Cornelius on the stand?"

"No prob. They'd be excellent witnesses," Garth answered with enthusiasm. In a more somber tone, he added, "If they knew anything."

"But," Cliff continued, "if Mr. Grant would turn the next disk he's asked to deliver over to us . . ."

"He couldn't tell you where it came from or who he's supposed to deliver it to."

"We could do surveillance on the pickup . . . perhaps supply a replacement package," Cliff pressed.

Martin held up a hand. "Whoa, son, that old dog ain't gonna hunt."

Cliff looked shocked. "Uh, beg your pardon, sir?" he stammered.

Garth noted that Dan was taking it all in, calculating.

Martin's voice took on an edge as he addressed Cliff. "Asking Mr. Grant to fail in making another delivery is out of the question. You saw the video. People who can do that wouldn't give a second thought to rubbing out a questionable mule. Think about it! You can bet your sweet bippy that they currently regard Mr. Grant as highly questionable. In fact, I'd give you good odds that the next delivery will be a dummy covered by their own surveillance. Mr. Grant has shown great courage in bringing this to us. He's already done more than we could reasonably ask. Asking any more is out."

"But, I merely thought . . ." Cliff blurted. Dan rolled his eyes.

Martin didn't let Cliff finish. "I'd suggest you confine your thinking to the legal weaseling and leave the cop thinking to us," he said with obvious impatience. "These guys are here to let us audit what they are doing with the funds we've made available. They're not asking for advice." He glanced Dan's way. "Nor do I think they need any."

Dan, picking up the cue, cleared his throat. "Yes, it would appear to me that we are deriving acceptable results. Detective Moore's preliminary work appears to validate his thesis. Therefore, we should continue with our present arrangement, using him to gather additional information. Naturally, we won't be able to determine whether the thesis is a useful premise for action unless it produces information that leads to an investigation."

Martin nodded in approval and picked up as soon as Dan finished. "Since there doesn't seem to be any of that yet, I see no reason to prolong this information session," he said to the group. Turning to the Old Man, he continued, "Charlie, lest you get the wrong idea from what my young colleague said, I need to reiterate that we are in no way suggesting any course of action. At this point, we are not in possession of sufficient information to give you either approval or disapproval. Your pursuit of validation for Detective Moore's thesis is strictly a matter for your discretion. Since this preliminary information suggests that you may be dealing with a sophisticated quarry, you can count on my understanding if you have to move fast at some point."

Garth was surprised to hear the familiar used in the group. He looked at the two men from the legal department. Cliff looked confused. Dan looked satisfied. What had happened?

"Ten-four," replied the Old Man, adding, "Lunch, Marty?"

Martin pulled out his PDA and tapped a couple of keys. "That old slave driver who guards my door has scheduled a working lunch for me. I'll have to pass."

Garth was pleased. There were a number of questions pressing on the inside of his skull. He wanted the Old Man to himself as soon as possible.

✳✳✳

Ordering a meal with the Old Man always felt like a tap dance to Garth. The august gentleman's many physical challenges required the waiter to take bits and pieces from several places on the menu to assemble an acceptable entree. Garth would feel guilty savoring something that the Old Man couldn't eat, so he sorted through the menu looking for something the Old Man could have or didn't like.

As they waited for the food to arrive, Garth said, "Mind tellin' me what went on in there? It sounded to me like we were cut loose."

The Old Man smiled. "That we were, my boy."

"Mind tellin' me why? I'm happy as hell that they did, but I don't understand why."

The Old Man looked up, surprised. "You don't? I thought you were doing a masterful job of steering the conversation to that end."

"Huh?" was all Garth could say.

"Pick your jaw up off the plate, son; I see that you didn't know what was happening. Here it is. For starters, Martin is a political creature. He's an excellent cop, but his current role has more to do with protecting his turf and budget—to say nothing of the bureau's reputation—than police work. Judge Grant's involvement in this put him on high alert. With her background, there is a better than even chance that she'll wind up on some law-enforcement oversight committee. Avoiding the displeasure of people who have the potential to be in a position of authority over you is a survival strategy for political animals."

"Sounds like a long shot that it would ever happen," Garth observed.

"Not as long as you might think. Martin did well to consider it. At any rate, keeping us at arm's length is a win–win situation for him. He has deniability if she is sucked into this thing; he didn't authorize whatever we did that involved her. On the other hand, he can claim credit for foresight and perception in recognizing the potential of a new investigative technique if we make a good collar."

"That makes sense. I'm sure glad it worked out that way."

The food arrived. The Old Man seemed lost in thought as he began to eat. Garth poked around in something that started life as yams and was now covered with a sauce described as "lite." Eating such stuff always made him wonder if being healthy was worth it. The two men ate in silence. Visions of grease burgers and fries with loads of ketchup danced in Garth's head as he pushed the empty plate away.

The waitress appeared. "Would you gentlemen like to see a dessert menu?"

"Uh, I don't think . . ." Garth began.

The Old Man cut him off. "We'd like some coffee and bring him a dessert menu."

Garth was surprised. He'd have thought that the Old Man would be itching to get back to the office by now. Instead, he pushed back from the table, applied the napkin to his mouth, tossed it on the plate, settled back, and crossed his legs. He regarded Garth thoughtfully for a couple of minutes. Finally, he spoke. "Are you telling me—in all honesty—that you went into that meeting this morning without a game plan?"

"I've told you more than once that's how I operate."

"And, I'm not having any easier time believing it now than I did when you first told me."

"What can I say?"

"I don't think you have to say anything—now. Your obvious ignorance of what happened this morning is proof enough that you didn't know what you were doing."

"But, I didn't 'do' anything."

"Oh yes you did. Even though you weren't aware of it, you played those guys like a guitar. You picked the right strings and pressed the right frets like a virtuoso. Can you tell me exactly what was going on in your mind during that time?"

"As little as possible. I try to stay calm and centered while taking in what's going on around me without thinking overmuch about it. What I should do or say occurs to me at the time action is required."

The waitress returned, placed cups of coffee in front of them, and handed a dessert menu to Garth. "Go ahead, indulge, son," the Old Man said. Garth didn't argue, he ordered apple pie with double ice cream. The Old Man seemed lost in thought as the waitress retreated, so Garth didn't intrude. He was well into his apple pie when the Old Man spoke again. "Tell me more about how this . . . er . . . approach of yours worked during one of those collars we've had to discuss." Garth didn't have to think twice about which incidents the Old Man meant. He put his fork down, took a sip of coffee, wiped his mouth, and took a deep breath. He'd never put what went on in his mind into words, but this seemed the time to come to Jesus.

"Ok, I'll tell you about losing that car," Garth began. "I'm driving into that alley. I don't expect any trouble. As near as I know, I'm surprising them with the arrest warrant. I've got backup following and another team in front of the building. Before I make the turn into the alley, I get real quiet, and I feel I should flip my holster open. I do. Since I hadn't thought about needing to have my piece at the ready, I'm beginning to think something is afoot that I don't know about. I press in on the quiet biz. Then, I get the feeling to open my door. I pull the handle as I turn into the alley. I wasn't more than a few car lengths in when I saw the flash in front of me. I was out the door and rolling as that shell blasted through the radiator and into the motor. As the smoke cleared, I was up against the wall with my piece pointed in the direction of the flash. Unfortunately, for them, they stood there, admiring the mess they'd made of my car. The one with the artillery went down without ever knowing what hit him; his buddy was turning toward me as he met his maker."

The Old Man shook his head and smiled. "I didn't think I'd ever see it," he said pensively.

"See what?"

"Do you know much Bible?"

"Can't say as I do."

"Well, it seems that Jesus told his disciples that they shouldn't worry about what to say when they were hauled before the law. That was a radical statement because his teachings alienated every power structure around. Instead of telling them to prepare their defense—it was a given that they would need one sooner or later—he told them to be quiet and promised that 'in that moment, it shall be given you what to say'. I've always wondered if that could really happen, but I guess I saw it this morning."

Garth was both pleased and embarrassed. He didn't know what to say. He forked up a mouthful of pie and ice cream.

"Now that I've seen you in action," the Old Man began, "I feel right about doing what I've known I had to do for quite awhile."

"Which is?"

"Do some delegating."

"Uh, I don't think I follow."

"It's no secret that I can't maintain this pace much longer. If I'm going to live long enough to enjoy retirement, I have to slow down. I know that. My superiors know that. They've told me to start working myself out of a job—delegate things until I've got somebody who can take over."

"I've thought that was the case for some time, but I don't want to think of working without you at the helm."

"How about being at the helm yourself?" the Old Man asked with a mischievous twinkle in his eyes.

Garth choked on the piecrust. "You can't be serious," came out between coughs.

"I don't see why not."

"Those other suits would have a guy like me for lunch."

"Not from what I saw in there this morning. In fact, I've spent a good deal of time, over the years, wondering just how in the hell you talked me into various things. Now, it becomes clear. No, I don't think you'd have any trouble holding your own. You'd need mentoring, but I think you've got all the basic equipment."

"Look, I'm a street cop. I don't . . ." Garth protested.

The Old Man leveled serious eyes at Garth. "Yes, you are a street cop and one of the best, but how long do you suppose it's going to last?"

"What's that supposed to mean?"

"It means that either your age or your record will catch up with you. Eventually, one of two things will happen. One, you will come up against someone whose reactions are a split second faster than yours are. Or, two, you will gun down another suspect, and I won't be able to keep you on the street."

Garth was quiet; the Old Man continued. "Do you have any idea how hard I've had to fight to keep you on the street? If there hadn't been heavy artillery involved in that last deal, you'd be pushing paper right now. The next one will probably be it. You are too good to waste through a scenario like that. It's time to get you in a position where your expertise is used to keep the next generation alive."

"I think I'm losing you."

"The young guys we've got coming up don't need an administrator in my chair. They need somebody who can help them understand how to use their instincts to stay alive. They need someone who has those instincts himself. Looking for the right replacement is what has kept me on the job way past retirement age."

"But, dealing with budgets and such . . ."

The Old Man tilted his head back slightly and closed his eyes. A contented smile spread over his face. "Ahhh, I can see it all now. I'm sitting in my boat, enjoying the warm sunshine. The fish aren't biting. I visualize you working on the budget and reflect how nice it is that I don't have to worry about you being Paladin or Florence Nightingale. At this moment, you're Bob Cratchet. I do hope I live long enough to experience that."

"Somehow, I don't think that's all that funny," Garth pouted.

"Forgive me, my boy, I do. I most certainly do."

18

LESTER DAHLRUMPLE BAGGED

Frank drove with one eye on the trip meter. Three . . . four . . . five miles since he had turned onto the gravel road. He pulled to a stop and turned the ignition off. His hands were moist and shaking slightly. He had never been this afraid. He took a deep breath and looked around. As his eyes adjusted, the moonlight revealed tall crops on both sides of the road.

The delivery instructions on the latest package were to take a specified route to this deserted spot. It was a perfect place to do him if that was their intent. Upon reading the instructions, he'd been sufficiently alarmed to take the chance of calling Garth. The latter hadn't liked the look of the instructions any better than he did and had advised him to bail out. It was good advice. He and Roz had both come clean with their spouses, so the threat of revealing their indiscretion was empty. For him, cut and run was the best option—except for two small factors. He couldn't shake the horror of that little guy dying in the video. He'd died alone and scared. Somebody had to stand up for him. Nor could he shake the Roz factor; her absurd hope that things would work out had infected him. If he ran, he deserted the murdered child. He didn't think that Roz would hold that against him, but it would always be between them.

As a youngster, Frank watched episodes of "I Led Three Lives" with his parents. Even then, with the immortality of youth upon him, he'd wondered what possessed a person to expose himself to the dangers associated with being a double agent. In fact, the dedicated agent thing had never looked attractive. Courageous he was not. He sat there. On the surface, he wondered what he was doing in this fix, but a cold, unbridled fury—more dangerous than bravado—burned deep within him.

222

Headlights came around the bend from behind. The van continued past. Another vehicle, following the van, pulled in and touched his rear bumper. The van turned around and parked within a few feet of his front bumper, trapping him. Both vehicles left their lights on, blinding him. Following the instructions, he sat and waited. After what seemed an eternity, a figure got out of the vehicle behind and tapped on his window. As he rolled it down, the person said the code word. Frank passed the package to him. Without a word, the man took the package to the van and climbed in the side door.

Frank was surprised. He was now inexorably involved—doing what Roz called the "Right Thing"—it felt good. His hands had quit shaking. He felt energized. He reviewed the instructions that Garth had given him.

After a time, his passenger door opened and the person he'd known from the Victoria house as "Carlos" got in. He let himself look frightened as he turned.

"Congratulations, you passed," Carlos said.

"Passed what?" Frank asked.

"This run was a test. Our tech says that you haven't monkeyed with THIS package."

"I didn't 'monkey' with the other one; I ran over it by accident."

"Yeah, that's what you told us, but we're careful. We wanted to be sure. So, tell me, what's it like being married to a judge? A used car sales man, married to a judge. It must be cushy."

Frank felt a twinge of elation he was careful to conceal. The guy was trying to demean him, to play the dominance game. No reason to do that unless they wanted his further cooperation. "You can see that I live a comfortable life."

"I understand that you did the Mr. Mom thing. Your wife didn't have much to do with raising your kids. She the one on top when you do it?"

"I'm used to hearing that she wears the pants, if that's where you are going."

"And, you want to avoid pissing her off. Is that right?"
"Yes."
"You've given some thought to what would happen if she got wind of your recent indiscretion. Tell me about it."
"She'd ruin me," Frank lied, as he tried to regain the frame of mind he'd been in as he parked. It worked, his gut grew cold, and his hands began to shake slightly. "She's cold and calculating. I wouldn't have a chance. With her influence, I don't think my business would survive."
"You might become a street person?"
"I imagine it would depend upon how far down she wanted to push me."
"Can't imagine what it would be like for a broad to have a big a stick over me. But, tell you what, chump, you behave yourself and you won't have to find out how far she'd go." With that, "Carlos" got out of Frank's car.
As the other two vehicles drove off, Frank basked in a glow he'd not experienced before. He'd done the "Right Thing." He felt elated, connected. As his eyes adjusted from the glare of the headlights, the moonlight falling on the crops looked more beautiful than anything he'd ever seen. It didn't look different than it had when he'd parked there earlier, but now he felt connected to it. With the intimacy, came a new beauty.

***

Little more than a week passed before Frank received another package.
"Detective Moore," said Garth, as he picked up the receiver.
Frank's voice came from the earpiece. "The next drop will be at the outdoor café on Linden and 96th. Tuesday at 2 p.m."
"Thanks, but you know you don't have to do this," Garth replied.
"Yes, I do," came the reply followed by a dial tone.

***

Tuesday afternoon found Garth and a surveillance specialist in an office that afforded a good view of the café where
Frank was to make the drop. "Either these guys are careless,
cocky, or setting Frank up," he thought. The corner of Linden and 96th boasted tall office buildings on all four corners. More than a hundred windows provided a view of the
café. He didn't see a hope in hell of getting anything useful.
Tailing whoever picked up the package would be walking
right into a set-up. That might well be what this was. About
all he'd get out of this were some photos that might be worth
something later.

"You say this guy's just a citizen?" the specialist asked.

"Yeah."

"Well, he's as cool as a pro. Sitting there, reading the paper, sipping on his java."

Garth looked through the telescope trained on Frank and
turned to the specialist. "Yeah, he is. I'd have never thought
it. Initially, I thought him a real wuss; it shows how wrong
you can be about people."

"Ahhh, company," the specialist exclaimed. Garth returned
to the eyepiece. A man was seating himself at Frank's table.
He zoomed in. The figure's expensive clothes didn't hide the
flab. Perspiration glistened at the edge of the fringe on his bald
head. His jowls moved nervously. Garth zoomed back to view
both figures. Frank put his paper on the table between them.
It was the Sunday edition—probably how the guy knew who
to sit with. The chance of this being a set-up remained, but if
the need for the paper was genuine, it was a mark for this being a real transfer. Frank and the newcomer exchanged a few
words. Frank drained his cup, got up and left. Chubs picked
up the paper as if to read it, scooped the package that was beneath it into his pocket, and sat back with his coffee.

✳✳✳

The following day, Roz frowned at the jangling phone interrupting her train of thought. "Roz here," she said curtly.

"This is Garth. Can you get a message to Frank for me?"

"Ummm, we haven't been seeing each other, but I guess so. What's up?"

"Frank told us where his last drop was to be. I advised him against it, but he wouldn't listen. The photos we took may be the mother lode. The guy who picked up the package is a well-heeled, known pedophile. We gotta be careful, because I still can't see why Frank would be trusted to deliver something to an end user when he was suspect a couple of weeks ago. Anyway, I wanted him to know."

"Thanks, I'll get it to him."

"One more thing. Is there any way to identify one of those disks by looking at it?"

"Sure, just a minute . . . um . . . the manufacturer's name, Alliance Magnetics, is printed close to the hub. It will be followed by a product number . . . um . . . lemme see . . . two-zero-eight-nine-six is the number for the self-destruct disk."

"Perfect," said Garth. "I'll keep you posted."

"When you get close, remember our bargain."

"You'll be as close to the take-down as I can arrange," Garth promised.

✳✳✳

Kitten opened the door of the B and B to admit Garth. Although she greeted him warmly, her countenance brightened further, and her hand brushed at her hair when she saw that he was accompanied by the tall, muscular, young man with the Sicilian features she'd seen at the Don's house. "C'mon in. We can use the parlor. The lady of the house is out for a while.

"Kitten, I believe you know Sebastian, don't you?"

"Saw him at the Don's. Never got introduced."

Sebastian stuck out his hand. "Sometimes, the Don treats me as a piece of furniture—that's the way in the old world. I'm pleased to meet you."

The guy was some hunk. "I'd like to have him furnishing my place," Kitten thought as she took the hand and got a nice little tingle. "Likewise," she said and led them into the parlor. "You guys want some coffee?"

"No thanks," said Garth. "I think we have some work to do tonight. We have a few things to get tied up, and you may want time to get organized."

After Garth had outlined his plan for the evening, he asked, "You see anything wrong with that?"

"Nah, sounds good to me," Sebastian replied.

Addressing Kitten, Garth asked, "Does it sound difficult?"

"Piece a cake," she answered.

Garth regarded Kitten soberly. "Are you crystal clear on the ground rules? Any alarms go off, you get the word from me, or you hear the mark getting up, you scram."

"Rodger that," Kitten answered.

Garth continued. "Going in, you double check your egress route. If there will be any problem getting out of there fast, you abort."

"Yes, Mom."

"I'm serious," growled Garth.

Kitten bristled. "Look, I give you that you're dammed good at what you do, so I leave the detectin' to you. How 'bout you give me the same space and leave the burglin' to me?"

Garth looked chagrined. "You need anything?"

Kitten looked at Sebastian. "For the operation, no. See ya about midnight."

✱✱✱

During the wee small hours of the morning, Kitten crouched outside the glass patio doors of an upscale residence. Coming through the back yard, she hadn't seen any signs of a dog in residence—that was good. She stuck the suction cup of the electronic stethoscope to the glass and tapped softly on the frame to make sure it was working. She wasn't used to working with one ear plugged up by a comm. set, but this stethoscope that worked through it was sweet. She sat listening for noises from inside and outside the house at the same time. After a few minutes, she thought she heard the occupant of the house snoring.

She waited a full fifteen minutes before cautiously shining her flashlight through the door. The dining area and kitchen beyond were in full view. No pet stuff—better yet. She stuck an ultra-thin blade between the door and the jamb and ran it down. About six inches from the floor, she ran into something. Damn. The place was protected by a security system. While releasing the lock, she was careful not to move the door. Extracting a piece of tape from her pack, she peeled the sticky off. With the tape tacked to the back of her hand, she jiggled the door slightly to allow her to slide the blade in front of the sensor. She felt the slight tug of the magnet and froze. She waited. Nothing happened. She pushed the door open. Careful to keep the blade in front of the sensor, she turned it vertical and taped it in place.

Flat on her stomach, Kitten inched her way across the dining area and into the hall. Looking toward the front door, she saw the security system panel. Slowly, she inched farther into the hall until she saw the front of the panel. It was unarmed. She rose and stretched. Returning to the back door, she removed the blade from the sensor.

A quick sweep of the first floor turned up one computer. It was in a room with a high-end entertainment system. Bookshelves lined one wall. An open bag of chips sat on the coffee table. Cups and other domestic debris were scattered here and there. "Interesting," thought Kitten. This was the single room showing evidence of habitation. She moved to the bookshelves. Her heart sank. There were hundreds of CD cases—the DVD she wanted could be in any one of them. Books, there were gobs of them too. Any one could be a hiding place for the DVD. She shone her light at an angle on a shelf. A collection of dust revealed typical guy house-

keeping. She checked the other shelves—no signs of disturbance. A few disks were scattered around the computer and
the DVD player. The ones she sought weren't among them;
she hadn't expected them to be, but it was easy and quick to
check them.

She looked around, searching for a clue. Suddenly, she realized that the room itself was odd. She stepped to the doorway and shined her light up the carpeted stairs and along
the bottom of the upstairs railing. Yep, all carpeted. She'd
thought it rather stupid to carpet the dining area and kitchen,
but now she realized that every square inch of the place—
except this room—was carpeted. Obviously, carpet was the
owner's floor covering of choice. It would have been easy to
miss that the den wasn't carpeted because the area rug was
huge. It extended to within a foot of the wall on all sides.
Possibly, it was custom made for this room. Why would a
person who preferred carpet have hardwood in the room
where he spent the most time?

She shined her light around the room again. In one corner
stood a large potted plant—the only piece of greenery she'd
seen in the house. In front of it, sat a longish couch. Thinking
that she'd have put the couch closer to the plant to open up
more floor space, she began to wonder. She walked over and
touched the plant. It was artificial. The space between it and
the couch was significant. She tugged gently on the pot. It
moved with little effort. She continued pulling to expose the
corner of the rug. Lifting the corner of the rug, she saw the
trap door. Beneath it, reposed a small safe. It yielded without
her having to use the stethoscope. Within were DVDs with
the product number two-zero-eight-nine-six on them. Kitten
put two in her pocket, closed the safe, and put things back as
they were.

After verifying that there were no signs of disturbance,
she moved to the patio. Carefully closing the door behind
her, she keyed her headset. "Phase one complete."

"Rog."

A few minutes later, Sebastian walked onto the patio.

"Good luck," she said, handing him one of the DVDs. "It was in a little floor safe located in the corner of the den. The den is front left."

"Nice work," said Sebastian with obvious admiration.

Kitten felt an urge to see where the admiration took him, but the present business caused her to say thanks and exit the premises.

Sebastian let himself in through the patio doors, examined the den, and moved upstairs.

Lester Dahlrumple awoke from a sound sleep as his bedroom lit up. A man whom he did not recognize stood at the foot of his bed.

"Les, you have been a very naughty boy," said Sebastian.

"Who are you? What do you want?" said Lester, as he fumbled for his glasses.

"You read 'The Godfather' or watch 'The Sopranos'?" asked Sebastian mildly.

"Yeah, but what . . ." Lester stammered as he struggled to put his glasses on with shaking hands.

"My name is not important, but it would be to your advantage to think of me as a 'soldier,' a young guy looking for an opportunity to become a made man."

"Th . . . th . . . Mmm . . . m . . . Mafia? I . . . is there really such a thing?"

"You don't want to know. That knowledge would have to come via an experience that would be your last."

Lester felt warmth between his legs. He'd peed his teddy-bear decorated jammies.

"Your second question—what do I want—is the one we need to address," Sebastian continued reasonably. He tossed a DVD to Lester. "Recognize that?"

Lester picked up the DVD, adjusted his glasses and turned pale. "Where . . . how?" he stammered.

"From that little safe in the floor of your den. By the way, that's a nice setup in there," Sebastian said pleasantly. Then, his voice took on an edge. "However, the important thing is that I know it's a snuff vid."

"How? . . . This thing's supposed to . . . Who?" Lester fumbled as he groped for understanding.

"More importantly, the police also know what's on that thing."

Lester's eyes grew wide as panic rose. "How . . . how . . . how . . . they promised I'd be safe . . . they . . . they . . ." he stammered, as tears filled his eyes.

"Well, I guess that the assholes you get these things from aren't as smart as they think they are."

"You said the police. But you . . . you're?" Lester babbled through tears.

"Les, snap out of it!" Sebastian said sternly. "I won't mind slappin' your fat puss if that's what's needed to get your full attention."

Lester wiped at his eyes with the sheet.

"Look at me; do I look Irish to you?" said Sebastian fiercely.

Lester looked at him timidly. "No, I'd say more Mediterranean, possibly Sicilian."

"Good. Do you know how important children are to us?"

"Uuuh . . . guess not."

"To us, nothing is more important. Their welfare is the reason we do everything we do. To us, abusing or mistreating a child is so despicable we don't even talk about it. Since my patriarch knows what is on those disks, I'm somewhat surprised that he sent me here to talk instead of making my bones with you."

Lester began quivering again.

Sebastian continued. "Non-cooperation with the police is fundamental to our world view. Denying them any information is a matter of ethics to us. But, my patriarch considers getting to whoever made those things so important that we're in bed with the cops on this one."

"You want me to finger . . .? No, I can't. They'd . . ." Lester said through sobs.

"Ok, for the sake of civility, let's list your options," Sebastian began in a reasonable tone. "One, having this disk is a violation of your parole; the cops haul you in. What happens then?"

"I . . . I'd go to prison."

"And, in prison?" Sebastian prompted.

"Th . . . there's bad people in there that would . . . abuse . . . and . . . and . . . hurt me."

"That's right," Sebastian said with an evil smile that didn't reach his eyes. "And, since we know about this, we'd make certain those people were not hindered in their dealings with you. You want to avoid the option of letting the cops deal with this. Let's consider option two. As we speak, my colleague is delivering another of the disks that was in that little safe of yours to the cops. If they bring the guy who made this DVD to trial, where they got it will become a matter of record. I'd wager he would have an even chance of beating the rap. I'd give you good odds that he wouldn't forget that the disk that led the cops to him came from you. I'd think he would be very unhappy with you."

Lester's whimpering increased in tempo.

"Ah, making those guys unhappy doesn't sound too good either, does it?" Sebastian continued. "So, let's look at option three. You don't help us. The cops don't find the guy who made this thing. We don't find him either. For one reason or another, your parole officer doesn't hear about this DVD. Life is good."

Lester brightened.

"But we still know," Sebastian scowled. "We still know and we don't forget. We don't forget that some lower form of life paid to watch innocent children abused and killed. That memory would provide an opportunity for some deserving young man to make his bones."

"You mean . . . you'd . . . even though I haven't done anything but watch . . . you'd . . ." Lester wailed.

"We'd consider it no more than pest control. We don't want your kind breeding."

Lester squirmed in the bed. Sebastian waited. After a time, Lester's tears dried; he was cried out. He hung his head. "What do I do?"

"Atta boy," Sebastian crooned. "You'll be told at your next meeting with your parole officer. You do your part to finger the maker of those DVDs, and we'll make a deal with you. We can't forget that you were part of this, but we'll show our appreciation for your help in taking it down. We won't bother you. Do we have a deal?"

"Yeah, I guess so."

"I can't say it was a pleasure to do business with you, but I'm glad you're cooperating. Whew, it's getting foul in here. I'm glad we're done," Sebastian said and walked from the room.

Lester squirmed and turned his head in disgust. He'd soiled his teddy-bear jammies during the conversation.

19

GARTH INTERVIEWS STEW

Garth noted that the digs of a parole officer were posh compared to his own, as he walked through the door signed "Nathan Brady." "Mornin', Nate," he said cheerily.

A thin man with an aquiline nose peered over accountant glasses as he curtly replied, "Morning."

Garth, unbidden, took a chair as the other arranged some papers.

Satisfied with the distribution of the documents, Nathan looked up and asked dourly, "What does a narc want with one of my sterling charges?"

"I want to talk with him for a few minutes. He might be able to finger someone distributing kiddie porn."

Nathan's countenance soured further. "Not surprised. Never did go for this bullshit of babysitting slime that ought to be in jail. 'Personal Recognizance.' Bull! The only thing I recognize about Lester is that he'll do it again. You got something on him?"

"At this point, I'm not prepared to lay any charges against Mr. Dahlrumple. I don't know if he has information that will help us. I'm just checking out a lead."

"I'd like to know what makes you to think he might have information."

"The operation we're investigating is large and sophisticated. At this stage, we have to keep everything close. Once our operation is complete, we'll be glad to give you anything relating to Lester."

Nathan brightened as he considered Garth's words. Well, Les was up to his old tricks. He'd suspected as much. There would be some good dirt when these guys were done. He could wait; he was a patient man. "Ummm, yes, I see. I'd appreciate your doing that."

The intercom buzzed. "Mr. Brady, your ten o'clock is here."

Nathan thumbed the button. "Give me three and send him in."

Nathan and Garth both stood. Nathan exited the office through a back door while Garth took the chair behind the desk.

Upon entering the office, Lester Dahlrumple was shocked to find the biggest, meanest looking Black man he'd ever seen sitting in the chair where he'd expected to see Nathan Brady. "Oops, sorry, I must have the wrong off . . ."

Garth cut him off as he started to back out of the door. "Nah, you got the right place, Les. Come on in and park it." As Lester took a seat, Garth noticed that the value of what he was wearing probably exceeded that of Nathan's car. He sat back comfortably and watched Lester fidget.

"Ah . . . er . . . Mr. Brady on holidays?" Lester asked timidly.

"Nah, he's here," Garth answered, and lapsed into silence.

"Then, who are you? . . . why? . . ."

Garth let a few seconds pass. "I'm a narc."

"A narcotics officer? I've never used any of that stuff."

"Yeah, I know, Les," Garth said, as he pulled the DVD from his pocket. "You get your highs from this." He held the DVD out to let Lester read the information surrounding the hub. The latter reached, but Garth held it out of his grasp. "I see you recognize this piece of work," Garth said with a note of triumph.

Lester sat back in the chair, pulled out a hankie, and began mopping at the sweat beads appearing on his brow. "Ok, I see. This is about that guy who broke into my house a few nights ago. What do you want?" he mumbled.

"A break-in?" replied Garth with mock horror. "Did you report it to the police?"

"No."

"Why ever not?" asked Garth, as he tried to remember how the face of compassionate concern felt.

"Except for the disk being missing, there is no evidence of a break-in. You probably know all that."

"Yes, I do; bless that Kitten," thought Garth. "A break-in that didn't break anything?" Garth mocked. "Next, you are going to tell me that you had a conversation with a Sicilian ghost."

"You know he wasn't any ghost."

"You can fulfill your agreement with that apparition by telling me who sold you this thing," said Garth, as he waved the DVD.

"I can't. Believe me, I would if I could, but I don't know who it is that supplies me with those disks."

"How did you make arrangements to start receiving them?"

"Well, there's this place where people can go to make arrangements for a . . . a little action."

"Isn't going there a violation of your parole?"

"No, no . . . it's not THAT type of place. It's upscale. Many corporate types relax there without knowing that it's used to . . . to make contact. It's on the twenty-eighth floor of a building about six blocks from my office. Their lunch special is ham hocks; they go great with a beer or two. I'd been in there a number of times without knowing, but a friend told me that if I were sitting with him in a booth, and we had a Shirley Temple placed as if it were for a third party, someone who could provide some entertainment would come and sit with us."

"This guy who came and sat with you, does he make those disks?"

"No, I'm certain he doesn't. He must be a broker of sorts. He has stuff for all different tastes. He's actually very nice, very discreet; he can determine what you want without making you feel the least bit uneasy."

"Les, save your admiration. You told this guy what you wanted. Did you pay him?"

"No, I received a credit card authorization form via email. I returned it; my card got hit and a few days later, I received instructions for picking up the package."

"Who hits your card?"

"Upscale jewelers, exotic liquor stores, boutiques."

"I gather you don't know this person's name?"

"No, I don't."

"Ever try to check out any of those places that are hitting your card?"

"Yes, but they didn't show on any of the searches I did."

"How about the source of the authorization form."

"I tried to send another reply, but the email address was no longer valid."

Garth sat quietly for a few minutes, thinking. "You haven't given me much to go on, Les."

Lester grew more agitated. "That's all I know. I swear, if I knew any more I'd tell you."

Garth looked down at the DVD. He began tapping it against his other hand. Without looking up, he said, "What if the person who sold you this knew I had it? Can you predict his reaction?" He studied the disk for a few more moments. When he looked up, Lester's hands had started to tremble. "Yeah, that's right, Les. I want you to think about what they do to those children. You can bet they wouldn't give a second thought to fitting you with concrete shoes if they suspected you had led the cops to them."

"B . . . b . . . but how? That disk was supposed to destruct," Lester stammered.

"How do we know what's on it? We were able to read one. Your friends aren't as smart as they think they are. In fact, we were able to get it back to them, and they didn't know it had been read," Garth replied smugly. There was no need to supply details that would lessen the mystique. "You know what Les? I'd bet those guys think the only way I could know what is on this disk is that someone—like yourself, for instance—had shown it to me."

Lester's eyes grew wide. "You wouldn't . . ."

"No Les, I wouldn't. Nevertheless, I cannot guarantee what conclusions they might come to on their own. Regardless of what you do, there will be an arrest and trial. Your only hope of coming out of this is to help us put them far enough away that they can't get to you."

Slyness crept across Lester's face. "Any chance they'd fry?"

"I'd love to make the case that tight."

"What do you want me to do?"

Garth put the disk in his pocket and looked at Lester. "Right now, I don't know. Act normal. Continue business as usual with these guys. We'll be in touch. I'm going to leave now so that you and Mr. Brady can have your scheduled conversation."

"Uh, does he know about the disk?"

"Disk?" said Garth, as he rose. "What disk?" He showed empty palms to Lester, turned, and exited.

✲✲✲

Roz, Garth and Kitten sat in her room at the B and B. "That's about the size of it," Garth said, concluding his recap of the interview with Lester.

"I'd have loved to watch his fat sacs quiver when Sebastian was talking to him," Kitten snickered. "Speaking of whom, is Sebastian still around?"

"Nah, he was on the plane that morning," Garth answered. Unmindful of Kitten's disappointment, he continued, "I thought Lester might be the mother lode, but all he can do is finger the broker. I'd bet that an approach to the broker would set off alarm bells." Garth looked from Roz to Kitten; neither one showed disappointment. They were intense, thinking, calculating. He appreciated that. "Roz," he began, "do you know if there is any way we can follow those credit card hits back?"

"You said that he'd tried to see who they were and been unable to find any such company didn't you?"

"Yes."

"Any idea of what length of time we are talking about between the time his card got hit and his trying to locate the company?"

"No, I didn't ask that."

Roz rested her chin on her hand, looked out the window, and nibbled on a fingernail. Garth and Kitten worked on their coffees. They had time for multiple sips before Roz wrinkled her nose and turned to them. "It sounds as if the credit card company is transferring the funds to a holding company. The outfits on the credit card statements must appear as members of that holding company. It's curious somebody hasn't noticed these companies disappearing after a single transaction, but I don't suppose we're dealing with much volume. Anyway, we are talking about somebody who knows a good deal more about the details of credit card transactions than I do. I'd guess it would take a full time professional to create these companies, use them to make a collection, and scrub them. I don't think a person with that schmaltz would work without building in good alarms. My guess is that any aggressive effort to follow the credit card hit back to the recipient would alert them. In addition, they'd know whose credit card hit was being followed."

"Humph," grumped Garth, "and that would seriously compromise Lester's usefulness to us."

"To say the least," interjected Kitten.

Garth sat back and sipped his coffee. Kitten refilled the cups. Roz looked out the window, tapping a fingernail on her teeth.

Garth turned to Kitten. "Could you describe that room again, please? I know you've been over it several times, but I want to be sure of my picture."

"Sure," replied Kitten, and described the room used to make the snuff videos.

Garth thought for a minute after she finished and then asked, "Can you imagine drawing a straight line from that vent to a point in the room that would put the kid on one side of the line and the people directing the thing on the other side?"

"Nope. The vent is in a corner of the room. I think I'd be looking at the backs of the people directing and running the cameras. Uh, I don't see where you're going with this," Kitten replied, puzzled.

Garth's brow creased. "Well, there's a problem with the take-down. Once you see them in the room with the kid, we can storm the front door. They'd go down their fire pole, and we'd gather them coming out of their escape route. It sounds tidy until you consider the kid."

Roz, who had been listening with one ear snapped around. "The kid?"

"Sure," Garth said slowly. "Think it through. They plan to do the kid at the end. The law comes busting in. The kid can finger them. They gotta do him before they leave."

Kitten and Roz both shook their heads. "Jeez, never thought about that," said Kitten. "We come bustin' in and he's toast."

"The problem is how to prevent that from happening," said Garth with finality. "If we could fire a smoke grenade between him and the scum, there's a chance they'd leave him in the confusion to escape, but it doesn't sound like that is possible."

"I'm afraid I agree," said Kitten.

"Garth," Roz interjected, "is there some way to make a person immune to tear gas?"

"Huh?"

"Bear with me. I'm asking if there is a pill or injection that can be administered to make a person immune to the effects of tear gas."

"Er, um, I don't know about tear gas, but I've heard that my colleagues in South America have an eye irritant that they blast a place with before they go in. Apparently, taking something or other about an hour before exposure will minimize the effects. I'm told exposure is still dammed uncomfortable, but you remain functional."

"In that case," Roz pressed in, "if we had someone in the room, doped with that stuff, he might be able to save the kid if Kitten laid irritant through the grate."

Garth's eyes darted from Roz to Kitten. His brows knitted together. He sat back and studied a corner of the ceiling. "A fifth column," he mused. "Never thought of that."

Everyone sipped coffee for some minutes. Finally, Garth spoke. "I can see that working. It's really thinking outside the box, but it could work. Do either one of you bright girls have any idea how we get someone in there?"

"Maybe start out with the honey pot," suggested Kitten.

"Honey pot?" asked Garth.

"Yeah, blind their caution with visions of mega bucks."

"Like Arab oil bucks!" Roz interjected.

"Yeah," said Kitten, continuing the thread. "They might get careless if they thought they had a chance of tapping into some Arab's billions."

"Ummm . . . that's an interesting idea," Garth offered. After some consideration, he continued. "With all the terrorism business these days, I'll bet somebody would have a legend we could use . . ."

"A legend?" Roz asked.

Kitten burst in. "Hey, somethin' you don't know, and I do, Ms. Smarty pants! A legend is a canned identity, family history, papers, and such, for somebody who doesn't exist. An operative assumes it in order to appear genuine to the quarry. Agent Slick tells whoever he's targeted that he is Alphonse Fudd. When the target checks, they find a history of a person named Alphonse Fudd, so they assume he is genuine."

"Yeah, the more I think about it," Garth began in speculative tones, "the more I think it might work. Les hooks our operative up with that broker. If the broker buys our guy as being the kinky son of some sheik, he'd smell enough bucks to introduce him to the guy making the disks. The smell of money could induce that slime ball to let our operative in on the making of a vid. There's a lot that might not work, but it would give us good chance of saving the kid."

Roz glanced at her watch. "Well gang, this has been fun, but I should run unless there's something else we need to go over."

"Nah, that's all I had," replied Garth. "I trust you'll update Frank."

"That I will."

"And, by the way, how is A.P.?" Garth returned, concern crossing his face.

"Not good. He uses more nitro all the time."

"Sorry to hear that. Y' know, if this is taking too much of your time . . . I mean time you should be spending with him . . ." Garth fumbled.

Roz smiled at Garth. "Sure, I know." She rose and turned to Kitten. "Catch ya later, girlfriend."

Kitten smiled back at her. "Later, smarty pants. Give A.P. a hug for me."

✸✸✸

Some days later, the intercom at Calvary Christian School came alive. "Mr. Collins, line three please." Stew tossed the basketball to a student, walked to the wall, and picked up the phone. "Stuart Collins here."

"Mr. Collins, this is Kitten. Did I get you at a bad time?"

"Ms. Jefferies! How nice to hear from you. How are you?"

"Doin' ok. You're probably busy, so I'll come right to the point. Would you be up to meeting me for dinner in the next day or two?"

"If there is something you wish to discuss relative to your education, there is no reason we can't meet here."

"This isn't 'zactly about my education. Once I explain, you'll understand why I don't want to bring it to the school."

A contest began inside Stew. No teacher in his right mind would allow himself to be alone with a female student. That was dynamite. But the thought of more time with Kitten contained considerable appeal; he found her fascinating. At any rate, she wasn't a student. In the future, she might be, but she wasn't yet. "Are you in trouble? Do you need help?" he asked, grasping for time to sort his thoughts.

"No. Somebody needs help, but it ain't me. Look, if this don't sit right, I don' wanna bug you. It was just an idea. Thanks anyway."

Stew found himself in panic mode. "No, don't hang up! It's not that I'm unwilling . . . it's . . . well, there are . . . ah . . . issues. I guess I could meet you. Would tonight work?"

"Hey, that'd be great. How's Luigi's at eight?"

"I'll be there," replied Stew. Hearing the line click, he replaced the handset. Why had he done an impetuous thing like that? He hadn't heard from her in weeks, and now she calls asking for a date . . . well, not a date, but a private conversation. Why had the thought of her hanging up thrown him into a panic? If he was going to be honest with himself, that wasn't hard to figure out. He wanted to see more of her—at any price.

✳✳✳

Gram looked up from her newspaper as Kitten breezed into the living room. "My, you look nice dear. Did you say you were meeting that teacher from Calvary Christian?"

"Yeah. Name's Stuart Collins."

Interest glistened in Gram's eyes. "I don't mean to pry, but is this about your education or . . . or . . ."

Kitten laughed. "No dearie. Mr. Collins is not a Nice Young Man in whom I am interested. The closest to an NYM that I've seen recently is a hunk who works for the Don, but he doesn't seem interested. Anyway, this meet with Stewball is about Garth's case."

"Stewball? That sounds a little familiar."

"Yeah, I shouldn't use it. I don't know him that well. It's hard though. 'Mr. Collins' sounds too stuffy for a guy who is that funny."

"Mmmm, I see," Gram replied with a smirk.

"I don't think you do," Kitten countered with her own grin. "Mr. Collins is fair good-looking and a real hoot, but I couldn't ever be interested in him."

"Care to elaborate?"

"Well, he's five or six years older than me for starters. The deal breaker is his teachin' at a Christian school. I donno what he believes. He didn't even start to push it at me. He must be religious though, to be teachin' there. Anyway, there's no buzz, no tingle."

"Was there with this boy who works for the Don?"

"Big time."

Gram managed to contain a surge of disappointment. "Have a lovely, platonic evening," she smiled.

"I won't be late," Kitten said as she left the room.

✸✸✸

Stew admired the rear aspect of the hostess as she led him to the table where Kitten was seated. Kitten greeted him with a broad smile. "Glad ya could make it."

"Great to see you again," Stew replied. As the hostess retreated, Stew inadvertently stole a glance at the way her long satin dress was stressed this way and that by the motions of her derriere.

Kitten arched an eyebrow. "You like nice buns?"

Stew's attention snapped back to Kitten. "Er . . . sorry. That was inappropriate of me. Still, the answer is yes. I make no apologies for being a male of the species in whom all the natural drives are operational."

The waiter appeared and offered drinks. Kitten ordered a glass of Viapolecella.

"What's that?" Stew asked.

"Red, not too dry. They serve a good one here."

"Ok, I'll have the same," Stew said to the waiter.

"Make that a carafe," Kitten added. Turning to Stew, she asked, "What are your Baptist buddies going to say about your imbibing?"

"Not much. They kid me about being more of a Buddhist" than a Baptist."

"Which are you?"

"I don't think I'm either," Stew replied, picking up the menu.

Kitten regarded her menu while wondering why Stew hadn't jumped through the opening she'd given him to explain his religious convictions.

The wine arrived; the waiter took their orders, and retreated.

Stew raised his glass. "Cheers."

"Cheers," replied Kitten, and sipped her wine. It wasn't the best bottle she'd tasted.

"Not bad," remarked Stew.

"The bouquet ain't up to snuff, but it's not bad."

"Boo . . . what?"

"Bouquet . . . the way the stuff smells . . . pretty important considerin' ninety percent of taste is actually smell."

Stew looked at Kitten. He was fascinated. He knew the meaning of 'bouquet,' but the following use of 'ain't and 'snuff' had made him doubt he'd heard correctly. Then, the ensuing display of knowledge about physiology—was there no end to the surprises this creature had in store? He continued looking at her, unaware that he should be saying something.

"What?" Kitten responded.

Stew shook his head and reached for his wine glass. "Nothing . . . sorry . . . got lost in thought for a minute. Uh, are you a wine connoisseur?" he asked, groping for a reply.

"Nah, I don't know much about wines. I like most of 'em. Fact is, I'm with W.C. Fields. I don't think I ever met the booze I didn't like."

"I believe it was Will Rogers who said 'I never met the man I didn't like", but I wouldn't be surprised if Fields said something close to that," Stew observed.

"Bravo, you pass Eng. Lit. 101," said Kitten with a smirk.

Realizing he'd been had, Stew didn't know what to say.

Kitten grew serious. "Last time we talked, you mentioned the rush you get from facing danger. Do you ever miss that?"

Stew struggled to follow the abrupt turn in the conversation. "Well . . . ah . . . umm . . . I guess. I don't think much about it, but I'd have to say I do. Still, I fail to understand where you are . . ."

The intensity in Kitten's face increased as she cut him off. She leaned forward. "Wanna feel it again?"

Stew was shocked. The look on her face was predatory and absolutely beautiful. The sight of how beautiful a predator could look was shocking. What was she asking? Whatever it was, the way she'd asked it had doubled the shock. He tried to look all business as he replied, "Ms. Jefferies, you'd better explain where you are going with this before I say anything further."

"Sure. Fair enough. I know it must sound like I'm jerkin' you around, but the truth is, I didn't know where to start. Here it is. There's a group of scum kidnapping young boys and using them to make snuff vids. We think we know where they make the videos and . . ."

Stew recoiled. "We? Are you a police officer? Was all this about your needing an education part of an . . . an . . . operation of some sort?"

Kitten held her hands up. "Sorry again. I'm gettin' ahead of myself. I'm not a cop. I am truly a girl with no formal education who has a grandmother bugging the hell out of her to get one. My Gram arranged for that visit I had with you. Shortly thereafter, I was approached by a police officer from Jackson Mississippi asking me to do some . . . some . . . er . . . consulting work for him."

Stew relaxed. "This 'consulting.' Does it have anything to do with the way you were able to open the lock on my car?"

Kitten looked down and toyed with her glass. "That was stupid of me—showin' off I guess. I'd be most grateful if you would forget it ever happened."

"Consider it forgotten as a token of my gratitude. I might have spent several hours extricating myself from that bit of stupidity. But, about this 'consulting' . . .?"

"Bein' an ex military type, you dig the principle of 'need to know,' right?"

"That is painfully correct."

"Ok, let's defer any further discussion about my role until you need to know," said Kitten with a twinkle in her eye.

The food arrived. They ordered more wine. Each ate for a while wondering what the other was thinking. Stew broke the silence. "Snuff vids? The real thing? Are you sure they are not staged?"

Kitten toyed with her fork as she used her tongue to work a bit of food from between her front teeth. "Actually, we've only seen one. The child on it disappeared about two weeks before the thing was made. He is still missing. We have a rough idea how often a DVD is made and there's a good correlation to unsolved disappearances of white males between nine and fourteen within a three hundred mile radius of Jackson."

Stew pushed his plate away. "Ugh, this is making me sick."

"The food? Mine's ok."

"No, the thought of some pervert killing innocent kids and selling videos of the act."

"Sick enough to want to help?"

"What can I do?"

"As I said, we think we know where the vids are made. We can raid the place next time they do one. The problem is, they'd probably do the kid as we came in. The place is a fort; there are three heavy doors to breach. They'd have plenty of warning and their emergency exit system is slick. Everybody's guess is that they'd kill the kid on their way out. The kid's only hope is for us to have someone in the room who can add to the confusion."

"There must be law-enforcement people who can do that."

"Yeah, but there is another problem. The slime uses an elaborate system to insulate itself from their clients. Letting someone outside their organization view the taping would represent a major compromise of their security. We hope to make them careless by giving them a smell of Arab oil millions. We are thinking to sell our operative to them as the kinky son of a sheik. We've got a legend for him, but the policeman running this investigation is having huge trouble finding the right person."

"And you think I might fill the 'kinky son of a sheik' role. Is that it?"

Embarrassed, Kitten stammered, "I . . . er . . . didn't . . . mean . . ."

Stew laughed. "Hey, I'm pullin' your chain. I know I could pass for an Arab. I'm willing to see if I might be able to help."

Suddenly, Kitten felt something cold inside her. "Uh, it would be dangerous as hell. You gotta realize that."

"Somehow, I get the impression that you aren't any stranger to dangerous situations."

"Not like this. I ain't never faced a gun. Before this is all over, there could be bullets flyin' all over the place."

"Been there. Done that. Still here. Got the T-shirt."

"Something tells me a 'wanna' is growin' inside you."

Stew twirled an empty wine glass between his fingers as he studied it. "Yeah, you're right. The government put a lot of training into me. I wondered if I would ever be able to use it for a cause I knew was right. Child rescue sounds right. When do I start?"

Kitten flushed slightly and said, "I'm afraid the question of 'if' has to be answered first."

"You lost me."

"Well, this cop, Garth Moore, who is running the show, will have to decide whether or not he's willin' to use your services."

"If he sent you down here to ask me, I can't see why he would have a question."

"Truth is, he didn't send me."

"Do you mean that you made this overture without his knowledge?" Stew asked, as alarm showed in his eyes. "Do you realize you might be compromising the whole operation?" he continued, as his grounding in military discipline took over.

Kitten folded her napkin this way and that. She didn't look at Stew. "Yeah, kinda."

"Then why, in god's name, did you do it?"

Kitten looked across the room as if searching for something, took a deep breath, and looked back at Stew. "Ok, I unnerstand you're spooked. I can't blame you. I know how you guys value the chain of command and all that. Gimme some space and I'll try to explain. There's this other lady involved in this thing. Her name's Roslyn." Kitten watched Stew begin to shake his head as if to tell her not to say any more, but she pressed on. "She's a real egghead—has a PhD in mathematics—but she has the most amazin' bunch of street smarts I've ever seen. Well, she has this goofy philosophy about bein' able to create your own reality by what you think. It sounds real off the wall until you see her in action. This gal don't miss. She's got it all, dream job, good marriage, money, and she credits this philosophy for everything. What's more, the more I watch her work it, the more I think she's onto something.

"The other day, she and I were doin' coffee and talkin' about Garth's not being able to find the right person to pose as our son of a sheik. It seems that, with the terrorism and all, undercover operatives with that Mid-Eastern look are in high demand. I mentioned I knew somebody who might fill the bill, but the thought of approaching him about doing it seemed plain silly. Well, she gets this real serious look on her face. She's a knockout, but when she gets that look, you feel she sees right inside you. She starts askin' me if it was an idea in my head or an urge from my gut. I didn't know what to say. I'd never thought about analyzing things that occur to me. We talked about it for a while and decided that it was more of an urge from down inside me than an idea. She said it's important to trust those urges and encouraged me to follow through. So, here I am—lookin' dumb as hell—but playin' it out."

Kitten felt drained; her mind was a blank. She fell silent, picked up the carafe, and poured herself another glass.

Stew's voice had an eerie quietness when he said, "I don't think you look dumb at all. I see that this new age thinking is unfamiliar territory to you. I appreciate your boldness for venturing into it. Thank you. Tell your policeman friend that I'd like to help."

✱✱✱

Garth sprawled on the loveseat in Rose's entertainment room. His feet were up on the ottoman. His arm was around Rose. She snuggled as they watched a stupid sitcom. During one of the many commercial breaks, Garth drawled a question with studied casualness.

Rose disengaged herself and looked at him in horror. "You want me to do what?"

Garth tried for the innocent face. "Hey, just askin' if you could. Kinda academic like."

"You want me to hack into the files of the Department of National Defense?"

"You did a good job of getting into the records for cops in the state of Mississippi."

"That was different!"

"Yeah, I know it was," Garth replied softly.

"And this . . . this is Federal! With the paranoia about national security . . . it . . . it . . ."

Garth held up his hands as if in surrender while he waited for her to run down. "Just askin' if it was possible . . ."

Her need for an emotional release satiated, Rose got up and refilled their glasses. As she handed Garth his, she asked, "Why do you need to know about a former SEAL?"

"He might have the skill set we need to put the lid on this child porn thing."

"Are you close?"

"Yeah, I think we can nail them in the act, but we need someone there to protect the kid as it comes down."

"Are you talking about having an undercover agent present during the making of one of these DVDs?"

"That's right. As soon as we see them come into the room with the child, we have all we need. We can storm the place, but we need to have someone there to protect the kid."

"And you are thinking about using a civilian for the role? That sounds crazy."

"This particular civilian is the first person I've come across who has the right looks and, possibly, the experience. Every candidate I've looked at has been too light on experience. Sure, they have had the training and most of them got top marks, but I can't send somebody in there who hasn't proven he has the instincts to stay alive."

"Instincts?"

"Yes, you can train a person until the cows come home, but if he doesn't have that special something that enables him to make the right decision and take the right action in a split second, all the training in the world won't keep him alive. It's not something you can teach a person. I call it instinct. The only way to know if a person has it or not is to find out if he makes it through dicey situations. I can't send somebody in there without proven instincts—both for his sake and for the sake of the kid."

"I think I see," Rose said, as she sat back down next to Garth. She pulled his arm around her. "You want to know if this guy has employed his training as a killer. You want to know if he has extricated himself from wet ops that went wrong. Is that it?"

"Wull, I wouldn't put it exactly that way, but you got the drift."

Rose began to chuckle softly.

"What's funny?" Garth asked.

"Most of the time you are so bright that I find some of the things you don't know amusing."

"Meaning?"

"Meaning that I can probably get you what you want without hacking."

"Not really? I'd think this guy's service record would be sealed."

"Really. Every so often, an attorney is asked to represent an ex special forces type. One has to be very careful about taking one of these cases because the client usually downplays how lethal he is. Often they are unbalanced and having a difficult time fitting into society."

"Yeah, I've run into a few of them. Even guys that have done well piloting choppers and fighters in battle zones find it difficult to fit into a world of stoplights and speed limits."

"It is a tragedy. We take these young men, train them and hone them to function in a lawless environment where the only rule is might makes right. Then, after a few years, we tell them that it's all over and dump them out into polite society. I don't think anybody understands the magnitude of the problem. At least, if they do, they are not making the information public."

"I'd think it's big. I'd guess that two or three out of four grasshoppers are ex military."

"Grasshoppers?"

"Guys who fly across borders in stolen airplanes loaded with narcotics."

"Oh, I see. Back to what I was trying to explain. Attorneys have found it necessary to protect themselves against potential clients who would try to sell themselves as pussycats when they are killing machines with a hair trigger."

"You mean they don't have to come clean with you?"

"They have to acknowledge that they have received the training. They know we can check on that. However, they can hide behind the classified thing when it comes to revealing how their training was employed. In response, we've developed a pipeline into the Pentagon. We don't get specifics, but we get an idea of how many ops the guy was on, how messy they turned out to be and sometimes, how many people went in vs. how many returned."

"Hey, that's slick. I'd like that phone number."

Rose snuggled against Garth and giggled. "I'll bet you would, big boy, but that's lawyer stuff . . . defense lawyer stuff. I'm surprised you cops don't have your own pipeline."

"Humph," Garth grumped. "I donno . . . gonna have to find out . . . Will you check on this one for me?"

"I suppose I'll compromise my principles this time," Rose replied, picking up the remote. "I can claim you used unethical means of persuasion." She pressed the off button.

✷✷✷

Garth worked at getting his pleasant face on as he walked into Calvary Christian School. He paused to check his reflection in one of the display cases. After a couple of adjustments, he continued into the office. "Garth Moore," he said, smiling broadly. "I'm here to see Mr. Collins."

"Welcome to Calvary Christian, Mr. Moore," said the pleasant-looking woman behind the desk. "Mr. Collins will be with you in a moment." She pressed an intercom button. "Mr. Collins, Mr. Moore is here."

"Thanks . . . be there in a jif," came from the speaker.

Garth looked around. The place was pleasantly appointed, tidy, and arranged for efficiency. He didn't have long to observe before a young man approached from the back of the office. The guy looked right. He was not much taller than Kitten. His features and coloring could well be Arabic. The muscles rippling beneath his tailored clothes—while not appropriate for the indulgent son of a sheik—gave him the look of a fighter. "Stuart Collins," he said, offering a hand.

"I'm Garth Moore, pleased to meet you," Garth replied, feeling the firm, confident handshake.

"Since it's nice outside, we can chat in the courtyard, if that's ok with you," Stew said.

Garth took an immediate liking to Stew. It wasn't exactly "nice" outside in the meteorological sense; the wind was blowing. Nevertheless, it would be "nice" for their chat because the wind made eavesdropping or recording difficult. "Sure, fine with me," he replied.

"Great," said Stew, motioning toward the back of the office. "We can take a shortcut through here."

Garth followed Stew through the back of the office and into a storage and workroom. Stew stopped by a photocopier and turned to Garth. "Mr. Moore, I assume you have identification." Garth was impressed. This man, almost two heads shorter than he, hadn't offered any apology. He'd stopped dead in his tracks, turned around, and made the request, as though he were talking to one of the kids. "Sure," Garth replied, pulling out his identification folio.

Stew didn't pay much attention to the badge, but he examined the card. "Do you mind if I give your card the photocopier test?"

Garth studied Stew for a second. Here he was, towering over a man who knew he was armed, yet the guy had challenged the validity of his identification without the slightest sign of nervousness. Obviously, he'd been around. "No, go ahead," he replied.

Stew removed the card from the folio and copied the back, not the front. Garth was impressed; the guy knew what he was doing. The characters designed to confuse a copier were on the back of the card. Stew tapped buttons to set the machine up for highest quality color and hit the copy key. As the copy came out of the machine, Stew put Garth's card back in place and handed the folio back to him. Stew smiled as he studied the copy and then offered it to Garth. "You probably want to personally dispose of this."

"Nah, feed it to the shredder," Garth replied.

The building that housed Calvary Christian school turned out to be an "L" shaped affair. The church building ran down the open side. A row of trees and shrubs at the back completed the enclosure of a courtyard offering walkways, green areas, flowerbeds, and numerous tables. Stew led the way to one in the middle and seated himself so he'd see anyone approaching from the building.

Garth opened the conversation with, "How much did Kitten tell you?"

"She told me some perverts are making snuff vids. You think you know where. You plan to raid the place during the making of the next one. You need someone on the inside to protect the victim. You are having difficulty finding that someone."

"Good," Garth replied, "you've got the gist. I realize that this someone I need is a person who can't give me a resumé of . . . of . . . ah . . . applicable experience."

Stew smiled. "I'd say that's a good way to put it."

"Instead, I'll pose a few scenarios about the experience I need. If any don't fit, tell me you are not interested."

Stew thought about the use of the words "fit" and "interested." This guy was ensuring he could deny having said anything about the operations he'd been on. In any case, what could he know about classified operations? "I can live with that," he replied.

"Oookay," said Garth as he considered where to start, "I need a guy with experience in black ops, the wet kind. And, to make it more interesting, say ops that had gone wrong."

Stew's eyes flashed with surprise.

Garth continued. "Say, a deal where he was the only one of the team to make it back."

Disbelief registered on Stew's face.

Garth went on. "Maybe to make it more interesting, say that it had happened more than once, like twice. And one of the times, he'd been considered a casualty because it took him a matter of months to return through hostile territory."

Stew was agape. "How do you . . ."

Garth held up his hand and shook his head slightly. "To quote Sgt. Schultz, 'Ve haff our vays,'" he said with a smile.

Stew tried to regroup. This guy knew more than any civilian was supposed to be able to find out. Was he CIA? DOD? Was this an effort to suck him back in? Was there a shortage of operatives, causing them to intimidate people into serving again? He searched his memory for details of his conversations with Kitten. "Tell me something. This Kitten, she came to me claiming that she had no education, but she displays an awe-inspiring range of knowledge. How does that square?"

Garth laughed. "Weird isn't it? Her conversation is a mishmash of street slang, college level English, ignorance, and knowledge. I'm constantly surprised."

"I'll give you that, but I'm asking how it happened. And, it better be good; I'm having a difficult time believing either one of you."

"Don't blame you," Garth began. "But, ask yourself this. If she were an educated person posing as uneducated, why would she drop in those four-bit words and displays of knowledge? It couldn't do anything but cast doubt on her story. Isn't that what is happening with you?"

"Well . . . yeah . . . I guess that's true."

"Anyway, this is how I understand it. Her mom and dad were circus people. They read a lot and mom taught her to read, but she didn't get any formal education. She lost both and is now living with her grandmother. The old lady is bugging hell out of her to get an education," Garth explained. He tried not to betray a boy in sneakers stealthily approaching Stew from behind.

Suddenly, Stew exploded. It was a cool move. He was up out of his seat and turning with both feet off the ground in one motion. He landed flat-footed in front of the boy, while yelling, "Wuff!"

The boy wilted. "Ah, gee, Mr. Collins, I thought I had you that time."

Stew mussed the boy's hair. "Better luck next time, Alex. Uh, could you put the word out that I'd like to not be disturbed while I'm talking with this gentleman?"

Concern showed on the boy's face as he said, "Uh, I'm sorry, Mr. Collins, I didn't . . ."

"Hey, no prob. I didn't say anything to anybody. You couldn't have known."

Garth watched the conversation with admiration. He was smiling when Stew sat back down. "Did I give him away?"

"No, I saw him duck back into the side door of the sanctuary. I figured he'd go out the rear and try to sneak up on me."

"Is this a game with you two?"

"Yes, I spend extra time with him, and he's fascinated that he can't surprise me."

"How'd you know he was back there? I could see him, but I couldn't hear him."

Stew's eyes narrowed, one eyebrow went up. He looked at Garth; he didn't answer.

"Ok, ok," said Garth. "I know; you felt him."

Stew's expression became pleasant again. "Right answer. Kitten said you were a street cop with a rep for action. I'd have doubted your story if that was a real question."

Garth grinned back. "Right answer. If you are the guy I need, you have to be able to feel people."

"I still remember the day I realized that most people can't 'feel' the presence of others," Stew reflected. "I was just a little duffer. I was sneaking up on my dad, wondering when he would feel me. I got right behind his chair and wondered why he hadn't turned around or said something. Then my mom called from the other room asking him if he knew where I was. His answer was so genuine that I knew he didn't know I was right behind his chair. I sat there for the longest time, thinking. I guess I'd suspected for awhile that people didn't 'feel' my presence the way I felt theirs, but I hadn't thought much about it. That time, I did. I went over various incidents and concluded that most people didn't feel the presence of other people. It felt cool to realize that I could sneak up on others, but they couldn't sneak up on me."

"I went through something similar," Garth replied. "I was always big, so I wasn't much good at sneaking, but I always knew if someone was around a corner or on the other side of a fence. As you did, I thought everybody knew. That was, until a friend got pounded by some guys that jumped out from behind a dumpster. When I asked him why he'd gone down an alley where those guys were waiting, he looked at me as though I had four eyes. In a flash, I realized he hadn't known they were there. The next flash was that he was the typical one, not I. Since being different is something to be avoided at all costs when you're young, I never mentioned it again."

Stew smiled and nodded knowingly. Garth felt they were connecting. His jacket had fallen open and Stew's eyes fell on the butt of his weapon.

"Garth," Stew said, "tell me something."

"If I can," Garth replied, making eye contact because the other had used his name.

"Ever use that thing?" Stew asked, glancing under Garth's jacket and back to his eyes.

"Yes."

The pain Stew saw in Garth's eyes was what he was looking for. "Not a nice memory, is it?"

"No."

"Mind pulling it for me?"

An efficient blur of motion brought the weapon into Garth's hand.

Stew smirked and nodded. "Thanks, that's all I wanted to see. Put it back before we scare somebody. Would you mind explaining how a missing-persons cop gets that good with a weapon?"

"I'm a narc. This is a special project," Garth replied, and explained how his foray into computer training led to this. He could see Stew relax as he explained; the interview was going well.

Stew felt himself begin to trust Garth. The guy seemed to be exactly what he claimed. Still, he needed to be sure. He searched his memory for things Kitten had said about herself. "What do you know about Kitten's grandmother?" he asked.

"Not much. Met her once . . . nice little old lady . . . retired nurse. She's heavy on Kitten about getting an education."

Stew looked earnestly at Garth. "Well, to be honest, I'm having considerable difficulty believing she has no formal education. What can you say to that?"

"I'd say I don't blame you. The things she knows are a constant surprise. I gather she's spent a lot of time in libraries."

"That's an odd place for a young woman to be spending time. Any explanation?"

"Not one that I'm free to share with you at this point."

"And, I suppose Kitten's involvement in all this is something you can't share either."

"That's right."

"Is she a consultant you use often?"

"Consultant?" Garth asked, surprise in his voice.

"Her word."

Garth chuckled to himself. "Yeah, I can tell you in all honesty that she has never worked with any branch of law enforcement, in any capacity, before."

Watching Stew, alarm bells went off in Garth. "You're not interested in her, are you?"

"Interested?" said Stew with a start. Then, he thought about it. Garth waited. "Well, I must admit I find her fascinating, but she's too young. I'd never let myself become interested in anybody that far out of reach."

Garth's tone grew ominous. "Ok, but you think about that long and hard. You know I can't afford to have any emotional entanglements cluttering up this operation."

"Anyway, she's spooked by what she perceives to be my religious affiliations. Her fears are groundless because she doesn't understand my belief system or motivation at all. But, my teaching at a school sponsored by a fundamentalist Christian church has her spooked."

"Would you mind leaving it that way until this operation is over."

"Not at all. Besides, I don't think there's any chance of her perception changing."

20

GARTH CONFERS WITH ROZ ABOUT STEW

Garth sat in his office, pondering about Stew. The man looked good: He had the right appearance. His credentials and work experience were perfect. Moreover, a fire burned inside him for the well-being of kids. It was obvious that he spent extra time with his charges—time that could be used to make money or chase skirts. He didn't seem to do much of the latter. Was that a good thing or not? The thought brought up the issue of Kitten. The guy was smitten. The way he'd lit up at the mention of her name spoke louder than his denial of interest. Would that muck things up? Since he had been a SEAL—and one entrusted with some dicey stuff—he probably knew how to compartmentalize his life. It was a good bet he'd guard against letting his feelings for Kitten get in the way of the operation. In addition, the religion card would help. Kitten's perception of Stew's religious convictions had her spooked. With a little feeding, it would become a useful aid in preventing her from giving him any encouragement. Yeah, since the Stew and Kitten thing was one-sided and the logical part of that one side said she was out of reach, the lid would hold until the operation was over. Stew's interest in Kitten wasn't a problem.

The real problem was the Old Man. What would he say to adding another civilian? He'd have a fit, pure and simple. From a legal perspective, their collective butts were already hanging way out. He cringed at the thought of presenting the idea to the Old Man. Perhaps he should wait until they found an insider who could do the job, that would make the best sense. Nevertheless, his gut told him that Stew was the man. Down deep, he couldn't see a future for the operation without Stew. Damn, how was he going to put this to the Old Man? He paced about in his office. He needed coffee.

He headed through his office door, but didn't stop at the bullpen coffee pot. Squad room swill wasn't going to cut it today. He thumbed a number on his cell phone as he walked.

***

When Garth arrived at the Bean Broker's cafe, Roz graced an outside table. Her head was back and the breeze ruffled her hair. "Damn," thought Garth. He never would understand women. Roz was one seriously fine-looking example of the species. What did she see in frumpy Frank? On the other hand, frumpy Frank was married to a nine-point-five. What did these lookers see in a neurotic little used-car salesman? Women, the eternal enigma, he grumped to himself as he slumped into a chair opposite Roz.

"Well, how's the big, badass, black cop biz these days?" she asked in a cheery tone.

"Been better. How's the egghead scene?" Garth replied gruffly.

"The eggheading is good. Uh, I didn't mean to be flip if you're not in the mood for it."

Garth waived a hand. "Aw, I guess I'm a little out of sorts . . . didn't mean to take it out on you . . . how's A.P?"

"Not good. He boots increasing amounts of nitro these days. I don't see how he can last much longer."

"That is a shame. If you're needed at home . . ."

"What I said last time we had this conversation still holds. You wouldn't even see my dust if I could do anything for him. Somehow, he doesn't seem to want me around any more than he ever did. The time we do spend together is better than it's ever been, but he wants nothing of altering our respective schedules. What's on your mind?"

"Got a conundrum I need to talk out."

"Lay it on me."

Roz sipped her coffee without taking her eyes off Garth as he explained the details regarding Stew. A smile played at the corner of her mouth as he explained his reluctance to get the Old Man's approval.

"A sticky wicket to be sure, m' lad," she observed.

"I guess that's why I'm talking to someone who thinks outside the box."

"Is it your gut or your head that's telling you Stew is the one?"

"My gut," Garth replied without hesitation. "If you had to make this decision, what would you do?"

"What I always do."

"Huh?"

"I'd approach this problem as I do every other. I don't tell many people about my methods because they'd think I'm crazy. I will tell you if you really want to know."

"I asked, didn't I?"

"Ok, let me start with a visualization exercise. Imagine we have these baddies all tied up with a red ribbon. Imagine that we've put a final stop to them. Try to imagine how that would make you feel."

"I . . . uh . . . don't," Garth protested.

"Humor me. Work at it. I'll go get you a coffee and mine refilled."

Garth was looking into the distance with a pleasant, relaxed look on his face when Roz returned.

"Feels good, doesn't it?" she asked, setting the cups down.

"Yeah. I'd expect it to. But I don't see . . ."

"I know you don't, but that's exactly what I would do. I'd work at basking in how good it will feel to have this scum put away. I'd work at relaxing and letting the universe or god or whatever work out the details."

"That works for you?"

"In spades. I discovered it as a little girl."

Garth was thoughtful for a few minutes and then shook his head. "Sounds new age or something like that."

"Actually, there is some good science behind it."

"Science?"

"Yes, one of the consequences of recent work in quantum physics is we have to admit that the observer affects the outcome of the experiment."

"What? If I experiment with the law of gravity by pushing this cup off the table, whether I'm looking at it or not isn't going to change the result."

"No," Roz laughed. "On the scale of our everyday experience, the effect is so small that it is negligible. However, when we start dealing with subatomic phenomena, the effect is profound. Heisenberg, in the 1920s, noted the effect, but the scientific community has only recently recognized the connection between physical phenomena and the way we think about them."

"Are we talking metaphysics here?" Garth groped.

"In a way. You might think of reality as a tree. Mystics understand the roots but not the branches. Scientists understand the branches but not the roots. Now, we're being forced to acknowledge a convergence between science and metaphysics."

"Wow, that's deep," Garth said, wrinkling his face.

"Yes, the science is esoteric, but we don't need to go any further into it. It is enough to say that good science is behind what I'm telling you."

"Are you're telling me that I just need to think about finishing these guys off?"

"No, I'm not suggesting you simply think about it. I'm suggesting you seek to maintain the good feeling. The feeling is the important thing. When we are feeling good, the channel is open to hear what universe wants us to do."

"Concentrate on feeling good? I don't know if I can do that. With what we have at stake here, I'd feel guilty if I wasn't trying to sort it out."

"I understand what you are saying. It's natural to worry at problems. It's a lot harder to relax and let the universe sort things out than it is to gnaw at the situation."

"Sounds like a cop-out to me."

"I understand where you're coming from on that one too. Let me suggest that it is more a case of employing something that is bigger than you are. Some authors call it the law of attraction. They present the idea that you attract into your experience whatever resonates with your emotions. If you are down because you are dwelling on the difficulties, your emotions attract more difficulties. If you concentrate on how good it feels to have the problem resolved, the positive emotions attract solutions. When you let your emotions go where they will while trying to solve a problem yourself, you are the only one working on it. When you take control of your emotions and keep them positive, you are getting the law of attraction—which is much bigger than you are—to work with you."

Garth's expression became one of puzzlement. "You say this stuff really works for you?"

"Yep."

"I mean, did you use it to get through school?"

"Yep. I studied the material and did the assignments, but I didn't cram. As the exam date approached, I concentrated on keeping my emotions positive and I always did ok."

"What would have happened if you hadn't studied?"

Roz grinned and shook her head. "I don't know. I'm not presenting a theology here; I don't have answers for all the 'what if' questions. I found it next to impossible to maintain a positive emotional state without studying, so I always did the work. Many times, I was surprised at how little studying I had to do to get that positive feeling going, but I never experimented with quantifying how little studying I could get by with."

Garth grinned back at her. "You don't suppose that the reason you did well is simply because you're one hell of a smart lady?"

Roz smiled back. "Thanks. There's no way to answer that, but I can guarantee you one thing; I made it through with a lot less stress than my peers. In addition, many of them rated much higher than I did on IQ testing. Whether what I'm presenting here is actually the way it is or not, it works for me."

"How about your work? The thing of reducing the stuff those research guys come up with into something that your chemists can use?"

"Same deal."

"Man, that's hard to get my head around. I always pictured you intellectual types working through reams of research data and formulae in a systematic manner."

Roz laughed. Garth watched. It was beautiful.

"Not so, comrade," she began. "Most cutting-edge science is done more by inspiration than deduction. The Einsteins and Teslas of this world start with an inspiration and work to confirm it with the math. The reason people outside the scientific community have the sequence backward is that scientists present their theories by starting where their colleges are. Ergo, their papers present the theory as the product of logical deductions that begin with present knowledge.

"I always approach a new project by seeking that good feeling which comes with satisfactory completion. As I review the material, I resist negative thoughts. Ideas about how hard it's going to be, or how this or that doesn't make sense, or how unreasonable the deadline is, always seem to hover about. It's a fight to keep them from landing. When I can maintain that good feeling, the solutions always pop out—most of the time, sooner than I'd expect. It's quite astonishing. From time to time, I find myself getting frustrated with a project, but when I sit back and look at what I'm doing, I realize that I'm trying to force a solution from my own abilities. Then, I work at getting back into feeling good about it, and it's as if a rush of positive energy takes over and the solutions happen."

"Similar to 'Use the Force, Luke; Use the Force'?"

Roz cocked her head and pondered for a minute. "Hey, that's good. I never thought about it in that sense; concentrating on feeling good is analogous to the Star Wars characters learning to employ the Force. As long as they relied on their own skill, training, and intelligence, they were no match for the dark side. But, when they learned to use the Force, their blows against the evil empire were effective."

"What you're saying feels right, but still, I donno . . ."

Roz beamed. "By Jove, I think he's getting it! Here's another slant on the same idea of getting this rational mind out of the way and connecting with the source of the answers. Do you know how Edison did it?"

"Edison?"

"Yes, Thomas Alva . . . light bulbs and all that. When he was working on something and ran into a wall, he'd take a nap. He'd lie down with a rock in his hand and drift off. When he got into deep or REM sleep—where he was dreaming—his body would relax and the rock would fall to the floor waking him up. Often, the dream would contain the answer to the problem."

"Why the rock?"

"You don't remember dreams that occur during REM sleep unless you are awakened while they are in progress."

"Weird system, but it must have worked."

"I'd say. He had over a thousand patents to his credit."

"Do you handle everything this way? I don't mean the way old Thomas did it, but your way, by seeking to feel good."

"Absolutely. I mean, I try to."

"Is it the source of your confidence?"

"Probably."

"Could I pry a little? It's not that I want to nose into your personal life, but I'm trying to get a handle on what you're saying."

"Go ahead. I don't mind telling you to 'f' off if you get out of line."

"Your relationship with Frank, did you feel good about it when you started fooling around?"

"For starters, I should clarify that we've only been in bed once. That time, I was too smashed to know what I was doing."

"Would you do it again?"

"I prefer to think not. At least, until things are sorted out with A.P. and Catherine. Still, I have to admit that some mistakes are just too much fun not to repeat," she replied with a sly grin.

"That's an odd way to put it. 'Until things get sorted out.' Most people would have said 'if'."

"Most people don't expect things to work out for them."

"And you do?"

"Certainly; it goes back to what I was saying about our reality being affected by—or a product of—our attitudes. I think a person creates their own reality by what they expect to happen. I know I made a mistake with Frank, but what we did is done. I can't change it. What I can do is to expect the final resolution to be beneficial for all. I think—and this is merely my kooky way of looking at it—that the best thing I can do is to inject positive energy into the situation by feeling good about the outcome."

"You honestly expect this mess you and Frank made to turn out well for everybody?"

"With every fiber of my being, I do."

"Got any ideas about how that might happen?"

"Not a single one. In fact, the openers have been so weird that I can't imagine what is next. When we told A.P. and Catherine, they both seemed relieved, each for their own peculiar reasons, but neither one was mad about it."

"Whaa . . ." Garth began, feeling he should scoop his chin up off the table.

"Without a word of a lie," Roz continued, "neither one of them seems mad at us. Things are better than they've ever been between A.P. and me. Frank says that an undefined tension that had been between him and Catherine since she announced her candidacy has evaporated. I don't have the slightest idea where this is going, but I'm smart enough to realize I'd never be able to guess the next move."

Garth was shaking his head. "That's hard to believe, but I'm very glad for you guys. Uh, tell me, does Frank buy into your view?"

Roz smiled tenderly. "No, the poor dear respects it, but he's having one hell of a struggle."

"Y' know, what you're saying sure sounds right. If I had any idea why it might work . . ."

Roz tossed her hair. "Here's an idea. Do you know what the corpus callosum is?"

"The whoseium?"

"The corpus callosum is the bundle of nerves that connects the right and left hemispheres of your brain."

"Oh yeah, that's the thing they cut to control epilepsy, isn't it?"

"Right on. We know that the right side of your brain functions in the realm of intuition and non-linear thought while the left side is specialized for rational, linear thinking. The left side is usually dominant. People who are very creative, and those who are able to think outside of the box, seem to have better access to the right side of their brain. We refer to musicians and artists as 'right brain' people, but they are far from being right brain dominant. Some people theorize that the right side of your brain knows and perceives a lot that is never used, because the information doesn't get across the corpus callosum. Information from that side is typically called intuition. For some strange reason, the left side of our brain seems to have evolved a mistrust of information that is not linear, so it shuts the corpus callosum like a valve."

Garth brightened. "Now, you're making connection. I know something about intuition. I call it instinct. As cops, we can train a recruit until we are both blue in the face, but if he doesn't have that special something that allows him to make decisions in a fraction of a second, and employ his training without thinking about it, he's not going to be any good on the street."

"Yes, that's it. Some researchers think that reacting to instinct is allowing the right brain to take control. These same researchers maintain that the right brain knows what to do a lot better than the left brain, because it is faster, and has access to information the left brain doesn't get."

"Mmmm . . ." Garth mused, as he sipped his coffee. "You mean, like being able to feel the presence of other people?"

Roz looked at Garth curiously. "Why, yes, I suppose. Are there people who can feel the presence of others without seeing them?"

Garth raised his eyebrows and nodded. "I'm here because I can do that. More than once, people who resented my interference in their affairs have tried to ambush me, but I knew they were there."

Roz was wide-eyed. "Really? How fascinating! Tell me more. Did you cultivate the skill? Can you turn it on and off?"

"Turn it on and off? I never thought about that. It's something that has always happened. As far as cultivating it goes . . . uh . . . do you remember my telling you about my great uncle?"

"The one who wrote music?"

"That's the one. Since he was the only person I could talk to about things that were out of the ordinary, I told him about it when I discovered other people didn't have the same ability. He said that it was a gift that I should 'follow' but he cautioned me to use it in the service of love."

"He must have been a beautiful man."

"He was. He practiced loving everybody. He wasn't too happy when I told him I wanted to be a cop, but instead of blasting me with his opinions, he talked with me for hours about why I wanted to do it. Finally, he said that although he didn't understand, 'Yo' heart, not yo' head er yo' pride's tellin' y' to do this, so I gotta give my blessin'.' He was a marvelous person."

Roz smiled and nodded in appreciation. "Good, that gives me something I can expand on. The researchers to whom I referred earlier would say that the reason your great-uncle could write the music he did, and that you can sense people and know what to do in dangerous situations, is because you can access the right side of your brain. They would postulate that you are able to open the corpus callosum valve in a way other people can't. I'd add that, in my case, that valve seems to open when I'm feeling good about things."

Garth was silent for some minutes. Roz watched different expressions cross his face; she waited and sipped her coffee.

After a considerable period of thought, Garth said, "What a concept. If we could teach recruits to get this corpus whoseium open . . ."

Roz held up a hand. "Hold on here, big boy. This is just a theory. It's a useful explanation, not a fact. I presented it because I thought it might help you get a handle on what I'm saying. It's not something you can run off and teach people. In fact, most of the current research indicates that the ability to use right brain function is hard-wired into us. Different people are able to use different right brain functions, but if you're not wired to use a particular function, you can't learn to do it."

"But, you said all I gotta do is to feel good to get it open."

"No, you asked me how I would approach solving your current problem and I said that's what I would do. I don't know if it will work for you or not."

"Well, you've given me a lot to think about. I knew you'd have some outside-the-box ideas, but I wasn't prepared for an entirely different box. Anyway, I best get back to the office. I've got a briefing from missing persons to attend."

✹✹✹

As Garth drove back to the office, he turned the conversation over in his mind. What Roz had suggested wasn't much different from what he was accustomed to doing. His practice of seeking to get quiet and centered when working on a problem was essentially the same thing, and it had always worked for him. The idea of seeking a positive emotion was no more than another slant on the same deal. What the heck, it was win-win anyhow. Feeling good was better than feeling frustrated. Even if it didn't work any magic, he'd be better off. Yeah, he'd give it a shot. He willed himself to stop agitating about how he was going to present the idea of Stew

to the Old Man and turned to thoughts of Rose. His insides
warmed.

✳✳✳

Garth was pushing the schedule as he walked back into
the cop shop, so he headed directly for the conference room.
An officer had just turned the projector on as he walked
in. The missing persons briefing started with an area much
wider than the one around Jackson, so his thoughts veered in
the direction of what he was going to tell the Old Man. The
pleasant feeling in his middle turned sour. He shook himself,
checked to see where the briefer was, and forced himself to
think about the pups that one of their police dogs had produced. Images of the fuzzy little outfits brought the pleasant
feeling back. The briefer droned on.

Finally, the presentation narrowed to his area of interest.
The first few cases didn't fit the profile. He was about to
relax when a missing person from Gulfport turned out to be
an eight-year-old white male. He was last seen a week ago.
The profile and timing were bang on. Garth's gut tightened.
Damn! He wasn't ready to move. Would another child lose
his life because big bad Garth wasn't ready? As his emotions
became riled, Garth caught himself. Although things fit, he
didn't know for sure his quarry had snatched the kid. Letting
himself get all riled up wasn't going to make him any more
efficient. Instead, it would play into their hands. He concentrated on the rest of the briefing and took comfort that only
one child was missing who fit the profile. He hoped that one
was a runaway.

✳✳✳

Back in his office, Garth noticed the lighted message indicator on his phone. He lifted the receiver and keyed message
retrieval. It was Terry's voice saying, "Tuesday." He checked

the call display. It was from the pay phone they'd agreed to use. Damn, damn, damn! His scumbags had pinched the kid and they were planning to make the vid in five days. Could he be ready by then? No way. He was going to lose this one. But, by god, he'd be ready next time. Stew was in. Maybe he wouldn't even tell the Old Man. He wondered how that might go down.

21
GARTH GETS THE BIG CHAIR

Garth spent a difficult night. He'd wake up with a sick feeling in his gut. Sometimes, about the fate of the missing child. At other times, about how he was going to propose using Stew to the Old Man. Knowing he needed rest, he'd turn to pleasant thoughts. Sleep followed the good feeling. He lost track of how many times the scenario repeated. During the morning drive to the office, he realized that he was in better shape than he'd been in on previous encounters with messy situations. Whether or not this feel good stuff worked, it had helped him to get a better night's sleep.

Garth answered his cell phone. It was the Old Man saying, "Get your ass over here. Use your light if you need to." Before he could reply, the Old Man hung up. The bottom fell out of his tenuous hold on a calm gut. What was wrong? The Old Man was often brusque, but not like this. He put the portable gumball machine on the car's roof and flipped the siren switch.

The Old Man's door stood open. Mildred Prentice, the guardian of the Old Man's door, waived him in. "Shut it," the Old Man said as he walked in. Garth looked around; boxes littered the floor. Packing was in progress. The Old Man wore sweats. Garth had never seen him in anything but a suit. "Whaaa . . ." Garth began.

The Old Man cut him off with "Sit."

Garth took a chair and said nothing.

"Can you get the shit in your office packed by noon?" the Old Man asked.

"Yes, but I don't . . ." Garth stammered.

The Old Man put his hands flat on the desk and leaned forward. "Do it. I'll be out of here by then. You move in."

Garth thought he'd heard right, but he was too dumbfounded to say anything.

273

The Old Man grinned although his face was ashen. "I finally got one up on the eternal smart-ass eh? That does me good . . . had a bit of a go-round last night . . . got rushed to the hospital about midnight . . . doc told me in no uncertain terms that if I didn't take time off—real time off—I'd be pushing daises damn soon. Therefore, you're in charge while we see how it goes with me. I don't want to hear about what you are doing, how any of the other guys' cases are going or anything else having to do with this office. You call 'em as you see 'em and we'll deal with the consequences after I get better."

The Old Man paused. Even this small amount of talking had tired him. He looked down, thought for a minute, and looked Garth in the eye with a grin. "Furthermore, if I don't get better, guess who will be left to deal with it on his own? Now, you get your ass out of here and get your shit together. Carl will call you when he has my stuff packed and moved. I'm not going to ask you if you have any questions, because I know you do. Sorry that I can't help you. There is an ambulance waiting downstairs to take me back to the hospital. The doc threatened to send the Marines if I wasn't back by ten o'clock."

Stunned, Garth stood and turned toward the door. Nearing the door, he turned around at the sound of the Old Man's voice.

"Garth . . . by the way . . . congratulations . . . and . . . and thanks. I . . . I couldn't have thrown this ball to anyone else. Now, scat."

✱✱✱

Back in his office, Garth's head felt like a blender trying to chew marbles. As he dumped stuff into boxes, his mind went in circles. He'd think of enlisting Stew. Since getting the Old Man's permission had been a part of his life for so long, his thoughts would go to ways of presenting the idea. However, his mind's eye didn't see the Old Man in that big, high-backed leather chair anymore. Nobody was listening to the presentation. He'd known for a long time that the pressure cooker was killing the Old Man. Every time the Old Man had mentioned retirement, he'd encouraged it even though he couldn't imagine working for someone else. Now that it had actually happened, he was in shock. On a superficial level, he knew the Old Man wasn't there anymore, but his subconscious was finding it hard to digest. Gradually, the marbles began to yield. As they broke down, he began to see somebody in that big, high-backed leather chair—him. In a sense, the Old Man was still there, but a presentation for needing Stew wasn't necessary; he was now the Old Man. A rapping on the doorframe interrupted his thoughts. He turned to see one of the maintenance men.

"Excuse me, Mr. Moore, but here's the hand truck you asked for."

"Thanks Eddie," was all Garth could think of to say. He thought it sounded a bit short, but he just couldn't think of anything else.

"Shore . . . uh . . . could you use a hand?" Eddie offered.

"Thanks man, but no. I got a lot on my mind. Doing this stuff helps me think."

"Yeah, I guess you do got a lot to think about. Donno whether to congratulate ya or say I'm sorry, but—for my money—the Old Man couldn't have put a better guy in that chair."

For the second time in as many hours, Garth was dumbfounded. It hadn't been two hours since the Old Man told him and even the maintenance people knew! "Uh, can you pick the truck up from the Old Man's . . . er . . . my office in an hour or so?" he asked.

"Betcha," Eddie replied as he turned to leave.

✳✳✳

As Garth pulled the hand truck loaded with boxes into the reception area of the Old Man's office, he got a horrified look from Mildred Prentice. She had been the Old Man's personal assistant since forever. Garth wondered what their relationship would be.

"Mr. Moore, we should have gotten somebody from maintenance to do that for you!" Mildred said, starting to rise from her chair.

"Nah, thanks Mrs. Prentice, but I'm in a state of shock. I need something to keep my hands busy while I get my head around all of this."

Garth pulled the hand truck toward the inner office, but stopped short. The plaque on the door was new. It now read "Garth Moore." Garth turned toward Mildred. "Mrs. Prentice . . . uh . . . how?" he stammered.

Mildred stood and walked to him. "Please call me Millie, dear. He's had everything ready for months. The plaque has been in my desk drawer. The Old Man wanted to change it himself as he left, but the medical Gestapo was already at the door. I had Eddie do it as soon as they were gone."

"Please come in for a moment," Garth replied, as he pulled the hand truck through the door to the inner office. He parked the truck against a wall and took one of the chairs without even looking at the big chair behind the desk. "Please," he said to Millie, as he motioned toward one of the other chairs. "I know this isn't going to be easy for either of us, but I want you to know this for starters. I realize that while I may be the man in charge, you are the woman who knows what's going on. I've got no delusions about that changing in the foreseeable future."

Millie preened. "Thank you, Mr. Moore, but I'm certain that . . ."

Garth held up a hand. "Let's start right there. I know 'Mr. Moore' will be appropriate in some situations, but, I want you to call me 'Garth,' 'shit-for-brains' or even 'kid.' You use whatever name pops into your mind. That way, I know what you're thinking and that's important to me."

Millie was wide-eyed. "I don't know if I can . . ."

Garth smiled. "Work at it."

"I will Mr . . . er Garth."

"Ok, I'll start off by acting like a real re-zecutive. Please get whoever is in charge of SWAT training on the horn for me. Or . . . do you have to send him a letter or something about the change of drivers here?"

"That's already been taken care of. The Old Man has had the letter ready for ages. I emailed it to all the department heads this morning. I'll have the hard copies mailed out by the end of the day. If you don't have anything else, I'll get Lionel on the phone."

"Lionel," thought Garth as Millie disappeared through the door. Unless he missed his guess, this office wouldn't contact SWAT training once a year, yet she still knew the department head by his first name. The lady knew her way around. The phone on the big desk buzzed. Garth walked over and reached, but drew back and straightened up before touching it. Eventually, he was going to have to do it. He walked around the desk and sat in the big, high-backed leather chair. He picked up the handset. "G . . . Ga . . ." What was he saying? Millie would be on the other end. "Yes, Millie?"

"I have Lionel on line 1."

"Thanks," Garth replied, and punched the line 1 button. "Mr. Frasier, how are you today?"

"I'm well, thank you, Mr. Moore. I'm looking at an email regarding the change of command over there. I'm not certain whether I should offer you congratulations or condolences."

"Y' know that's the second time I've heard that sentiment today."

Lionel chuckled. "I don't doubt it. You have big shoes to fill. But, if it's any help, one thing your predecessor excelled at was choosing the right people."

"Wait a minute," Garth blurted without thinking, "I'm not his replacement; I'm just filling in until he gets better."

"Humph, I can't believe that he'd replace himself with anyone that naïve."

Garth recoiled. He paused for a minute. "Uh, thanks . . . I guess it was wishful thinking."

"I was hoping you'd see it that way. Even if he does get better, he deserves some life outside the pressure-cooker. He's done one hell of a job—made a huge contribution to society. He needs to be able to relax and enjoy himself for whatever years he has left. Anyway, my apologies. You didn't call for a sermon. What's on your mind?"

"I got a guy that needs a little refresher training."

"Background?"

"Navy SEAL."

"Name and Social Security Number?"

Garth fumbled for his notebook and gave Stew's name and SSN.

"You need this ASAP?"

"Yeah, please, if you can work it out."

"You want his reaction times and situation analysis honed, is that right?"

"Yeah, he hasn't been active for about three years. He's going into something dicey. I don't want him to be rusty."

"Can I have him for two weeks?"

The sinking feeling returned as Garth remembered that he'd not be able to protect the current abductee. "We may have longer than that," Garth said in a downcast voice.

"Ok, have him over here Monday. I'll touch base with you Wednesdayish to let you know how it's going."

"That's it?"

"Yes, unless you have something else."

"Er . . . no . . . and thanks."

"My pleasure."

Garth replaced the handset and sat back. Wow, that was easy. No questions, just "yes sir" and "how high?" He wasn't used to having this much stroke. A person could get to liking it. It gave him a nice feeling, but the thought of the child he was unable to protect intruded. "No," he thought. "I'm not going to let that happen." He walked over to the hand truck and began moving boxes. As soon as he found the one with the pictures, he began placing them around the office. He considered the people in each. The good feeling returned.

He sat back down at the desk and pressed the intercom button.

"Yes, Garth?"

"Millie, would you please call the Calvary Christian Academy in Miami and get Stuart Collins on the line for me?"

"Certainly."

Thoughts of the missing child began to trouble Garth again, so he looked at the pictures. This setup had possibilities. Since his own fingers didn't have to do the walking, he'd have more time to get centered.

Millie's voice came over the intercom. "I have Mr. Collins on line 1, Garth."

Garth thanked her and punched the blinking line 1 button. "Hello Stew."

"Hi Garth, I don't remember your having a secretary."

"There have been a few changes around here. I'm holding down my boss's chair while he convalesces."

"Oh, sorry to hear he's sick . . . nothing serious I hope."

"Serious enough. Heart trouble, high blood pressure, the usual consequences of hypertension. There is no prognosis for when he might be out. Anyway, you still want a piece of this action?"

"I don't like your asking."

"Sorry. Could you get up here on Sunday? I've got a refresher exercise arranged for you. It starts Monday."

"Sure. Where am I staying?"

"The Starlight Motel. 5028 Henderson Drive. It's half a dozen blocks from the training facility."

"I'll be there . . . and . . . and thanks."

"Maybe you should wait until this is over to thank me."

"I don't think so. Whatever way it shakes out, I've been looking forward to it."

Garth replaced the handset, got up, and resumed emptying the boxes. With all of his belongings distributed, the office still looked bare. He put the empty boxes on the hand truck and pulled it through the door. "Uh, Millie," he began.

She turned a pleasant smile toward him. "Yes Garth?"

"Uh, y'know that fake palm tree in the corner? Is it important to the Old Man?"

Millie's hand went to her mouth. "Oh, my goodness. I'm sorry. He told me to trash it. I forgot."

"Hey think nothing of it," Garth said, as he turned back through the door. Presently, he returned and deposited the tree and pot on the hand truck. "There, Eddie will be up directly to get this," he said as he maneuvered the hand truck against a wall.

Millie pressed the binding tabs of a report folder into place and held it out to Garth. "Here's some light reading."

Garth took the folder. "What is it?"

"A few weeks ago, the Old Man asked me to review your caseload and make recommendations regarding who should pick up your cases if this should happen."

"Pick up my cases?"

"Yes, he was quite insistent that I do my best to persuade you to assign all of your cases except the child porno thing to other investigators," she answered matter-of-factly. "He also made me promise to do everything I could to keep departmental affairs off your back until you wrap that one up."

"Sounds like he gave this a lot of thought."

"He's known it was coming for a long time. We both have. To be honest, I've come to work every day for the past six months fearing that I'd find he'd waited too long."

Garth pursed his lips and nodded. He turned the folder over in his hands. "You guys are right. I'm not going to be able to do right by this job if I'm running cases. I don't think I can give the child porn thing to someone else, though. And, I got no problem with you exercising your judgment about what gets passed to me until I put a wrap on it."

"You tell me when, and I'll dump the whole truck on you," Millie replied.

"Maybe you can start spoon feeding me when the time comes."

Millie raised an eyebrow. "This is going to work out well."

Garth retreated into the big office, settled in the leather chair, put his feet on the desk, and began perusing the folio Millie had handed him. As he read, he became increasingly impressed with how well Millie understood the ongoing investigations as well as the strengths and weaknesses of the individual investigators. Her recommendations were sound. Only one would he call differently. After considering her reasoning, he had to confess his opinion was based on insufficient information. He thought about that. Having an assistant who understood things this well gave him a warm feeling. He pressed the intercom button. "Millie?"

"Yes Garth?"

"We'll go with these recommendations of yours. Please arrange appointments with each one of the individuals concerned within the next few days. Let them call the time. I don't want my first official act to be getting in the way of their investigations."

"Certainly. But, I think your first official act should be signing a document I have ready for you."

"Bring it on."

Millie came through the door and placed an Authorization for Expenditure in front of him. He'd seen many in his time, but never pictured himself approving one. Millie seated herself while he studied the document. He looked up, confused.

"Uh, why do we need a radar van?"

"We don't need the van. We are buying it for traffic. Jemez interrupted a street deal. The perp ignored the order to get out of the car and fled. Jemez pursued. The chase ended with the perp creaming a photo radar van."

"Because our boy was chasing this guy, we have to replace the van?"

"Strictly speaking, no. Nevertheless, funding is easier for us than it is for them. Drug enforcement is a glamour department. The public is always willing to ante up more money for our operations while the opposite is true for traffic enforcement."

"Ah," said Garth, as he began to understand. "We're doing traffic a favor?"

"It's more a matter of interdepartmental relations," Millie continued.

"Uh, what sort of favors might we need from traffic?"

"Can't think of any, but the gesture will go well with the other departments."

"Ah, I see," Garth said as the picture clarified. "It's a matter of our department appearing interested in the other shows as opposed to being myopic about our own."

"Precisely. But, we have to be careful."

"Careful?"

"The financial watchdogs are always on the lookout for mismanagement being covered up by interdepartmental transfers of funds or assets. Therefore, I alerted Carol to what we are doing. This AFE will go straight to her so it will bear her signature as it filters down through the desks at finance."

"Carol? You know the Chief Financial Officer?"

"We play bridge. The only avenue her signature won't cover is IA, so I let Josh know what we're doing. They don't worry about things they know about beforehand."

Garth rubbed his chin as he pondered the faces of the pariahs at Internal Affairs. "Josh, Josh," he muttered. "Mind telling me what your connection is there?"

Millie took a breath. "We were . . . er . . . involved a few years ago."

Garth looked thoughtful, then puzzled. "Are we talking about the same Josh? Josh Whittaker?"

"Yes." Millie straightened in the chair and smoothed her skirt. "You're wondering about the age difference, aren't you?"

Garth began to feel embarrassed. "Well, yeah, but it's none of my . . ."

"Yes it is. Eventually, you need to know about my personal life. You may disapprove, and you have a right to.

"You know that I've been a widow for . . . ah . . . fifteen years now," Millie said, as her eyes became moist.

Garth grabbed the Kleenex box out of his desk drawer and handed it across the desk. "An industrial accident, wasn't it?"

"Yes, we each went to our work one morning and before lunch, I was a widow. This year, I've been without him for as long as I was with him. His name was Gustav. I called him Goose."

"Gustav sounds German. I can't imagine any German allowing himself to be called 'Goose'."

"As with most people of that nationality, he did take himself very seriously, except where I was concerned. He treated me as a fragile china doll. He was a wonderful husband. He let me get away with anything. I still talk to him. I don't hear any replies, but I still have these one sided conversations at his gravesite, in the room where I've arranged memorabilia of us, and in the Mercedes.

"This yellow Mercedes SLE convertible was his pride and joy. We used to get in that thing and go for the joy of going. Those were special times together so the car is dear to me. I spend a lot on keeping it in mint condition. Sometimes, I pile in it on a Friday evening and just go. Where I go doesn't make any difference, I drive to feel that connection with Goose. Most of the time, I don't have any destination in mind; I go until I have to turn around to make it back to work on time.

"I suppose it was a means of coping at first. After a few years, I began to wonder if it was a sign that I wasn't getting through the grief. Some well-meaning friends have suggested as much. It did bother me for a while, but I've come to terms with it. If this need to get out on the road so I can connect with Goose, is an indicator that I haven't made it through, so be it. I don't even wonder about it any more.

"Those well-meaning friends are still concerned about how I'll ever be able to maintain another relationship when

I take off every so often to be with my deceased husband. They have a good point, but I seem to have stumbled upon a solution.

"It was eight . . . no, more like nine years ago now, when I interrupted one of those jaunts to stop by an old friend's house. When she heard that I was on my way back to Jackson, she asked if I'd consider giving her nephew a ride. At first, I recoiled at the idea of another man in the SLE, but I rationalized that giving this boy a ride wasn't the same as having another man in Goose's car.

"This boy turned out to be a graduate student. Maple and I are about the same age and this nephew is the son of her older sister. He'd been through one program to get a degree in business and then decided to go back and pursue his real love—anthropology. He turned out to be within fifteen years of my age, so he's not exactly a boy. He got off on the right foot by thanking me profusely for the ride. I found myself in stitches as he explained that finances were tight because people didn't line up at the door with job offers for anthropologists. He was doing his thesis on the Mayan civilization, and since I've always had a mild interest in the culture of Central America, we enjoyed great conversation on the way back.

"A week afterward, he surprised me by calling to ask if I'd like to have coffee with him. I'd enjoyed his company but hadn't given a thought to seeing him again. He said he'd enjoyed my company and would like to pursue a friendship if I felt so inclined. He was quite gallant about assuring me that he understood that I was still dealing with grief and that his intentions were purely platonic. The overture was understandable, since he was a good deal more mature than most of his peers and needed someone to talk with. I accepted the invite for coffee and it turned to walks in the park, which became meals and TV watching at my place.

"At one point, his landlord hit him with a huge increase that he couldn't afford. It was at the beginning of a term. Space was tight and he was having one heck of a time finding something else. I offered my basement suite until he found something. After he'd been there for a while, he confessed that he was attracted to me. He was so sweet about it. He said that he wanted to make love to me, but that he understood my situation. He was careful to say that if I wasn't ready, or if I wasn't attracted to him, it was cool. He assured me that he valued our friendship and that—having made himself clear—he'd let me take the lead. My initial thought was to tell him to move out immediately, but I didn't. The more I thought about it, the more I thought why not? The Friday morning I woke up with him in my bed, I felt like an adulteress. I drove the SLE to work and was gone as soon as the Old Man left the office.

"It was a weird trip. The connection with Goose was as it always had been. I kept starting apologies and explanations, but I'd get a few thoughts in, and they'd seem pointless. I finally quit fretting and enjoyed the connection. I didn't know whether I'd find Luke there or not when I got home on Sunday night, but he was. He didn't ask me where I'd been; he asked me if I was ok, and if I was ok about him being there. I just hugged him. After we ate the dinner he had waiting, he retired to his own bed. I appreciated that.

"The next evening, we had a beautiful, frank talk about our relationship. He thanked me for a great night of sex but said that if I wanted something long-term, he couldn't deliver so we shouldn't go any further. That was great news to me because I wanted more of him, but not forever.

"Having him there for the next months provided a great transition for me. He had no problem with my taking off for a weekend now and then or with time I spent in the memorabilia room. He never intruded. He accepted not belonging in those parts of my life. After getting his doctorate, he landed a research grant. We both understood it meant his moving into a phase of his life which had no place for me. Neither of us even mentioned an ongoing arrangement. I helped him deal with the few belongings he'd accumulated and bade him a fond farewell. During the first year, he wrote a few times telling me about what and how he was doing. He always thanked me for the time we'd spent together and for the painless parting when it came time for him to move on."

By this time, Garth was suffering a case of detail overload. "Uh, is this the first time you've explained all this to anyone?" he asked.

Millie was quiet for a time. "Yes, I guess it is," she began thoughtfully. "The Old Man watched it happen. My close friends know bits and pieces, but I've never felt the need for any of them to know everything." She began to look concerned. "Am I boring you with detail? Am I taking up too much of your time?"

"Neither of the above," Garth said gently. "Getting to know each other is an investment in our working relationship. I'll admit to being a bit in awe of you. I appreciate seeing your human side. Please continue and tell me as much or as little as you want."

Millie smiled with relief. "I met Josh through Luke. He was another late bloomer; he'd begun a career in the military but decided he wanted to study criminology. When the school term following Luke's departure began, Josh kept calling with points of law-enforcement he wanted to discuss. It wasn't hard to see he wanted to move in on the comfortable deal Luke had vacated. One evening, I asked him directly if that was his plan. He looked terribly embarrassed, but admitted to those intentions. We started dating. I was flattered by the pursuit of a younger man. Eventually, he moved in.

"After graduation, he received a job offer from the department. As we were discussing it, he mentioned an interest in the Internal Affairs end of things. He thought this job might be an avenue for eventually getting into IA. I'd had some misgivings about whether or not our relationship should continue if he went to work for the department, but the idea of him winding up in IA finished any deliberation. I told him we should terminate our relationship before he made a decision either way. He agreed and moved out the next day. We've continued an amicable, platonic relationship since.

After he moved into IA, the Old Man asked if I should continue having coffee with him, but the contact has proven useful from time to time.

"My subsequent relationships have continued the pattern established with Luke and Josh. I hook up with a younger guy, we seem to meet each other's needs for awhile, and then we go our separate ways. Being the senior partner in the deal, I can be draconian about the part I expect them to play, and I don't put up with any nonsense. My employment at the cop shop probably helps, but I can't say I've had a bad experience yet.

"Now you know. The personal assistant you were left with is an older woman with a string of younger lovers."

Garth was smiling. "Millie, that's beautiful. You are an amazing woman. If ever there was an example of somebody making lemonade out of the lemon that life handed them, that's it."

"You don't mind?"

"Mind? Hell, I encourage it. In fact, count on my support. If any of those young bucks sticks a toe over a line you've drawn, I'd consider it a privilege to be introduced as your back up."

Millie relaxed. "Thanks, I needed to get it out into the open."

"You ever start getting serious about one of them?"

"No, I find them shallow. It's not their fault. They lack experience. I usually tire of the deal before they do."

"Well, I've heard it said that a good man is hard to find."

Millie arched an eyebrow mischievously. "That's true. But, a hard man is also good to find . . . for awhile."

Garth stared at her with his mouth open, but no words came out.

"Oh, dear, I've shocked you," she said.

"It's just that . . . that . . . well, I've always seen you as Mrs. Decorum and propriety. It's nice to know that you are not an uptight, puritan prude. I'd have trouble working with that. Nevertheless, I have a lot of revelations to cope with right now, one of which is how well you understand the cop business." He tapped the report she'd given him. "This is a great piece of work. And the way you knew how to handle the subtleties of that van for traffic makes me think you belong in this chair more than I do."

"Hold it right there, Mr. Shit-For-Brains," Millie said, as she cut him off with a stern look. "I may be a pretty fair bureaucrat, but that's not what the people of this fair city need in that chair. We need a cop there. I'm not saying someone employed as a cop, but someone who IS a cop—through and through. Navigating the bureaucratic sea is something a person can learn, but being a cop is something you are or you are not. You can learn the politicking, but a political or bureaucratic animal could never learn to be a cop."

Garth squirmed. "Yeah, you're right . . . sorry, I guess I was feeling overwhelmed."

"If you don't feel that way from time to time, I'd think you didn't understand the situation. In addition, you bring something really special to this job—something even the Old Man couldn't deliver."

Garth looked surprised. "Which is?"

"Knowing how to stay alive. Even though the Old Man was a cop at heart, he'd never had to shoot his way out of an ugly situation. He spent many an hour agonizing over how he could transfer your expertise in that area to our youngsters."

Garth looked puzzled. "Huh? He was always bawling me out about it. He'd growl and snarl and pick apart every detail of those encounters."

"And after you left, he'd have himself a big laugh about it."

"Really? Sometimes, he'd be curt about dismissing me. I thought he was completely pissed."

"Probably, he needed to get rid of you before he started laughing. He'd call me in and tell me all about it between bouts of laughter. It did him good to share those episodes with me. Recently, those conversations have been ending with talk about how much more valuable you'd be communicating your survival techniques to other officers rather than employing them."

"Yeah," Garth began in a pensive tone, "I guess it is time I concentrate on passing what I've learned down the line. That idea has been working on me for some time, but I guess I can't put it off any more." He squirmed in the chair. "But, on a more mundane level, this chair . . ."

"It's not comfortable for you, is it?"

"It's a nice chair, but no. Any idea why?"

"One, it is the wrong size. Two, it has taken on the Old Man's contours. We need to get you a new one. Any idea what your K-T-S measurements are?"

"My what?"

"Knee to Tush to Shoulders dimensions. An inch or two makes all the difference in the world. I'll take yours and get a chair for you to start shaping."

"Excellent," Garth replied. "When the new one arrives, don't throw this one out. Put it over in that corner where the fake plant used to be. And, could you get a nice portrait of the Old Man for me? I'd like a small table to go next to this chair and put his picture on it."

"No problem . . . it's a beautiful gesture. I'll go get my tape measure."

As Millie departed to fetch her tape measure, thoughts of the abducted child's plight returned. There had to be a way. Was it possible to interfere with the scumbags' production schedule?

22

PLANS TO PUT THE LINE OUT OF ORDER

Garth stepped out of the elevator and stood looking at the outer door to the Old Man's . . . er . . . his office. It felt weird. Previously, the few steps from the elevator to that door were made with a slight sense of foreboding since the Old Man had, more often than not, wanted to chew him out. As he walked into the reception area, Millie greeted him pleasantly. "No trouble getting you a chair; come see," she said, rising and preceding him into the inner office. Behind the desk was a new chair. It was similar to the previous one, but distinct from it. Garth turned to the corner. The Old Man's chair was there. On a small table beside it, a discrete lamp illuminated an excellent portrait of the Old Man taken in healthier days. Garth went behind the desk and lowered himself into the new chair; it felt much better than the old one. Smiling, he looked at Millie. "This is perfect. How did you do it so quickly?"

Obviously pleased, Millie shrugged. "A couple of calls and the delivery guys were here. The instructions for adjusting it are on the desk in front of you."

"That portrait is excellent and the little table is perfect. You didn't get them with 'a couple of calls,'" Garth said with a raised eyebrow.

"The lamp came from the same place I got the chair. I have their catalogue. The table and portrait are things I had around."

"Well thanks, but I didn't mean for you to . . ."

"Chalk it up to vested interest. The more comfortable you feel around here, the easier my job is," Mille said with a wink. "You enjoy and I'll get on with the paper shuffling."

As Millie left, Garth regarded the setting in the opposite corner. It gave him a good feeling; his mentor would be there to guide him. He sat back and began to think about the case at

hand. The sour feeling started to return as he remembered—
a youngster's life was in danger and there didn't seem to be
anything he could do about it. He fought the urge to fret by
thinking of the superb job Millie did in picking people to assume his active cases. Yes, a true jewel, that one. He became
amused as he thought about her confession. Suddenly, he sat
bolt upright, dialed the number for Arbutis Security and left
a message with their receptionist. Less than an hour later, his
direct line lit up.

"Terry here, Garth.".

"Terry, what do you suppose would happen if you told
those guys their alarm wasn't working when you checked
it?"

"They'd tell me to fix it."

"Do you suppose they'd delay production of their next vid
until you got it fixed?"

"Probably."

"How long could you stretch the repair out, saying you
needed parts or something?"

"Day, maybe two. It's all standard stuff."

"Rats," said Garth, as his heart began to sink.

"Are you trying to buy some time? Are you trying to delay
their making the vid until you are ready to move?"

"Yeah, it just occurred to me that we might be able to save
the kid if we could get two weeks."

"Mmmm . . ." said Terry, as though he were trying to recall some details. "I . . . uh . . . think it might be done with
the line instead of the alarm system itself."

"The line?"

"Yeah, I could render the line inop. They'd have to get the
phone company to look into it. If you could get the cooperation of somebody down there, it wouldn't be hard to fake the
request getting lost or misplaced. I'd think a two week stall
could be done without anybody getting suspicious."

Garth's spirits lifted. "Yeah, I should be able to get the
cooperation of Ma Bell. Please plan to go ahead with the
disable unless you hear from me to the contrary."

"You got it."

Garth hung up, pondered for a few minutes, fished through the drawer in which he'd deposited his notebooks, withdrew one from a few years back and began flipping through it. There he was! Glenn Cochrane had been the maintenance supervisor for Southeastern Bell at the time. He dialed the number.

The call was answered on the second ring. "Hello, this is Glenn Cochrane."

"Bingo," thought Garth. "Mr. Cochrane, this is Garth Moore from Narcotics; do you remember me?"

"Moore . . . Moore . . . Narcotics . . . uh, yes! You're that big, ug . . . er . . . officer who I helped with a wiretap a few years ago. That was exciting. You took down a big operation there. It was gratifying to read about it in the papers. Do you have another warrant?"

"No, I don't have a warrant, but I'm after even bigger quarry than the last time we worked together. I need to discuss what I need with you—nothing more than a preliminary conflab to see if you can help."

"My schedule is fairly loose for the rest of the day. When would you like to drop by?"

Garth started to say he'd be there in a few, but stopped. This office was designed to impress. Why not take advantage of it? "Actually, Mr. Cochrane, it would be better if we met in my office. I know it would be an inconvenience, but can you possibly come over here? You will understand after we discuss the case."

"Inconvenience or not, you've got my curiosity up. I'll be there within the half hour."

"Much obliged," Garth answered, hung up, and thumbed the intercom button. "Millie?"

"Yes Garth?"

"A Mr. Cochrane will be by in a few minutes. Please show him right in."

"Will do."

A few minutes later, Garth came through his office door, but instead of approaching Millie's desk, he lounged against the doorframe, ill at ease.

"Yes?" Millie said with a pleasant smile.

"Uh, this Cochrane guy, I asked him to meet me here instead of going to his office because I'm asking for a favor."

"And you want to impress him with this layout?"

Garth shuffled. "Yeah, I guess."

Millie smiled approvingly. "You're learning fast."

"Well, it just seemed like the way to work things. I want him to feel impressed, but when the guys come up to get their new assignments, I want them to feel comfortable. I always knew what to expect when I walked in here by looking at you. Somehow, your demeanor set the stage. Did you and the Old Man have a code to tell you what impression to create?"

"D and P 1 meant most formal. D and P 3 meant neutral. D and P 5 is downright folksy."

"D and P?"

"Decorum and Propriety."

Garth grinned. "Gotcha. D and P 2 for Mr. Cochrane," he said, and retreated into his office.

Garth wasn't yet comfortably in his chair when the intercom buzzed. "Mr. Cochrane here to see you, Mr. Moore."

"Thank you, Ms. Prentice. Please show him in."

Garth rose as Millie ushered Glen Cochrane into his office. He stretched out a hand across the desk. "Good to see you again and thanks much for coming."

"Good to see you again too," replied Glen, as he took the proffered hand.

Releasing the hand, Garth motioned to one of the two chairs at the low table to the left of his desk, "Please."

Glen seated himself as Garth came around the desk to take the other chair.

"Would you gentlemen like something to drink, coffee, tea?" asked Millie.

"Bless her," thought Garth. It had occurred to him this minute that offering a beverage would be appropriate, but he didn't know if Millie fetched coffee. She was still way ahead of him.

"Coffee, black, would be great," said Glen.

Garth started to open his mouth, but Millie was gone as though she was expected to know what he wanted. He turned his attention back to his guest who was looking around the office.

"This is some layout," Glen began. "I didn't know narcotics officers rated receptionists."

Garth chuckled. "They don't. Narcs are lucky if they can get somebody from the steno pool to type a report for them. Last time we worked together, my office was about the size of a large broom closet. Since then, things have changed. I'm not exactly a narc anymore, it's more like I'm Mr. Narc."

"You are running the narcotics division?"

"Yes. It's only temporary until we see whether my former boss' health will allow him to return to work," Garth answered, gesturing toward the portrait of the Old Man.

Millie, with a professional smile, put coffee and condiments on the table, and noiselessly retreated.

Glen took a sip of his coffee and looked across the cup at Garth. "This case must be important for the division head to be directly involved."

"It's more a case of my not being able to let loose of it. I'm dumping the rest of my open cases on other officers, but I have to see this one through."

"Big time drug operation?"

"No. Child pornography. Somebody in this town is kidnapping young boys and selling videos of them being sexually abused."

Glen looked disgusted and then puzzled. "But, you're narcotics . . ."

"Yes. I'll tell you how I came to be involved if you want to know, but, the less you know, the better."

"How so?"

"Politics. You've been a manager for years, and I've only been one for a few days, but one thing my former boss, over there, made sure I knew about was deniability. I'm asking for a favor. I can't make a formal request on this one . . . get a warrant or anything like that. If you decide to help me and something goes sour, you need to be able to deny knowledge of what I'm doing."

"Fair enough. What is the favor?"

Garth pulled a piece of paper from his pocket and put it in front of Glen. "In a few days, this number will be reported as not working. I'm asking if you can intercept that call so the repair department doesn't react, and then route the queries regarding why the repairs haven't been made to this office for a couple of weeks."

Glen pursed his lips in thought. He took a sip of coffee. Garth waited. "Yes, that can be done. Umm . . . after this 'couple of weeks,' am I correct in thinking that this line would become functional again?"

Garth nodded.

"And, the purpose of routing queries to this office would be to give the inquirer the run-around concerning why the repair hadn't been made?"

Again, Garth nodded.

"If I went along with this, and there was a fire, there could be legal recriminations."

"The alarm system on that line is stolen, not registered, and not connected to any monitoring company."

"Are you absolutely certain of that?"

"I can put you in touch with the guy who installed and maintains it."

Glen grinned. "No need to do that. Actually, you are not asking me to do anything that doesn't happen on its own all too often. Yes, I'll be happy to help you with this. When will the line go dead?"

"Next Tuesday."

"What number should the calls be routed to?"

"Woops, that's too technical for the man in charge to answer. I'll have to ask the woman who knows what's going on." Garth said, as he rose from the chair. Reaching across the desk, he punched the intercom.

"Ms. Prentice, do we have a number that isn't normally used? We're going to be answering calls from a certain party in a different manner, so we need to know when that party is calling."

"Yes, 1176 is dedicated to special use. It is not assigned to anything at the moment."

"Please reserve it for my child abuse case."

"Yes sir; done."

Glen rose as Garth turned back toward him. "I got that," he said, and held up the paper Garth had given him. "Any calls regarding this number will be routed to your 1176 number until I hear from you. Do you have the capability of recording those conversations?"

Garth raised an eyebrow. "Donno—one second." He pressed the intercom button again. "Ms. Prentice, do we have the capability of recording conversations on 1176?"

"Yes sir."

"Thanks," Garth said, and released the button. Turning back to Glen, he said, "You want those conversations recorded?"

"Yes, since your people will be posing as us, I need to know what was said in case there is a violation of policy."

"Sure, we'll make recordings for you. Uh, do you have a manual for your customer service people? I'll have my troops scan it so they know what not to say."

Glen stuck out his hand. "I'll have one sent over. Please don't copy it and get it back to me as soon as this business is concluded. It's a pleasure to do business with you again, Mr. Moore."

After Glen's departure, Garth sat looking around the empty office. That was easy, a lot easier than such things were when he was an ordinary narc. Maybe he'd get to enjoy this job.

✳✳✳

After several days of talking with the officers in his department, Garth felt fried. All of them had expressed enthusiastic support and accepted the cases he transferred to them as though they were gifts. He'd just concluded the last interview. He felt gratified and humbled at the same time, but this much talking without any action or time for reflection in between, had been trying. He put his hands behind his head and leaned back to relax.

The intercom buzzed. "Lionel for you on line 1, Garth." He stabbed the line 1 button as he picked up the handset. "Mr. Fraser, good to hear from you," he said with forced cheerfulness.

"That Collins cat you sent over for refresher training—you got any more like him?"

The jovial tone pleased Garth, so he answered in kind, "I don't think so. We don't normally stock them. But, tell me, are you asking because you're having a good or a bad time with him?"

"I want to offer him a job."

"He's already got one. It's not in our field. His giving me a hand has nothing to do with his regular employment."

"Can you tell me what he does for a living?"

"He teaches history and, I think, English at a private, Christian school."

"You gotta be shittin' me. That guy is the best example of lethal I've ever seen. He has moves none of us here ever thought about. And fast—watching him work is like looking at a Tasmanian devil cartoon—there is a blur and the work's done."

"The job he's doing for us will involve him and one other operative going into a situation where there will be eight to a dozen bad guys. At least four of them will be muscle. The others will be boss or techno types. The scum will have a child with them. As soon as we see them with the child, we'll move in. His job is to protect the child while they try to make their escape. What do you think his chances are?"

"Who has the element of surprise?"

"He does. We'll lay a flash grenade in the room followed by an irritant that he and the other operative will be doped to withstand."

"My money would be on him. I wouldn't want to be on the other side if surprise was on his. Speaking of that irritant, have you ever used it?"

"No, it comes via some colleges in South America."

"Would you like me to give him a test slash familiarization run with it?"

"Would I? I hadn't even thought of that one! It would be terrific if you could."

"Have that other operative bring the substances and paper over. I'll have to get our medical people to clear it, but if it's ok, I'll arrange for Mr. Collins and your other operative to get some live action with it. That is, if I can get some volunteers to play the bad guys."

"If you have any trouble getting volunteers, I can bring over an example of what these scum are doing."

"That bad, huh?"

"That bad. It couldn't get much worse."

After a few more pleasantries, Garth hung up the phone. He sat back and put his hands behind his head. He hadn't even thought about a test run. Either Stew or Kitten could have an adverse reaction. The antidote might not work for them. Hell, he didn't even know if the irritant worked. He'd been planning to send them into an ugly situation doped with something that might not work or worse have bad side effects. Damn, how stupid could you get? Thoughts of inadequacy began to pummel him. How could he handle a division with a couple dozen people if he couldn't take the necessary precautions to protect two? The intercom's buzzing interrupted his morose thoughts.

"There is a Ms. Winters here to see the new division head," Millie said cheerfully.

Garth scrambled to his feet. Did they have a lunch date he'd forgotten? He couldn't remember one. He burst through the door ready to apologize for whatever he'd missed, but Rose spoke before he could.

"Pretty impressive," she said, scanning the outer office. "And, a plaque on the door. Is there Bigelow on the floor?"

"I . . . uh . . ." Garth stammered.

"I was in the neighborhood to take some depositions over to the court house, so I stopped by on the chance you'd have the time to show me your new digs."

"Always got time for you," Garth said gallantly, as he crossed to where she stood. "Have you girls introduced yourselves?"

Rose and Millie gave each other the conspiratorial girl-smile. "Yes. In fact, we've had a nice chat," Rose answered.

Garth took Rose's hands in his. She was wearing the engagement ring. That was a good sign. Try as he might, he couldn't figure why she wore it at some times and not at others. He took her wearing it at times—even though she'd not accepted his proposal—to mean that she wanted to accept. "You look great; hope you haven't been waiting long."

"Thank you, kind sir," Rose answered. "I've only been here a few minutes."

Garth released her hands, moved to the inner office door, and held it open. "Well, come see the rest of the place."

When she got to the middle of the office, Rose stopped and surveyed the layout. "Quite a contrast to your former abode."

"Reflects the different purposes, I'd think," replied Garth with a grin. "The other place was designed to be as uncomfortable as possible, so I wouldn't spend more time than necessary in it. The purpose of this one is to impress the other high level bureaucrats with whom I will have to deal."

"I don't think I follow."

"A lot of this job is going to involve enlisting the cooperation of other government agencies, interfacing with poli-
ticians and greeting dignitaries. This layout is designed to
give people the impression that the guy sitting in the chair
over there has a lot of stroke," Garth said with a touch of embarrassment. "But, here, let's sit over here," he said, sliding a
chair out from the low table. "I'll get us some coffee."

As if on cue, Millie came into the room and set coffee and
condiments on the table as Garth seated Rose.

"A real professional, that one," observed Rose, as Millie
closed the door behind herself.

"You got that right," replied Garth, seating himself. "As
long as I keep in mind that even though I'm the man in
charge, she's the woman who knows what's going on, I'll do
ok."

"You don't seem comfortable with all of this."

"I'm not."

"Want to tell me why?"

"I was good at my old job. I was contributing. I don't
know how I'll do in this one."

"Is this a permanent appointment?"

"Officially, no. Until the Old Man applies for retirement
or . . . or . . ."

Seeing the look of pain on Garth's face, Rose interrupted.
"Yes, I understand. Let's assume he retires; what then?"

"I'd need to submit a letter of application."

"Do you expect him to be back?"

"No."

"I know it's early, but have you composed that letter?"

The finality of writing the letter caused feelings of inadequacy to flood Garth. "Not sure I will," he pouted.

Rose regarded Garth for a long moment. He fidgeted. She
took a sip of her coffee, set the cup down, and studied him.
"You want me to level with you?"

"Shit, walked right into that one," Garth thought. "Uh,
sure," he replied.

"When you walk into a dangerous situation, do you approach it with more or less caution than you did at first? Don't answer right away; think about it for a second."

"Damn lawyers," thought Garth, but he did as he was told. He took a long swig of coffee and considered the question. "I'd have to say, less," he admitted, after a few minutes.

Rose smiled. "Good, any other answer would have been evading the truth. Over time, it's part of our nature to become increasingly complacent about the performance of any activity we repeat."

"But the years have honed my instincts . . ." Garth protested.

"Be that as it may, the years have done something else. Your reactions aren't what they were when you were twenty."

Garth cringed. Numerous things of late had suggested this might be the case, but he'd done his best to ignore them.

Rose continued mercilessly. "I'll grant that experience gives you an advantage which offsets the disadvantage of slower reaction times, but it's only for the time being. Ultimately, the latter will win. You have a limited number of quick draws left in you and every damn day, somebody is born who will grow into a punk wanting to take you on. If you don't quit while you are ahead, one of them will eventually beat you."

"I'm not about to let that scare me . . ." Garth blustered, when Rose paused to take a breath.

Undeterred, she cut him off. "This isn't about you, who you are, or who you are not. This is about the investment society has in you. Whether or not you realize it, you owe me and every other law-abiding citizen. You now have the opportunity to multiply yourself. On the street, you take on one miscreant at a time. Now, you can teach the younger generation how to stay alive. Each one of them can rid us of an undesirable. In effect, you will be taking on several at once. You've done an exemplary job of discharging your oath to protect and preserve, but that oath didn't say anything about limiting your efforts to what you can do as an individual. If you can multiply yourself, that promise requires you to do so."

Garth didn't reply for the space it took both of them to take several sips of coffee. When he did, it was in a pensive tone. "That's the second time in as many days that I've heard the same sentiment. I wonder if it means something."

"It means that the truth of what I've said is blatantly obvious to anyone with the perception of a rubber duck."

23

STEW MAKES CONTACT

Stew and Lester Dahlrumple sat in a yuppie watering hole on the twenty-eighth floor. A Shirley Temple, placed on the other side of the table, lent the impression they were waiting for a third party to join them. Stew nursed a ginger ale as Lester downed his second double-malt Scotch. "Better go easy on that stuff," Stew admonished.

Beads of sweat stood out on Lester's forehead. He mopped them with a napkin. "Yes, yes, you're right," he replied.

Stew studied the man. He was nervous as hell. Was he going to make it? Moreover, would his obvious agitation blow the operation? Could he remember the script?

For his part, Stew felt good. In fact, he was invigorated. It felt good to be back in a dangerous game.

After Lester waived the waitress off for the second time, a well-dressed man took the seat opposite them. "Good morning, Les," he said.

"Good morning, Charles," Lester replied, "I'd like you to meet Gabriel Donnely."

"Pleased to meetcha, Gabe," Charles said, offering a hand.

Stew took the hand, being careful to make his grip gentle, effeminate. "I don't believe I caught your surname," he said, releasing the hand after the briefest of contacts.

"Didn't give one. Charles will do." Turning to Les, he asked, "How long you know this guy?"

"We met in a bar a few days ago."

"So, you can't vouch for him?"

"Not really."

"So, why you bring him to me?"

"Mr. Charles, if I might," Stew interrupted. "I approached Mr. Dahlrumple. I'm looking for a source of exotic entertainment. Therefore, I've sought out places where others with those tastes are comfortable. Mr. Dahlrumple has told me nothing beyond that he may know of a source."

Charles eyed Stew suspiciously. "What kinda thing you interested in? I probably don't know anythin' that will help ya, but it don't hurt to talk."

"Since Mr. Dahlrumple and I don't actually know each other, I'd prefer to explain what I want to you in private."

"Works for me," replied Charles. "Scram, Les."

The relieved Lester Dahlrumple beat a hasty exit.

Stew placed a business card in front of Charles. After studying the card, Charles grinned and grunted. "Ali Ben-Adden, eh? I didn't figure you for no Donnely. Pricey card, too. What's your business?"

"I'm attached to the embassy here, but I actually have no 'business.' I'm free to pursue whatever interests me."

"Which embassy?"

"Saudi."

Interest glistened in Charles' eyes. "Are you tellin' me that you're the son of a rich sheik or sumpthin' like that?"

Stew produced a picture of a Lear jet. "This is my personal transportation. Draw your own conclusions." He pushed the picture toward Charles in a manner causing his sleeve to ride up and reveal the watch. He watched Charles' eyes go from the picture to the watch. The eyes registered recognition. Charles did appreciate expensive things.

"Don't think I've seen one of those before—nice." Charles offered.

"Rolex didn't make many."

"It don't seem too smart to me—wearn' that in a place you don't know, around people you don't know," Charles observed, his eyes narrowing.

Stew smiled indulgently. "Please notice that rather large man at the bar. If anyone were to make a move toward me that appeared the least bit threatening, he'd intervene most decisively. And, since we have diplomatic immunity that could mean anything."

"You got a bodyguard?"

"To be correct, that should be plural. You don't know who else in this place works for me."

"You go everywhere with a staff of muscle?"

"To be certain, I do. There are many people and groups who would kidnap me for ransom."

"Y' know, I don't hear no rughead accent."

Stew caused a flicker of annoyance to cross his face. "I was educated at Harvard."

"While you was there, did you study or did your family buy your way through?"

"It was an entertaining time. My peers accused me of majoring in campustry. However, enough of this chitchat. I've sought contact with you because I wish to become a distributor of one of the products for which you provide contact."

"You wanna go into competition with me?"

"No, I wish to expand the market for that product into my part of the world."

"I thought you Islamic types was pretty straight-laced."

"The value of a product varies in direct proportion to the degree to which it is forbidden," Stew replied with a sly smile.

"I heard they deal damn rough over there with people who break their laws. You don't need the money. Why you want to take the risk?"

The sly smile remained on Stew's face. "It is said that life without risk is like food without salt."

"Donno if I can dig that. I think that if I was you, I'd be enjoyin' the company of Playboy bunnies. But, whaddya want and what's in it for me?"

"I need an introduction to the person who makes the videos having graphic conclusions. For this introduction, I'm prepared to offer generous compensation."

"Like?"

"Ten large up front and we forget you exist or two points on the action."

"We?"

"I'm not alone in this quest."

"You a point man for somethin' like a rughead mafia?" Charles asked. The words were hardly out of his mouth when the big, dark man who had been lounging at the bar appeared at the table, casting a menacing presence.

Stew's eyes were narrow, threatening. "You like need a lesson in respect?" he said with a Sicilian inflection.

Charles' eyes darted anxiously from Stew to the big man. "Hey, I didn't mean no . . ." he began.

Stew's mouth curved upward, but his eyes were still cold. "Certainly, you didn't. You were just acting stupid. I'm not altogether certain I can accept that level of stupidity." Stew nodded toward the big man and the latter ambled back to the bar.

Charles regarded Stew with admiration. "Wow that was good. I didn't see you signal him."

"Perhaps you were too preoccupied with making cute remarks about my ethnic background."

Charles put his hands on the table, palms upward. "Hey, look, I apologize."

"Your apology is accepted, but the stupidity issue remains. Lawmen are dogs who can smell stupid. Your smart mouth could be a serious liability. Consider the offer of points on future action withdrawn."

"Look," Charles entreated, "I'm used to dealin' with sickos and weirdies. It works good to put 'em down. I ain't used to dealin' with a class guy like you. I been in this business a long time and the fact that I'm still around should tell ya that I ain't stupid."

Stew didn't reply; he waited and began to look bored. Charles' expression clearly indicated that he saw opportunity slipping through his grasp.

"How 'bout," Charles began, "I arrange a meet for you with the guy who makes those disks? It won't be easy; he's super cautious, but I think he trusts me enough that I can swing it."

Charles' attempt to raise his stock pleased Stew, but he didn't show it. He took a sip of his ginger ale, put the glass back on the table, and tipped the glass one way and then the other, studying the flow of the liquid.

"And . . . and . . . I'll do it without anythin' up front if you'll reconsider the two point offer."

Stew pulled a gold pen from the inside pocket of his jacket, wrote a number on the back of his business card, and pushed it back toward Charles. "You've got three days to check me out and make the arrangements. I'll expect a message at this number by Friday detailing the time and place." With that, he rose and started for the door. Charles noted that a man sitting by the door rose at the same time and preceded him out. The big man followed. A third man motioned to the waitress and paid the tab for the four of them before leaving. "That's stroke," thought Charles admiringly. If he played his cards right, this guy might be his ticket to something better than dealing with the likes of Lester Dahlrumple.

✳✳✳

The following day, Garth, Stew, Roz and Kitten sat in Kitten's B and B room listening to the playback of the conversation between Stew and Charles. Kitten was enthralled. Garth and Roz were pleased. "Boy, you played him like a violin," Garth said after the tape ended.

"Yeah, that was great; you sucked him right in," Roz added.

"Now, let's hope that the number-one scum takes the bait," Stew said thoughtfully.

"Dang, I guess I'm starting to think like a white collar, but I still can't believe you got him to arrange contact without some up front dough," Garth said in mock disapproval of himself.

"I think the whole thing is totally amazing," Kitten commented. Turning to Stew she asked, "Where did you learn that technique?"

"To tell you the truth," Stew answered with a matter-of-fact tone, "I've never done anything similar before. I've never had any training that directly relates to it."

"Then how . . .?" Kitten pressed.

"The same way I approached any other assignment," Stew answered. "If you stop to think in a combat situation, you won't survive. You have to relax and let your training take over. I talked as the words formed in my mind."

Garth smiled knowingly. "That's it, but I've never seen the instinct thing work in conversation. It's cool."

"Remember our conversation about the right-left brain thing?" Roz asked Garth.

"Are you saying that Stew knew what to say because his corpus-whooseum valve was open?"

"Don't get hung up on the idea of the corpus callosum being a valve. That's just a useful way of thinking about it," Roz began. "What you heard was a beautiful example of a person using his right brain. Stew's right brain was receiving messages about Charles' reactions and state of mind. Since Stew has conditioned himself to right brain input, he was able to respond with precisely what would prod Charles in the desired direction. The actual mechanism of how that happened isn't important. You saw the results."

"Yeah, that's right," Stew interjected. "I've never thought about it in a right versus left brain context before, but that is what happens. It's similar to taking a test. If you go with whatever pops into your head as soon as you read the question, you have, statistically, a much better chance of getting the question right. If you stop to think about it, something happens to muck up that first impression and your chances of getting the question right decrease. The phenomenon is getting a lot of study lately, but I've never equated it with combat training. Learning to rely on your training to prompt the correct reaction is exactly the same thing."

Garth's cell phone buzzed. He answered, listened for a short while, thanked the caller, and put the device back in his pocket. "This is better than ok," he said with a grin. "That was Millie. A message was left at the number. They want a meet down in the warehouse district tomorrow night."

Everyone gave each other high-fives, but Garth's elation evaporated quickly. As the others continued celebrating by toasting with their cans of pop, he retreated into silent thought.

"Ok, gloomy Gus, what now?" asked Roz.

"These guys are good," Garth began. "We were right to be careful about underestimating them. Asking for a quick meet makes it difficult to set up surveillance. I don't think they're on to us; it's just a common precaution. Nonetheless, it confirms our thinking that they're damned sophisticated. The short notice makes trying to get a stakeout position risky. Even if we had time to contact the building owners in the area, I'd bet it would get back to them. Damn, I'd sure like to get a look at whoever Stew talks to."

"How 'bout I take a walk around down there and see if I can find a vantage point?" asked Kitten.

Chagrined, Garth rolled his eyes. "Guess I forgot about our secret weapon. Yeah, why don't you do that?"

✳✳✳

The following evening, as the midnight hour approached, Kitten settled into a niche formed by the Gothic cornices on a building adjacent to the meeting place. "Why," she wondered, "had somebody thus adorned a building in a warehouse district?" It didn't make sense, but it was damn handy. She hid easily among the round contours of the gargoyles.

Some blocks away, Garth groused about the quality of the coffee they'd obtained en route. The stuff was supposed to be fresh. It may have been—several hours ago. As the technician twiddled knobs and adjusted displays, Kitten's channel lit up. "In position . . . aiming the camera . . . howzat look?"

Garth turned to the bank of small monitors. One of them showed the meeting place. "Put number three on primary," he said to the tech. A wide-angle view of the corner where the meeting was to take place appeared on the large high-definition monitor. He punched onto Kitten's channel and keyed his mike. "Great picture here. Zoom in on something." The field of vision narrowed until part of a fireplug filled the whole screen. Even with the false color produced by the night vision equipment, the sign warning against unauthorized usage was legible. He keyed his mike again. "Man, that's beautiful. I can even make out a stain; damn dog probably couldn't read."

Kitten broke in, "Company." The view expanded to show two SUVs moving toward the corner. One made a U-turn and parked while the other nestled to the curb half a block down from the corner. Kitten panned from one to the other. Six men exited each vehicle. Abruptly, the field narrowed as she zoomed in on one who had walked up to the door of a darkened building. He entered without difficulty. "Look to you like he had a key?" Garth asked.

"Yeah," Kitten replied. "Looks like they all did."

"Well connected bunch; good thing we didn't try to set up in one of those buildings," Garth observed.

"You got that right," Kitten replied. "From the looks of things, they either own this whole area or know who does. They're checkin' the place out as if they belong here. I see lights going on and off in each window that has a view of the corner."

The tech tapped Garth's arm as he keyed into Kitten's channel. "Could you give us close-ups of the SUVs?" The images of one SUV and then the other filled the screen. "Kill your cam transmitter right now! No more pix UFN." The tech shouted. The screen went dark.

"Whaa . . ." Garth began to say.

The tech cut him off as he brought up a still of the last SUV. "See that antenna? It's a wideband monitor. They may be checking for electronic emissions in the area. How many people did she say got out of each unit?"

"Six."

"That's good. It doesn't look as though they left anybody behind to use that rig, but we'd better lie low until we get a feel for whether or not they did. The voice should be ok because the encoding makes it sound like a fax signal."

Garth keyed his mike. "Kitten, that SUV with the Buck Rogers antenna on the roof may be able to detect the transmissions from your camera. Don't send anything else without hearing from me. You may have to tape the meet, so use your best judgment about what to save."

"Right, Scotty."

"Boy, she's great," offered the tech. "No 'why' or 'what about.' She immediately does what you tell her and waits for further instructions. What unit does she usually work for?"

"Uh, let's see if there is some way to get that picture back."

"Ah, sure," the tech replied, reaching for a book.

Minutes passed, the tech flipped from one reference to another.

"Looks like the check of one building is done; I see the guys going into another," Kitten announced.

"See if you can get a look at those guys and save any face shot shots you get. What was your first impression of them?"

"Soldiers, all."

"Try for a good look at the guys in that unit with the antenna and tell me if any of them look like techno-weenies."

The tech grumped and punched keys to bring up something on the Internet. After studying some screens, he turned to Garth. "I think this techno-weenie has figured out a way to get our picture back."

Embarrassed, Garth turned to him. "Uh, I didn't mean . . ."

"Sure, you did. But it's ok. I'm used to people thinking I'm not a real cop. Anyway, that rig Kitten has will broadcast on a frequency used for aircraft radio navigation. Luckily, I find that freq isn't in use these days. I'd be surprised if the rig in that SUV would even look in that band."

"Let's give it a shot," replied Garth appreciatively.

The tech punched himself into Kitten's channel. "Kitten, can you change your transmit frequency?"

"I'm lookin' at the LCD panel now. What do I do next?"

"About half way along those buttons at the top of the screen, there is one marked F-R-E-Q. Touch it."

"Ok, the screen now shows three dashes, a dot and two more dashes."

"Great, use the keypad to enter 111.95."

"Done."

The tech manipulated some controls and said, "Give us a shot of that corner."

The meeting place appeared on the big screen.

"Ok, Kitten, that's great. I think we put you on a frequency they won't detect. You can switch to continuous transmit now. Let us know if there is any unusual activity around that SUV with the antenna, or if it cruises the neighborhood."

"Will do."

The tech turned to Garth. "God, she's good—just does what she's told without asking any questions. What department did you say you got her from?"

"I didn't," Garth replied firmly, and pointed to the monitor. "Looka this." A couple of men had been loitering around the SUV with the antenna. Four more were walking toward it. They all got in and the vehicle moved away. Kitten followed as it drove down the street. Suddenly, the picture jerked back to the meeting place in time to see a stretch limo park at the curb.

"It looks like they gave the all clear. Must've been waiting somewhere close," Garth observed.

The patch from Stew's cell phone rang. "This is Ben-Adden," Stew answered.

"C'mon in," the caller said, and broke the connection.

Minutes later, the view on the screen panned up the street to show the approach of a Mercedes SUV. It parked in front of the stretch. The driver alighted and another large man got out of the passenger side. After scanning the area, one of them held a rear door open for Stew. As Stew got out, another large individual emerged from the other rear door.

Cautiously, the two men in the front seats of the limo got out. One of them opened a rear door. A man in a light colored suit emerged. The picture zoomed in on him. As he looked around, the camera picked up excellent images of all sides of his face.

"Whatta piece of camera work!" the tech exclaimed.

"And some luck," Garth observed. "He must be cocksure that nobody's watching. Can you get those shots off for ID?"

"As we speak."

The man in the light suit approached Stew with one of his goons on either side. "What is it you want?" He said, stopping a few paces in front of Stew.

"I wish to explore the possibility of becoming a distributor of your videos in my part of the world."

"Which is?"

"Saudi Arabia."

Interest showed in the eyes of the man in the light suit. "I don't know how it would work. I don't give out masters for copying."

"I have no interest in getting into the technical aspect of producing the disks. Perhaps 'distributor' is the wrong word. What I have in mind is assisting you to set up a distribution network."

The man in the light suit thought for a minute. "In this 'set up,' whose people would be making the disks?"

"Yours."

"Where would they be made?"

"Your call."

The interest of the man in the light suit increased; his features softened. "What do you suppose this product might be worth over there?"

"Easily five figures per copy to begin with. Once the product became known, you could probably name your price. The potential market has considerable disposable income."

The man in the light suit struggled to keep his excitement in check. "And, I suppose you'd want some of your people on my staff, to insure you got your cut and all that."

"Well, yes, we would want representation within your organization."

"And, for this little service, what cut would you expect?"

"Only the client list."

"What do you mean? I'm asking what percentage you expect to get out of this."

Stew took on an apologetic tone. "Please, I don't mean to insult you, but the amount generated from this enterprise would be of no consequence to me. All I want for my assistance is to know who gets the videos."

The man in the light suit began to look suspicious. "I'm not following you."

Stew pursed his lips and looked around as though in thought. "Shall we say that knowing the weaknesses of one's friends and enemies can insure that the friends stay friendly and that the enemies are neutralized."

The eyes of the man in the light suit lit up. "Ah, you want to use the product to blackmail people."

"Let's say that we desire to gain some leverage."

"Mummm, I think we may be able to work something out."

"There is one caveat which we should clarify."

The suspicious look returned. "Which is?"

"Well, the product's considerable value is derived from the graphic termination."

"Yeah, so?"

"For the product to have the value I'm suggesting, I would have to personally verify that said conclusion actually took place and was not the product of the electronic trickery for which your entertainment industry is famous."

The man in the light suit began to look alarmed. "You don't mean . . ."

"Yes, I would have to witness the making of a video."

"No fucking way!" the man said and turned back to the limo.

Stew waited silently.

The man didn't make a step before turning back to Stew. "Do you think I'm stupid or something?"

"I had hoped you were a better business man," Stew said calmly. "You were my first choice. Naming the USA—the 'Great Satan' as it is called by many of my countrymen—as the origin of the product would have given it extra . . . what is the word? . . . er . . . pizzazz. Nevertheless, the British product will do as well. Thank you for your time."

"The British?"

"Did you forget? They invented the snuff video."

"Have you been talking to someone else who makes a . . . a . . . similar product?"

"Yes. In fact, we were starting to iron out the details when I heard about you."

"How many of you guys would have to be in on it?" the man in the light suit asked, motioning to Stew's bodyguards.

"Myself and one other."

"Perhaps that can be worked out . . ."

"But, I must stipulate that we would come armed."

"Why?"

"For a person in my position, abduction for ransom is always a present possibility. The premises you use for the taping are, presumably, secret. The risk I'm taking going to such a place is at least commensurate with the risk you are taking by having me there."

Satisfaction registered on the face of the man in the light suit. "Fair enough. We'll expect you and your muscle to come heavy. I'll be in touch." With that, he turned and walked back to the limo.

"That was short," observed the tech.

"Let's hope it was sweet," answered Garth.

"It would have been nice to get audio too," mused the tech, "but I still think you made the right call."

"Yeah, it's too bad that they can't get the size of the dishes on those parabolic mikes down. The thought of her trying to aim the camera and that dish while trying to stay concealed wouldn't compute."

"From the performance she just turned in, I'd come down on the side of her being able to pull it off. She must have a lot of experience at this sort of thing."

"Far as I know, this is her first time," Garth said without thinking.

The tech looked at Garth, stunned. "How . . . why . . ." he began.

Garth cut him off. "Sorry, that was verbal diarrhea on my part. End of discussion regarding her. Let's pack up and get back to the store."

24
STEW REPORTS

Stew related his conversation with the man in the light suit to Roz, Kitten, and Garth as they sat in Kitten's B and B room. Garth's cell phone buzzed. Garth answered, grunted acknowledgement a couple of times, thanked the caller, and hung up. "Got a positive ID on the guy," he said to Stew. "His name is Maurice Authier, indicted four times on charges related to child molestation, never been convicted, successful business man, made a couple of piles in risky ventures." Turning to Roz he continued, "Your profile was bang on. We're dealing with someone who is successful, ruthless, a sexual deviant, and smart. That is, if this Authier is the guy."

"What does your gut tell you?" asked Roz.

Garth was silent while he turned to gaze out the window. Everybody else remained silent and worked on the refreshments provided by the B and B owner. After some minutes, Garth nodded and looked at each of the others saying, "Yep, I feel he's the one." Turning to Stew, he asked, "What was your impression?"

"As far as I'm concerned, every iota of your caution is warranted. To me, he looks as slippery as a greased eel. One misstep on our part and he'll be as gone as the smoke from yesterday's cigar."

"How's your refresher training with Lionel's group coming?"

Stew grinned. "To be honest, I'm not certain who is training who. I have a few moves they've never seen. We seem to spend as much time discussing how I'd do something as drilling. Overall, though, the opportunity to work out every day is great. You never know how rusty you are. I really appreciate your arranging this for me."

Garth nodded. "Did you get a chance to test that dope?"

Stew grimaced. "That irritant is wicked stuff. The scum won't be worth a nickel if you can lob some into the room. The antidote isn't much better. It's the worst stuff I've ever tasted, but it does work. After a shot of that stuff, you can still feel the irritant, but it doesn't bother you."

Garth looked puzzled. "Taste? I thought that stuff was administered by injection."

Stew grinned. "It is, but right after you get stabbed, you begin to taste it. Furthermore, it is some ugly tasting hoojar."

"Any after effects?"

"None that I noticed."

"Do you think using the irritant will give you guys an advantage?" Garth asked.

"You bet. If you get a can of that stuff lobbed between us and them, they will be in too much pain to notice that we're covering the kid."

Garth puzzled for a second. "How about following the irritant with a flash grenade?"

"Better yet. We can cover when we see the smoke. They'll be in a lot of pain and unable to see. It should neutralize them."

"I'm hoping they will all bolt for that fire pole and leave you two there with the kid."

"That would be the best scenario," Stew agreed. He glanced at Kitten and back at Garth. "Has she been exposed to the irritant and the dope?"

Garth looked blank for a second and then exclaimed, "God, no! Hadn't thought about it. Glad you did—something we gotta do."

Kitten's eyes grew wide. "What's this?"

In a soft voice, Stew explained. "You're going to be in that ventilation duct. Some of that irritant is bound to make its way up there. You don't want to feel the effects of that shit in an enclosed space, believe me."

Hearing Stew use profanity for the first time, Kitten paused. Thoughtfully, she said, "Yeah, I guess that's right."

Garth nodded. "I'll get a familiarization run for you lashed up with Lionel."

"The boys see her drive up in that 'Vette and we'll lose the day," Stew said, with a wink.

Kitten felt herself flush. It was a new experience. Sure, young men showed interest in her, but she'd never considered herself enough of an item to interfere with the work of a mature group of professionals. It was shocking to think of herself in that league. Shyly, she looked at Stew. He gave a slight shrug. The look on his face disarmed her. It was pure admiration. She knew what it was to be desired; to be admired was something new. It had been cool to experience Garth's open admiration of her skills, but to be admired as a woman was something else. She felt slightly giddy and not quite in control. That, she did not enjoy at all.

"Speaking of the people you'll meet at the training center," Garth began—ignoring the remark about her interrupting work—"if any of them ask you what unit you are with, say '13.' That's the polite way of saying, 'You don't need to know.'"

Surprised, Kitten took a few seconds to digest what she had heard and then asked, "You don't mean somebody might mistake me for a cop, do you?"

"The tech I had in the surveillance van did. He even got pushy about why he hadn't worked with you before. I finally had to get curt to shut him down."

Kitten found the thought of being mistaken for a law enforcement professional strangely pleasing. From the first time she'd given any thought to the concept of society in general, she'd realized that she was on the fringes. That's where circus people were and that's what she was. Although she wasn't with a circus anymore, she still saw herself as belonging on the fringes of society. To be mistaken for a contributing citizen warmed her; it made her wonder if that wasn't what she really wanted. Inwardly, she shook her head. It didn't matter. It could never be. Too much bad water had passed under the bridge.

A voice interrupted Kitten's reverie as Roz addressed Garth. "You don't have any idea where they are keeping the child, do you?"

"Not a clue. The street people haven't seen anybody around 1295, so I don't think he's there."

"Do you remember the reference to 'Acme'?"

"Sorta."

"Ok, try this on for size," Roz began, searching for words. "The connection with Wiley Coyote may indicate this guy is an insatiable predator. We know that in addition to being careful, he's cocky. That's an unusual combination. Showing up for that meet in a light suit—knowing it would be the only one there—indicates a serious need to let people know he can do anything he wants. Put those two ideas together and it might lead you to think he's keeping the child at his place of residence to, perhaps, sample the merchandise."

Garth considered the idea while the others in the room looked at each other. "Damn!" he exclaimed after a few minutes' thought. "Those dots do connect. I don't think I'd ever have seen it, but there's no question. In fact, it opens up an interesting line of speculation." With that, he pulled out his cell phone and selected a number from the auto dial.

"Hi Curly. Garth here. Do you have a current address on that Authier that you ID'd for me? Great . . . pretty classy area of town." Pulling out his notebook, he wrote the address down. "Thanks much," he said, and hung up. Turning back to those in the room, he said, "We have a good address on him. It's in a posh area of town." Punching another number on his cell, he returned to it. "Hi Millie, Garth here. Could you see who might be able to drop by 1812 Manchester Drive and size it up for a stakeout? If somebody was out in a delivery or postal van that would be perfect. We want to be very careful not to make anybody suspicious. Also, I want our JW ladies to do that area . . . Just like that? No questions? You're a doll. Thanks."

After Garth hung up, he saw everybody looking at him. "What?" he said.

"JWs?" Roz asked.

"Yeah," Garth chuckled. "We've got the sweetest-looking pair of older ladies who do the JW thing like you wouldn't believe. They go from door to door chatting with the residents. Although they talk the proselytizing line, they are actually looking for someone with some animosity toward the residents of the target property—someone who would let us do surveillance from their house without saying anything about it."

Kitten was wide-eyed. "Boy, you guys have some arsenal," she said, looking at Garth.

He grinned and raised an eyebrow as he replied, "Frankly, my dear, you haven't seen the half of it." Kitten wanted to retreat into her own thoughts, but Garth continued. "In addition, lady, when you are at that training center, try to avoid referring to them as 'you guys.' They will assume you are one of them, and it's best for all if you maintain that fiction."

"I dig that," Kitten replied, and lapsed into silence.

"Well, guys, this has been a slice," Roz began, as she looked at each one in the room and settled on Garth. "But I'd best get back to the salt mines if there isn't anything else on your mind, Garth."

"Nah, that's it. Can't tell you how much I appreciate your help."

As Roz rose, Stew got up also. "Guess I'd better run along too. Got a night exercise later; I want to catch a nap before then."

Kitten looked at Garth. "Could you hang tough for a few minutes?"

"Sure," he replied, and poured himself another cup as Roz and Stew departed.

After the door closed, Kitten sat silently. It was obvious to Garth that she was weighing something, so he took one of the two remaining pastries and settled back. While Kitten thought, he munched and sipped contentedly. As he reached for the remaining pastry, Kitten spoke. "Thanks for giving me time to find the words."

"Gave me a good excuse to do those goodies. That land-lady of yours is a mean hand in the kitchen. What might be those words you were searching for?"

Kitten took a breath as she looked up at the ceiling. "It's been a real eye-opener to see the array of resources you guys have at your disposal. I thought cops just asked questions and wrote things in their little notebooks. I suspected that you might employ technology, but nothing like that camera I was using last night. And ECM—that was outta sight."

Garth frowned, "ECM?"

"Electronic Counter Measures. That stunt of switching me to a frequency used for aircraft navigation to foil whatever might be in that SUV was Star Wars stuff."

Garth was surprised. "I don't remember discussing any of that with you."

"You didn't. I've taken a few flying lessons. I recognized the frequency. The antenna on that SUV looked like some-thing off a nuclear sub, so I—as you say—connected the dots.

Garth shook his head. "You are amazing."

"Not as amazing as you guys. It was cool working with you last night; you guys are damn good at techno-wizardry. Watching you combine that with Humint, blows me away."

Again, Garth frowned. "Humint?"

"Boy, you don't read many spy stories, do you? Human In-telligence, the time-tested method of using people to gather information. I would never in a thousand years think you guys had a resource like your JW ladies."

"Technology does things that people can't, but it goes the other way also. It's a matter of using the right blend."

"Watching you manipulate that 'blend' is downright scary."

"Scary?"

"Yeah, it makes me realize that you guys could have had me anytime you wanted to put the weight of your resources into it. The only reason I was getting away with it was be-cause I wasn't doing enough to get anybody serious."

A look of genuine pleasure took over Garth's face. "That is absolutely correct," he said with obvious satisfaction. "Your MO kept the interest level down, but it was a double edged sword."

"Yeah, I see that now. You guys wouldn't have developed an interest in me before the organization did. I'd have never thought they might put me in the white slavery you described, but it makes perfect sense."

"Vertolio had your name on the tip of his tongue when I asked about a cat burglar. Does that tell you anything?"

"Yeah, lots—I've been giving a bunch of thought to it," Kitten replied with a shudder she couldn't suppress. "He must have been watching for awhile; maybe he was close to making a move on me."

"Wouldn't be surprised," Garth said kindly, "But, that's part of the past we're going to make go away." He waited for her to reply. After several minutes had elapsed without her saying anything, he asked, "Would you mind taking a physical exam this afternoon?"

"A what?"

"A physical exam and have blood taken for lab work. Before we can run you through a drill with that irritant and the antidote, we have to get doctor's clearance."

"I don't mind, but won't it take weeks to set up a doctor's appointment?"

Garth smirked, "I think not." He pulled out his cell phone and dialed a number. "Hi Grace, this is Garth . . . not bad, not bad at all, and yourself? . . . She's doing great too and no, she hasn't said yes yet. Uh, can I get someone in for a physical this afternoon? . . . Yeah, that's right, I'm trying to cover my poor planning by making a crisis for you. Same deal as Stewart Collins . . . Yeah? You're a doll. She'll be there at four." He replaced the cell phone in a pocket, pulled out the notebook, wrote an address in it, tore the page out, and handed it to Kitten. "If you'll be at this address by four, the doctor will see if you're warm."

"Wow," was all Kitten said as she took the paper. Any time she or Gram needed to see a doctor, they were lucky to get an appointment within the month; being around somebody with this much stroke was neat.

✳✳✳

At three fifty, Kitten walked into the reception room. She had tried for the professional look. She wanted to appear as mature as possible. The receptionist looked up and asked, "Ms Jefferies?" while giving her the maternal smile.

"Yes," replied Kitten while thinking, "So much for looking mature."

"We haven't seen you before, have we?" asked the receptionist, as she pushed forms and a pen across her desk.

"No," Kitten answered, as she took the forms.

"I didn't think so," the receptionist said amiably. "You must be a recent graduate. What unit are you with?"

"Uh . . . uh . . . thirteen," Kitten replied.

The receptionist's eyebrows bounced and settled onto a face that had become all business. "It's like that, is it? Please be seated at that desk over there and complete these forms."

Kitten took the forms and turned toward the desk thinking how slick that had worked. She had been wondering how to avoid the obvious effort to chat her up, but the opportunity to use "thirteen" had done the trick. She seated herself and filled out the forms. She hadn't more than looked up from completing the forms when a lady in a lab coat appeared, smiled pleasantly, took the forms and asked her to follow. The gal in the lab coat perused the forms as they walked down the hall and held a door open for Kitten. The room was obviously the office of a lab tech. Kitten plopped herself in the chair with the armrest. The tech was good; she got the blood sample with one poke. She started to speak as she held out the urine analysis bottle, but Kitten cut her off. "Yeah, I know, piss in the bottle, and leave it in the window."

The tech grinned. "Almost. Hand it through the window to me. I'll be waiting on the other side."

"Waiting?"

"Yes, the doctor will want the results right away. I'll run these while he's examining you."

"You can do it that quick?"

"Most of it is computerized, so it doesn't take long," the tech answered and then regarded Kitten with an apologetic smile. "Please don't take Grace's reaction to you saying you're 'thirteen' the wrong way."

"It was obvious she didn't appreciate it."

"She likes to mother people. She thinks it's 'just awful' that Garth would want to involve someone like yourself in the 'terrible stuff' he gets involved with."

"Like me?"

"Yeah, young, female."

"What's your opinion?"

"Professional people know what they sign on for. Garth knows what he's doing. I'm grateful that you are willing to get mixed up in some of his 'awful stuff' because I wouldn't have the courage," the tech said, as she opened the door to the examining room.

"Thanks," Kitten replied as she walked through.

The tech winked. "You're welcome, but I should be thanking you," she said, and closed the door.

Kitten sat patiently while the doctor peered, poked, and prodded. "Great muscle tone," he observed, "you work out regularly?"

"Yeah, in this line of work, it pays to keep in shape."

"It would seem that way to me, but a lot of your colleagues don't seem to get it. I deal with a lot of sprains, strains, and other muscle trauma that are the result of flabby muscles being called upon for sudden, strenuous activity."

"Perhaps the result of too many doughnuts and too much paper work," Kitten observed, thinking that she was getting good at this ruse.

The doctor chuckled and turned as he heard the door open. The lab tech handed him some paper, smiled at Kitten, and retreated. Kitten returned the smile and waited as the doctor studied the paper. After several humms, ahs, and other unintelligible sounds, he looked up. "Well, young lady, you are good to go."

Kitten couldn't resist needling him. "No pelvic?"

The question didn't net the expected rise. "Not unless you think you might be pregnant, but there's nothing here to indicate you are," the doctor replied in a droll tone.

"You can bet your ass I'm not," Kitten replied, as she slid off the examining couch.

"Things not going too well in the romance department?" he asked kindly.

"Big nada, zilch, there," Kitten grumped.

"I'm not surprised," the doctor began in the same kindly tone. "People who get involved with these thirteen type operations often have a difficult time maintaining relationships."

"Nice to know," Kitten replied in the same sullen tone.

"If you want to talk about it, I'm qualified to do some counseling," the doctor offered.

Kitten bristled. "Hey, not havin' a boyfriend don't mean I need a shrink."

Unperturbed, the doctor continued in the same kindly tone. "I didn't mean to imply that you were in need of psychotherapy. Over the years, I've observed that many people in your profession don't understand the unusual stresses that are part of the job. I'm merely offering to explore whether or not I can help you understand and, perhaps, give you some tools."

"Ain't that a little outsida the doctorin' biz?"

"I suppose some would think that it is, but I consider the 'doctorin' biz'—that was a nice turn of phrase, by the way—to encompass the whole spectrum of your well-being. A person needs healthy relationships as much as they need food. Helping you satisfy that need is equally as important as prescribing pills."

"That's neat," Kitten observed, "double dippin' as an M.D. and a shrink."

"I don't bill the department for counseling—it's something I do pro bono."

"A doctor, doin' something for free? Mind tellin' me why?"

"My, you are the candid one," the doctor said with a grin. "Let's call it my investment in the community. I know that the things you do are necessary to keep my family safe. Those activities produce stresses that can poison relationships. In a sense, you may be picking up baggage which prevents you from enjoying your life as you protect mine. Since I wouldn't have the courage to do your job, the least I can do is to help you—if I can—keep the dragons at bay."

"Yeah," said Kitten. "Yeah, that makes a lotta sense. I need some time to digest it though. Can I get back to you?"

"It will be my pleasure if you do," said the doctor, as he opened the door for her.

✶✶✶

Driving back to the B and B, Kitten felt a strange sense of elation. "Respect," she thought. Experiencing respect was something new and intoxicating. Acknowledgement as someone who provided an important service was somehow exciting. She'd always thought of citizens as people who led dull lives punching cash registers or taking orders for fast food. The people she was now meeting were anything but dull. It was proving to be a great trip. As she thought about it, she got the impression that something within her was being filled. Even though she hadn't been aware of a void, she felt an emptiness being satisfied.

25

KITTEN GETS GASSED

The following morning, Kitten sat on the front steps of the B and B. Her blond ponytail cascaded from the back of a blue ball cap. A package containing the cap, a grey sweat-shirt, and pants that matched the cap was waiting for her at the B and B when she returned last evening. Although the ensemble sported no logos, she assumed it was cop-issue stuff. The quality was a surprise. They were nice threads, not unisex or three-sizes-fit-all. The sweatshirt fit her nicely al-though it could accommodate more than she had to put into the bust line. The pant hems were a touch shorter than she would have done them, but the garment was cut for a woman and zipped up the side. She'd liked the comfortable, profes-sional, image of herself in the mirror.

She absentmindedly twirled a lock of the ponytail while waiting for Stew. For some reason, she found waiting for him pleasant. Ordinarily, she chafed while waiting for any-thing. Today was different. The chirping of the birds sounded musical and the puffball clouds drifting through the brilliant blue sky imparted an idyllic quality to the scene. "Why am I noticing birds and clouds?" she wondered. Maybe being part of the way Garth made things happen was more intoxicating than she'd thought.

At precisely the agreed upon time, Stew pulled up in front of the B and B. Kitten was on her feet and reaching for the vehicle's door handle before it stopped. "Nice outfit," Stew said, as she climbed in.

"Garth sent it over."

"The guy thinks of everything. You'll blend right in."

"Never thought I'd want to blend in with a bunch of cops."

"Does it bother you?"

"No. In fact, I'm enjoying it. Surprised hell out of me, but I'm havin' a ball."

Stew was thoughtful for a few minutes and then asked quietly, "Do you care to elaborate on the 'surprised' term?"

Kitten reacted instinctively, "Why?"

Catching the defensive tone in her voice, Stew kept the tone of his voice quiet. "Because I'm interested, that's all." He turned his head toward her, gave a quick smile, and turned back to the road. "If you don't feel comfortable talking about it, I don't want you to. I just enjoy hearing you talk about yourself."

"Well, I guess you could say that Garth and I ain't been 'zactly on the same side of the fence."

Stew's lower lip covered his upper lip as he nodded. "I surmised as much."

When Stew didn't push for more details, Kitten felt an odd compunction to add them. "Family thing—daddy and in-laws involved—didn't know nothin' else until Garth came along." She fell silent. Why had she said that? Was she trying to make what she was more palatable to a citizen? Why would she do that?

"Thanks," Stew said in the same quiet tone. "I know it's difficult for you. No need to say any more."

For the remainder of the ride, Kitten struggled with both wanting and not wanting to reveal more of herself. Pulling into the training center parking lot was a relief. Inside, they were greeted by a lady in a halter top and shorts that were obviously from the same issue as Kitten's outfit. "Hi, Stew. You must be Ms. Jefferies, I'm Georgia Mathias," she said, offering Kitten a hand.

Still off balance from the conflicting emotions she'd been experiencing on the ride over, Kitten reverted to type. "Uh, just call me Kitten, everybody else does." She failed to notice Stew's expression of dismay.

"Good," answered Mathias. "Call me Rhino. Everybody else does."

Relieved, Stew laughed.

Kitten liked the handshake. It was firm and confident. Rhino was much like herself—all muscle, and sinew. If this was how she'd look in twenty years, it wasn't bad, not bad at all.

As Rhino released Kitten's hand, she said, "If you're ready, we'll get this show on the road."

"Lead the way," Kitten responded. Rhino was all business; she liked that.

Rhino led the way into a locker room. "Strip down to the skin—socks, undies, everything," she instructed. "Put your stuff in any empty locker. In that green cabinet, over there, you will find some paper coveralls. Put a set on and meet me on the other side of that metal door."

Kitten did as instructed. Through the metal door was a windowless room with tiled floor and walls. It smelled strange. Within, Rhino was chatting with Stew who was also clad in a pair of paper coveralls. Approaching Stew and Rhino, she held her arms wide and said, "Twins!"

Both Stew and Rhino grinned. "Have you ever been exposed to tear gas or anything similar?" Rhino asked.

"No."

"Ok, here's the drill. I'm going to be on the other side of that glass over there. You'll be able to see me at all times. Should you feel distressed to the point you want out at any time, hit that red button under the glass, and head for that door under the EXIT sign. The one you entered through will not open while this is in progress, so be certain you head for the exit. After I'm out of the room, I'll ask you if you can see me through the glass, and if you are ready to begin. Answer normally; the intercom is good. When you are ready, the green light above the window will come on. That means the irritant is being pumped into the room. Don't take deep breaths; breathe normally. Start counting. When you get to fifty, head through the exit door. On the other side, you will be in a shower room. The water will be running. Shower in the coveralls and then take them off. Barf right on the floor if you feel like it. Shower as long as you want to, soap and rinse several times. I'll bring you a robe. Any questions?"

"I don't think so," Kitten began, and looked at Stew. "But, uh . . ."

Rhino grinned. "Usually, this is not a co-ed exercise, but Galahad insisted on being in the chamber with you. He's had the antidote, so he'll be able to make it to another shower room."

"That's nice of you," Kitten began, "but I don't think . . ."

"Good idea. Don't think," Stew said firmly, "Just do what she says. You don't have any idea what this shit does to you. Humor me."

The profanity added emphasis to what he was saying. Kitten shrugged and said, "Carry on."

Rhino walked through the exit door and appeared on the other side of the glass. "Ready?" came through the intercom.

Kitten looked at Stew. "Whenever you are," he said.

Kitten looked back through the glass. "Fire away," she said.

Rhino smiled and nodded. The green light came on.

Kitten started counting. What could happen in less than a minute? Eight, nine, ten . . . she smelled a floral odor. Nineteen, twenty . . . her throat began to burn and her eyes felt gritty. Would she push the red button before she got to fifty? No way . . . she'd do a full minute before she went through that door. Thirty-five, thirty-six . . . everything from her eyes down through her throat seemed to be on fire. Forty-one . . . forty-two . . . it was getting hard to concentrate on the counting. Forty-nine, fifty . . . she bolted through the exit door.

Before she reached the shower, breakfast erupted down the front of the coveralls. She didn't care. Her only thought was to get to the shower. Without bothering to test the temperature, she plunged into the shower, held her face up, and batted her eyes. The burning lessened as the water washed through them. She found a bar of soap and lathered her hands. After rinsing them, she scooped handfuls of water into her mouth. The burning in her mouth and throat became less intense, but as soon as the water hit bottom, it came up again. She didn't pay any attention to where the puke went;

she rinsed off and repeated the process. She didn't think about where Stew had gone or who else might be in the room as she ripped the coveralls off and gave them a vicious kick. Showering had never felt this good. She lathered and rinsed several times. She gratefully took deep breaths of the steamy air and forced as much air as possible out of her lungs when she exhaled. A couple of times, the exercise produced more retching, but as soon as her gut calmed down, she went back to getting the crap out of her lungs.

As Kitten began to feel better, she noticed a bottle of shampoo on the shelf under the showerhead. She palmed a big gob and worked it into her hair. It was great stuff. After the third shampoo, she was feeling almost human again. "Dammed ugly shit," she heard someone say. She turned toward the voice and saw Rhino holding a terry cloth robe. "Put this on. Don't bother to towel," Rhino continued.

Kitten allowed Rhino to put the robe on her. It was luxurious, went down to her feet, and it was warm! As the warm cloth drew the moisture from her body, it felt like the last of the poison followed it. She knew it was probably an illusion, but it sure felt good. "God, that feels good—thanks," she said.

"Donno why that feels so great, but I know that it does," Rhino replied.

"Yeah, I'll say," Kitten answered, wringing water out of her hair.

Rhino produced a towel. "Here."

Kitten took the towel and began to dry her hair. "I suppose you've been through that?"

"Yeah, and lots of others."

"Do they all act that fast?"

"No, this one is faster and meaner than anything I've seen yet. It should be a great tool."

Kitten snuggled the warm robe about herself. "This is some neat . . . they teach ya to do this?"

Rhino smiled. "No, it's something I tried once and it seems to help the girls recover from the shock."

"The girls?"

"Yeah, I told the guy who runs this exercise for his gender. He tried it once or twice without much positive effect—probably has to do with the way guys don't appreciate a nice shower and shampoo the way we do."

"Could be," Kitten mused. "Uh, you said this business isn't usually done co-ed?"

"Yes, you are monitored at all times for signs of distress. I've had to drag girls out of the chamber, strip them, get them under the shower, and even give mouth-to-mouth once."

"Ugh, that couldn't have been nice."

"Un-nice in the extreme, but I won't go into the details. Anyway, we'll give you a couple of hours to recuperate. Then, we'll shoot you up with the antidote and do this again. Through the exit door of this room, you turn left and the second door on your left is the locker room where your clothes are. If you want to exercise, you may get some sweats out of the grey locker in there. If you want to kick back, continue straight out of the exit door to the patio. There are vending machines out there if your appetite returns. I'd encourage you to get something down before the next session."

"I'm starting to feel like I could chew right through the damn door to get to the goodies."

"Excellent," Rhino observed with a smile. "You not only look to be in superb shape, but appetite indicates that your general state of health is good."

"You a doctor?"

Rhino put her finger to lips and grinned. "Yeah—sports medicine specialist—but don't tell anybody."

Kitten followed Rhino through the exit door. Kicking back sounded best; she headed for the patio. The place could have belonged to a luxury hotel. A fountain graced the middle. Planters full of flora and hanging baskets of seasonal flowers were all over. A chaisse lounge in the sun beckoned. Passing the vending machines, she noted no coin slots. Everything looked interesting and uninteresting at the same time. Most of her felt hungry, but her stomach still felt queasy. She decided to pass on food for the moment, plopped down on the lounge, put her head back, and was out.

Kitten was unaware of any passage of time before she heard her name and felt a hand on her wrist. Rhino was kneeling next to her, taking her pulse. "Uh, are you checkin' up on me?" Kitten asked, as the fog cleared.

"Monitoring is the term," Rhino answered. "That shit plays hell with your electrolytes. Yours seem a little wonky. I'll be right back. Try not to go back to sleep."

"Wouldn't think of goin' nowhere," Kitten mumbled, as the fog cleared.

Rhino returned with a sports drink container that she offered to Kitten. "This should get things back on track."

Kitten sat up and took a couple of slurps. "Not bad. How long was I out?" she asked.

"About thirty minutes. When you hadn't awakened on your own by the third check, I decided we should do something about it."

"Every ten minutes sounds more like mothering than monitoring," Kitten grumped.

"Actually, your boyfriend kept shooing me over here to check on you."

The last wisps of fog vanished as Kitten's mind went to high alert. "My who?"

Rhino looked surprised. A slight frown passed across her face before she smiled. "Stew . . . the way he looks at you, I just assumed . . ."

"Dead wrong, girlfriend; we're working together, that's all."

Rhino's expression became sly. "So, you wouldn't mind my letting that stud muffin know he could eat crackers in my bed anytime?"

"Hey! I didn't say that!" Kitten blurted. She started to continue, "Besides, I don't think he'd . . ." but trailed off, realizing that her reaction was uncontrolled.

Rhino stretched and turned a satisfied smile on her. "I thought so. You don't seem to realize what a lucky girl you are."

Kitten wasn't accustomed to handling the same straight up, in-your-face treatment she dished out. "Meanin' what?" she said in a surly tone.

"Aside from being cute and built like a brick shit house, he's real. You can take anything that comes out of his mouth to the bank. If I had a guy like that looking at me, I'd have his bones jumped and hauled off to the altar before you could say scat."

"In that order?"

"Donno—depend on the situation."

Wanting to deflect the direction of the conversation, Kitten asked, "You been workin' with him here?"

"Yes."

"How good is he?"

"Better than good, he's lethal."

Stew? Lethal? Kitten couldn't make the concept compute. "Whaddya mean, 'Lethal'?" she asked, swinging her legs off the lounge.

Rhino sat beside her. "The other day would be a good example. Stew said that he'd prefer having a knife in a particular situation. None of the rest of us had any idea what he meant, so we asked him to demonstrate. He came back from the armory flipping this knife that he'd picked out. It wasn't as though he was fooling around with it, more like getting the feel of a new tool. After flipping it into the air a few times and catching it by the handle, he did a number that reversed his grip on it. He did a few more things, threw it into a tree, walked over, pulled it out, and said he was ready. 'Neck,' he said and disappeared behind the bushes. We were all listening and watching the bushes, but we never saw him until he poked out of them for a second and threw the knife into the dummy's neck. Then, he said 'Heart' and repeated the performance burying the knife into the dummy's heart. You don't see him coming or going when he doesn't want you to, and he seems to have an unlimited number of ways to create a corpse. Even though he may be the nicest guy I've ever met, he can be a killing machine."

Kitten felt a stirring in her groin as she listened. The picture of teddy bear Stew becoming a serious badass was fascinating and stimulating. "Good to know he can handle himself," she said, trying to keep her tone casual.

Rhino looked puzzled. "You haven't worked with him before?"

"Nah, Garth introduced us," Kitten lied. Likely, lying to Rhino was an exercise in futility, but she didn't know what else to do. Stew saved the day by bounding onto the patio.

"Hey, what are the haps? Is she ok?"

Rhino grinned as she raised an eyebrow at Kitten and stood to face Stew. "Yeah, yeah, Mother Hen, she's just fine. Her electrolytes are a little scrambled, but that'll pass. We were having some girl talk."

"Thanks," Stew said to Rhino and turned to Kitten. "Wanna do the obstacle course with me? Exercise will pump that junk out of your system."

Although her truest desire was for both of them to leave so that she could snooze in the sun, Kitten seized upon the opportunity to escape from the conversation with Rhino. She jumped up saying, "Gimme five to get some sweats on."

✳✳✳

The course failed to present anything that was a real obstacle for Kitten. The best way over, through or up any of the "obstacles" was apparent to Kitten as she approached them on a dead run. Stew stayed with her for the first few. She supposed that he was holding back to keep pace with her until she noticed the sweat running down his face. The idea that he was really trying fired her competitive tendencies and she kicked the pace up. Stew began to lose ground. A vertical obstacle appeared ahead and she noted a niche in the face that would provide purchase. She adjusted her stride to make a flying leap. The purchase was good; she yanked hard. Momentum carried her up to get a firm grip on the top.

Once over the obstacle, she didn't see any more of Stew. She finished the course and headed back for the patio.

✻✻✻

Now seriously hungry, Kitten punched up a couple of bottles of grapefruit juice and a roast beef sandwich.

The sandwich was gone by the time Stew came panting onto the patio. He plopped down beside her while wiping sweat out of his eyes. "Man, you smoked me good!"

"Peace," she said, opened the other bottle of grapefruit juice, and handed it to him. Stew downed it in two draughts.

"Want another?" Kitten asked.

"Sure, and a water," Stew answered, burying his face in the towel.

Stew downed the water in one long pull and began nursing the juice. "You are some good," he observed as his breathing returned to normal.

"Well, if you don't mind me saying, that 'obstacle course' is more of a pussycat run."

"Obviously, you have some specialized and highly developed skills. I surmise that they have something to do with this, er, enterprise that you and your family were involved in."

Ordinarily, someone getting this close would have alarmed Kitten, but she found it, rather—er, nice—from Stew. "Yeah, sorta," she answered.

"Most impressive!" came from across the patio. Stew and Kitten turned to see Rhino striding toward them. A stopwatch dangled from a lanyard around her neck. "You just broke the record for the obstacle course by almost three minutes. Mind telling me how in hell you managed that?"

"Just a young Jewish girl, trying to make a living," Kitten said, with a grin.

Rhino didn't smile back. Her expression was both exasperated and calculating. "I don't know where Garth came up

338   John A. Burnham

with you two, but I'm beginning to suspect a pool of talent exists to which we don't have access. If that's true, it pisses me off big time!"

Stew held his hands up. "Whoa, I can assure you that nobody in the law enforcement community is holding out on you. I understand your desire to have some of the things we are showing you in your curriculum. Once this operation is concluded, I don't see any reason why that might not be arranged."

Rhino continued to look sulky. "Yeah, ok. Kitten, how are you feeling? Ready to try that gas on again?"

Still high on endorphins, Kitten chirped, "Fight, fuck, or go for your gun, I'm ready."

Stew looked shocked, but the remark broke Rhino's sulk. "Hey then, let's do it," she said with a grin.

✷✷✷

In Rhino's office, Kitten grimaced as Rhino injected clear fluid into a vein in her arm. "Ugh, there's an awful taste in the back of my mouth."

"That's a good sign. It means that this stuff is interacting with your mucous membranes so that they won't be vulnerable to the irritant."

Kitten thought about that statement as she showered to wash off her second exposure to the irritant. 'Won't be vulnerable' was a bit optimistic. Her eyes, mouth, and throat hurt, but she had been in the chamber, breathing that junk for a full two minutes, and she was still functional. She had not experienced the panic for relief she'd felt the first time through. Moreover—as far as she could tell—she retained the ability think and make decisions. The antidote must have worked. As she dressed, she found herself thinking about the showdown. If she did her part right, Stew wouldn't be feeling any worse than she was now, while the bad guys would be in the same state of panic she'd experienced earlier in the day. He'd have a huge advantage. The thought was comforting.

Stew greeted Kitten as she came into the foyer. "Tough day's work, eh?"

"Been through worse, but I can't remember 'zactly when."

"Hungry?"

"Starvelous."

"There's a nice little Malaysian place a couple of blocks from here if you'd like to join me."

"I was thinkin' more along the lines of a steak."

"Montana's?"

"Now you're talkin'."

After they were in the car, Kitten ventured, "Glad we didn't run into Rhino on our way out. She was gettin' some intense—donno if I'd have known how to answer her."

Stew nodded. "That she was, but it's understandable. She sees us showing off moves and techniques that she's never seen although she's been working in an elite, inter-jurisdictional training center for fifteen years."

"That place ain't just for Jackson cops?"

"No, I gather that people from all over the country are trained there."

"Makes her a heavy hitter in this business."

"Yes," Stew agreed. "I think she is an acknowledged expert in the field of self-preservation and she's good—lots of fun to spar with because she's tough, fast, and able to change disciplines before you know what you're dealing with."

"So, besides bein' a doctor, she's an instructor?"

"Yes, her area is teaching people to recognize what martial art their opponent is using, and how to deal with it. You can see why we were upsetting to her."

"No, I can't. Maybe you can 'splain to me."

"She's dedicated her life to keeping cops alive. It's her job to know every trick in the book and the job of her boss to get her apprised of new ones. We show up with stuff she knows nothing about. My background has been alluded to.

She accepts the idea that the military doesn't want to admit some training. I gather that this isn't the first time the lack of interchange with the military has come up, so she has a pigeonhole for me. Then, you show up and blow the obstacle course record. She knows that SEALS and Rangers aren't co-ed, so she begins to suspect that you got your training at a civilian facility unknown to her."

"She don't twig onto the idea that I got my stuff outside of formal training?"

"Remember, she thinks you are a career law enforcement person."

"Ah, I got it now. She's not thinkin' outside the box. There's no place in her box for me to come from unless somebody ain't playin' nice with their colleagues."

"That's a bingo, lady."

26
Interest Declared

At the steak house, Stew watched in amazement as Kitten shoveled offerings from the salad bar onto her plate. "I could ask if they have plates with sideboards," he observed.

"Yeah, that would be good," she replied, balancing an artichoke heart on the macaroni salad.

In their booth, she began an assault on the plate, but became aware of Stew watching her. "What?" she mumbled through a mouthful of coleslaw.

"Oh, sorry, nothing," Stew replied and went to work on his plate.

About half way through the heap on her plate, Kitten looked up and asked, "Now that we're sittin' here all cozy and enjoyin' a meal, are you gonna try to convert me?"

Stew looked up, astonished. "Do what?"

"Y' know, tell me I'm a sinner and that I need to come to Jesus."

Stew put his fork down. "Why do you think I would do that?"

"Ain't that what you Bible thumpers do?"

Stew slowly removed the napkin from his lap, wiped his mouth, and placed the napkin on the table. Without making any effort to hide his annoyance, he turned cold eyes on Kitten. "I believe you have made some assumptions that are both unfair and erroneous."

The move sent chills through Kitten. Had his approval become that important to her? She sought to regroup. "Well, I thought your teachin' in a Baptist school and all that . . ." she began, but words to complete the thought failed her.

To Kitten, it seemed an eternity before Stew said, "I take grave exception to the accusation that I would have a religiously motivated agenda."

"What makes you different from other born—again types?" Kitten said with a pout.

"Again, you are making an unfounded assumption; I make no claim to being born-again. Since I have no recollection of my birth, it must have been sufficiently traumatic that my mind erased it. I have no desire to repeat the experience."

The lightness of Stew's tone as he delivered the last sentence lifted a huge weight from Kitten. "If you ain't intent upon leadin' all those little duffers down the path of righteousness, why are you teachin' in a church school? I know teachers make better bucks in the public system."

"Fair question. But the answer is complicated; are you sure you want to hear it all?"

The thought of Stew telling her about himself sounded better than a hot fudge sundae. "Yeah, every bit; but let me grab some entree before you begin," she said, rising from the table.

Returning, Kitten had a plate in each hand. As she set the plates down, one thumb slipped into the gravy. She put the thumb in her mouth and slurped the gravy off. "Ok, let's have 'The Life of Stew'."

"I come from a line of military people. My great—granddad flew fighters from carriers in world war two. My granddad died doing the same thing during Viet Nam. My dad was in the Navy. He is the original military buff. He bought every Tom Clancy novel as soon as it was on the shelves. He took my brother and me to every war movie as soon as it hit the theaters. We watched M*A*S*H and every other program or special having to do with armed combat on TV.

"Dad was none too pleased when I announced that I intended to pursue a major in history instead of joining as soon as I was out of high school, but he was always supportive of whatever my brother or I wanted to do. He let it go with a few remarks about history being a sound foundation for a military career. At that time, I had no idea of what I wanted to do. I intended to do a stint in the military, but I was interested in history, and thought I'd sniff out the academic world first.

"Although my dad's core philosophy was, 'My country right or wrong,' I had developed an interest in why people and nations do the things they do. At the time, I wasn't questioning whether the things this country did were right or wrong; I just felt a need to understand why. History seemed a good place to start. At that time, I was naïve enough to think that history was a record of past events."

"Ain't that what it is?"

"Unfortunately, no," Stew began with a smirk. "It's more a catalogue of whatever opinion best served the vested interests of the time."

Kitten sat back and laughed. "That's rich. It sounds right on. Can you give me an example?"

"Sure. I decided to concentrate on the B.C. to A.D. transition period because the events of that epoch are foundational to our society. For years, history texts dealing with that period have used the writings of a guy named Josephus as the primary reference. There are many reasons for that reliance, but the main one was availability. His writings are well preserved, and appear to be a fairly complete record of the Jews from antiquity through the first century. For decades, he has been regarded as a critical and authoritative historian. As more ancient documents have been discovered and deciphered, it has become apparent that he was a turncoat Jew who, in the interest of preserving his own skin, rewrote history for the pleasure of his Roman patron."

"No kiddin'?" Kitten answered thoughtfully.

"It's been a surprise to scholars, but it shouldn't have been. The idea of objectively recording events is a recent, Western idea. The ancients regarded writing as a means of teaching moral truths, as opposed to a vehicle for preserving a record of events. Old Josephus was portraying the Romans as the rightful rulers of the world. To him, rearranging, embellishing, or suppressing events was part of the job. To be certain, he was no more than what we would now think of as a spinmeister, but to give him his due, we need to understand that he lived in a remarkable time. He had played a dangerous card to gain favor with Vespasian and to avoid execution. Vespasian's subsequent rise to the position of emperor was the result of unprecedented events. He had every right to think that his time was unique and that the cosmos was undergoing a fundamental change, so he wrote from that perspective."

"Ok, I see, but back to you . . ."

"Yeah, right . . . As I began to doubt the accuracy of information in the history books, I started to feel as though everything stood on shifting sand. It was a time of confusion and disorientation.

"In a sense, I was saved from my despair by a Naval Recruitment Officer. He suggested I consider a career in Naval Special Ops. I jumped at the idea. It offered an exciting relief from my quandary. More importantly—I came to realize later—it pleased my dad. After I told him, he was on cloud nine. I've never seen him happier. When I was in boot camp and training, he wanted to know everything I could tell him. He saved every one of my letters in a loose-leaf notebook. He did the same thing with letters from my brother—everything from boot camp through flight training to his current deployment on a carrier. His apartment is filled with pictures of us in uniform, but there's only one or two of us as children."

"Is he living out a desire for a military career through you guys?" Kitten queried.

"I think so."

"His dad and grandfather were both military men. Do you have any idea why he didn't follow them?"

"As the son of a naval officer who died in the line of duty, he should have been a shoo-in for an appointment to the Naval Academy. Instead, he served four years as an enlisted yeoman."

"Yeoman?"

"The Navy's name for a person who performs clerk or secretarial type work."

"Lemme get this straight. His pedigree qualified him for an education that would have put him drivin' an airplane or a ship, but he wound up pushin' paper. Is that right?"

"Unfortunately, yes."

"Any idea why?"

"No. None at all. My brother and I spent a lot of time wondering about it between ourselves, but we've never asked him. By the time we understood enough to ask the question, we were also able to understand that if he'd had any inclination to discuss the subject we'd have heard about it before that time. I surmise something happened early in his enlistment that scuttled his chances of a military career. If that's the case, it would be extremely painful for him to talk about it."

"Ok, thanks . . . but back to you . . ."

"Yeah, I keep going off on rabbit trails, don't I? Well, my mindset was typical for the first couple of years. I derived great pleasure from following orders in a professional manner. I never questioned those orders because unquestioning obedience was basic to the job. When or where my skills were to be exercised rested with somebody higher up the chain of command. My upbringing and training had led me to believe in the moral correctness of the orders that came down that chain. That is, until I was on R and R after a messy job."

"R and R?"

"Rest and Recreation. It's paid time off. Well, as I was sitting on the veranda of a nice resort, browsing through the paper, I skimmed an article about the conviction of an individual who had killed a drug lord and his two bodyguards. I stopped skimming and read it over carefully because it was an image of my last job. He and I had done almost exactly the same thing. It hit me like a ton of bricks. His reward was a trip to the chair and mine was a paid vacation. The only difference was a matter of who gave the orders. I'm not questioning that the victims, in both cases, richly deserved what they got. I'm certain that the world is a better place without them, but the question is whether any person has the right to give those orders. The obvious answer is no. Therefore, what I did was wrong. The realization was a profound experience. In an instant, I realized one of the foundational components of my personal philosophy—the idea that it was morally right to obey the orders of my lawful superiors—was, in fact, completely wrong. A concept for which I'd put my life on the line several times was fundamentally flawed. The experience shook me to the core. In one fell swoop, the justification for everything I had become and everything I was doing evaporated. I went around in a daze for the next few days. I was back to the disorientation I'd experienced in college. I'd been raised to believe in the enterprise of war. Now, I knew it was wrong. But, what was right? I descended into a cloud of gloom, confusion, and guilt. I knew where it was headed. I didn't want to go there, but it was like quicksand sucking me in. The harder I struggled, the faster I sunk.

"On a particularly gloomy night, I gave up and reached out. I didn't have a clue as to who, or what I was reaching for. It was a final act of despair. The act of reaching out to something beyond myself transported me to place where I could see what was right—my inner compass. In that instant, I sensed that I was part of the infinite. Although my recent actions were not consistent with the grand scheme of things, I perceived that I was still part of the grand design and that following my inner compass would bring me into alignment with it. I saw that my confusion was the result of seeking a philosophy or system of ideas that was right. Since any philosophical or political theory is the product of fallible people like me, it can't be entirely right. In that moment of clarity, I perceived that the best any of us can do is to follow our inner compass, because that spark of the infinite will lead us—step by step—toward that which is right.

"I'd done that in following my inclination to understand history. I'd done that by staying in school instead of joining the military right off. When the going got rough, I stopped listening to my inner compass. When I saw an opportunity to get relief from my academic quandary and please my dad at the same time, I quit following my own inclinations and began following what other people dictated.

"In that instant of clarity, I could see how I'd accepted bits and pieces of information over time and built a house of cards that led me to blindly follow orders to do that which is morally wrong. I saw I have a responsibility to subject everything I believe to critical examination. Somehow, from that lofty place, I understood that being faithful to my inner compass and constantly subjecting my belief system to scrutiny are opposite sides of the same thing.

"Without actually realizing it, I became a person who would never again lay his life on the line for something he believed because—in the words of Bertrand Russell—'I could be wrong.'

"It was an experience like none other I've had before or since. Because of that confrontation with myself, I realized that what I really wanted to do was to teach, to help youngsters avoid the trap and unfortunate consequences of thinking what other people, the media and society in general tell them they should think.

"That, in a nutshell, is why I teach at Calvary. The environment there allows me to pursue those goals better than in the public system."

Placing her fork on the table, Kitten said, "That's a shocker. I'd have thought a school run by Baptists would require any staff to fit into a doctrinal straight jacket."

Stew grinned. "I don't blame you for thinking that, but there are as many kinds of Baptists as there are breeds of dogs. The folks at Calvary lean way toward the liberal end of the spectrum. They are so far left that I wouldn't be surprised to hear that some of their more conservative brethren are considering sending missionaries into their midst."

The remark struck Kitten as immensely clever. Or, was it the infectious twinkle was in his eye she found so engaging?

Stew continued. "The other thing is that the school isn't a part of the church as such. Although it rents premises from the church, it is run by an independent board of directors who are dedicated to providing a quality education."

"Ok, I guess I see," Kitten said thoughtfully, "but it still seems to me that being faithful to your opinions and not offending them at the same time, would be a tightrope act."

"It gets that way, but no more than maintaining the 'politically correct' guise one needs to function in the public system."

"Point taken." Kitten answered. "You gotta girlfriend?" she asked, looking into his eyes.

Stew nearly choked, but managed to recover enough to reply in the negative.

Kitten picked up her fork, munched a few more bites, and asked, "Mind my askin' why not?"

Stew put his fork down, wiped his mouth with the napkin, and sat back. Thoughtfully placing the napkin beside his plate, he answered, "I believe the psych people would term it a male-dominated youth. My father was a super-dad. As far back as I can remember, he was playing with my brother and me. Every weekend, he'd take us to a sporting event, movie or camping. Looking back, I don't know where he found the time, but he was always there to take us to ball practice, athletic events, and who knows what all. Whatever we wanted to participate in, he was right there, encouraging and facilitating. He must have spent a young fortune on gear of one kind or another. Larry—my brother—and I had the normal interest in girls, but it was the physical thing. We were typical jocks. We dated to get laid and that was it. Our involvement was with sports and the things we did with dad; the idea of a relationship with a girl never surfaced.

"In military special ops units, you develop a bond with the other members of your team as you train and face danger together. I guess the shrinks would say my military years were a male dominated extension of my childhood. They'd probably say that I've never had an emotional attachment to a woman because association with other men has always met my need for companionship.

"While that may be true to an extent, the larger truth is that I simply find women too fussy."

"Fussy?" Kitten puzzled.

"Yeah, they're always fussing with their nails, their hair, or something. They fuss about why they shouldn't eat this or that. They always seem to be tugging at a skirt or top that's too short to begin with.

"It's always the same old story. In the early stages of a relationship, I don't seem to notice the fussing, but the more time I spend with someone, the more I notice and the more it bugs me. I used to start out with high hopes that things would be different this time."

"Used to—meaning past tense?" Kitten asked.

"Yeah, I've stopped kidding myself. The problem is not with my dates; it's something I carry. After I realized that, I worked on becoming more tolerant and even tried living with someone. That ended as soon as I realized that the personal fussing now extended to the living quarters. Anymore, I don't even ask for dates without asking myself if the person is my type—which, I suppose, means fussless."

During Stew's confession, a question had been building in Kitten's mind. At first, she fought it, but the more she listened, the more important it became to know where Rhino stood with Stew. She had tried to ignore the tightness in her gut that the latter's expression of interest in Stew had caused, but now, the desire to know if that interest was reciprocated had built to a crescendo. The "Type" statement opened a window of opportunity, and she dived through. "How 'bout Rhino? She your type? There sure ain't much fussy about her."

"In a general sense, Rhino is the type of person I find attractive, but I have a hard time thinking about getting cozy with a girl who has been able to deck me a couple of times," Stew said with forced casualness.

The flip answer irritated Kitten. "Look, tell me it's none of my biz, but don't try to fake an answer."

"Sorry," said Stew as his countenance became pensive, and he began to toy with his glass. "I'm not so dense that I haven't noticed Rhino's interest, but it wouldn't be fair to encourage it." His eyes rose to meet Kitten's. "I will explain why if you want to know, but I'd advise against it."

"Advice denied. Spill the beans," Kitten blurted, now completely out of control.

"At this time, my interest is consumed by someone else."

Kitten rocked back. "I thought you said you didn't have . . ."

Stew held the eye contact steady as he carefully said, "I don't. The term 'girlfriend' implies reciprocity. That someone is you. With the difference in our ages, I don't see you having an interest in me. But, it would be unfair of me to start a relationship with Rhino when I spend most of my time thinking about you."

Kitten managed an appreciative smile as a hurricane of emotions raged inside her. She was relieved to know Stew wasn't interested in Rhino, but panicked at the thought that he felt a relationship with her was out of reach. After several awkward moments of silence, she managed, "Always the consummate gentleman, eh?"

"I try to extend the same courtesy to other people that I'd like them to give me."

"Rhino did think we were an item."

"Yes, I did notice a slight difference in her demeanor toward me today."

"Howzzat?"

"Well, before today, it was clear that she thought of me as available. Today, it was obvious I'd been shifted to the 'taken' category."

"Mmm, pretty sensitive for a guy."

"The ability to read unspoken communication is a survival skill for a teacher."

Kitten was pensive for a few moments. She munched down a couple of mouthfuls as she studied Stew. Then, she asked, "Is the age difference the only thing that's botherin' you?"

Stew looked puzzled. "Yes. Why do you ask?"

Kitten's head was down. She almost looked through her eyebrows as she said. "You've already scoped out that I'm workin' for Garth because I've spent some time outside the law. You're an educated guy. Culture and correctness ooze out of you. I have to work to make people think I'm not straight off the street. Getting hooked up with someone like me could jeopardize your job, your friendships, everything you are."

Stew smiled with understanding. "That's not quite right. Permit me to set you straight. If other people's opinions in this matter were of the slightest concern to me, it would indicate that my self-image is in jeopardy. Fortunately, I think I'm still intact because those considerations have never crossed my mind."

Kitten raised her head and locked eyes with Stew. "Maybe you oughta give it some thought because I don't see the age difference as a big deal."

Stew's eyes widened. He looked away from Kitten and around the room. He felt his composure crumbling. Thoughts of delights previously kept safely outside the attainable barrier in his mind came crashing into his consciousness like invading Huns.

When he looked back at Kitten, her chin was resting on interlaced fingers. A mischievous smirk danced in her eyes. "Gotcha," she said quietly.

Stew closed his eyes as he lowered his head and shook it slowly. "Damn," he said.

Kitten grinned. "That ain't 'zactly the most romantic thing a girl has ever heard after declaring her interest in a guy."

Stew looked up sharply. "Oh, I didn't mean to . . . I mean I'm sorry . . . I . . . I . . ."

Kitten reached across the table and put a hand on his. "Relax, Galahad. It's ok . . . you're in shock . . . can't tell ya how great it makes me feel to have that effect on you."

Stew looked at her. His eyes became moist. "You truly are the most amazing and exotic creature I've ever encountered."

"So why the damn?"

"It's the job. As long as I thought the only thing between us was a one-way crush on my part, I felt I could deal with it so my performance wouldn't be affected. Knowing that you feel for me puts a whole new dynamic in the equation."

Kitten mulled Stew's statement over before saying, "Yeah, I think I see what you mean. Now, there's a danger we're going to be thinking about one another's welfare when we should be giving full concentration to our own."

"Your perception never ceases to amaze me. Are you certain you were never in special ops?"

"Some of my ops have been special alright, but I'm merely street smart."

"I hope you'll tell me about them sometime."

"Yeah, I want to . . . sometime. However, right now, I propose we establish a boundary sign. I want to know everything there is to know about you, but I realize there is stuff you can't tell me. Moreover, there's probably stuff that you won't feel comfortable talking about until I've earned more of your trust . . . I know that's the way it is with me. Therefore, I propose we say 'whoa' if the other is approaching any of those areas."

"That's brilliant," Stew replied, as he beamed at her. "For the moment, I'll assume there is a 'whoa' on anything regarding your past."

"You're ok with that?"

"Ok and then some. Another thing that's always sabotaged relationships for me is the things I can't talk about. Women consistently regarded those areas as a threat. I can't express how much it means to have someone understand."

"Gotta been there to understand . . . ain't many people been where we have."

Stew shook his head. "I hadn't thought about that, but it's a darn fine basis for a relationship."

Kitten floated through dessert and the ride back to her B and B. She was jolted to reality when Stew double parked in front of her building, jumped out, and opened the door for her. She looked up at him from the seat. "Uh, ain'tcha gonna come in?"

"No."

Feeling a cold rush of disappointment, Kitten got out, looked at Stew, and asked, "Why? Don't you want to?"

"I 'want to' more than I've ever wanted anything. But, there is an innocent child who is depending on us being clear headed. I think he deserves that we not carry this thing between us any further until the op is over."

"Boy, are you one cold fish," Kitten said, as she alighted from the car. Stew closed the door and started around the car. "Ain't you even gonna kiss me?" Kitten said to his back.

"Please don't make this any more difficult than it is," Stew answered with longing in his voice and eyes.

Kitten watched the tail lights disappear. "Whatta guy," she thought. Turning down an opportunity to get laid because it might—not would, but might—interfere with his ability to help a kid he didn't even know. At that moment, she knew she loved him more than she'd thought it possible to love anyone.

27

A.P. Confesses

On the same evening that Kitten and Stew declared their mutual interest, Roz walked toward the door of her house. A.P. had left a message saying he wanted to talk with her that evening. She opened the door expecting bad news. A.P. had spent much of the previous week undergoing tests in the hospital. Since then, he'd seemed more preoccupied than usual. Had the tests suggested bad news?

A light came from the library doorway. She heard a fire crackling in the hearth. Tossing her coat over the newel post, she walked in. A vase of roses on the coffee table greeted her. A.P. lounged comfortably in his chair. Taking her chair, she noticed a glass of wine on the end table. She picked it up. "Are we celebrating or toasting?" she asked.

A.P. held up his glass. "That remains to be seen," he said with a smile, and took a drink.

Roz followed suit. It was good plonk, better than their usual stock. "Ok, what's up, bucko?" she said.

In an uncharacteristic gesture, A.P. feigned being hurt and replied, "Don't you like the flowers?"

"I love them, thanks, but I can't remember the last time you bought flowers and the idea of your taking the trouble to buy a special wine has me wondering."

A.P. nodded. "You are most correct. I'd be wondering if I were you. I think this occasion is special. At least, I hope you will regard it that way. I wanted to do everything right. I want to begin by acknowledging that I haven't been the husband you deserve . . ."

Roz interrupted when he paused. "And blah, blah, etcetera. We've been over that. Let's get to the real stuff. It's not just the wine and flowers, but it has been a long time since your mood was this jovial."

A.P. blushed slightly. He took a deep breath. "I . . . I . . . guess it has to do with . . . with being in love."

Roz felt a wave of shock that subsided into relief. She knew her eyes were wide when she said, "Do I know her?"

"No, no you don't. And, it's not her; it's him."

"Whaaat?" Roz blurted, her eyes going wider yet.

"The first day I was in the hospital, I was visited by the Chaplain. We hit it off well. Each day, his visits got longer. Finally, we had to admit a considerable physical attraction," A.P. said, looking at his wine glass. He paused, looked up at Roz, and studied her face for some seconds. Seeing no disapproval, he ventured, "You're not repulsed."

"Should I be?"

"Were I looking at a similar situation from without, I think I would be. Nevertheless, from within, I find it beautiful. I didn't know this about myself. Perhaps that's why I've never been much good as a husband. I have not been excited. I'd come to think something was wrong with me, like I didn't have the capacity to become sexually excited, but he excites me—intensely."

Roz closed her eyes and slowly shook her head. "That does explain a lot."

A.P. waited a full minute before asking, "That's it? You're not mad?"

Roz looked at him with loving eyes. "You old dog. How could I be mad? I was the unfaithful one in this deal."

A.P. put his wine glass down. "I'd hardly call one romp in the hay when you were drunk unfaithful . . . particularly with someone like me at home . . ."

"Whoa, stop!" snapped Roz with a frown. "I won't listen to you dissing yourself any more." The frown softened into a sly grin as she said, "You perverse old hound—porkin' a padre—how was it?"

A wide grin split A.P.'s face. "God, you are wonderful. Nobody else would have reacted that way. I love you."

"Yes, and I love you. But I still want to know."

"Unbelievable. Now I know what people mean by earthquakes. It popped the wax in my ears."

Roz hooted, drained her glass, and held it out for a refill. "Let's toast to new relationships."

A.P. poured. They toasted and sat quietly with their own thoughts for some minutes.

"Uh, do you think I should move out?" asked A.P.

"Why ever would you think that?"

"Well, I'd like to have Roy over once in awhile, and I'm supposing that you'd like to live with Frank eventually."

"All we need to accommodate Roy is separate bedrooms. It would be awkward if I had to come into the room for a pair of panties when you two were snuggled up in the sack."

A.P. looked incredulous. "You'd be ok with that arrangement?"

"Sure. I'll move into the guest room."

"Y' know, I could move out, leaving the house to you and Frank."

"Nah, if there is any future for us, it's going to be in a house he provides. He's been Mr. Catherine for too long. I'm not going to ask him to be Mr. Roslyn."

A.P. looked at her admiringly. "You are certainly one of a kind. I love you. If you weren't married already, I'd propose."

"Look at you now! How the mighty have fallen! Mr. Ultra-respectable Barrister turns out to be a closet gay who is now suggesting bigamy!"

They laughed their way through the rest of the bottle. When it was gone, they hugged and Roz retired to the guest room.

✳✳✳

The following morning, Kitten awoke to the buzzing of her cell phone. Thoroughly annoyed, she fumbled it to her ear and muttered "Yeah, goddamn, yeah."

"My, what a lovely greeting." It was Stew's voice.

"Wha timezit?" she replied.

"Seven-ish. Do you still love me?"

"Don' remember sayin' I did."

"You didn't need to."

"I'm pissed that you had to call. I'd have preferred a nudge."

"My apologies. How about breakfast?"

"That sounds good. Gimme half an hour."

After hanging up, Kitten jumped out of bed and began her ablutions. Her efficient routine didn't go as well as usual; replays of the previous night's dreams continued to interfere. It was a first time experience. Sweet dreams about a man were a most delightful way to spend the night.

It was closer to forty than the promised thirty minutes when Kitten bounded down the steps and through the door Stew was holding open for her.

"Sorry 'bout bein' late," she said as Stew slid behind the wheel.

"No prob. I can't believe you got yourself ready this fast as is."

"Normally, I'd have made it ok, but I guess I'm a little distracted," she said, sneaking a look at his profile and feeling herself blush.

"I find myself in the same condition, but can't say that I mind at all. However, I do feel that we need to let Garth know what is up with us."

"Ain't been much 'up' so far."

"You know what I mean. He needs to know we are emotionally involved."

"Yeah, I suppose. What do you think his reaction will be?"

"You can bet he won't appreciate it. As far as what action he might take in response, I don't know him well enough to guess."

"Ummm . . . about you not spendin' the night with me. Is there any more to it than limiting our involvement for the sake of the kid?"

Learning to follow Kitten's abrupt changes in conversational direction is going to take practice, Stew thought.

"Usually, it's the guy who gets accused of having a one-track mind," he quipped, groping for time.

"Yeah, you're right," she replied. "Normally, girls gotta fight guys off. Now, here I am, more than willing and the guy won't cooperate—it's got me wondering."

"Things happened quickly last night. I had difficulty keeping my head together. There is another aspect to why we can't have sex yet, but I couldn't imagine explaining it last evening. I want to be a good role model to my kids. Young people are constantly perplexed about sex; it's a normal part of growing up, but our society makes it hard for them to make appropriate decisions. I make no bones about being promiscuous during my jock days, but I now openly admit that it was wrong, selfish, and could be considered a form of bullying. I now maintain that sex should be reserved for a totally committed relationship—one which takes full responsibility for the entire welfare of any children that might result."

"You mean married?"

"Fortunately, I've never been called upon to define exactly what I mean by 'fully committed' because I don't know myself. I know many people who are legally married but are not totally committed. On the other hand, I know couples who, though not legally married, are. Therefore, I can't say that ecclesiastical or legal sanction makes the difference. I don't know what does. Therefore, I don't know what to tell my kids when they ask how to know whether they are totally committed. The best I can say now is that willingness to exchange vows and become liable for each other's credit cards is a good indicator."

"So, you wanna be able to tell those little duffers there hasn't been any panky going on between us until we are married, engaged, or something like that?"

"Yes, I do."

"Would a teeny fib hurt?"

"Sweetheart, you do need to understand that duplicity isn't part of me. I accept it as part of your background, but I can't go there. I'll never lie to you, but I also will not lie to anybody else."

The term of endearment softened the mild rebuke. Kitten felt both chastened and warmed. "Boy, you do know how to ruin a girl's day," she said through a mock pout.

✳✳✳

Millie looked up with a cheerful "Hi, Kids," as Kitten and Stew walked into Garth's reception area.

"Good morning, Ms. Prentice," Stew replied.

"Don't be a stuffed shirt—call me 'Millie.' Anyway go right in. Garth's waiting for you."

As Stew moved toward the door to Garth's office, Kitten put her hand to the side of her mouth and said to Millie in a mock whisper, "You gotta admit though, he stuffs that shirt well."

Stew felt color coming up his neck. Millie replied with a knowing nod.

Before they got to Garth's door, Kitten looked over her shoulder. Catching Millie's eye, she reached down, gave the cheek of Stew's butt a firm squeeze, and winked wickedly. Millie answered with an approving grin. SEALS had a reputation for being able to handle anything. She hoped to have the opportunity of watching this one deal with the tiger he had by the tail. Even through his dark complexion, she saw the blush on the back of his neck deepen.

Feeling apprehensive as they moved through the door to Garth's office, Kitten and Stew inadvertently locked hands.

Garth looked at them and said, "Oh damn! Goddam it all to hell!"

Stew went into shock at Garth's reaction.

Kitten was surprised for a moment, looked down at their locked hands, and began to giggle. "That's the second time I've received that reaction. D' ya' suppose it means anything?"

Garth remained stern. "I was afraid of this, but I was ho-pin' to hell that it would wait until the operation was over. Anyway, plant your butts."

Stew, with military obedience took a chair. Kitten went to the side of another chair as though she intended to push it closer to Stew. "Leave the furniture where it is," growled Garth. He leaned back in his chair, rubbed his eyes, and ran his hands through his hair. He saw the whole operation coming apart. "Civilians! Damn! For shitsake, what was I thinkin'?"

"I'm thinkin' you throw a good tantrum," Kitten observed. "You two guys will have to pardon me, but I can't see the problem."

Garth turned on Kitten with fierce eyes. "The problem is, Ms. Mouth, that having operatives who are more than professional associates in the same operation can get people killed." He studied Kitten. His countenance or the tone of his voice should have intimidated her. Instead, she sat there as though nothing more threatening than having her nails done was happening. His anger began to subside. She was exactly what he needed for this op. His tone of voice moved toward reason as he continued. "There is a danger that your, er, involvement could cause you to second-guess me during the operation. If I tell you to do something that you think might put himself over there in a pickle, you might ask me why instead of doing it. The delay could hand the advantage over to the opposition." He turned toward Stew. "Isn't that right, Mr. SEAL?"

"Yessir! Absolutely, sir. There can be only one person making decisions and giving orders if an operation is to be successful. Immediate execution of said orders without a second thought is critical to the success of the mission," Stew replied, as though he were in boot camp.

"Well said, Mr. Gung-ho," Kitten thought without saying it. Obviously, Garth's demeanor intimidated Stew.

"How in hell you gonna do that when there's somebody you're fuckin' in the op?" growled Garth.

Kitten saw the expression on Stew's face indicate that he was gaining some composure.

"Please allow me to clarify," Stew began. "Although Kitten and I have a mutual attraction, we have not been involved physically in any manner. By mutual consent, we have postponed anything of the sort until this operation is concluded."

"Yeah," Kitten interjected. "The clod hasn't even kissed me. The first time we've held hands is when we came through that door, just now."

Garth looked from one to the other with narrow eyes. "You tellin' me that you want to continue?"

"Yes sir," Stew chimed in. "I signed on with the welfare of the abducted child and that of future victims in mind. That has not changed. I will do my job with that single consideration in mind. I promise you that I will not consider Kitten's welfare during the operation."

Garth began to entertain hope that the operation might survive. "Yeah, I can believe that your training might enable you to do that," he said to Stew. Turning to Kitten, he asked, "What about you?"

"If you think it through," Kitten began, "you'll realize that I've been in more than a few situations where thinking about anything but the job at hand would have meant curtains. I'm gonna be there to get that kid out and put the scumbag under. I understand what your problem is now, but you can bet that I won't be thinkin' about sweet lips over there when I'm in that air-conditioning duct."

Stew felt the color rising from his collar again, but Garth began to feel better. "Ok," he began with eyes moving between Stew and Kitten. "But I want you to think long and hard about this. Put yourself in the position of being in the middle of the operation and hearing me tell you to do something that appears to put the other in jeopardy. Ask yourself if you can do it without questioning."

"Been there," Stew said. "On an op, I'm in the zone. You say jump and I'll be halfway up before you tell me how high."

How the order might affect anybody else won't enter my mind. It's a survival skill."

"And you?" Garth asked Kitten.

"Please give me some credit. The only view I'm gonna have of things is what I see through that grate. I've got enough sense to know that I won't have the big picture of what's going on. Thinkin' of anything but how to do what you tell me to do would be suicide."

"I like to hear that. However, it would take a lot more discipline than most people have to pull it off."

"Can you squat on a balcony, fifteen stories up, behind a goddamn begonia planter and concentrate on nothing but listening for thirty minutes?" Kitten asked with annoyance.

Stew's eyes went wide as he looked at Kitten.

Garth put his elbow on the desk and leaned his head to rub his eyes with the heel of his hand. When he looked up, he was grinning. "I guess I should take the remark about 'civilians' back."

The intercom on Garth's desk came alive. "Call coming in on the reserved line. Do you want to listen?"

"Yeah, put it on the speaker," Garth answered. "Looks like the scum are getting worried about their phone," he said to Stew and Kitten.

"Good morning, this is Eastern Bell, how may I help you?" It was Millie's voice.

A gruff voice answered. "You can get my goddamn phone fixed."

"What is the number please?"

"736-6219."

"Please give me a moment to retrieve that file . . . oh, my goodness. You requested that repair a week ago, and it hasn't been fixed yet?"

"That's right, lady. What's the holdup?"

"I can't see why it hasn't been done yet. Perhaps the order was misplaced. I'll reissue it with a priority tag."

"When will it be fixed?"

"Sometime within the next five to seven days."

"That ain't good enough for me. Lemme talk to your boss."

"Certainly, sir, please hold for my supervisor."

"They are getting antsy," said Garth, with a wink. "We may get some good intelligence out of this call."

"Hello, this is Mrs. Jacobsen. How may I help you?" came from the speaker—it was Roz's voice.

"You can git my goddamn phone working."

"Yes, I see that you requested repair a week ago. Please accept my apologies that it is not working yet. I note that the address for this number is a building listed as unoccupied. Sometimes our repair people take it upon themselves to put such requests on low priority. I know that is of little comfort to you, but it may be an explanation."

"Look, I don't care about why or what. You just jerk a knot in that clown's tail. I need that phone working."

"Certainly, sir. As a token of our apology for the tardiness of this repair, I am pleased to offer you some additional services free of cost. If you would please describe the nature of your enterprise, I shall see what might be appropriate."

"Don't need nuttin but that phone workin'."

"Well, sir, we are always interested in how businesses make use of their properties—particularly when they have been unused for a time."

There was a pause. Muffled sounds indicated that the caller was conversing with someone else with his hand over the microphone. Nervousness was apparent in the caller's voice when he replied. "Look lady, what we're doin' there is none of yer business. Can ya just guarantee me the phone will be workin' by this time next week?"

"Yes, sir, you may be assured of that."

Clicks indicated that the caller was hanging up. Garth grinned. "That Roz is amazing. She had him going by getting nosy. It appears they want to do that vid next week. Stew, will you be ready?"

"I feel ready now, but that gives us a good time frame. It's not good to train right up to the time of the op. A three-four day break is optimum."

"Perfect," Garth answered. "I'll tell Terry to give them back the line over the weekend. You should get a call from them Monday or Tuesday about a date for the debauchery."

A broad grin took over Stew's face. "Glad to see this show on the road. If you don't have anything more, I'd best get over to the center and finalize things."

"No, I don't have anything more for you," Garth answered. Turning toward Kitten, he continued, "But, as for Miss Muffett over here, we have something else needing attention. I'll get her to wherever she needs to go afterward."

Kitten and Stew looked questioningly at each other. Then, without a word, Stew got up and left the room.

"Love those military types," said Garth as the door closed. "They know when they're dismissed." He rummaged in a file drawer.

28
WILHELMINA NAHJIR

A wicked grin crossed Garth's face as he said to Kitten, "What do you think of the name 'Wilhelmina'"?

"Pretty dumb; can't imagine anybody hangin' that on a kid. Why'd ya ask?"

Garth's grin became sly as he handed Kitten the folder. "Have a look at this."

Within the folder, Kitten found the birth certificate for a Wilhelmina Nahjir. The date on the certificate was within a few years of her own birth. Flipping the certificate over, she saw a high school transcript. The grades were good—not outstanding, but consistently good. Under the transcript were pictures of a pretty girl with a creamed coffee complexion and black hair. Strangely enough, the eyes were as blue as hers. None of the pictures showed a child; all were of a young adult. The person was slightly heavier, but Kitten judged her to be similar in height and build to herself.

Looking up, Kitten said, "Ok, this Nahjir sadist named a daughter Wilhelmina."

"I didn't think you'd like that name."

"You're so right. So what?"

"I'm afraid you're going to have to get used to it."

"Whaddya mean?"

Pointing to the folder, Garth answered, "That's you. Amanda—a.k.a. 'Kitten'—Jefferies doesn't exist anymore. That's your birth certificate and high school transcript."

"I don't think I follow."

"My part of our bargain is to make your past go away. You now have a different past. Since Vertolio will have a continuing interest in Kitten Jefferies, you qualify for the resources of the Witness Protection program. Welcome to your new world, Wilhelmina. May I call you 'Willie'"?

Kitten looked down at the folder while she tried to assimilate what she'd just heard. She looked at the pictures and transcript. Was Garth telling her that the life of Miss Clean, average, young lady would now be attributed to her? She groped for something to say. "Why'd you guys come up with 'Wilhelmina'? Couldn't you do any better?"

Garth smiled indulgently. "We didn't 'come up' with it. Wilhelmina Nahjir is, or was, a real person. The birth certificate and transcript are genuine. Now that she doesn't have any more use for them, you can continue the life she started."

"But . . . but . . ." Kitten protested, "Her complexion is much darker than mine and her hair is black . . . and her facial features . . ."

"I'm assured by our people who deal with such things that the tanning bed and beauty salon will take care of all that."

"Ya mean," said Kitten, as it all started to sink in, "I can show this transcript and it will be just like I'd gone to school?"

"That's right, Willie."

"And people will think the parents and childhood this girl had are mine?"

"Right again, Willie."

"Jeez, I never liked 'Amanda,' I guess 'Wilhelmina' ain't much worse . . . could get to likin' 'Willie,'" Kitten mused. Then, she looked up and made eye contact with Garth. "Uh, we ain't done with this op yet. I didn't think the biz of makin' my past go away would happen before then."

Garth became grave. "Our deal wasn't conditional on the op being finished. In any case, you've already done enough to earn this."

"And?" Kitten pressed, not letting him escape.

"And," Garth began, raising one eyebrow. "I wanted your payout to be a done deal before this thing actually comes down."

"Whyzat important?"

Garth sighed, sat back, and looked at the ceiling. "Ok, ok, if this thing turns messy, I may wind up in a position where I couldn't deliver on my promise. This way, you have your payout before the curtain goes up on the last act."

Admiration and gratitude flooded over Kitten. She couldn't think of a thing to say. Garth broke the ensuing silence. "About your Gram."

"Gram, Gram!" Kitten thought. She'd been so immersed in her own considerations that she hadn't thought about Gram. "Yeah, what about her?" she asked.

"There's a little retirement community in Corpus Christi that is favored by retired law enforcement people. It wasn't planned as such; it just happened that way. Your Gram is getting to the age where she won't be able to look after her yard much longer. With you out of the picture, that aspect will be increasingly important. Her moving to a gated community providing yard maintenance is a natural step. Nether Vertolio nor any of his ilk will have any interest leaning on a person whose friends and neighbors are retired cops."

"Why does that make a difference?"

"Think it through. Older people are infamous for keeping track of everything that goes on in their neighborhood. Retired police types are no different; if anything, they are worse snoops. In addition, they are snoops with connections and time on their hands. Anybody prowling around that neighborhood runs the risk of having an identification run on them. Plus, nothing excites ex-cops like a chance to 'get back in the game.' If anyone tried to lean on your Gram for information about you, it would be like handing a pair of their shorts to a bloodhound. Vertolio et al would consider approaching anyone in that community an unacceptable risk."

"That sounds cool. How long will she have to wait to get in there?"

"As we speak, she is negotiating for the quarters of a deceased Chief of Police."

Kitten grew silent as she thought about the finality of severing her connections with everything and everybody in Florida.

After some minutes of silence, Garth handed her another piece of paper. "Here's your itinerary for the rest of the week. We need to get you looking like Willie before we can make up a driver's license and other identification."

Kitten looked at the paper. The next four days were packed. While she was studying the schedule, Garth spoke. "Is a trip up to Tennessee on Sunday ok with you?"

"A who, where?"

"Willie's parents live in Tennessee. He's of Syrian descent; she's German. He's retired FBI. He wasn't a field agent, some sort of technician. You need to meet them. You can drive up there Saturday night to meet them on Sunday and come back that evening."

"Yeah, I'm cool with that. I've been wantin' to stretch the 'Vette's legs."

"While I understand that, it does bring up another little matter. That 'Vette of yours is too distinctive. For safety's sake, I don't think you should be seen driving it with your new look."

"I gotta get rid of my 'Vette? No damn way!"

"Look, Vertolio knows the car. When you don't show up in Florida after this is over, he's going to put out feelers. We need your 'Vette to show up on some used car lot in Florida. That will make the trail cold."

"You want me to take it to Florida and sell it?"

"No. I don't want you to set foot in Florida again—not ever. You remember Frank Grant, don't you?"

"Yeah, Roz's unauthorized piece. It still boggles me to think of a dish like her playin' around with a nondescript like him."

"I've done some wondering about that myself, but Frank is an automobile broker. He has agreed to move the 'Vette for you, and he has a possible replacement. You take it to Tennessee and see if it suits you."

Kitten was in a daze as she exited Garth's office. "See you later, Willie," said Millie.

Startled, Kitten looked at her. The older lady had a kind smile on her face. "Uh . . . oh yeah . . . see ya later," Kitten stumbled.

✳✳✳

On Friday, Kitten bid a fond farewell to the B and B proprietor. She threw her stuff into the 'Vette and drove to Sunland Motor Cars. Frank came out of the showroom doors as she entered the parking lot. He motioned for her to follow the driveway leading to the back of the building. She found a parking spot, shut the 'Vette down, picked up a magazine, and waited. It was a full quarter hour later when Frank came out of the back door of the building. She rolled down the window as he approached.

"No sign of your being followed," Frank said, smiling.

"Garth seems to think of everything," she answered, shaking her head.

"That he does. Well, hop out and I'll show you the wheels I found for you."

Frank led the way to a rather pedestrian-looking powder blue two-door sedan. It was the sort of thing driven by young, professional women.

"What is it?" Kitten asked, not trying to hide her disdain.

"It, or at least the body parts, started out life as a Buick."

"A Buick for chrissake!"

Unperturbed, Frank continued. "I don't think many Buick parts remain."

"Whazzat mean?"

"Here, have a sit," Frank said, opening the door.

Kitten settled into the softest leather seat she'd ever encountered. "Mmmm, nice," came out before she thought of anything snarky.

"The adjustments are on the side of the seat."

An array of buttons greeted Kitten's probing hand. She looked over at the panel. "You'd need a flight engineer to run that damn thing," she remarked.

"It has three axis adjustment, plus lumbar support, heat and massage."

The rich wood steering wheel felt marvelous. A large screen stood where the console ran up into the dashboard. "T.V?" asked Kitten.

"GPS and views from the low light cameras mounted front and back."

As Kitten turned the key, a plethora of lights, around the instruments, in the dash, on the console, and overhead began to glow. Further turning brought forth a throaty grumble. Light pressure on the accelerator caused the tach needle to hop toward ten grand. "Wow, what kind of mill is that?" Kitten exclaimed.

"I believe it started out life as something Volvo makes. It's a V-6, turbo, intercooler, etc. I think the horsepower rating is close to three hundred."

"You keep saying 'started out life as.' I take it most of this rig has undergone extensive modification. Who made it? Who would want a car like this under an econo-Buick body?"

"I can't honesty tell you who did the mods, although the technical details are extensively documented. As far as why they were done, I can't tell you that either. Part of my deal is that I can't reveal the source of these vehicles. There are more of them around than you'd think."

✳✳✳

Kitten pulled the Buick into a motel and looked around. This is what it was going to be like for a while. One, at the most two, nights at a motel and then move on.

✳✳✳

Saturday was bright and clear. Kitten flicked the Buick over the twisty roads of Mississippi and Tennessee. Begrudgingly, she admitted that this thing would smoke the 'Vette in any situation. Moreover, the ride was wonderful! She'd always equated the 'Vette's stiff ride with good handling, but this thing was cushy over the bumps and would out-corner the 'Vette anywhere.

A chime sounded. The radar detector was sensing something. She downshifted and decelerated to the speed limit. The chime became more insistent. Was the thing also telling her how close the radar was? She glanced at the console display. A red triangle had appeared ahead and on the left side of the road. As she came abreast of the triangle, she caught the glint of hubcaps behind a signboard. With the triangle showing behind her, the chime began to slow down—sweet! The Buick seemed to be equipped with every gadget known to man.

Although Kitten was having a ball exploring the car's trinkets and handling qualities the kick kept getting interrupted by anxiety over the impending meeting. Up until now, aggression had proven to be an effective way of dealing with the unknown, but how could you be aggressive with people who were giving you their lost daughter's identity? Try as she might, she couldn't formulate a battle plan. Would these people like her? Would she like them? What would happen if they found her disagreeable? Lord knows, enough people had, but it wasn't important in the past, now it was.

Each time her thoughts returned to the troubling subject, she found it more intractable and she felt herself feeling lower. This would never do. She cast about in her mind and found Roz's face. Crazy Roz who thought that you could make things go your way by feeling good about them. Roz's description of the process was more elegant, but that's what it amounted to. Crazy as hell. Crazy? Really? How could somebody so crazy have a track record like Roz's? That stuff wasn't a fad with Roz. It was a cornerstone conviction. Maybe she should try it. What did she have to loose?

Kitten tried to imagine how good it would feel if the meeting with the Nahjirs went swimmingly. Since she had no idea of what particulars might result from a positive meeting, she was trying to imagine the feeling without knowing the details. It was tough, but she worked at it every time her thoughts returned to the meeting. Gradually, she was able to experience the glow. Whether there was anything to this approach or not, it was better than fretting.

✳✳✳

Early—for Kitten—on Sunday morning, she studied her reflection in the hotel room mirror. The face looking back at her had a creamed coffee complexion framed by black hair in a pageboy cut. It amazed her what a few sessions in the tanning bed and some makeup had done. The latest picture of the original Willie hung on the side of the mirror. She studied it, picked up an eyebrow pencil, and made an adjustment. It was incredible. For all the world, the face in the mirror was Willie a few years after the picture was taken. Satisfied with the morning maintenance routine, she put on a white blouse, blue skirt, low heels, and a blazer that matched the skirt.

The GPS in the Buick led her down a pleasant tree-lined street and stopped in front of a modest rancher with beautifully tended gardens and lawn. Kitten parked, shut the growling steed down, took a deep breath, and stepped out. Practicing relaxation exercises, she walked up the curving walk. At the door, she smoothed her clothes, took another deep breath, and pressed the doorbell.

A sixty-ish, matronly woman opened the door. Looking at Kitten, her eyes went wide. (Kitten noticed that they were the same blue as Willie's eyes.) She stepped back as though trying to regain her balance and shouted "Oh, my God! Haj! Come quick!"

Not certain what to do, Kitten stood quietly.

A large man with olive skin appeared from behind the woman. As he came to her side, he put an arm around her and smiled appreciatively at Kitten. "Please pardon my wife; it is a shock to see someone standing at our front door looking like our little girl all grown up."

"I understand," Kitten began unsteadily, "I'm K . . . er . . . Amanda Jefferies; I believe you were expecting me." The woman continued to stare at her.

The man maneuvered the woman out of the doorway as he said, "Yes, we are . . . so glad you could come up to meet with us . . . please come in."

The woman gained some composure as she turned down the hallway muttering something about cookies. The man stepped aside as Kitten entered. He motioned toward the living room. "Please sit with me in here."

The tastefully appointed living room featured pots of growing things and minimal furniture. Artwork, probably limited edition prints, adorned off-white walls. Kitten seated herself on the Danish Modern sofa as the large man took a chair that was obviously his. Gesturing widely, he said, "Welcome to our home, Miss Jefferies . . . or, may I call you Willie?"

"Willie would be best, and it ah . . . isn't Jefferies anymore, I guess," Kitten replied, as she struggled to recall the diction lessons.

"Ah yes, quite so," Haj responded. "This is going to seem a little strange to both of us for awhile, but Willie, Willie Nahjir is who you are now. Therefore, that's the name we should all use." He folded his hands beneath his chin and looked earnestly at Kitten. "Willie Nahjir, Willie Nahjir," he repeated softly to himself. His eyes became moist. "It's so good to be able to look at you and say that."

The sight of emotion from a big, solid, man put Kitten off balance. She didn't know what to say. The discomfort of the moment was broken when the blue-eyed woman glided into the room and placed refreshments on the glass-topped coffee table with blinding efficiency. "Well," thought Kitten, as she noted the bloodshot eyes, "a good cry has morphed the basket case at the door into the ultra-capable Teutonic hausfrau." She and the woman exchanged smiles. Straightening, the woman looked at the man in the chair. "Oh, Haj, you've been blubbering again." She crossed the room, pulled a tissue from her pocket, and handed it to him.

"Thanks, Ingie," the man said, mopping his eyes.

The woman seated herself on the one unoccupied piece of furniture in the room. "Please pardon my performance at the entryway," she said to Kitten.

"S' . . . er . . . That is understandable," Kitten said with effort.

"You might think you understand, but you cannot . . . not really," Inga replied.

"A straight shooter," thought Kitten. This was good.

"You see, dear, the final year of our daughter's life was most difficult," Inga continued. "She deteriorated rapidly. As the end came, it was hard to recognize her as the healthy, vibrant girl we'd raised. Seeing you standing there, beautiful and full of life, it was almost as though her sickness had never happened."

"I think that's the mindset we need to cultivate," Haj interjected.

Kitten looked from one to the other as she worked out a reply free of contractions and slang. "I think I'm a little lost here. Could you please help me with some background?"

"Certainly, dear, certainly," Inga replied. "This has happened very quickly. Probably, we all suffer from information deprivation. Willie was always an active person. She was active in sports as both a participant and cheerleader. During her senior year in high school, she became unable to maintain her schedule of physical activity. After graduation, she was diagnosed with leukemia. It was a particularly aggressive form. She was gone less than two years later."

Inga paused. Sensing that she didn't have anything more to say now, Haj related an anecdote from Willie's days as a cheerleader. As he finished, Inga related how she and Willie had enjoyed doing crafts together. The narrative hand off from one to the other continued until Kitten drained the last cup of coffee from the carafe. Haj fell silent as Inga bustled off to the kitchen.

Kitten was impressed. Instead of the one-upmanship, interrupting, and attempts to dominate that characterized conversations with most couples, the Nahjirs waited patiently for the other to finish, said their piece and handed the ball back. Obviously, they each considered their partner's contributions as valuable as their own. It was refreshing. Kitten had not been looking forward to listening to a couple of people talk about their kid, but this wasn't what she'd dreaded. The longer they talked, the more comfortable she felt.

Inga returned with more coffee. She augmented the offering of cookies with muffins. Kitten snagged one with cinnamon frosting. It was Dutch apple and excellent. As she ate with relish, she noticed that Inga and Haj were looking at each other and smiling. Resisting the habit of licking her fingers, she demurely wiped them on a napkin, looked up, and said, "Yes?"

The couple looked at each other as though trying to decide who should answer. Finally, Inga said, "You used to fight what you thought was a weight problem. When you were in high school, you would never have downed a pastry that way."

Noticing the change of reference, Kitten replied, "I suppose that's not the case anymore. People tell me I eat like a horse. I never give it any thought."

"That's wonderful," Inga replied, beaming. "Although I could understand your concern, I always had the mother's worry about eating disorders. They seem to affect so many young women these days. In fact, as we were talking, I felt a twinge of worry because you are so trim."

Inga and Haj lapsed into silence as they sipped their coffees.

The subtle change of reference wasn't lost on Kitten. In a measure, they were starting to think of her as Willie. It felt weird, but surprisingly good. She decided to follow suit. After a couple more bites of the muffin, she ventured, "Uh, if you don't mind my asking, why did you make my identity available?"

The silent exchange between Haj and Inga about who should answer ensued. Finally, Haj said, "I assumed we'd get around to that. We don't mind you asking. In fact, you need to know. It's our way of building a memorial to Willie. She had such potential, so many dreams . . . her death seemed such a waste. Offering her identity to someone who had performed a service to society seemed a way to ensure that the life she had started wasn't wasted."

For the first time in her life, Kitten experienced a feeling of profound unworthiness. "Uh, how much do you know about the 'service' I'm performing?" she asked.

"Detective . . . er . . . I guess it's 'Director' Moore now . . . outlined the case and your role in the investigation," Haj answered.

"We're most impressed with your courage—a little thing like you—taking such risks," Inga added, beaming.

For a person whose primary personality trait was impertinence, the feeling of a blush rising up her neck was unnerving. Kitten ducked her head and asked, "Did Garth mention why I'm helping in this investigation?"

"No," Haj answered, "I wouldn't have expected him to, either."

Without being able to help herself or meet their eyes, Kitten dumped the whole truck—her family story, history of burglary, and deal with Garth—on them. When she looked up, she was astounded to see them looking at each other and smiling contentedly. "Knowin' who I really am didn't put you guys off?" she asked.

Haj sat back and laughed. "Hey, my parents may have come over on the boat, but it wasn't the one last night. Your story isn't any different from what I expected."

"I don't understand," Kitten said.

Haj held up a hand and began ticking off points. "One, you are not a law enforcement type because you need witness protection. Two, the people you are after can't represent the danger to you, so you must have expertise that organized crime wishes to exploit. Three, your contribution to the current investigation indicates that said expertise lies in the area of clandestine entry. Four, who—other than a burglar—has that expertise?"

"You guys don't mind a person with my past taking your daughter's identity?" Kitten asked, hardly able to believe what was happening.

Inga took the lead. "On the contrary, my dear, it fulfills our deepest desire. Willie intended to study criminology because her goal was law enforcement. She had a dream of being in law enforcement to help young people headed down the wrong path. She didn't want to be a counselor. She wanted to be out where she'd make contact with young people before they even knew they needed counseling. In short, she wanted to be able to do exactly what Mr. Moore has done in your case."

As Inga talked, the idea that had been flitting around in Kitten's mind like a will-o-the-wisp, crystallized into a lifetime goal. Her composure returned. She looked confidently from Haj to Inga. "I'll do my best to honor her memory."

Haj smiled. "I have no doubt that you will. Do you have any plans for the future that you'd feel comfortable sharing with us?"

"Well, the first order of business is school. Although I now have a transcript that would get me in, my fiancé thinks I should fill in some gaps before attempting university."

"Mmm," Haj began, "that seems reasonable. Does he have any projection regarding how long that will take?"

"He figures he can have me ready for next year's fall term."

"Will you devote the time between now and then to study?"

"Yeah, I guess."

Haj's countenance became serious. "Tell me if I seem to be prying, but have you considered where this study is going to take place?"

The freedom she felt to reply surprised Kitten, but it felt good. "Not actually. Even though my fiancé teaches in Florida, it wouldn't be wise for me to go back there. He feels obligated to finish off this school year there. It looks as though I'll be lighting somewhere without him. We've had some brief discussion on the subject, but we haven't come up with any plan yet."

Haj looked at Inga. She nodded at him. He turned to Kitten. "You may light here. You could have Willie's . . . er . . . your old room back. We've talked about this and we think it would help your transition if you could be immersed in her things and get used to thinking of us as your parents . . ." Haj looked startled for a second and then embarrassed. "Oh, please forgive me. I didn't mean to be presumptuous. I don't mean that we would, in any way, replace your parents . . ."

Kitten laughed. "I think it's a great idea." She looked from Inga to Haj. "Mom, Dad, one does not refer to the queen of the big top as 'Mom.' Even though I called my father 'Daddy,' I could never think of him as the head of the household, the provider; he was more my buddy. Therefore, the two cubbyholes in my psyche labeled 'Mom' and 'Dad' were unoccupied until this afternoon."

Haj began to sniffle. Inga handed him a Kleenex and grabbed one to dab at her own eyes.

Kitten waited for a few moments before continuing. "Living here sounds great, but what about neighbors, brothers and sisters, friends, the people who knew Willie?"

"There aren't any of those around here. Willie never occupied the room we are offering. The plan to build her a memorial by giving her identity to someone else germinated during her last year. We moved from the west coast immediately after the funeral. Our parents have passed on, and she is an only child," Haj explained.

Kitten brightened. "Staying here would work out perfect. It's a long haul from Florida, but I'd be distracted if Stew were anywhere close. He's going to be making applications for a position at other schools, so I don't suppose we'll be getting married until we know where his next job is. You might have me around for a good while."

"He shouldn't have any difficulty finding another position," Inga observed. "I'd think he could have everything put together before the term ends. You'll probably be able to set up housekeeping as soon as school is out."

"That could be," Kitten replied as her face took on a sly look. "But, I plan to throw him a curve that might make the relocation a tad more difficult."

"And that would be?" Haj asked.

"After I complete my junior year, I'm going to apply to the Police Academy. There's no sense in making another move to be where that is."

Haj and Inga beamed, speechless.

Kitten tried to look innocent. "After all, isn't that what I was going to do?"

✳✳✳

The growl of the engine became a song as Kitten danced through the gears to hold it between seven and eight grand. When the tach read in that range, the car had wicked acceleration out of corners. She'd found a switch that caused driving lights to illuminate the road like noon. She made a mental note to find out where they'd come from next time she stopped. It was close to midnight, but she was higher than a kite, and having a ball. "Crazy Roz, Crazy Roz," ran through her mind. If things always worked out as this day had, the lady was crazy like a fox. In fact, she was onto something that should change the world. Kitten hoped that the change she and the rest of Garth's team planned to make in a certain little corner of the world, later in the week, worked out half as well as today.

29

THE OPERATION COMES TOGETHER

Kitten's cell phone began to jangle. She pulled a pillow over her head and ignored it. The noise stopped, but immediately resumed. The caller was redialing without leaving a message. She reached out and swept everything, including the lamp, off the night table. The crash was satisfying, but the phone continued to demand attention. She'd left the damn thing in her jacket pocket. The ringing paused and resumed. "Somebody is in a real sweat to talk," she thought while swinging her legs out of the bed. She found the phone, thought about smashing it, but flipped it open instead.

"Willie! Good morning!"

"I . . . I . . . think y' got the wrong number."

"No, I don't honey. It's Millie. Wake up. Garth needs to see you as soon as you can get down here."

"Can't you transfer me to him?"

"No, he was very clear. He can't discuss this over the phone."

"Yeah, tell him I'll be there in forty-five."

"If I have a breakfast bagel and coffee waiting, can you make it in twenty?"

"Yeah, ok, but make it two of the kind with sausage and egg."

"You got it . . . see you in twenty."

"Damn, this must be important," thought Kitten as she dressed. As her head cleared, she realized the case must be heating up. Excitement replaced her morning mad. She packed everything, paid for the room, settled for the damage to the lamp, and headed downtown.

As Kitten hurried into the office, Millie handed her two bags and motioned her through Garth's door. Stew was there. She gave him a smile and settled into the unoccupied chair.

Garth looked at her critically. "Where's the Willie makeup?"

"One, some asshole is in an all fired panic to see me; I didn't have time to put it on. Two, I busted a lamp in the hotel room. I thought it best to avoid the Willie look when I told the desk clerk to add the price of the lamp to the tab; people remember that kinda thing."

Garth nodded at Stew. "By Jove, I think she's getting it!"

Without acknowledging, Kitten dug into the bags and began munching.

"We gave the scum their telephone line back on Saturday," Garth began. "That evening, they told Terry to check out the alarm system. Yesterday, they left Stew a message saying he could view a taping on Wednesday."

"Hot damn!" said Kitten around a mouthful of bagel. "Party time!"

Garth didn't share her elation. Gravely, he addressed Stew. "You ready?"

"Yessir," Stew replied crisply.

"Lionel and Rhino agree," Garth said, tapping a pencil on the pad before him. Turning to Kitten, he asked the same question.

Kitten swallowed the food she was chewing, took a sip of coffee, and looked directly at Garth. "Yes, I am."

Garth put his elbows on the desk and began rolling the pencil between his fingers. He looked from Kitten to Stew and back again. "Are you two still dead certain you can obey my orders during the op without consideration of what effect they might have on the other?"

"Yes . . ." Stew began.

Garth cut him off by holding up a hand. "Before you answer, consider this. The first priority here is the safety of the child. Second is your safety. Third is taking this guy down. That's the way it's gotta be; that's the way I'll call the shots. Can you guys take my orders without thinking of anything but how to carry them out?"

"Yessir!" replied Stew, straightening in his chair.

Kitten's posture was more casual. "Have you seen anything in my performance thus far to indicate I'm thinking about anything other than how to do what I'm told?"

Garth put the pencil down. "No, in fact, your performance has been exemplary; few professionals do as well."

"That will continue. I know my view will be limited. I'd be stupid to outguess the guy with the overall perspective," Kitten replied matter-of-factly.

"Sir, if I may," Stew interjected. "Our relationship is on hold. As we promised, we have seen little of each other since our last conversation on the matter."

Kitten bit her tongue. The way Stew reverted to treating Garth as a military superior was nauseating. Nevertheless, this was not the time to say anything.

Garth sat back and rubbed his eyes. "Don't get me wrong guys, I appreciate your talent and dedication, but it's just that . . . that . . ."

Kitten sat up straighter and interrupted him. "It's just that if much goes wrong, you're toast."

Stew looked at her—horrified.

Garth chuckled. "Yeah, I guess."

Kitten continued. "I may be nothing more than an uneducated, small-time thief, but I see the picture: If we rescue the kid and catch the scum with a smoking gun, you are a hero. On the other hand, if anything happens either to the kid or to one of us, you are toast. The shit will be so deep you'll never get out. I know that, you know that, but it's the kid's only shot. I don't see that we—you, the Stewball, and I—even have a choice. If we let anything deter us now, the kid's gonna meet an end that nobody deserves. None of us wants to live with that on our conscience. We are in a spot too, and our one hope of jumpin' slick is to do exactly what you tell us."

Garth visibly relaxed. He'd needed to hear that from her. He hadn't recognized the need, but it had been there. He'd been able to impute that understanding to Stew, but Kitten was an unknown quantity until now.

"Ok, here's the drill," Garth began. "The scum have told Stew they'll pick him up sometime after 11 p.m. We'll maintain the stakeout on Authier's place. They will be designated 'Stake.' The officers disguised as street people observing all four sides of the building will be designated 'North,' 'South,' 'East,' and 'West.' The stakeout observing the door of the escape tunnel will be designated 'Exit.' Kitten will be designated 'Eyes.' The SWAT teams who will storm the front and rear entrances will be designated 'Front' and 'Rear'. I'll be in the command van. My call sign will be 'Nero.' I don't want anybody to forget who's running the show.

"As soon as it gets dark, I'll take up a position a few blocks from 1295. North, South, East, and West will then take position. Eyes can scale the wall as soon as she thinks it's safe. We'll then wait for the baddies to show up. Once we are certain that everybody is inside, Front and Back will move to positions within a block. As soon as Eyes reports seeing the kid, we'll move in, but here's where things will get dicey.

"Ideally, Eyes will fire the grenades into the room at a time when Stew and the kid will be on one side of the blast and the scum on the other. Stew, you'll have to try to produce such an opportunity. You'll have to be bushy-tailed all the time. As soon as Eyes reports a favorable arrangement of the people in that room, I'll tell her to fire.

"Eyes will get out as soon as she fires the grenades into the room—no holding back to see what effect they had—just fire and get out.

"I'll bring the control van into a position that blocks the street to the East of Exit's position and a White Door will move in to block the street to the West. Hopefully, the scum will be disoriented and preoccupied with getting out."

"I don't think there will be any other thought in their minds," Stew observed. "I've experienced some ugly stuff, but nothing that induces panic like that crap."

"And the antidote? It really works?" Garth asked. In spite of Rhino's assurances, he needed to hear it from the participants.

"Absolutely," Stew exclaimed. "You can tell you've been exposed to the irritant, but the effects don't happen."

Garth looked at Kitten and waited.

"Aside from putting a pig-farm-taste in the back of your mouth, the stuff does work. I can't claim to be as enthusiastic as Mr. Gung-Ho over there, but with it in my system, the irritant didn't make me dysfunctional."

Garth looked from one to the other. "Any doubts at all about using it?"

"None whatever. It's our edge," Stew replied.

"Nah, it's probably what will make this thing work," Kitten agreed.

Garth distributed handouts. "Here are diagrams of the area around the building, where our people will be, and a list of their handles. Practice visualizing each position while saying the designation. Any questions?"

Stew piped up. "Let's imagine the following: Eyes sees me close to the child; she hasn't reported seeing Authier yet; there is space to lob the grenades between us and the others in the room. What would be your call?"

"Think about the priorities," Garth answered.

Stew thought for a minute. "You'd tell her to fire."

"Exactly. I'd encourage you to think about different scenarios. Try to answer them according to the priorities. If you run into any difficulty, give me a rattle, and we'll discuss it."

"Yessir," said Stew.

"Gotcha," said Kitten

"Any other questions?" Garth asked as he sat back.

"Not now," Stew answered.

"None that I can think of," Kitten replied.

Garth took a deep breath. Kitten thought it looked like a sigh of resignation. He turned his palms up. "Well, I guess it's a go. Now that I know you guys are ok, I got other ducks to line up. Scat and get all the rest you can."

"Yessir," said Stew as he stood.

"Scatting . . . Nero," said Kitten.

Thirty minutes after the departure of Stew and Kitten, Garth hung up the phone for the umpteenth time. Everything was coming together beautifully; he was having no trouble lining up the resources. If things had gone this well when setting up a previous op, he'd have been on cloud nine. This time, however, he was uneasy. He sat back, rubbed his eyes, and considered why. After a few minutes of reflection, he thumbed the intercom button. "Millie, please locate Ms. Cornelius for me."

"One each Roz comin' right up."

Garth went back to his checklist and tried to think of contingencies for each item, but he couldn't focus. Mercifully, line one lit up in short order.

"Hi Garth, Roz here."

"Hi. Uh, you busy?"

"Are you inviting me up for a cup of Millie's coffee?"

"That or I could meet you someplace."

"Actually, I'm oot and aboot at this moment. I can be there in ten."

"That would be much appreciated," Garth answered, and hung up. He looked around the office for a minute, got up, and walked to the outer office. "Millie, please whip up some of that road tar Roz likes. She'll be here in a few minutes."

"One Americano coming up. I'm glad you called her; you've been looking in need of some shrinking."

"Whaa . . ." Garth started. No use trying to hide anything from this lady. "Yeah, it's the idea of using these civilians. It's against policy, good sense and a number of other things."

"It is that," Millie answered, "but I'm amazed we are this close to the people who make those videos. I'm sure our usual investigative techniques would have tipped them off. Your outside-the-box thinking appears to produce remarkable results."

"Have you been talkin' to Roz?"

"No. Why?"

"She's always talkin' about thinking outside of the box."

"Once this operation is over, I want to get to know her better; she seems full of challenging, interesting ideas."

"That she is. Send her right in when she arrives."

Garth went back to his office and paper, but it didn't go any easier than before. Millie announced the arrival of Roz within a few minutes. Without realizing it, Garth settled back to enjoy watching her walk in. As the office door opened, he realized what he was doing and privately reprimanded himself while trying to gain a more professional frame of mind. He had no need to bother. The person who walked in was wearing geeky horn-rimmed glasses with her hair pulled back into a bun. The loose-fitting tweed business suit made her look more like a sack of potatoes than the slick tomato he knew her to be. Where was the entertaining walk? Did the suit hide it too? He stood.

"Roz, good to see you."

"Nice to see you too," she replied. Garth was relieved that the intellectual trappings couldn't hide the smile that made him glad to be a man.

"I didn't know you wore glasses."

"I usually wear contacts—vanity, you know—but glasses are better for the egghead look."

"Here, have a sit," Garth said, moving around the desk and holding a chair for her. After Roz had seated herself, Garth took a chair on the other side of the coffee table. "Millie should be in shortly with your coffee. So, you been egghead-din' this morning?"

"Egghead marketing is closer. The company made a presentation to a potential client. I was there to advertise their intellectual depth. All I did was look geeky, present my résumé, and put some techno-babble on them."

Millie appeared with coffee and condiments. After placing them on the coffee table, she turned to Garth. "I won't put any calls through unless they are urgent."

Garth gave her a warm smile. "Thanks."

"Mmmm, superb!" Roz said after sampling the Americano. "Millie, you could put Starbuck's out of business."

"Thank you, but the credit should go to the beans. Great coffee isn't that difficult if you have the right grind. Starbuck's would go down on their own if they paid what we do for that coffee."

Roz raised one eyebrow. "Are you trying to hide a secret recipe behind modesty?"

Millie giggled. "Not at all. I'll be glad to show you how I do it—the beans, the grind, the brew, and the rest."

While the girls talked, Garth stirred his coffee, lost in thought.

As Millie closed the door behind her, Roz interrupted his reverie, "I hope this is a positive update."

Garth shook his head slightly as he came back to the present. "Uh, yeah, it is. The scum are going to do a vid on Wednesday night, and we're ready for them."

"Are you certain they have the child?"

"We're not a hundred percent on that, but your suggestion that Authier might be holding him at his residence may have paid off big time. Our JW ladies found most of the neighbors are suspicious of him. He rebuffs any attempts to get acquainted or to involve him in neighborhood activities. The lady across the street is particularly suspicious because the comings and goings of his muscle look to her like something out of a gangster movie. She has allowed us to use her house for surveillance. It's perfect. The angle gives us a view of the front of Authier's house as well as a look down the driveway that goes from the street around to a garage in the back. Authier's house backs onto a green area. We mounted a camera in the bushes. It gives us a view of the back door and the vehicles parked back there. The garage is detached; there's no way anybody could get from the house to a vehicle without us seeing them."

"Nice. Have you seen anything interesting yet?"

"We haven't, but the lady who owns the house we're using said she thought she saw a child's face appear briefly from behind the drapes a few days ago. It disappeared immediately, so she didn't get a good enough look to give us a description, but she was certain that it was a child."

"Well, it does sound as though we are closing in."

"Thanks—in a large measure—to your input."

"You are more than welcome," Roz replied.

Garth savored the delicious smile for a few moments and then grew pensive.

Roz sipped her coffee while watching Garth turn his cup back and forth in his hand. After a few turns, she asked, "Something bothering you?"

"Yeah . . . no . . . it's just that . . . I donno, I guess I need to talk about it."

"So talk."

"It's this idea of using civilians . . . I mean Kitten and Stew . . . it's unorthodox . . . I don't think my predecessor would have let me do it."

"Are you troubled about going ahead with the operation?"

"I don't see how I can do anything else. It's the kid's only shot."

"But, if it doesn't come off the way you have planned, you are in deep doo-doo. Is that right?"

Garth nodded solemnly.

Roz returned the nod, looked out the window, and sipped her coffee. It was a full minute before she turned back to Garth. "I think you are assuming too much responsibility. It is getting in the way of your knowing what your next step should be."

Garth grinned. "I knew your opinion wouldn't be anything I expected. Proceed."

"Let's start with how the case has built up to this point. You are a narc. Your even being on this case is the result of a rather remarkable set of coincidences. Right?"

"Yeah, I'd have to grant you that."

"And, your big break—Frank and me coming to you with the disk—dropped into your lap."

"Right again."

"Whatever help I've been, Kitten's turning out to be more than you hoped for, Stew—Mr. Perfect for this assignment— coming out of the woodwork, all of these things were more or less handed to you."

"I've mentioned before that a cop's job is connecting the dots."

Roz's expression took on the mischievous look that Garth had come to associate with her getting ready to drop a zinger. She didn't disappoint him. "Ever get the idea that some-one—or something—is handing you those dots to connect?"

Garth became quiet. He rose, walked over to the desk, and thumbed the intercom. "Mille, could we please have refills?" He returned to the chair, but instead of looking at Roz, he looked to the corner of the room and studied the Old Man's picture. Neither he nor Roz said anything until Millie had retreated from delivering cups of fresh brew.

Garth took a sip, set his cup down pensively, and made eye contact with Roz. He arched an eyebrow. "Do you real-ize that you are forcing me to consider something I've been avoiding?"

"That wasn't my intent, but if it is happening, I'm pleased."

"As I mentioned in previous conversations, my MO isn't standard cop issue. You're the first person, other than my uncle, I've ever discussed it with. I'm not real comfortable talking about it, even with myself. It's always worked and I've become good about knowing how to work it, but I guess I've avoided thinking about the why."

Roz's expression became soft, caring. "Please let me in-terject something. I consider your reaction understandable. All of my adult life, I've enjoyed being in situations where kookiness is expected and is, sometimes, an advantage. Peo-ple like you don't have that luxury. Usually, being different is a huge handicap. I think the way you've managed to capi-talize on your uniqueness without spooking other people is admirable."

"Yeah, the thought has crossed my mind that something or someone bigger than myself hands me stuff from time to time, but I don't see how it impacts on the decision I have to make."

"Ok, I'll lay it out. In my opinion, that bigger someone, call it God, the universe, serendipity, whatever—the label makes no difference—has a grand scheme. There's no way that we can know the goal of that scheme. We can perceive it as making the world a better place, enlightenment, any number of things, but our ability to understand is too limited to grasp even a fragment of the ultimate intent. The only thing we can do is play our part. I see everything that has happened from the beginning of the universe until now as elements of an unfathomably large mosaic. We each fit into a particular place in that design. Our role is not to influence the design, but to come into harmony with what the designer is doing. Therefore, the question for you is not whether or not to go ahead with the operation, but what the next step is for you."

"But I'm the guy in charge . . . it's my responsibility to . . ." Garth protested.

Roz held a hand up. "Back off stud. Think for a minute. Consider your last take-down. You paused before driving into that alley. Once you felt centered, you went in. Did you stop to think whether or not it was the right decision?"

Garth looked slightly exasperated. "Of course not! I was concentrating on the next move."

"Bingo. I'd suggest, at that moment, you knew you were operating in concert with your intuition, your right brain, or whatever, so you had complete confidence that things were going to pan out as they should."

Garth pursed his lips. He looked from Roz to the Old Man's corner. His brow furrowed. He looked out the window. Slowly, his head began to nod and he turned back to Roz. "Yeah, I guess that's what happened. I'd never have put it that way, but thinking of it in those terms is as valid an explanation as any other."

"As you turned into that alley and opened your door, did you feel responsible for the results?"

"Why . . . I . . . ah . . ." Garth began. His eyes widened. He looked at the Old Man's corner again. He turned back to Roz. "No. I've never given it a second thought. In those situations, I know I have to let my intuition take over, so I guess I hand the outcome over to it. Yeah, at those times, I know things are out of my hands."

Roz smiled broadly. "Yep. Isn't that the story on the rest of life? Isn't that why they say that the best laid plans of mice and men usually amount to the same thing? We can scheme and connive all we want, but things have a way of going where they will regardless of where we try to push them. Why not concentrate on the next step and leave the overall outcome to the universe?"

"Yeah, that's right on. I need to concentrate on the things requiring immediate attention. The final go or no go won't happen until we deploy troops on Wednesday night."

"Now you're thinking. Uh . . . have you ever called an operation off at the last minute?"

"Coupla times."

"What was the reason you called them off?"

"They just didn't feel right."

"Did cancelling them turn out to be the right call?"

"Damn right. In one case, we had bad information. We'd have looked like supreme fools if we'd acted on it. In the other situation, the people weren't where we thought they were. Moving in would have tipped our hand. Backing off gave us the chance to nail 'em when we could."

"Let me be certain I have this right. In both cases, you had conducted a thorough investigation and all the information you had on hand indicated that a bust would be appropriate."

"Yep, that's the way it looked."

"And, the only thing that stopped you was because, when the time came, it didn't feel right. You hadn't received any additional information that would change your mind. It was strictly a matter of your intuition telling you something wasn't right."

"Thass what happened."

"The ole intuition has been bang on every time, but now that the stakes are higher, you're having trouble trusting it."

"Sounds sorta dumb when you put it that way."

"Perspective m' man. It's an exercise in maintaining perspective. Our culture, our institutions, our education, and even our entertainment teaches us to ignore the right brain and to try to do everything with the left. It's no wonder that you, when presented with an unfamiliar situation, try to do a left brain analysis instead of waiting for your connection with the cosmos to show you the next step."

"Weird the way that works isn't it?"

"Not exactly. The left brain doesn't appreciate things that can't be classified and measured, so it doesn't trust intuition and instinct. Whenever we face an unfamiliar situation, we naturally try to deal with it via left brain techniques. It takes discipline and practice to maintain a right brain orientation."

Garth sat back comfortably in the chair. He raised his cup and smiled. "Ok, teach. Right brain it will be, all the way."

30

THE TAKE DOWN

Kitten clung to the wall of 1295. The night was perfect for kitten burgling. Warm temperature allowed minimum clothing. The clouds formed an overcast that blocked starlight while being too high to reflect city lights.

Headlights flashed down the street to the north! She flattened herself against the side of the building. The headlights disappeared without passing. Had the vehicle turned down the street at the west end of the block? She waited. Her headset came to life, "Nero, Exit. A black Escalade tag NKG-465 just went in. Make and color positive. Lights come on in the tunnel when the door goes up. Occupants unknown. Windows are heavily tinted."

"Nero copies," returned over Kitten's headset. Aha, the vehicle had gone into the escape tunnel. The party was beginning. She tightened the strap holding the launcher and grenades to her back. The extra weight and bulk made the climb different—not difficult, but different. She didn't need the extra weight swinging around.

As Kitten reached up for the handhold to pull herself onto the roof, another set of headlights appeared on the street to the west. No place to go. She froze. As before, the lights disappeared without passing.

"Nero, Exit," came over the headset. "Light blue Ford panel van tag PSF-663 just went in. Two occupants visible."

"Nero copies."

Kitten hoisted herself over the parapet wall and down onto the roof. "Nero, Eyes. On the roof," she said into her mike.

"All stations, Nero. Anybody see her?"

"North, negative."

"East, negative."

"South, negative."

"West, negative."

Kitten resisted the impulse to giggle. Garth had begun the evening with a stern lecture to the whole team about radio discipline. The discussion about protocol seemed silly to her at first. The idea of beginning each transmission by identifying yourself, and following with the tag of the person you were addressing, sounded like war movie stuff. As the team discussed coordination details, she saw the necessity. It was the only way to keep everybody on the frequency appraised of the big picture.

"Eyes, Nero. Carry on."

"Eyes copies."

About twenty feet to her left, a fixture that hadn't had a bulb in it for years looked over the parapet wall and down onto the street. She moved to it, put her feet on the wall to either side of the conduit, and pulled with all her strength. It didn't budge—good! She clipped the escape rope to it, made certain that the coil was neat, and that the little beacon Garth had supplied was on the end she'd grab. It was another neat touch. Damn good thing, she reflected, that she hadn't known how tricky these cops were. She moved from the shelter of the parapet wall. After about a dozen steps, her headset came alive. "Nero, Red. I have Eyes about halfway between the east wall and the equipment enclosure. No visual, IR only."

"Damn," thought Kitten. Yesterday, Garth had found that he could add a surveillance point atop one of the adjacent buildings without risk. That one had been designated "Red" because he was equipped with infrared detection equipment. Red had spotted her. She ducked and made herself as small as possible behind a vent pipe.

"Nero, Red. Contact lost."

"Eyes, Nero. Don't be cute. Just get on with it."

Kitten became peeved. Since this would be her last burgle, she wanted it to be perfect. Damn techy shit anyway.

"Nero, Red. Got Eyes moving toward the enclosure."

Kitten stopped against the enclosure. The scum might use the ventilation system when they were in the building. She couldn't hear the sounds of machinery. She pulled the stethoscope out, connected it to her headset, and put it against the wall. No sounds of machinery running, only . . . only . . . voices! They were too faint to understand, but definitely voices. They were three stories down, but some sound was coming up through the ducts, into the plenum and this giz was picking it up. Sonofabitch, this stuff was sweet. She undid the access cover and carefully moved it out of the way.

"Nero, Eyes. Going in."

"Nero, Red. Lost contact."

"Eyes and Red, Nero. Nice coordination."

Inside the enclosure, Kitten used her flashlight to check the fan. The locks were still in place. She inspected the blades. They had not banged against the locks. Probably, the thing didn't work—good. She spoke into her mike, "Nero, Eyes. Fan appears inop."

"Eyes, Nero. Proceed."

Kitten moved through the fan, along the duct, to the plenum access. She put her ear against the access door—nothing. She put the stethoscope against the door—voices again. Slightly louder this time, but still too faint to understand. Slowly, she opened the door and used her flashlight to look around the plenum. It looked exactly as it had the last time. She moved into it and began her descent. At the third floor access door, she repeated the listening exercise. Now, she could make out the words with her ear against the door, but it was much clearer with the stethoscope. She listened for several minutes. The conversation revolved around equipment checks and lighting—exactly what would be expected. She spoke into her mike, "Nero, Eyes. In position to go silent. Can hear techs setting up equipment."

"Eyes, Nero. Anything to indicate that either the child or Authier is on the premises?"

"Nero, Eyes. Negative on both."

"Eyes, Nero. Proceed."

"Nero, Eyes. Copy—going silent."

Kitten pulled up her left sleeve. The buttons on the wrist unit glowed faintly. She pressed the one with the check mark on it.

"Eyes, Nero. Receiving check."

Kitten pressed the button with the Y on it.

"Eyes, Nero. Receiving Yes."

Kitten pressed the button with the N on it.

"Eyes, Nero. Receiving No. Proceed."

Kitten slowly moved the access door latch to halfway open. It hadn't made a sound, but she listened through the stethoscope for a full minute. No change in the voices. She put the stethoscope away and moved the backpack and launcher around to her front. She opened the door. Now, she heard the voices. She moved her body halfway through the door and froze, listening. The sounds emanating from below didn't change. She moved into the duct on hands and knees. Carefully, she checked under the backpack and launcher—nothing hanging down to make noise. She moved a hand forward and listened. Then, she moved the opposite knee forward and listened. Proceeding in this manner, it took about ten minutes to get to the grate, but it enabled her to do it without making a sound. The light coming up through the grate made seeing easy. She pressed the check button on the wrist unit.

"Eyes, Nero. Confirm that you are in position."

Kitten pressed the Y button on the wrist unit.

"Eyes, Nero. Receiving Yes. Proceed."

Kitten unbuckled the backpack and launcher. She opened the pockets of the backpack and placed it where she could reach in easily. She affixed the flash grenade to the launcher, armed the device, and positioned it where she judged that she'd be able to lift the grate and fire the grenade with one motion. She positioned the irritant grenade where she'd be able to grab it as she pulled the launcher out of the hole. Then she squirmed around, trying to make herself comfortable.

Even though everything had gone exactly according to plan, Kitten was anything but comfortable. She studied the room below. She saw a small stage affair with straps hooked to the walls. Lights shone on it. In front of it, a video camera stood mounted on a tripod. Microphones hung from the ceiling and cables ran everywhere. Four burly men stood around observing. Had Kitten known of them, she'd have recognized three of them as the persons known to Frank as Carlos, Jamie Herron and the menacing young man who had received the mangled disk. Three other people were involved in testing the equipment.

She considered the upcoming sequence of events. Bring the kid in, put him on the stage, everybody else move behind the camera. The best time for getting a grenade between the scum and the kid would be after they put him on the stage. Stew needed to get in front of the camera. She tried to figure out how that might happen, but couldn't make it gel. Stew would try to produce an opportunity, but she couldn't see it happening. If they came in together, he might be able to do it, but there was no reason to think it would go that way. From where she was sitting, it didn't look good.

According to instructions from the scum, Stew and his "bodyguard" were sitting in a limo a few blocks away. There hadn't been any instructions regarding whether they were to be escorted in, or led in, or what. The time and location were the only items in the communiqué. It was a good bet they would not be in the room until just before the camera began rolling.

Kitten's gut tightened. She couldn't fathom how this was going to work. For the first time, she wondered if it would work at all. Now that she could survey the scene below, the thought of Stew being down there brought pangs of panic. This would never do. She took a deep breath and let it out in stages. If this op was going to have a chance in hell of working, she had to get control of herself.

She forced herself to look away from the troubling scene below. A memory of her delivery from the clutches of consternation a few days ago flickered through her memory. Roz—crazy Roz! She needed to keep an eye on what was

398 John A. Burnham

going on. As she looked back trough the grate, she deliberately thought about a girl talk session she'd had with Roz.

She'd been fascinated with the calmness Roz displayed regarding the situation with Frank. It was obvious—though she couldn't understand why—that Roz wanted Frank with all her being. However, she seemed content to wait. Kitten, on the other hand, could never see herself waiting if her relationship with Stew was in jeopardy. She'd always seen herself as a person of action—a woman in control of her own destiny, someone who moved the pieces where she wanted them. Now it was obvious that the idea had been a deception.

The cops on one hand, and Vertolio on the other, could have made the rest of her life a hellhole anytime they chose. Yeah, Roz had something when she said that the best we can do is to listen for the next step. In fact, she was right in saying that we get in the way of what the universe wants to do when we try to steer things. Suddenly, it dawned on Kitten that her relationship with Stew was indeed in the same type of intractable jeopardy as was Roz's relationship with Frank. The details were different, but the overall situation was similar. Well, she might be nothing more than a minor thief but she knew enough to go with the best track record. Roz's was a whale of a lot better than hers, so she determined to concentrate on hearing the next move. She didn't have long to wait. Her headset came to life.

"Nero, Stake. Authier is on the move. Black BMW, no other persons in the vehicle. No sign of the child."

Kitten looked at the launcher. The safety was off. The ready light glowed green. She practiced controlled breathing. Ten minutes went by before the radio came alive again.

"Nero, Exit. Black BMW going in."

"Hot damn," thought Kitten. She adjusted her position to keep an eye on the door. Within a few minutes, Authier came through it. She touched AU on the wrist unit.

"Eyes, Nero. Understand that you have Authier in sight. Any sign of the child?"

Kitten touched N on the wrist unit.

***

Officer Arnold Barrett shifted in his chair. He'd been gratified when Garth assigned him the stake position. It acknowledged him as number two man in the operation. He thought the promotion of Garth to the Old Man's chair to be a good move. Perhaps he would now occupy the same position with Garth that the latter had enjoyed with the Old Man.

A soft beep and a red light above the monitor displaying the back of Authier's house grabbed Barrett's attention. The system was detecting movement. A figure had emerged from the back door, moving toward the black SUV parked in front of the garage. A second figure emerged. Barrett studied the monitor closer. Was that one figure or two—a large person and a small one? Suddenly, the figures separated. The smaller one ran past the SUV. Both of the larger figures pursued. Barrett made a split second decision. He grabbed the microphone attached to one of the radios at his elbow, made an effort to control his voice and said, "Unit 38, Stake. Block the driveway."

"Stake, 38. Moving," came from the speaker.

The two men cornered the child against the hedge. As they grabbed him, he turned directly toward the camera. "Get me a face," Barrett said to the technician at his side. The tech punched keys furiously. The face of a terrified child appeared on one of the monitors. It was the right one! Barrett hit the priority button on his comm. unit. A squeal came through everybody's headset.

Kitten winced as the priority screech assaulted her ear. It was the signal for everybody to give way to a message having precedence over anything else.

"Nero, Stake. Positive ID on the child as they tried to muscle him into the SUV. White door moving in to block the driveway now."

Barrett grabbed another microphone. "Dispatch, Barrett. We need backup, now."

"Barrett, Dispatch. Unit 87 is within ten blocks of your position."

"Barrett, 87. We're on our way"

"87, Barrett. Approach from the east with lights and siren."

Squad car unit 38, with lights flashing and siren wailing, screeched to a stop, blocking Authier's driveway. Officers Wade and Svensen alighted and took up positions on the street side of the vehicle as the siren died.

The child struggled against the beefy arms to no avail. His captors looked at one another in shock. They crouched behind the SUV.

Squad car unit 87 pulled to an abrupt stop facing unit 38.

The child fastened a vicious bite on a fat thumb close to his mouth. The owner of the thumb yelled in pain and released his grip. The child thrashed, kicking him in the nuts. The man bellowed again and bent over as he clutched himself. The child's kicking feet caught him in the ear. He stumbled backward, looked up at the flashing lights, and ran around the back of the garage.

Officer Lansing was opening his door of unit 87 as the figure emerged from behind the garage and began to run across the grassy area toward the bushes. Throwing his hat on the seat, he gave chase. The contest wasn't even close. The fleeing pasta-pot panted as he tried to force his bulk toward the bushes while the uniformed figure behind him closed the distance with lithe, powerful, coordinated strides.

Officer Herman stood on the street side of unit 87 and watched. The figures of pursued and pursuer merged. He felt a pang of fear for his partner as a scream of anguish broke the night. He relaxed as Lansing's voice began reciting the Miranda with more than necessary volume and enthusiasm.

By this time, Barrett was behind the car with Wade and Svensen. A bullhorn was in his hand. He pressed the trigger. "Release the child and come out with your hands up."

The child gasped as the arm tightened around his neck. The arm's owner peered over the hood of the SUV. "Lemme go or the kid gets it!" he shouted.

"That's some tough talk for a guy whose survival odds have just been reduced from 50-50 to zero," came from the bullhorn.

"Whaddya mean, pig?"

"Before your partner bolted, our sniper could have been looking at either one of you. Guess who he's got in the cross-hairs now?"

The child felt the gripping arm began to tremble. As soon as it loosened, he kicked his way free and ran around the SUV. Seeing the small figure emerge from behind the SUV, Svensen shouted, "Cover me!" and ran up the drive. In one motion, he scooped the boy into his arms and turned around, shielding him.

Officer Wade looked at Barrett. "Sniper?" he queried.

Barret shrugged. "It was the best I could think of at the time. Now, go cuff that goon."

✹✹✹

Upon hearing that the child had been positively identi-fied at Authier's house, Garth keyed his mike. "All stations, Nero. Do not acknowledge UFN. Stew, abort. Front and Back move in. Eyes, fire both. Acknowledge in rotation."

"Nero, Stew. Moving, no contact yet."

"Nero, Front. Moving."

"Nero, Back. Moving."

A wave of elation and relief washed over Kitten as the radio chattered. They hadn't contacted Stew yet. He was on his way out of the battle zone without participating. He'd be disappointed, but she'd try to console him. She jerked the grate up, shoved the barrel of the launcher through, closed her eyes tight, and pulled the trigger. A sharp crack preceded a flash that looked bright through her closed eyelids. She pulled the launcher back, fitted the irritant grenade, and fired again. As the gas erupted, so did bedlam in the room below. Screams and curses followed as she scrambled down the duct. As she approached the access door, a couple of sharp cracks indicated that someone was firing a pistol through the hole where the grate had been. As she scrambled up the plenum ladder, she shouted into her microphone. "Nero, Eyes. Grenades detonated. On my way out." As Kitten scrambled toward the fan, she heard reports that Front and Back were through their respective doors without incident. Then, the best news of all came over the radio.

"Nero, Stake. The child is recovered. He appears unharmed."

Although she was still several feet from the fan, Kitten had to pause for a moment to give thanks. She didn't know who or what she was thanking, but she felt an overpowering need to express gratitude. She moved on through the fan and out to the access panel.

"Nero, Stew. Clear," sounded in her headset. He was back at the rendezvous point. He was safe! It was all over. She paused with her legs hanging out the access opening. She put her head in her hands. "Thanks, thanks . . ." she mumbled.

As if choreographed, the command van and a police cruiser screeched into position blocking the street to the east and west of the escape door and illuminating it with their headlights. Officers emerged from both vehicles, weapons drawn. A car from the pound had been parked directly across the street from the escape door. The officer manning the "Exit" station was behind it. Garth ran to his side. They crouched down.

As they waited, Garth considered the situation. It was wonderful that the kid was safe, but they hadn't actually seen him with Authier. That would make obtaining a hard conviction difficult. And Authier's lawyers were going to have a ball with the methods he'd employed to get this close to the scum. Secretly, he found himself hoping that Authier would come out shooting. He resigned himself. Whatever way it went from here, it looked like old Garth was toast.

Kitten was still sitting in the access opening when a thunderous noise broke her reverie. Before it quit, she was on her feet, running while she thumbed the button on her belt.

From Garth's vantage point, the noise seemed distant. He looked around to see where it came from. His headset came alive. "Nero, Front. There appears to have been an explosion in the basement."

Team "Back" was through the back door and starting down the stairs when a hurricane of heat, dust, and noise flattened them. "Stay low and abort," shouted the leader.

"Front and Back, Nero. Exit the building now and report status."

"Nero, Front. Wilco. We're all ok."

"Nero, Back. The blast caught us on the stairs. Everybody seems to be moving. Will report as soon as we're outside."

Under Kitten's running feet, the building shook and seemed to tilt. She lost her footing and stumbled sideways, ending up in a heap on the gravel. Dust, dislodged by the blast, clouded the air around her. As she got up, another rumble, not as loud as the first, caused the building to sway.

Team "Back," as one man, flattened themselves against the floor of the hallway.

From Garth's perspective, this second noise was closer. What the hell was going on?

The beacon lit up to show Kitten the end of the escape rope. She grabbed it, threw it and herself over the edge. As she rappelled down, a muffled rumble shook the rope. She hit the ground running in the direction of the pickup vehicle.

This noise almost deafened Garth. The steel door of the escape tunnel bulged and flew off its hinges. A ball of fire followed it. Everyone covered their eyes and ducked. Heat rolled over them. The car they were pressed against shook. The steel door clanged and scraped against the pavement. Garth wondered if it had hit either the command van or the patrol car. Breathing became difficult as dust filled the air. Pieces of brick, mortar, and other debris rained down. Garth pushed himself tighter against the side of the car. Desperately, he wanted to check things out, but the chunks hitting the car continued to sound sizeable.

After what seemed like forever to Garth, the racket stopped. Covered with dust, he looked up, wiped his eyes, spit a couple of times, and keyed the mike of his headset. "All stations, Nero. Report status in rotation." He leveled his weapon at the pile of rubble that had been the face of the building across the street.

"North, ok."

"East, ok."

"South, ok."

"West, ok."

"Front, ok."

"Back, one broken arm, otherwise ok. We'll need medical."

"Red, ok."

"Eyes, ok."

Garth looked at the officer next to him. The man grinned and said, "Exit, ok."

Garth keyed his mike again. "Front and Back, Nero. Withdraw. Maintain watch on the doors from a safe distance."

"Nero, Front. Any idea what happened?"

"Front, Nero. Apparent detonation of explosives in the escape tunnel while occupied by the suspects. Do you have any feel for how badly the building may have been damaged?"

"Nero, Front. It shook the hell out of us, but I can't see anything indicating structural damage."

While the other officers maintained watch on the rubble strewn portal, Garth checked the command van, ordered an ambulance, and checked the patrol car. Everyone was dirty, but unhurt. As he returned to his former position, he keyed his mike. "Eyes, Nero. Status."

"Nero, Eyes. On my way to rendezvous."

Garth breathed a sigh of relief. The citizens and the kid were ok. Mission accomplished. He keyed his mike again. "Eyes, Nero. You now have clearance to give your boyfriend a big kiss when you get to rendezvous."

"Nero, Eyes. Will comply."

As Garth dusted himself off, he felt another presence. He turned. It was Terry. "What the hell . . .?" he started.

Terry was shaking his head. "What a mess," he observed.

Garth looked at the rubble and then back to Terry. Lights began to flash inside his head. "What the hell are you doing here?" he growled.

"Just a law-abidin' citizen come to see the local constabulary dispense a little law and order," Terry replied with an innocent grin. "What do you suppose happened?"

"I think I should ask you that question."

"Donno," Terry began. "My guess would be that the scheme for covering their escape by blowing that tunnel backfired. I told you that the electronics weren't top drawer. Not bein' much on explosives, I don't know more than that, but I'd suppose that the electronics malfunctioned and set the charge off while they were in the tunnel instead of going off as they got clear."

Garth grabbed Terry by the front of his shirt and lifted until the little man was on tiptoes. "You suppose! You guess! My black ass! Don't play games with me!"

Terry calmly looked into Garth's eyes. "Please put me down and I'll explain."

The calm in Terry's manner began to defuse Garth's mad. He released his hold. "This had better be good," he growled.

Terry brushed at dust that had found its way from Garth's hands to the front of his shirt. "By way of making this both complete and good," he began, "please imagine yourself standing in front of a grand jury. They are asking you questions about the situation we have here. They are going down the list of people involved. They come to me. Now, consider two alternate scenarios:

"One, you have knowledge that I had something to do with this. Questions about who I am, what my capabilities are, and how carefully you checked into where I've been would follow.

"The second scenario is that you are able to honestly say that all you know about me is that I'm an alarm installer.

"Which would be more likely to result in a conclusion that would be amicable to all?"

Garth looked away from Terry to the pile of rubble. He reviewed the case in his mind. Terry had warned him about there being explosives in the tunnel. Terry had opined that the electronics were flaky. Terry had been the one to suggest that he not risk anybody going into the tunnel. Hell, he didn't really know that the scum had installed explosives in the tunnel. All he had was Terry's word. There certainly had been explosives in there, but they could just as well be Terry's work. Whether or not he had the skills, he had motive. If the scum beat the rap, his name would be high on their shit list. Terry had made several remarks that betrayed paranoia about the ineffectiveness of the justice system. That attitude probably extended to the witness protection plan. Perhaps this was Terry's personal insurance plan. Maybe he was an explosive expert. Maybe there was access to the escape tunnel that he'd lied about. Hell, he may have been in position to know when all the vehicles were in the tunnel. Maybe, maybe, maybe, but he didn't know. At this point, it was all a guess; he didn't have any solid reason to think Terry was anything more than an alarm installer. A person could do that by following the instructions with the alarm systems. No, with what he knew now, there was no reason to connect Terry with the explosion. If he unearthed any reason to suggest that Terry might have been involved, it would open up a can of worms regarding how thoroughly he'd checked Terry out. There hadn't been any reason to at the time and, knowing no more than he knew now, he could defend not doing so. The more he thought about it, the less he wanted to know about what had actually caused the explosion. His suspicions, after all, were nothing more than speculation. He visualized Terry in front of a grand jury. He'd look geeky, ugly, and harmless—the type of person often disregarded by the rest of humanity. The august seekers of truth on the grand jury would be no exception. Terry could easily lead them to arrive at the conclusion that the tunnel booby-trap had backfired. He could visualize Terry dropping hints here and there and the members of the jury becoming impressed with their own insight and perception as the picture formed in their minds. It would be a tidy conclusion. He reflected on his inability to rattle Terry. The little dude appeared to be unflappable. With someone like that planting ideas that would lead to a tidy conclusion, the case might be marked closed without many questions. Pushing Terry for further information wouldn't serve any purpose, but he had to know one thing. He turned to Terry and tapped his headset. "Er, Ter. Do you know anything about these?"

"High quality headset probably connected to a police frequency comm. system. Just the usual stuff that anybody in the electronics biz would know."

"How secure do you think they are?"

"I don't think you'd be able to eavesdrop with a standard police frequency scanner."

"But, if the eavesdropper were one step further up the ladder of sophistication?"

"I'd bet on the spy."

Garth nodded. "I thought so. Sooo, you knew that the kid was safe?"

A smile of genuine delight spread across Terry's face. "Is he? That's wonderful news!"

Garth fought for self-control. It was obvious that Terry had been eavesdropping on their radio conversations; it made him mad. So Terry knew about the child's rescue. It was also more than a good bet that Terry had engineered the explosion. But the little dude was being careful. He wasn't playing games; he was merely making certain that most of this conversation could be related verbatim later. Garth began to appreciate Terry's moxie. He studied Terry. He rubbed his chin. Should he risk the clincher? "Yeah, it was a lucky break that the child was rescued en route."

Terry looked at him with a knowing smirk. "Yes, most fortunate for the child. But, not being able to put the prime suspect in the same place as the child could have made obtaining a conviction difficult, couldn't it have?"

"Yes, it could have."

"Sometimes, things have a way of working themselves out," Terry observed. He winked at Garth, turned, and walked away.

Garth heard the ambulance siren at the back of 1295. He keyed his mike. "Back, Nero. From your perspective, where were the explosions?"

"Nero, Back. From the escape tunnel would be my guess."

"Back, Nero. How do you feel about going in for another look?"

"Nero, Back. The injured officer is in the ambulance. I don't have any problem going back in."

"Front, Nero. Reenter—work your way up to the third floor. Exercise extreme caution. If you see any evidence that the building has sustained structural damage, abort."

"Nero, Front. Wilco."

"Back, Nero. Proceed in to the basement. There may be people needing help down there. If you see any evidence that the building has sustained structural damage, abort."

"Nero, Back. Wilco."

Garth walked over to the command van and addressed the tech. "Ron, get coffee orders from everybody and give the list to one of the uniforms in the patrol car. Everybody is gonna have to maintain position for another couple of hours."

Garth pushed the earpiece of his headset forward as the refreshment orders poured in. Everybody was relieved, but all were doing a good job of maintaining discipline because the two SWAT teams could still be facing danger. He was proud of them. He fiddled with his cell phone for a few minutes and hit a speed dial number. He put the instrument to his free ear. After a considerable number of rings, a groggy voice answered.

"Yeah . . . What the fu . . . do you know what goddamn time it is?"

"Yes, Mr. Kinkaid, I do know that it is two o'clock in the morning. This is Garth Moore, I apologize for calling at this hour, but I have a life-threatening situation that needs your expertise."

"Moore . . . Moore . . . you're that big . . . ug . . . er . . . narc?"

"Actually, I'm now the head of narcotics. We did a bust tonight at 1295 Industrial. The suspects tried to escape through a vehicle tunnel to another building. Apparently, they had lined the tunnel with explosives. The charges went off as they were trying to use the tunnel. I need an engineer down here to assess the condition of the buildings and to supervise digging the vehicles out of the debris."

"You think anybody survived?"

"I doubt it, but we can't go on that assumption. We must work like there's somebody still alive until we know differently."

"Ok, I'll get a team together and be down ASAP."

"Thank you, sir."

"Don't expect me to be bringin' no dammed doughnuts, either."

"Bad cop?"

"A damned annoying one."

Garth smiled as he put the cell phone in his pocket, but it rang almost immediately.

"Garth here."

"Hi Chief, this is Arnold. I rousted the Juvie people out and took the child over to them. That Tyler is one plucky kid. He made a break for it as soon as they had him out the back door. He made it to a hedge and couldn't get through before they ran him down, but it gave us a good look at him. The Juvie gal gave him a cuddle and some hot chocolate, put him to bed, and he was out like a light. She's planning to stay at his bedside all night in case he wakes up with bad dreams."

"I don't see how he could avoid bad dreams after what he's been through. Uh, he didn't say anything about what went on while he was in Authier's clutches, did he?"

"Uh, uh. In fact, he hasn't said more than a dozen words. He ran to one of the uniforms sobbing. That officer—Svensen—picked him up, took him over to the patrol car and held him while we dealt with the remaining goon. He'd calmed down by the time we got to the centre, but he wouldn't let go of Svensen until he saw the Juvie gal."

"Poor little tyke. Nobody should have to go through what he's experienced. Uh, you said 'remaining' goon?"

"Yeah, one tried to run for it. Officer Lansing gave chase. When Lansing hit him, the fat bastard did a face-plant in the grass. It seems that most of Lansing's weight was on the back of his head when he hit. His face is a mess. Lansing is in the ambulance with him."

"Lansing's hurt too?"

"Nah, he knows how to do that stuff. He was a running back in high school. I understand he didn't miss the pro cut by much. I had to send someone to keep an eye on that scum. I thought it would do him good to see Lansing there."

Garth chuckled before keying his mike, "Er, Arnie, how are you doing?"

"Ok, why?"

"From the looks of things, it's gonna be quiet around here until the engineers get some digging done. I'll have a ton of questions to answer tomorrow. Could you stay on duty and look after things here until Donaldson comes on duty in the morning?"

"Does it mean I can turn my cell off for the weekend and have Monday off too?"

"Yeah," Garth replied and pocketed the cell phone.

Garth's headset came to life. "Nero, Back. Nothing on the main floor. We are now in the basement. Nothing down here either. There is debris all over. The tunnel is blocked about thirty feet in."

"Three vehicles went in there. Any sign of them?"

"Negative. One of them laid some rubber getting into the tunnel, but all three must be in there."

"Ok, post someone at the mouth of the tunnel to listen for any sounds. The rest of you stand easy for awhile."

"Nero, Back. Wilco"

"Front, Nero. Status."

"Nero, Front. Currently searching three. No sign of anybody yet. All the equipment in the studio is in place and the lights are still on."

"Front, Nero. Establish tight security over that room. Nobody in until the crime scene techies arrive. When your search is complete, stand easy for awhile."

"Nero, Front. Wilco."

Garth listened with satisfaction as the officers who had fetched the doughnuts called each station to find out where they wanted the refreshments delivered. The conversations over the comm. lightened. Discipline faded. No problem; everybody had done an excellent job. They deserved to relax. He was munching his third pastry when an unmarked sedan pulled up alongside the command van. The occupants identified themselves as engineers employed by a consulting firm. Garth dispatched them to examine the ends of the tunnel. After another half hour, trucks with lights arrived. Another car parked alongside the command van. A disheveled and obviously unhappy Mr. Kinkaid stepped out. He surveyed the situation for a moment and walked over to the tunnel exit without acknowledging anybody else's presence. Garth licked the frosting off his fingers as he followed. Kinkaid had a powerful flashlight in hand with which he examined the door, the hinges, the rubble and the side of the building.

Kinkaid turned to Garth. "Them two hirelings show up yet?"

"Yes, they looked this end over and then went into the other building to examine the other end."

Kinkaid pointed to Garth's headset. "Can you use that thing to get their asses over here?"

"Certainly," Garth replied and keyed his mike. "Back, Nero. Please have someone escort those two engineers back to the tunnel exit. Tell them that Mr. Kinkaid wants a consult."

Kinkaid studied Garth. "You got yourself one helluva mess here," he observed.

"Yes, I do."

"This musta been one mother of a drug operation."

Garth thought for a minute. "Uh, it didn't have to do with drugs. Our information indicated that a snuff video was going to be made in that building tonight."

"A what? A . . . a . . . snuff . . . where they tape a whore bein' killed?"

"Our information indicated that it would be a young boy."

The petulance vanished from Kinkaid's face. "My god! A child?" He turned toward the tunnel exit. "Is he in there?"

"No, he's safe. The Juvenile authorities are looking after him."

"Thanks, Moore. You've probably told me more than you should have, but I appreciate it," Kinkaid said and returned to his examination of the tunnel exit.

Some minutes later, the other two engineers arrived and went into a huddle with Kinkaid. Garth returned to the command van and found an unopened coffee. It wasn't cold yet, so he began working on it. As he sipped, he could feel tiredness taking over. He seated himself and rubbed his eyes.

A rush of cold air awakened Garth. His right trouser leg was wet. The empty cup lay at his feet. He looked up to see Arnold Barrett in the open door of the command van. "Damn, must have dozed off," he said while reaching for a paper towel.

Barrett took a seat and waited while Garth mopped up the puddle of coffee at his feet. As Garth deposited the last of the toweling in the wastebasket, Barrett asked, "Uh, Garth . . . I hope I made the right call. I know it would have been best to nail Authier with the kid . . . but . . ."

Garth looked at him and smiled warmly. "Hey, you followed the priorities exactly. The child's safety was paramount."

"Well, at first, I was a touch worried about getting a conviction, but from what I heard over the comm., it may not be an issue."

"That crew is digging them out. For my money, there isn't anybody left to line the pockets of slick lawyers."

"That's good. Things have a way of working themselves out."

"That is the second time tonight I've heard that," Garth replied in surprise.

"Come again?"

"It's not important. About that tackle Lansing made; isn't it a bit odd that his weight came down on the guy's head?"

"Yeah," Arnold answered pensively. "I asked Lansing about that. His answer was that he'd misjudged when to jump because of the darkness. I don't exactly buy that. For my money, if Lansing had intended to hit him in the waist, that's exactly what would have happened. However, I intend to accept Lansing's version as he gave it."

"It was good thinking for you to get that scum off to the hospital right away. We may be looking at a police brutality charge here. Perhaps I should have a talk with Lansing about excessive force."

Barrett was unable to suppress a grin.

"What?" asked Garth.

Barrett shook his head. "Garth, everybody knows about those 'excessive force' lectures the Old Man used to lay on you every couple of months."

Garth looked at the floor. "Yeah. He doesn't work for us anyhow; just put something about it in your report to his Captain."

"Sure, Garth."

The conversation was interrupted as Kinkaid poked his head in the door. "Moore, you look beat."

"Yeah, it's been a long day at the office."

"Well, you can go home. As near as we can tell from what we can see the charges were near the ends of the tunnel. The placement caused the main force of each to go down the tunnel. You said that vehicles were in there when the explosions went off?"

"Yes, we believe there were three vehicles and three explosions."

"Well, I'd guess that the explosions sandwiched all three into a heap in the middle of the tunnel. We can't account for the third explosion yet. I'll get some equipment down here to dig them out, but it's going to be slow going. We'll have to shore the tunnel up as we go."

Garth thanked Kinkaid, cuffed Barrett on the shoulder, and headed home as the sky became grey with dawn.

31
Epilogue

The ringing of the phone awakened Garth. Who in the hell wanted to talk to him at this hour? It shouldn't be Rose; he'd left a message on her machine that he was ok. "Yeah?" he grumbled into the handset.

"Garth, it's Millie. It's four in the afternoon. I have the debrief set up for five."

The fog from the sleeping pills began to clear. Since dawn was breaking when he got home, he'd popped a couple of zonkers before hitting the hay. They, or coming down from the adrenalin, or the combination, must have hit fast. He remembered leaving a message for Rose, but the one he'd left for Millie was hazy. No wonder he still had one sock on. He stumbled into the shower, did his morning ablutions, and dressed on autopilot. He drove to the office thinking of the coffee he knew Millie would have waiting.

Millie didn't disappoint. She handed him a cup as he came through the office door. "Aaah, thanks," he said. "Do I have a raft of calls waiting?"

"No, there isn't anybody that needs a call back. Donaldson took over as scene supervisor when he came on duty at nine. By that time, the SWAT teams had been through every room in both buildings. As you supposed, there was nobody found. Per your instructions, Arnold came by to fill me in before he went off duty. I made a call to the task force and gave Martin a quick synopsis of the events and status. He requested a working supper with you this evening."

"He's not exactly my first choice of a date for tonight, but he deserves the get-together. What time and where?"

"Gergio's at eight."

"Ok, what else?"

Garth perched on a corner of Millie's desk and sipped the coffee as she related the status reports. It was anticlimactic.

He didn't feel like doing the five p.m. debrief, but the players deserved to know.

Stew and Kitten walked through the door as Millie finished. Kitten had her "Willie" look on. She and Stew were holding hands. Garth was pleased; they looked like a typical Mediterranean couple.

"Hi, kids," Millie said, mirroring the happy looks on their faces.

"Good morning, Millie, Sir," Stew replied as he looked from Millie to Garth. At the "Sir," Kitten rolled her eyes toward the ceiling.

"Hope you two were able to get some rest after all the excitement," Garth offered.

"Oh, yeah, no prob. there," Kitten began sarcastically. "After you told us to secure, this clod took me to the motel, gave me a couple of kisses, and drove off. He was gallant enough to pick me up for breakfast this afternoon, but I'd have been up for something more."

Stew began to blush. Garth and Millie struggled to hide laughter. Kitten continued to look impish.

Terry's arrival broke the awkward moment. "Hello, all. I'm glad to see things haven't started yet; I want to hear everything."

All four greeted Terry and headed for Garth's office. Millie was distributing coffee as Roz and Frank walked in, also holding hands.

"Well," Garth began, "thanks to the efforts and courage of all of you, it looks as though the scum have been put out of business.

"In a nutshell, this is the way it came down. They planned to bring the child in after everything was set up. All of the major players were at 1295 when our stakeout saw the goons take the child out of Authier's house. We blocked the driveway. One of the goons tried to run for it. An officer named Lansing tackled him. The other goon surrendered. The kid was out of the goon's grip and into the arms of a uniformed officer before anybody knew it. His parents picked him up from the Juvenile authorities this morning.

"Once we had the child, I told Kitten to lob the grenades in. It worked like a charm. They left everything—lights, camera, and even some tapes of previous stuff. Missing Persons is now trying to identify the victims. We didn't expect that bonus. As we did anticipate, they went down the escape pole, into their vehicles, and into the tunnel. An explosion in the tunnel buried all three vehicles. We have people digging, but they have not yet reached the first vehicle. Our best guess is that we won't find anybody alive."

"An explosion?" Frank asked.

"Yeah," answered Garth as he tried for the casual face. "Terry warned us of explosives in there. Ter, would you give us your opinion?"

Terry fidgeted and appeared to look uncomfortable, but Garth knew it was an act. "Uh, well . . . when I was in that tunnel, hooking up the alarm for the rear door, I saw what I thought might be explosives along the walls. Not knowing anything about such stuff, I wasn't certain, but they looked like what you see on TV. While I was working, I checked out where the wires attached to them went. It was to a circuit board mounted on the same backboard as the alarm system. It wasn't a commercial job, just something cobbled together. The muscle was watching me real close, so I couldn't spend much time looking at it, but I'd guess—if those things hooked to it were explosives—that it was a detonator that could be triggered by a garage door opener."

"Beautiful performance," thought Garth. He took the cue and prodded.

"Thanks, Ter, but can you give us your opinion of what happened?"

"Uh, yeah, I guess. You said there was an explosion?"

Garth played along. "Yes, after all three vehicles were in the tunnel, there were three explosions. The last one blew the escape door off its hinges. All we could see from either end of the tunnel was rubble."

"Whoo wee," said Terry. "I was afraid of that—if I was right about those packages being explosives."

Garth addressed the group. "Terry had warned us there might be explosives in that tunnel. That's why we didn't have anyone in there." He turned to Terry. "Please tell these other members of the team about your fears."

Terry shifted in his chair and looked at the floor. "Well, you know, garage-door openers can be sort of flaky. Most everybody has come home to find his or her garage door open at one time or another. Other openers, automotive ignition systems, and a number of other things, trigger them because they are cheap, unsophisticated devices. That board looked like a garage-door opener control. Whatever it was, it wasn't high tech. My guess is that something unexpected triggered it; it could have been an interference pattern set up by three vehicles close by at once, perhaps a cell phone, the alarm system itself going off, who knows?"

As Terry talked, Garth scanned the group. The face on each person, except for Roz, was a mask of rapt attention. When he got to her, she glanced at him and raised an eyebrow slightly. He returned a barely perceptible nod. She pursed her lips and returned her attention to Terry. She wasn't buying it, but they were communicating. After Terry finished, she laughed and addressed Garth.

"I gotta hand it to you, boss cop. You said that a lot of law enforcement amounts to waiting for the bad guys to outsmart themselves. It looks like that's what happened here in spades. Their clever scheme put them out of business and saved the taxpayers a lot of money in one fell swoop."

"What a swiftie," thought Garth. Roz was seeing through Terry's story, but she got the signal that it was important for everybody to buy it.

Garth scanned the group again. Relief was registering on all their faces. The truth that a final, satisfactory conclusion had been reached was sinking in. As the tension drained, an animated conversation developed. Garth relinquished control and let everybody enjoy the victory. Congratulations and quips made the rounds. Each talked about how they felt during different phases. Roz and Kitten exchanged girl talk about the "Willie" look. Millie popped in and out with coffee refills. Garth sat back and enjoyed the scene.

As the chatter died down, Terry addressed Garth. "How about our deal, boss?"

Garth was surprised. "I'd intended to discuss that with you in private."

"No need for that, I think these folks would be interested in knowing."

"Sure, if that's the way you want it. There is a spot reserved for you in rehab the first of next month. I've spoken with your employer. He is granting you time off with pay. Since your source of junk has dried up, I need to ask you if you have enough to last you until you report to rehab."

Terry didn't flinch or look the slightest bit embarrassed. "No."

"Ok, don't do anything on your own. I'll arrange for you to talk with a doctor tomorrow. He'll take care of you. Do you want to get into the matter of your daughter while we're here?"

"Sure, why not?"

"The rehab people think that your goal of becoming a part of her life will be therapeutic. With your permission, they will attempt to establish dialogue between you and her mother."

For the first time, Terry began to show emotion. He swallowed hard and said, "Thanks, Garth. That's more than I'd hoped for."

An awkward silence followed. Kitten struggled with something that had been swirling in her head. Finally, she addressed Garth. "Uh, I think you said that I can now apply for college. Is that right?"

"Yes," Garth replied, "your transcript shows that you have completed high school, so you can apply."

"Does that mean to any institution of higher learning?"

"Well . . . yes . . . I suppose . . ." Garth replied hesitatingly, and looked at Stew.

"We've formulated a plan to get her ready to handle the work by the fall of next year," Stew said with obvious pride.

"In that case, I don't think I see what you are asking," Garth said as he turned back to Kitten.

"I'm askin' if my new identity is solid enough that I can apply for the Police Academy."

Murmurs of approval filled the room. Garth couldn't help registering surprise. "You want to become one of us?"

"Yeah. That's what the first Willie was going to do and since I'm gonna become a citizen, I just as well go all the way."

More congratulations and a few hugs followed. After the group left, Garth sat at his desk feeling as if he'd been to an encounter group.

✳✳✳

Later that evening, Garth entered Gergio's restaurant dressed in his most dignified togs. Martin, the agent who headed the federal task force on missing children, sat in a secluded booth. He rose and offered a hand as Garth approached. "Garth, good to see you."

Garth took the hand. "Likewise, sir. Uh, sorry about not getting with you earlier . . ."

Martin cut him off as they took their seats. "Nonsense, it was good timing. Your secretary gave me enough to go see Charlie. That was the first order of business."

It still unnerved Garth to hear the Old Man referred to by his given name. "And, how is he, Sir?"

Martin looked at Garth. "You can knock off the 'Sir.' Call me Martin—we're peers now. Charlie's doing great. He was elated to hear how this thing turned out."

"That's excellent S . . . I mean, Martin. How about the prognosis?"

"It is better than any of us hoped for. He's a tough old bird. He might outlive me or even you. Getting rid of the pressure enabled him to spring back like you wouldn't believe."

"Did he say anything about missing the pressure?"

"Yes. He says he misses it like an ingrown toenail. He told me to tell you to get used to that chair. He's looking forward to doing a lot of fishing. When I was there, he had brochures of boats scattered all over the place."

Mixed emotions swirled within Garth. He busied himself with the menu.

Martin saw the struggle, so he waited until after the entrees arrived to pick up the conversation. "I guess we should get to the case."

"Yeah, sorry. The excavation crew reached a Chev Suburban late this afternoon. It was a couple of feet shorter than when it drove in. The engineer's first thought, after his preliminary examination, was that the position of the charges directed the force of the blasts down the tunnel from each end. He was right. They recovered remains of four occupants. We'll have to rely on fingerprints or dental for I.D. We've tried to locate the owners of both buildings, but they are numbered companies and the trail to the principles is cold. It looks as though somebody has done a serious job of wiping data."

"My guess is that we'll never find out who owned them," Martin offered. "The tax and utility payments will stop and the city will own them before long."

"That would be my guess also," Garth agreed. "I don't think that anybody will be interested in becoming connected with what we found on the tape in that camera."

"Pretty ugly, eh?"

"Worse than that. Our analysts are tough, but one had to go home sick. Another has asked for relief from assignment to this case."

"Speaking of the case, have you considered when to turn the investigation over to us?"

"Whenever you say. I want to see my people rid of this thing as soon as possible."

Midnight approached as Garth and Martin completed their discussion of the case and transfer details. Leaving the restaurant, Garth began to share the sense of closure that the rest of the team experienced earlier in the afternoon.

✸✸✸

Garth was in the office early the next day, dealing with details. As noon approached, he gathered the things that Millie had purchased for him and headed for Rose's office.

Garth waited in front of the receptionist's desk while the ample lady put her nail file back in the drawer.

"May I please see Ms. Winters?" he asked, when she looked up.

"She's with a client."

"I . . . uh," Garth stammered.

"I know. I know. You gotta ketch a plane or sumpthin'," said Ample as she reached for the intercom. "Miss Winters?"

"Yes."

"Kin y' come out fer a minute? Tall, dark 'n ugly's here bearin' gifts."

Garth was disappointed. He had been trying for the suave face.

Rose walked into the reception area and noted the large box of chocolates and the flowers Garth was holding. "Let me guess. Those mean you can't tell me where you're going, Thursday night is off, and you don't know when you'll be back," she said sourly.

"Wrong, wrong, wrong," said Garth, as he handed her the offerings. "I'm not going anywhere. I'll be here Thursday. In addition, I'm asking for a date tonight to celebrate my making official application for the position of Narcotics Director."

Ample watched in horror as Rose grabbed Garth and kissed him fiercely while entwining him with a shapely leg—right in front of the clients.

LaVergne, TN USA
08 February 2010
172254LV00004B/4/P

9 781606 933800